I0726687

Love In Springtime: A Regency Romance Easter Collection

Five Delightful Regency Easter Stories
from

Arietta Richmond

Catherine Windsor

Isabella Thorne

Katherine Keats

Kelly Anne Bruce

Dreamstone Publishing © 2017

www.dreamstonepublishing.com

ISBN: 1925499510

ISBN-13: 978-1-925499-51-3

Disclaimer

These stories are works of fiction.

Names, characters, places and incidents are the product of the author's imagination and are used fictitiously. Any resemblance to events, locales or actual persons, living or dead, is entirely coincidental.

ARIETTA RICHMOND, CATHERINE WINDSOR, ISABELLA THORNE, KATHERINE KEATS, KELLY ANNE BRUCE

iv

Introduction

We hope you enjoy this Easter Collection of Regency romance stories. As authors, we each have a different style, but we are brought together by our love for Regency Romance. This collection presents some very different heroes and heroines, but the common theme is that they all find love, despite trials and tribulations along the way, at Easter, or in some way related to happenings at Easter.

We have each also given you a bonus, with some previews of our other books. We hope that you love reading these stories as much as we enjoyed writing them, and that you will also go on to enjoy all of our other Regency books!

Thanks for reading 'Love in Springtime: A Regency Romance Easter Collection'!

Arietta Richmond

Catherine Windsor

Isabella Thorne

Katherine Keats

Kelly Anne Bruce

ARIETTA RICHMOND, CATHERINE WINDSOR, ISABELLA THORNE, KATHERINE KEATS, KELLY ANNE BRUCE

Table of Contents

ARIETTA RICHMOND, CATHERINE WINDSOR, ISABELLA THORNE, KATHERINE KEATS, KELLY ANNE BRUCE

His Majesty's Hounds – Book 4

Sweet and Clean Regency Romance

Being Lady Harriet's Hero

Arietta Richmond

Books by Arietta Richmond

His Majesty's Hounds

Claiming the Heart of a Duke

Intriguing the Viscount

Giving a Heart of Lace (a prequel to Winning the Merchant Earl)

Being Lady Harriet's Hero

Enchanting the Duke (coming soon)

Redeeming the Marquess (coming soon)

Winning the Merchant Earl (coming soon)

Healing Lord Barton (coming soon)

Loving the Bitter Baron (coming soon)

Rescuing the Countess (coming soon)

Attracting the Spymaster (coming soon)

The Derbyshire Set

A Gift of Love (Prequel short story)

A Devil's Bargain (Prequel short story - coming soon)

The Earl's Unexpected Bride

The Captain's Compromised Heiress

The Viscount's Unsuitable Affair

The Count's Impetuous Seduction

The Rake's Unlikely Redemption

The Marquess' Scandalous Mistress

A Remembered Face (Bonus short story – coming soon)

The Marchioness' Second Chance (coming soon)

A Viscount's Reluctant Passion (coming soon)

Lady Theodora's Christmas Wish

The Duke's Improper Love (coming soon)

Other Books

The Scottish Governess (coming soon)

The Earl's Reluctant Fiancée (coming soon)

The Crew of the Seadragon's Soul Series, (coming soon - a set of 10 linked novels)

Dedication

For everyone who had the grace to be patient while this book, and every other book that I have written, was coming into existence, who provided cups of tea, and food, when the writing would not let me go, and endured countless times being asked for opinions.

For the readers who inspire me to continue writing, by buying my books! Especially for those of you who have taken the time to email me, or to leave reviews, and tell me what you love about these books, and what you'd like to see more of – thank you – I'm listening, I promise to write more about your favourite characters.

For my growing team of beta readers and advance reviewers – it's thanks to you that others can enjoy these books in the best presentation possible!

And for all the writers of Regency Historical Romance, whose books I read, who inspired me to write in this fascinating period.

ARIETTA RICHMOND, CATHERINE WINDSOR, ISABELLA THORNE, KATHERINE KEATS, KELLY ANNE BRUCE

Chapter One

Lord Geoffrey Clarence tapped on the rickety door before opening it carefully. No matter how many times he had been here, the whole place still felt fragile to him – he was a big man, and worried that, if he pushed too hard, the stairs or the doorframe would simply break.

On the other side of the door, the room was warm as the early winter afternoon's sunlight streamed in through the large glass windows. Cecil Carlisle, Baron Setford, waved him to a chair and handed him a cup of coffee, which was, as usual, perfectly prepared, and exactly as he liked it. One day, Geoffrey thought, he would find out how Setford managed that – the miraculous appearance of perfect hot coffee, when there seemed no-one else in evidence, and there had been no exact time for the meeting.

For now, he simply accepted the cup, and sipped with pleasure. This was a place in which he could be totally relaxed, certain that there was no danger – which was a sensation to treasure.

"You've done well these last few months, m'boy. The Prince Regent appreciates still being alive."

Geoffrey raised an eyebrow, a somewhat cynical expression on his face.

"Is that 'appreciates' in a 'here's your reward' way, or in a 'since you're so clever at this, here's your next nasty job' way?"

Setford guffawed and leant back in his chair, his piercing pale grey eyes sparkling. Once the laughter had run its course, his face took on a more serious expression.

"You always were damn sharp – straight to the crux of it. And you're right about it being able to go either way. But in this case, it's actually a bit of both. There's a reward, but there's also another 'nasty job' as you so aptly put it."

He reached over to the table beside him, and produced a folder. From the folder, he withdrew a large sealed document. Sealed with the Prince Regent's seal, if Geoffrey wasn't mistaken. Silently, Setford passed it to Geoffrey.

"That's the reward."

Geoffrey broke the seal carefully. A minute's perusal of the document revealed that he was now the owner of a rather large estate, located not too far from Charlton's country seat, Pendholm Hall. An estate called, apparently, Witherwood Chase. He wondered what it was like. Gifts from Prinny had an alarming potential to come with 'issues'. Who knew if the estate had been well maintained or not? He may have just been gifted an expensive repair and maintenance bill.

"Do you know anything about it?"

Setford shook his head.

"Nothing at all, beyond the fact that it has reverted to the crown after the previous owner proved treasonous. So you may find interesting things within its walls. And that's the 'nasty job' bit. We are not at all sure that we have all of the conspirators in the treason. So, you need to develop a sudden desire to look into your new property – in VERY great detail. I would be personally extremely grateful if you manage to find the papers and other evidence that we believe are hidden there."

Geoffrey grimaced – digging through dusty cellars and trying to find secret compartments in wainscoting might have amused him when he was a boy, but it certainly wasn't exactly appealing now! Still, a decent estate wasn't a gift one received every day. It might even turn out to be a pleasant place. With Charlton's family nearby, he'd even have good company if he wanted it.

And... far better to spend the next few months, and then the holiday season, in a place of his own, rather than in his miserable brother's house, watching him bicker with his miserable wife. Alfred's opinion of what Geoffrey should do with his life stopped at 'being a good heir and doing everything the way I do'.

Setford watched him carefully, and smiled wryly as the expressions flowed across Geoffrey's face.

"Yes, I rather thought you'd appreciate having a bolt hole of your own, and a damn good reason to stay there."

"Astute as ever, sir. I just hope it's not quite a crumbling ruin – this 'reward' doesn't happen to come with any convenient cash, to help deal with any repairs needed, does it?"

Setford laughed again.

"A gift from Prinny, that came with money?? Surely you know better!"

Geoffrey sighed, and went back to the excellent coffee.

~~~~~

Five sennights later.

Lady Harriet Edgeworth arrived in the morning room at Pendholm Hall like a whirlwind (which was not an uncommon occurrence...). Her brother looked up with an amused smile on his face. Charlton Edgeworth, Viscount Pendholm, was quite used to his sister's tendency to be all energy – behaving like a good little society miss was challenging for her at the best of times, and here at Pendholm Hall, where they had grown up, she simply didn't try most of the time.

The two dogs lying by the hearth looked up, their sleep disturbed by her arrival, but, after a few thumps of their tails, they settled back to rest.

"Did you have a good ride Harriet?"

"Wonderful! Thank you again for buying Moonbeam for me – she is just the best horse that I have ever had! Poor John can barely keep up with me, and Miss Carpenter quite refuses to ride with me anymore."
~~~~~

Charlton knew that the last statement was the most important to Harriet. His sister's long-suffering companion had never been much of a rider, and Harriet had been making her life miserable by causing her to ride as often as possible during the last year.

"Where did you ride to today?" Lady Pendholm asked her daughter, smiling at her exuberance.

Harriet's face took on an expression which could be described as 'false innocence', if one was to be uncharitable.

"Oh, just across the park to the river near Witherwood Chase." Whilst her tone of voice was casual, the whole effect was spoilt by the blush that coloured Harriet's cheeks. Her mother's eyes sparkled with a mischief that made it quite obvious where Harriet's volatile demeanour came from.

"It's a lovely ride, isn't it? You didn't, perchance, happen to see Lord Geoffrey did you? I wanted to invite him to dinner tomorrow."

Harriet's blush deepened, to a colour that was not exactly flattering against her dark gold hair. Her family teased her about her interest in Lord Geoffrey. They were sure that she would grow out of it. She was equally sure that she would not. It was not a childish infatuation, not at all.

She had decided, when she had first met him, just after he had heroically saved her brother and mother's lives, as well as the lives of four other people, that he was wonderful. He looked like the hero he was.

And he was going to be her hero. No matter how long it took for her to convince him.

Whilst she had been the toast of the Season earlier in the year, and had been flattered by the attention of a large number of eligible gentlemen, she had not wanted to marry any of them. She had shuddered at the thought. She knew what she wanted, and she planned to get it.

"He did ride by, in the distance. Unfortunately he didn't see me." She sighed in disappointment, firmly telling herself that he had NOT ignored her, that he simply hadn't seen her. "So you'll have to send a footman over with a message to invite him."

Watching Harriet's eyes light up at the thought of Lord Geoffrey coming to dinner, her mother had a hard time not laughing. But it really wouldn't do to belittle her daughter's *tendre* for the man – that would, of a certainty, only make her more stubborn.

"I will do so this morning."

Harriet produced a large smile at her mother's words, and whirled out of the room again, to change from her riding habit to a gown suitable for luncheon.

Chapter Two

Lord Geoffrey's first sight of Witherwood Chase had not been inspiring. The gates were uneven and looked not to have been shut for a very long time, the drive was rutted so badly that he feared for the wheels of his carriage, and the winter bare trees that lined it did nothing to improve the prospect.

The house itself was larger than he might have expected – a graceful and well-proportioned H shape, where the side wings enclosed a formal garden and a grand approach to the porticoed entry at the front, and a terrace onto a once elegant herb and scent garden at the rear, which was protected from the elements by a decorative wall between the ends of the wings. An impressive four stories of windows had looked down on him as he alighted from his carriage and approached the doors.

Everything had shown signs of some recent neglect, but not so much as he had feared might be the case. He had discovered, upon his arrival, that the property had come with staff – a point which had not been mentioned in the missive granting him ownership.

The staff (a butler of a rather venerable age, a housekeeper, an estate manager, two footmen, a cook, two maids and two grooms, plus a gardener) had responded to his arrival with courtesy, but obvious suspicion. Now, a month later, as Christmas approached, that had at least faded to them treating him with cordial distance. That suspicion and distance was not aiding his investigations one bit.

He had added another two footmen, and a valet, to his staff – men who came well recommended, via Baron Setford, and who had skills and knowledge not commonly found in footmen or valets – which they took great care not to reveal to the other staff. The house had also seen a continuing parade of persons in the business of providing various types of repairs, cleaning services, furniture supply and restoration, and more. The costs were rather alarming, but the ledgers presented by the estate manager had at least given him hope that the place might actually be capable of funding itself, with a little attention to the tenant farmers.

That realisation had led to a round of visits to the village, and all of the tenant's cottages, to assess what repairs would be needed, and to start the long process of building their trust. It was increasingly obvious that the previous owner, apart from having been foolish enough to commit treason, had never been a very likeable man, and had never put the slightest effort into caring about those whose work generated much of his income. Geoffrey hoped that, eventually, the tenants would trust him enough to actually reveal exactly what they had so disliked about the previous master of Witherwood Chase.

On this particular day, Geoffrey had just returned from checking on the repairs to various farmers' cottages. He was well pleased with progress, as the fact that their cottages had been restored to a weatherproof state, before the worst of winter, had led to a markedly more positive attitude from the farmers and their families.

The day was brisk, and the early snow had partly melted in the weak sunlight. He had enjoyed being out and moving, as he always did. At one point, in the distance near the small river that bounded one side of his land, he had seen Lady Harriet riding that quality grey mare that Charlton had bought her a few months ago. He had admired her seat, and, if he was honest, her fine figure, from a distance, but had carefully pretended not to notice her. However attractive the chit was, she was only eighteen, and the sister of one of his closest friends – definitely not a girl that he should be getting interested in!

Handing Rajah to the waiting groom and leaving the horse to his well-earned rub down, Geoffrey took himself inside, via the kitchen door – why walk all the way around the house in the cold and the sleet which had begun to fall? The Cook gave him her best disapproving look, glaring at the small trail of wet slush left on the floor from his boots. He swept her a somewhat mocking bow.

"I must apologise, Mrs Chester, for trailing mud in here. But I quite refuse to freeze for any longer than necessary. I am certain that the maid can manage to deal with it expeditiously."

Her expression suggested that his frivolous attitude was unsuitable for a Lord, but she said nothing of it, simply turning back to the preparation of what looked like a sumptuous meal.

As he stepped into the hall, on his way to his study to warm up with a glass of good brandy in front of the fire, his butler intercepted him.

"Good afternoon, my Lord. A letter has just been delivered for you." Barnstable proffered the letter on an aged and elegant silver salver.

"Thank you, Barnstable." Geoffrey swept the letter up as he continued towards the study, determinedly ignoring Barnstable's rather pointed look at the final drips of muddy snow which had fallen from his boots onto the patterned marble floor. This having a collection of staff was still a strange experience. So many years of looking after himself during the war had made him unused to needing others, or paying any heed to their fussiness.

Still, there were some advantages – such as the excellent meals that Mrs Chester produced each day. Brandy in hand, he dropped into his favourite chair with a sigh, and brought his attention to the letter. It was addressed simply 'Lord Geoffrey' in a hand which he recognised. He wondered what Lady Sylvia wished of him.

Opening it, he smiled. It was, for a letter from a member of the *ton*, utterly short and to the point. It invited him to dine with Lady Sylvia and her family, at Pendholm Hall, the following day. A relaxing, and likely entertaining, evening in Charlton's company was definitely appealing.

Lady Sylvia was also an excellent conversationalist, and a pleasure to speak with, as she was intelligent, and not afraid to have opinions. The only thing which gave him a moment's pause was knowing that it would also be an evening spent in Lady Harriet's company.

Since the unfortunate incidents of early in the year, when he had been forced to dispose of some ruffians to save the lives of a number of people, including Charlton and his mother, Lady Harriet had conceived a vision of him as some sort of hero. Which idea rather horrified him. He was certain that she harboured a *tendre* for him, and he found dealing with her somewhat obvious regard difficult. Especially as the girl was so damned attractive!

So be it. He would not let the chit's obsession with making him out as a 'hero' stop him from spending time with Charlton. Charlton Edgeworth, Viscount Pendholm, was, like Lord Geoffrey, one of a group of six men who had, during their service in France and Spain, come to be called 'His Majesty's Hounds' for their tenacious ability to sniff out French spies and troop movements, and deal with them. For all of those years, they had been closer than family – each owed the others his life, multiple times over. Geoffrey was overwhelmingly glad that Witherwood Chase was so close to Pendholm Hall.

Leaving his brandy on the side table, he went to his desk and quickly dashed off a reply, accepting the invitation with pleasure. Once his note of acceptance was sanded and sealed, he rang for Barnstable and settled back into his chair. The door opened rapidly and Barnstable came into the room at a rate that belied his appearance of great age.

"Yes, My Lord?"

"Please have Peterson deliver this letter to Pendholm Hall immediately."

Barnstable took the letter, bowed, and left the room.

Staring into the flames, and sipping his brandy, Lord Geoffrey contemplated his progress with his mission. Digging into the secrets of the house had become more of a pleasure for him than he had expected. For, as he did, he discovered fascinating things about the building, and he was, as well, making it his own. He had not quite realised, until he came to Witherwood Chase, how soul destroying it had been to live in his brother's house, dependent upon him. The gift of Witherwood Chase may have come with a mission which was frustrating and slow, but it had been a gift without price as far as its impact on his state of mind.

He was beginning to realise just how deeply blue-devilled he had become after his return from war. Working for Setford had begun to turn that around, but the simple fact of having his own place had been the biggest factor in shifting his view of the world. He still had days when it all seemed pointless (usually after digging through yet another few rooms of the house, and finding nothing more thrilling than mouse droppings and tasteless paintings), but they were less now.

He was, however, beginning to be annoyed. Setford was so certain that there was something here to find, yet he had been singularly unsuccessful to date, in finding any trace of either papers, or possible hiding places. But, he reminded himself, he had barely begun.

He had searched, in detail, barely more than a quarter of the house so far – he could not expect this to be easy, or Setford's men would have found everything when the treasonous previous owner was captured. The house was old – at least 500 years old - and had been extended many times. There was a warren of cellars and a tangle of tiny attic rooms, as well as the large quantity of rooms on the main floors. Add to that all of the outbuildings, and the scope for potential hiding places was extensive.

He had the feeling that some of the staff knew more about the house, and the events here before the conspirators had been caught, than they were telling him – he would simply have to find a way to get them to talk of it. He wondered, not for the first time, if the house had hidden passages and rooms. It was old enough to have been here at a time when hidden rooms, priest holes or secret passages and tunnels might have been needed, to escape the ravages of civil war. But if those things were there, he had yet to see any sign of them.

Perhaps, tomorrow, he would take a different approach. Leaving the rooms in the main part of the house for later, he would start with the attics, and see what interesting things he found there, then work his way from there down, a floor at a time, until he reached the deepest cellars. Attics in houses this old often contained items stored generations ago, so, if nothing else, he might actually have fun discovering items from bygone eras. And, should they include further truly ugly paintings, at least he could sell the damn things, to recoup some of the costs of putting the place back in order!

Having a plan made him feel more cheerful about it all.

Leaning back, he eyed the faded tapestry on the wall in front of him and sighed – another thing needing cleaning and care. Now that the drapes on the windows to the side of it had been replaced, the sad state of the tapestry was very obvious. Oh well, it could wait for now. Right now, as he sipped the last of his brandy, food was the most pressing thing on his mind.

Barnstable, as if he had heard the thought, chose that moment to appear at the door, announcing that dinner was served in the dining room. Lord Geoffrey rose and followed him from the room.

Chapter Three

The following day Lord Geoffrey took himself up to the attics, much to Barnstable's horror.

"My Lord! The attics are full of… um… a… rather historic… collection of… things… Not to mention dust, dirt, and probably rodents! Surely a gentleman like yourself doesn't wish to dig about in all that!"

"Oh, what fustian, Barnstable, stop fussing. I will, eventually, stick my nose into every nook and cranny this rather curious construction of a house has to offer. A little dust and dirt never hurt anyone. I might even find something of value – at least I can hope. If nothing else, I can ascertain whether the roof is leaking anywhere!"

Barnstable managed to look both offended and dignified at once (rather an achievement, Geoffrey thought) and, bowing stiffly, took himself out of the room. Geoffrey followed. As he entered the hallway, he saw one of the footmen moving hurriedly in the direction of the servant's stairs. Idly, he wondered what the rush was.

Putting that from his mind, he made his way up a rather impressive number of stairs, finally arriving at the door into the attics. It was a rather small door, and Lord Geoffrey, being a rather large man, squeezed through it carefully. He noted, with amusement, that Barnstable was right – he had already acquired smears of dust and dirt on his clothing – and that by just going through the door.

The attics proved to be a warren of rooms, spread across the under roof space of all of the main part of the house and the wings, sometimes in multiple levels, with small flights of stairs between them. To start with, all he did was wander from room to room, trying to get a feel for the scale of it. He found a section with a large rainwater cistern – no doubt responsible for the luxury of running water which was present in parts of the house, and a multitude of rooms full of stored furniture, paintings, and God knows what else, all covered in dust sheets.

Mid-afternoon, just as he was contemplating returning downstairs in search of luncheon, Lord Geoffrey opened another door. All thought of food left him instantly. This room, unlike the others, was ordered. Its walls were covered in carefully structured racks, stands and display cases were placed neatly about the space, and, on every rack, in every case, on every stand, were weapons and armour.

This one room was a museum collection of weaponry from centuries past and times recent. It was, in one room, more weapons that Geoffrey had ever seen before – including the armoury tent in their field camps during the war!

For a man whose distinguishing ability was consummate skill with weapons, this was the ultimate find. He felt rather like a small child presented with a room full of toys.

The swords, in particular, called to him. The light of his lantern reached into shadowy corners, drawing sparkling glints from sharpened metal. Even through the light layer of dust, he could see that they had been well cared for – as if someone, until very recently, had come here often, dusted, polished and oiled everything, to keep it in the best of condition. He wondered who. It did not matter.

The next few hours disappeared into a haze of delighted exploration, as he opened cases, lifted weapons down from the wall, and generally did an inventory of the contents of the room. This was certainly not what Setford wanted him to find, but, for himself, this alone was reward enough for all of the tedious time he had spent, and would spend, searching for the blasted treasonous papers.

"My Lord! My Lord?? Where are you?" Barnstable's voice came to him, distantly echoing through the attic rooms.

"Here Barnstable – in the north-west wing, I think."

Footsteps approached after a few minutes, and Barnstable peered through the door.

"Oh my!"

Barnstable's shock was obviously not feigned, as he stared in some awe at the contents of the room.

"I gather that you were not aware of this collection?"

"No, my Lord, not at all. It is... impressive, isn't it?"

"Quite. Even if I find nothing else of interest in the entire house, this is worth any amount of dust dirt and poking about. Now, what was it you came to tell me?"

"My Lord, it is nearly five – I believe that you are due at Pendholm Hall at seven, for dinner?"

"Is it? I quite lost track of time up here, with no light but my lantern. I'd best hurry then. Thank you."

Lord Geoffrey turned, and, with a last longing look at the beautiful collection of weaponry, closed the door and followed Barnstable out of the attics.

~~~~~

Lady Harriet was fidgeting. She had tried to read, and found herself unable to concentrate, even on the new novel that had just arrived. She had considered embroidery, and instantly discarded the notion – she did not do it well at the best of times. So now, she was wandering about the family parlour, randomly picking up the various small statues and items on the mantle and shelves, fiddling with them a few moments, then replacing them, just to keep herself busy. For sitting still was an impossibility, when, at any moment, Lord Geoffrey might arrive.

Had they been in the morning room, she might have sat at the pianoforte, and allowed herself to release her tensions into the music. That always worked. But, alas, this room did not contain an instrument, so she was left to fidgeting beneath her mother's amused and tolerant gaze.
~~~~~

Lady Sylvia observed her daughter with interest. Harriet had, it seemed, put more effort into her appearance this evening than usual, even allowing for the fact that they were expecting a guest. That would be because of who the guest was, she surmised. She was still quite uncertain about Harriet's obsession with Lord Geoffrey – he seemed to be of a temperament rather more quiet than Harriet's bright volatility. Perhaps that was part of why he appealed to her? But, for a man like that, would Harriet seem appealing, or merely childishly annoying?

For now, given that Lord Geoffrey's behaviour had always been utterly correct and polite, and that he was a man to whom she owed her life, as well as being one of Charlton's closest friends, she was willing to simply let things proceed as they would. Her thoughts were interrupted by the sound of the front door knocker, followed by the measured tread of the butler's feet on the marble foyer floor.

At those sounds, Harriet froze, arrested in mid motion as her hand reached for yet another trinket, and she stood a moment, a flush rising to her cheeks, and her heart beating hard, as she composed herself, ready to greet Lord Geoffrey when he was shown into the room. Then, with a deep breath, she moved again – turning to face the door just as it opened.

Lord Geoffrey was, as always, immaculately presented. The dark blue superfine of his perfectly cut coat displayed his powerful shoulders in a manner that quite stole Harriet's breath. It was ever so – no matter how much she prepared herself for his presence, each time the impact was just as great. Her breath stalled, her heart beat harder, and her ability to think became alarmingly dimmed.

He advanced into the room, bowing over her mother's hand, then hers. Somehow, she stammered a greeting in response to his. He turned to greet her brother. Her eyes drank him in as he spoke with Charlton, who was laughing at some comment Lord Geoffrey had made.

They all settled into the comfortable seats around the fireplace, and conversation flowed freely. As the initial effects of his presence wore off, Harriet regained her ability to think, and found that she had missed, apparently, quite a bit of conversation – it seemed that Charlton and Lord Geoffrey were discussing the events of the last year.

"It seems so surreal to me, Charlton, that it is, this week, a year since we returned from the war. So much has changed! Then, we were exhausted, heartsick from years of war, and unsure of how to go about life again, here. Now, we are all so much more settled, Hunter is married, you will be married in little more than a month, Raphael is off travelling and actually enjoying life, Gerry has been given a title – deservedly so – and Bart thinks he's found the perfect place to breed his horses. And as for me – I am finding that Witherwood Chase is far more interesting than I had expected. Having a place of my own has its challenges, but it is infinitely better than living on Alfred's sufferance."

Lord Geoffrey's rich, deep voice flowed over her, and she had to agree with his sentiments – it had been a remarkable year. It seemed that Charlton also agreed.

"Indeed, Geoff, it is hard to believe that Christmas is almost upon us. I will be glad to see the others at Meltonbrook Chase for twelfth night, although it seems that Raphael will not return in time – he will be sorely missed!"

"I have to assume that there is some great profit to be had from this venture, for it to have dragged him away for so long. We will simply have to wait to find out though – he's been remarkably close about it all. It's bad timing from my point of view – being purely selfish – Witherwood Chase, it turns out, is full of a great hoard of things that have been shoved away in its attics, rooms and cellars forever – perhaps centuries! Including the largest collection of ugly paintings that I have ever seen. I will be selling them, with Raphael's help, I hope. With a bit of luck, our canny merchant can help me actually make the place pay for all of the repairs I've done since I got here!"

"The previous occupant had bad taste then?" Lady Sylvia's voice was amused. "I never met the man, even though we were close neighbours. He never seemed to be here when we were. The villagers did sometimes remark on the state of his tenant's cottages though – it seems that he was not a good manager at all, and certainly not popular with his tenants, or anyone else in the district."

"That is very much true my Lady, this month has been one long tale of woe as far as the condition of the cottages, and of the house and outbuildings. I don't think the man had spent a penny on maintenance in the last few years at all. The tenant farmers are beginning to at least talk to me, now that I've had their cottages repaired in time for the worst of winter. How they survived last winter I've no idea, some of those cottages were so run down."

"I'm glad to hear that you're making progress – no-one deserves to go through winter without adequate shelter." Charlton spoke emphatically.

For both Charlton and Geoffrey, the memory of nights on cold winter ground, and peasant cottages ravaged by war, was close to the surface at that moment. Each knew, without words, what the other was thinking. After a moment's silence, Lord Geoffrey chose to turn the conversation to lighter things.

"Witherwood Chase has turned up some things rather more interesting than ugly paintings, disintegrating drapes and mouse droppings."

"Oh?" Charlton raised an eyebrow and waited for Lord Geoffrey to continue.

"Yes. Today, I decided to explore the attics – well, to start on that, at least – they are enormous, with rooms full of the discarded possessions of centuries of inhabitants. I found yet more ugly paintings – I can only assume that generations of that family had matching poor taste! But, late in the day, I found something quite wondrous." His voiced conveyed a sense of excitement that Lady Harriet had never heard in it before, and she gazed at him in some astonishment, suddenly desperate to hear more.

"There is a room up there which might best be described as a museum. A museum of perfectly cared for, neatly stored and displayed weaponry! Enough weaponry to outfit a regiment or more. I could spend weeks exploring the possibilities of what's in that room."

A boyish enthusiasm lit up Lord Geoffrey's face. Charlton smiled, caught up in the energy emanating from him.

"Well – it's yours now – you've got weeks to play with your new toys." Charlton grinned, and Lord Geoffrey laughed at his teasing.

"If only that was all I had to do! I've barely touched on the place, even though I've been digging into it for over a month now. I've made it my mission to explore every inch of it before I allow myself to indulge too much – God knows what the place has hidden in its crevices!"

As he spoke, his eyes were on Charlton's, and there was a slight emphasis on the words 'mission' and 'hidden' – an emphasis that Charlton did not miss. Unfortunately for Lord Geoffrey, Lady Harriet did not miss it either, as her adoring eyes were soaking in his every move. She found herself, when in his presence, unable to look away for too long – her eyes simply found their way back to him, as if that was the only natural place for them to rest.

She decided that there was more going on here than the apparent. And a puzzle was not something that she could leave alone. Nor was a secret. The idea of things hidden in Lord Geoffrey's house, of a potential treasure trove to be discovered, took her right back to her not-so-long-ago childhood. Before she could stop herself, words were falling from her mouth.

"Oh! I love digging through old things and finding treasures! Can I help? I am sure that Miss Carpenter would love to help too. If the house is that big and full of old things, surely more people going through them will get it done faster – and give you more time to explore those weapons." Harriet understood the value of bribery... surely he would agree to let her help, if it got him what he wanted, faster?

Lady Sylvia watched, fighting an urge to burst out laughing. The moment of what was almost terror in Lord Geoffrey's eyes did not escape her.

"Err, I... I am sure that you don't really want to get covered in dust and spider webs?" Lord Geoffrey spoke hopefully, having, for a moment, obviously forgotten that Lady Harriet was not your ordinary genteel young Lady.

Harriet laughed.

"Oh I don't mind dust and spider webs – it's no worse than I've found in the stables and the garden outbuildings, and I've been poking around in those all my life. I especially don't mind if there's something interesting to find!"

Lord Geoffrey glanced at Charlton, then at Lady Sylvia. When it was obvious that neither of them intended to rescue him, he took a deep breath, silently promising Charlton retribution for this later, and spoke.

"Well, umm..., in that case, I errr... I will be glad of your assistance, when you can spare the time. But you must be certain to bring Miss Carpenter – you must have a suitable chaperone with you, after all."

Lady Harriet tried, almost successfully, to repress her grin of triumph. Her heart beat faster at the very thought – she would get to spend whole days in his company! Surely, with such proximity, she could get him to start seeing her as a woman, not a child?

~~~~~

Unbeknownst to Lady Harriet, at that very moment, Lord Geoffrey was most decidedly seeing her as a woman.
~~~~~

He had been, quite unsuccessfully, trying to avoid looking at her all evening. From the moment that he had been shown into the parlour, he had been acutely aware of her – of the sensation of her leaf green eyes following him, of the delightful shape of her beautiful body, the flushed red of her lips, the slightly dishevelled fall of her dark gold curls, that seemed never to stay quite as tidy as her maid had intended, and the subtle rich floral scent that she wore – a mixture of rose, and daphne, with perhaps a tiny touch of lemon sharpening the sweetness.

He had never met another woman who used that combination of scents – a combination that instantly took him back to the scent garden of his grandmother's house, so long ago. It made him want to simply soak it in, for it brought him a sense of peace and safety that he had not felt since his childhood years. Which felt odd to him, as, at the same time, her presence roused in him a much more carnal appreciation of everything about her. No matter how often he told himself that such an appreciation of his closest friend's sister was not a good idea, his body refused to obey his mind, and flamed into awareness the instant he found himself in the same room as the delectable Lady Harriet.

Her childlike manipulation of the conversation had charmed him, even whilst it brought him a sensation of sheer terror – for how could he possibly carry out his mission to search the house for evidence of the traitors if he was to be continuously distracted by her presence? He would have to make sure of her safety, and still somehow search, whilst concealing what he was really looking for. His head hurt at the very thought of how hard that would be.

For Lady Harriet's keen intelligence and bright curious nature would ensure that she cheerfully investigated everything…

He had been sure that Charlton would save him, but the rogue had just sat there, and let his sister gull Geoffrey into doing as she wanted. They would have words about that later!

Still, he couldn't help but be warmed by the sight of the glowing smile on her face, now that he had agreed to allow her to help. Perhaps it was worth it, to make her look that happy.

Chapter Four

The staff at Witherwood Chase has greeted the additional two footmen and the valet with suspicion, having all been working at Witherwood Chase for many years. They had their own routines, their own unstated, but agreed, divisions of authority, and had, largely, got over interpersonal politics years ago. Which wasn't to say that there were no secrets, or that they all trusted each other.

Newcomers, however, had caused them to silently close ranks and defend their territory, without any discussion required. Peterson, as one of the newcomers, was acutely aware of the wall of silence that they presented to him. Cold politeness hid secrets, but whether those secrets were a previous complicity in treason, or simply a resentment of the invasion of the place that they saw as their own, he had not yet discovered.

In time, he would do so. Baron Setford had chosen him for his skills, which included things unusual in a footman, such as weapons training, lock-picking, tracking and investigation, amongst other things.

Lord Geoffrey was a man he could respect – a man who appreciated his capabilities, and left him to get on with things. There was nothing soft or foppish about Lord Geoffrey, and his reputed skill with weapons was something any man would admire.

This evening, with Lord Geoffrey away visiting Viscount Pendholm, Peterson was using the time to apply those investigative skills of his. Most of the staff were in the servants' hall, enjoying a quiet evening. But at least two were not. After Peterson had excused himself from the gathering, supposedly to take to his bed early, he had quietly waited in a small storeroom just outside the servants' hall.

His patience was rewarded when Jobs, one of the grooms, and Ashley, one of the footmen who had long been with the house, quietly left the room. They paused a moment, not far from the storeroom door, and spoke in whispers.

"Ash, if his Lordship keeps a'diggin around like this, he's sure to be findin a door soon. Things aren't safe. Not up here. They'll have to go deep with t'others."

"Aye, but how'll we get 'em moved? Can't be a'doin it now – we don't know when His Lordship'll be back, and you'll have to be in t'stable to take his horse when he gets here."

"So I'll be in t'stable. But you go now and make sure all's still where it ought to be, and pack em up so's we can move em the next time he's away – or sooner, if'n he gets too close."

"I don't like it, but ye have the right of it, we can't do more'n that tonight."

The two moved on, from the sound of their steps in two different directions, and moments later Peterson heard the door to the back garden open as Jobs headed back to the stable. A lone set of footsteps echoed along the corridor towards the servants stairs.

Peterson eased out of the storeroom, moving along the corridor on silent feet, listening to the footfalls ahead. With great care, he followed Ashley up the servant's stairs to the floor above, and along the servants' corridor there. The corridor turned, a short distance after exiting the stairs, and Peterson paused at the corner, peeking carefully around to assess Ashley's progress. The corridor was empty. Peterson shook his head. That wasn't possible – there were no doors off this corridor for quite some distance – he couldn't have gone that far yet. Yet the corridor was empty.

Peterson eased around the corner, and walked the length of the corridor – no door, no sign of Ashley. He shook his head and took himself to his bed, mulling over what he had heard, and seen – or rather, not seen.

~~~~~

The next morning brought two visitors to Witherwood Chase. One was expected – Lady Harriet, with the long-suffering Miss Carpenter (who, unlike Lady Harriet, *did* object to dust and spider webs...) in tow, and one was unexpected, but most welcome.

Barnstable, still recovering from the shock of Lady Harriet's somewhat energetic arrival, turned in surprise at the second knock on the door.
~~~~~

Upon opening it, he discovered a sprightly gentleman of middle years, dressed in fashionable clothing better suited to a young dandy, on the doorstep. The gent stepped inside, doffed his hat, and presented his card.

Winston Featherstonehaugh Esq.

Valuer of Artworks

Bowing, he looked Barnstable in the eye and declared -

"I am here to see Lord Geoffrey Clarence. Sent, at his request, by Mr Raphael Morton. Please let his Lordship know that I have arrived."

Barnstable, rather flustered by this apparition, showed him into the visitors' parlour, and went in search of Lord Geoffrey.

Lord Geoffrey, who was just in the process of settling Lady Harriet and Miss Carpenter into the morning room, and offering her tea (whilst he worked out how on earth he was going to keep her occupied and entertained, without giving up on his own investigations completely), was as startled as Barnstable had been, when handed the gentleman's card and told of his arrival.

After the surprise wore off, however, he was rather pleased. He had written to Raphael shortly after arriving here, when he had come to the conclusion that the place was packed with horrible art, asking if he might advise on getting it valued, as a step towards disposing of it profitably. It would appear that Raphael had gone one better than simply advising, and had, before setting off on his travels, engaged a valuer on Lord Geoffrey's behalf.

How typical of Raphael! He was always generous, and often chose to simply act, rather than fuss about anything. And, perhaps, this was also a solution to occupying Lady Harriet, at least for a while, and doing so in a way where he did not have to be in her presence (and thus tortured by his awareness of her). He turned to her, smiling, and waited a moment whilst a maid delivered the tea, and left the room. Once the maid was gone, he spoke.

"Lady Harriet, might I ask you to carry out an important task for me?"

"Why of course, Lord Geoffrey – what can I do to help?"

She sounded genuinely delighted that he had a task for her, and he found himself charmed yet again by her positive, energetic nature.

"I am sure that you heard me mention, yesterday, that this house contains a vast quantity of artworks that are… not to my taste… shall we say?"

She nodded, wondering what was coming next.

"A gentleman has just arrived, whose skill is in valuing artworks. I have need of someone to go from room to room with him, and to take down notes for me on what he says about each painting, and to also make those notes very clear about the exact position of each painting, so that, later, we make no mistakes when sorting them for sale. I can provide Peterson, my footman, to be guide and escort from room to room, if you, and Miss Carpenter, will be my scribes, and capture this information for me?"

It wasn't exactly the sort of task that Harriet had hoped for, but still, it was a start. And Lady Harriet found, rather to her own surprise, that, because it was Lord Geoffrey who was asking, she was willing to take on this task, even if it sounded rather less adventurous than what she had been imagining.

"Certainly, Lord Geoffrey. I would be pleased to assist."

Had his shoulders just sagged with relief? Surely not, she pushed the thought away. That must have been her imagination at work.

"One moment."

Lord Geoffrey left the room, and went to greet Mr Featherstonehaugh. As he stepped into the room, he suddenly better understood Barnstable's reaction. The man was unusual, to say the least. Still, Raphael had recommended him. A few minutes conversation confirmed Lord Geoffrey's faith in Raphael.

However eccentric the man might appear, he seemed to know his field, providing a rapid and somewhat passionately enthusiastic assessment of the painting on the parlour wall as demonstration of his knowledge. And the number he named as a value for the painting left Lord Geoffrey a little shocked, and very pleased. If all of the paintings had similar values, he was about to be a wealthy man indeed.

After enquiring as to Mr Featherstonehaugh's arrangements, and sending a footman to pay off his driver and bring in his luggage, then to see the housekeeper about having a room prepared, he led the man into the morning room.

Upon introducing Mr Featherstonehaugh to Lady Harriet and Miss Carpenter, he was surprised to see that, within minutes, Lady Harriet had charmed Mr Featherstonehaugh, and that Mr Featherstonehaugh had charmed Miss Carpenter — which, based on his past observation of the woman, was quite an achievement! Leaving them chattering enthusiastically about the paintings on the morning room wall, he sent Peterson to fetch some pencils and suitable paper, as well as a slate to rest the paper on. Stepping back into the room he breathed a sigh of relief — perhaps his day would contain useful work after all, for the ladies appeared to be forging a firm friendship with Mr Featherstonehaugh already.

When Peterson returned, he explained the requirement, and that Peterson should, for the next few days, or until such time as the inventory was complete, place himself at Mr Featherstonehaugh and Lady Harriet's command. Given that the inventory would also need to deal with those paintings currently in the attics, which would need to be brought down for inspection, it was likely to take some considerable time.

As they set off into the house, Lord Geoffrey breathed a sigh of heartfelt relief — even though a traitorous part of him regretted letting Lady Harriet out of his sight.

~~~~~

Lady Harriet was delighted when Lord Geoffrey actually seemed to be taking her wish to help seriously. Expecting a tedious task, and quite prepared to be a martyr to her regard for him and do it anyway, she was pleasantly surprised.
~~~~~

For the gentleman valuer was entertaining, passionate about his subject, and quite willing to treat a Lady's assistance with respect. He was, she suspected, the only other person that she had ever met, who was quite as… vigorous… a personality as she herself was. And, even better, Miss Carpenter appeared to actually like him! Perhaps she might not moan about the whole process after all.

Therefore, when Peterson has supplied her with pencils, paper and a slate, she was happy to leave the room and begin the apparently extensive task of cataloguing the paintings in this rather large house. Happy that is, all but a little anguished regret at not being able to stay in the same room as Lord Geoffrey, who, it seemed, had other work to do, elsewhere. She was sure that it was important. He would surely not, after all, be avoiding her company.

Chapter Five

Two sennights passed, and Christmas was upon them. It was two sennights of tedium, interspersed with moments of humour, frustration and delighted discovery. Lady Harriet, in a manner that quite astounded her family, stuck to her stated intentions, and went, accompanied by Miss Carpenter, every day, to continue the work. Such persistence, from the normally volatile Harriet, made her mother begin to think that, truly, it was possible that her *tendre* for Lord Geoffrey was more than a passing infatuation.

What astounded them all more (including Harriet herself), was that Miss Carpenter also went willingly and cheerfully, without complaint. For once she seemed to actually be happy with being dragged along by Harriet, willy-nilly. No-one mentioned either fact. But the general interest in what might be found in the rooms and attics of Witherwood Chase was high.

Lord Geoffrey was both pleased with the progress and utterly frustrated.

Pleased, because Mr Featherstonehaugh's valuation list was providing growing evidence that the dusty collection of paintings, antique furniture and tapestries in the house represented an astounding amount of wealth – even if Geoffrey only sold a small portion of them.

Frustrated, because he was still only marginally closer to fulfilling his mission for Baron Setford.

Peterson had confirmed that at least two of the staff who had come with the estate, appeared to have been party to the treasonous conspiracy, and that he suspected the house contained secret passageways or rooms. But he had been unable to find an entry, or to get enough detail of the men's involvement for Lord Geoffrey to take any action.

In addition, the daily interaction with Lady Harriet was a source of constant stress. The more he saw of her, the harder it became for Lord Geoffrey to think of her as 'Charlton's sister', and the easier it became for him to see her simply for herself – an attractive young woman, who had more determination and less fussiness about her than any other woman of his acquaintance. That she stuck at the dusty and somewhat boring work impressed him, and his respect for her grew daily. As did his attraction to her. He wanted to know more about her – how she thought, what on earth possessed her to want to do this for him, why she saw him as anything more than her brother's friend. Surely she could not still be casting him as some fairy-tale hero, based on the events of nearly a year ago?

Her scent had subtly infiltrated the house, and he was, even when in another wing of the building entirely, always aware of her.

~~~~~

They had fallen into the habit of gathering in his study each afternoon, to go over the achievements of the day – the latest finds in various rooms, as far as paintings and other items of value (for they had, some time ago, dealt with the items he had already seen, and headed into previously unexplored territory in the long unused wings of the house), the progress of repairs and renovation of many parts of the house, and the plans for the morrow.

When it was but a few days to Christmas, Mr Featherstonehaugh spoke up, after reporting his latest finds.

"Lord Geoffrey – I would like to make a pause in this work. Whilst I am keen, extremely keen, to see this through to the end – for never before have I had the privilege to assess such a remarkable collection -..." his eyes shone as he spoke, and he almost bounced on the spot, his enthusiasm still as bright as the day they had begun, "- I am also keen to return to my family for this holiday season. Now that my wife is gone, whilst they are happy in my mother's care, my children will want to see me at this time If it is agreeable to you, my Lord, I would take leave of you until just after twelfth night, then return to your most gracious hospitality to continue this work."

Whilst Lord Geoffrey felt ready to grind his teeth in frustration at the thought of another few sennights of delay to his mission, he could not, in good countenance, refuse such a request. Added to that, he, and Charlton's family, had committed to spending twelfth night at Meltonbrook Chase, where most of the other Hounds would be present.
~~~~~

He would need to devise a way to ensure that the servants suspected of being conspirators had no chance to remove anything in his absence.

"That seems, Mr Featherstonehaugh, to be an admirable plan. I must commend your good work to date, and that of Lady Harriet and Miss Carpenter in documenting your findings. I wish you the best of the season and will gladly release you to your family for now. Peterson will see to making travel arrangements for you."

He turned, unable to prevent himself, aware, as always, of Lady Harriet. She was watching him, her face a picture of conflicting emotion. Her emotions often showed on her countenance, and he was beginning to understand more of her thoughts, just from watching her face. It seemed that she felt as he did – both glad of the rest and the holiday, and reluctant to lose the excuse to spend each day, at least partly, in company with him. He most certainly felt that way with respect to her.

He had come to look forward to her arrival each day, to her bright enthusiasm lifting his spirits and to watching her sparkling green eyes light up with delight each time some new and interesting treasure was unearthed, revealed by the removal of a tattered dust sheet, or the unlocking of a previously locked chest. When she spun about exuberantly with childlike joy in the discoveries, he sometimes had to stop himself from sweeping her up and spinning with her. The impulse rather shocked him, for he had never been one for such outward show of his feelings. But stop himself he did, for he suspected that, should he take her into his arms like that, it would not stop at simply spinning about.

He was terrifyingly certain, that, should he gather her to him, he would be unable to stop himself from kissing her.

At this moment, watching the flicker of sadness cross her face, followed by what seemed... could it possibly be... like longing... he wanted more than ever to kiss her. Propriety be damned. Somehow, in the last month, he had come to care for her in a new and different way. He pushed the thoughts aside and firmly repeated to himself, mentally *'Charlton's sister – not for you!'*.

Lady Harriet took a deep breath and the normal bright smile appeared on her face. She spoke politely, granting Mr Featherstonehaugh a curtsey.

"I wish you well of the season, Mr Featherstonehaugh, and your family. I will look forward to making new discoveries with you when you return."

Her words were followed by another soft voice, hesitant but clear, surprising Lady Harriet into turning slightly to look.

"As do I Mr Featherstonehaugh – this has been a most enlivening few sennights, which I have much enjoyed." Miss Carpenter actually blushed slightly as she spoke.

Lord Geoffrey and Lady Harriet shared a startled look, and both, at the identical moment, raised an eyebrow. The understanding between them was instant, and they found themselves then repressing laughter. It would seem that the usually somewhat stiff-necked Miss Carpenter had been charmed rather more than might have been expected!

Mr Featherstonehaugh swept them all a flourishing bow, thanked them for their words, and took himself off to pack.

~~~~~

As they swept up the drive of Meltonbrook Chase, Lord Geoffrey felt a little ridiculous. Here he was, arriving in his own new carriage, with a groom, two footmen and a valet. After all of those years at war, this entourage seemed excessive, yet he had no choice. He had left Walters, the other unusually skilled footman sent by Setford, at Witherwood Chase to keep an eye out for anything suspicious. With him, he had Peterson, his valet Hurst, Ashley as the second footman, and Jobs as groom and driver.

He had concluded that the simplest way to prevent his two suspect conspirators from removing evidence while he was away, was to to take them with him. They could scarcely refuse his command, but their surly expressions upon being told that they had been chosen to accompany him had seemed a good indication that Peterson's suspicions were correct.

His thoughts were brought back to the present as the house came into sight through the winter bare trees – magnificent, and imposing. And a scene of mild chaos, with multiple carriages vying for space before the doors. It would seem that everyone had arrived at once.

When he alighted from the carriage, he was swept up into exuberant greetings and laughter, leaving poor Peterson and Hurst to deal with unloading and managing the distribution of his belongings to the appropriate places, whilst he tried to keep straight all of the new faces and names through a whirlwind of introductions which only slowed down once they were all ensconced in the parlour with refreshments.
~~~~~

With a few exceptions, they were a far happier group than they had been a year ago. The year had wiped the outward traces of war from the lines of their faces, had softened the edges of their bodies a little and removed the gauntness of years of hard living, and, most importantly, had brought love and family back into their lives.

Hunter Barrington, Duke of Melton, was a transformed man – he had returned grief stricken and lost in so many ways, yet here he was with his delightful new Duchess and obviously very happy. Charlton was equally happy, and was seated beside his betrothed, Lady Odette, who, with her aunt Lady Farnsworth, had been invited to their gathering as well. Bart and Gerry were tucked away in the corner, probably talking horses – but, whilst they were the quietest in the room, and perhaps still carried the strongest after effects of the war in their minds, they too looked cheerful. Hunter's sisters, Lady Sybilla and Lady Alyse had joined their conversation and appeared to be holding their own on the topic of horses.

The Dowager Duchess of Melton and Lady Sylvia had settled with Lady Farnsworth, and seemed deep in discussion of the plans for Charlton's wedding. The only others in the room were Lady Harriet and Miss Carpenter, Hunter's brother Charles was away, apparently dealing with estate matters elsewhere, much to his mother's displeasure.

Lady Harriet had settled on the seat of the pianoforte near the large windows to the rear of the room, her hands stroking its surface almost reverently. Miss Carpenter seemed rather lost, but, faithful shadow to Lady Harriet, she had settled on a small elegant chair off to one side, and simply watched.

It seemed wrong that Raphael was not there too. What could be so important that he would sail off and miss this gathering?

The thought was fleeting and Lord Geoffrey found himself drawn into conversation with Hunter, Charlton and their Ladies and the afternoon disappeared into the flow of discussion.

Somewhere along the way, Lord Geoffrey realised that a quiet, yet beautiful thread of melody was winding its way through the room. Not loud enough to disrupt any conversation, but soothing and relaxing in the background. He was drawn, as always to watch Lady Harriet, whose fingers on the keys were producing the marvellous sound. She seemed more still, more relaxed than he had ever seen her, and her eyes were closed – she played from memory, by feel alone, seemingly unaware of her audience, just lost in the music. He had not thought it possible for her to look more beautiful than she usually did – but like this, she was stunning.

With a start, he realised that one of the others had addressed him – had possibly spoken his name more than once.

"My apologies – I am a little... distracted."

"So I see." Hunter laughed good-naturedly and returned to the topic. "I must show you Nerissa's plans for the grounds – come spring, you won't recognise the gardens. We will have the most beautiful park of any estate in the county. But enough of us – what have you to tell us about your new estate? How goes your restoration of Witherwood Chase? I hear that it's a huge rambling place that needed quite a bit of maintenance?"

"That is an accurate, if rather understated summary! It's five or six hundred years of rambling additions to the building worth of unmaintained mess."

Hunter laughed at his expression, whilst Charlton added his own commentary.

"It is, at least, an elegantly proportioned building – through all of those additions, and no matter how tangled the interior layout is, at least they managed to keep the exterior attractive!"

"True." Lord Geoffrey turned to Lady Nerissa, "I believe you would enjoy the gardens, my Lady, for the front between the wings of the house is a lovely formal pattern, and the rear, enclosed between the other wings has been a well-designed herb and scent garden. They appear to have had little good care for some years, yet retain the evidence of their design. I would be honoured should you be willing to apply your skills to helping me plan their restoration and improvement."

The young Duchess favoured him with a glowing smile which lit up her face and clapped her hands together in delight.

"Nothing would please me more, Lord Geoffrey – I will be sure to inspect them in great detail when we gather at your estate for Easter."

Conversation flowed, and Lord Geoffrey drifted from one group to another, more relaxed than he had been in months, yet always aware of the music winding through the room, his eyes drifting, again and again, back to Lady Harriet as she played.

This was something of her that he had not known, and it intrigued him that one who was normally so active and energetic could be so still and peaceful.

Eventually, dinner was announced, and Miss Carpenter stepped forward, diffidently, and gently touched Lady Harriet's shoulder, bringing her back to awareness of the room. Lady Harriet flushed, and looked rather surprised to find that so much time had passed. She stood, composed herself, and stepped forward.

Somehow, Lord Geoffrey found that he was in the perfect position to offer her his arm, and lead her in to dinner – and to discover himself seated between her, and Lady Odette. Dinner was both delightful and torture, for Lord Geoffrey was acutely aware of Lady Harriet's presence, so close beside him, her scent winding its way around him, and of the fact that he should not be reacting to her the way that he was, the way that he always did, no matter his resolve to not do so.

To add to his discomfiture, Lady Odette insisted on thanking him, yet again, for his actions in saving her life, and Charlton's, earlier in the year, even though those actions had meant the death of her father. Lady Harriet's eyes shone with that alarming hero worship again, as the story was told for those who had not been present at the time. And he had been hoping that she had stopped seeing him that way! How could he ever live up to such a perception? He was no hero, he was simply a man who did what must be done, when it was needed.

By the end of dinner, he was heartily glad to escape to the library and a glass of port with the other men.

With only Hounds present, Lord Geoffrey felt comfortable enough to discuss, a little, his mission for Setford, and his current frustrating lack of progress. They all agreed to keep an eye on the behaviour of Jobs and Ashley whilst the men were at Meltonbrook Chase. Charlton regaled them with the tale of Lady Harriet trapping Lord Geoffrey into letting her help with the exploration of Witherwood Chase, and great merriment and teasing resulted. But it was not without sympathy.

Geoffrey followed up with a description of the findings so far, including the weapons 'museum' in the attic – a find that they were all keen to see for themselves. His tales of dust sheets and mouse droppings, ugly paintings and archaic furniture were greeted with less enthusiasm, until he mentioned some of Mr Featherstonehaugh's astounding valuations of the pieces. He was slapped on the back and congratulated on his luck. In his opinion, it was only fair compensation for all his, so far fruitless, searching for hidden compartments or passages.

They settled to talking about possible places a door could be hidden, or a mechanism to unlock one, in a room or a hall. Lord Geoffrey took careful note of their ideas – anything was worth a try if it got him a step further towards finding the blasted papers for Setford.

This was the point at which, again, he missed Raphael's presence – for Raphael was the one who would have immediately 'seen' a logical plan of attack to test for, and undoubtedly find, the hidden passages. His sharp mind had always been able to lay out an approach better than any of them could.

Ah well, surely he would see Raphael at Charlton's wedding, although, god willing, by then he would have found the papers and be done with this mission.

~~~~~

Lady Harriet had excused herself from the parlour and gone in search of the necessary. That urgent business dealt with, as she returned along the hall, she heard the murmur of the men's voices through a door she was passing.

She stopped. Eavesdropping was wrong... but... she wanted to know what they spoke of... what was men's conversation about, when they were by themselves?

Feeling guilty, she applied her ear to the door. They were discussing the many ways that hidden doors and passages, rooms and compartments could be made or unlocked, in a house! What a remarkable thing to talk about. But wait... they seemed to be discussing how Lord Geoffrey could find such a thing in _his_ house! At the faint sound of a servant's footfall, imagination aflame, she stepped away from the door, and returned to the parlour.

~~~~~

Peterson, leaving Hurst to wait for Lord Geoffrey in his guest suite, went out to the stables to make sure that the carriage and horses had been suitably cared for, and to check on Ashley and Jobs.

The two had been given a small room to share in the stable block, whilst Hurst and Peterson had been given an equally tiny room in the servants' quarters of the house. With this many people, and all of their staff, in attendance, space was at a premium.

He stepped into the shadowed stables and paused. The two men were there, alone, at the far end of the row of stalls, talking quietly. Peterson froze, easing back into deeper shadow behind a rack hung with horse rugs, the scent of horses and hay rich around him, and listened. They were not speaking loudly, yet the words carried to him clearly by some trick of the building's structure.

Horses snuffled, but apart from that, there was only the men's voices to hear.

"It'll be right 'til we's back. He can't be a'searchin through the place while he's here." Ashley didn't entirely sound like he believed what he was saying.

"True, and that silly lookin' little art man's gone off home for the holiday too. So with Lord Geoffrey and Lady Harriet here we should be good."

"Still, soon's we's back, we'd better git 'em moved. 'E might find the top spot, but 'e's not like t'find the deep one."

"But Ash, what about later like. D'ye reckon any of them fancy blokes'll be ever comin' back? 'R we hidin this stuff fer nuthin?"

"Shut that thinkin Jobs! Old master paid us good to keep t'stuff safe, 'n we will. That's all there is to it."

"Right then. What'll we do if'n he gets close then? D'ye reckon as we could scare 'im off the place?"

"Not likely. 'E's a tough one – you seen 'im with them swords. Right scared me proper that. We don' wanna be buying any trouble. Just keep the stuff hid. We can worry about what to do else when we has to, 'n not afore."

At that, Jobs absently stroked the nose of the nearest horse, and the two took themselves off through the row of stalls and out the door into the grooms' quarters.

Peterson waited a few minutes, then eased out of shadow, checked on the horses, and the carriage in the next section of the building, and headed back to the house. It was good that the men had, apparently, seen Lord Geoffrey at weapons practice, and been scared by his skill. So they should be!

He was no closer to knowing what it was, exactly, that the men had hidden, but the conversation at least confirmed that it was still at Witherwood Chase, and that they wouldn't be taking it elsewhere any time soon.

They were canny, but they'd have to eventually make a mistake – one way or another, Peterson intended to find the entry to the secret passages – he was, more than ever, convinced that the papers, if that was what they were 'keeping safe' must be hidden in secret rooms or passages somewhere in the upper floors of the house. By now, there wasn't a lot of the main area of the house left unexplored, so secret places became more and more likely.

Chapter Six

With Christmas and Twelfth Night gone, Lord Geoffrey was ready to tackle the mystery of the hidden papers again. His conversations with the other Hounds had filled him with renewed determination to prod and poke at every possible piece of the walls and framing, until he found a way into the hidden passages – for he was convinced that such passages existed. What Peterson had overheard whilst they were at Meltonbrook Chase had just added to that certainty.

They were watching Ashley and Jobs closely since their return, in the hope that the two might accidentally reveal an entrance. At this instant, though, Lord Geoffrey's biggest concern was Lady Harriet. For, once the nearly complete assessment of all of the paintings and antique furniture was done, how was he to keep her occupied, should she insist on continuing to 'help', so that she was not always with him, so that she wouldn't notice his rather eccentric looking behaviour, when he started poking and prodding at the walls of his house?

As if his thoughts of Lady Harriet had summoned her, she and Miss Carpenter arrived at that moment.

Mr Featherstonehaugh had arrived just a few hours ago, and settled in, newly enthused about his task, and keen to finish the assessment. Although, it had seemed to Lord Geoffrey, he was rather sad that it was coming to an end. He had asked, with studied casualness, if any new rooms, or storage spaces, had been discovered?

'I wish' had been Lord Geoffrey's internal thought, although he wasn't wishing for quite the same sort of new hoard of treasure that Mr Featherstonehaugh seemed to be.

Interestingly, Miss Carpenter blushed like a schoolgirl when Mr Featherstonehaugh greeted her with his customary flourishing bow and a kiss on her hand. Lady Harriet observed it with a raised eyebrow again, and said nothing.

A plan was devised, mapping out which parts of the house had yet to be checked for paintings, cleaned and set to rights, and they all set about their appointed tasks. Lord Geoffrey stood in his study, staring, unseeing, at the faded tapestry before him, as he decided where he would start.

Perhaps, given the conversations that Peterson had overheard, with mentions of down, and deep, he should work in the cellars and the servants' belowstairs rooms. It would be braving the wrath of Mrs Chester, and possibly disrupting his dinner, but it had to be done.

Days later, he was no further advanced, and had achieved little but convincing most of his staff that he was mad.

His obsessive need to have seen, touched and inspected every single corner of his home utterly puzzled them —no member of the nobility they had ever met before had given a damn about such things.

And so it went.

Mr Featherstonehaugh, with the able assistance of Lady Harriet and Miss Carpenter, and the guidance of Peterson, worked steadily through the remaining rooms, as well as the large quantity of paintings and objects which Lord Geoffrey had instructed be brought down from the attics, for their convenience.

Lord Geoffrey, with ever increasing frustration, worked steadily through the entire house, for what felt like the thousandth time, poking and prodding at walls, carvings, architraves and anything else, likely or unlikely, which might conceivably conceal a mechanism to open a hidden door or panel.

He drove the frustration from his mind by spending a few hours at the end of each day on weapons practice, trying out progressively, all of the remarkable collection of swords and other weapons that the room in the attics had provided.

Meanwhile, repairmen came and went, new items of furniture were delivered, old ones were repaired, rooms were painted, or papered with new, brighter and more appealing colours, drapes were replaced and the house was generally being brought back to the state it deserved to be maintained in.

The tenant farmer's cottages were in better condition than they had been for many years, and the farmers themselves had come from grudging politeness to cheerful respect and liking for their new Lord. Were it not for Baron Setford's mission, he could almost be happy. Almost... for a traitorous voice in his mind whispered that, without the mission, he would have no excuse to spend so much time in Lady Harriet's company.

~~~~~

A month passed, and, with only a few days' work remaining on the assessment of valuables, the neat ledgers of Mr Featherstonehaugh's findings, so ably written in Lady Harriet and Miss Carpenter's hands, showed totals so large that it made Lord Geoffrey's head spin. Gifts from Prinny might rarely come with cash attached, but this one had certainly come with more wealth included than anyone might ever have imagined.

He was now so wealthy that it might even bring him close to the wealth enjoyed by Raphael, or by Hunter, now that the mismanagement of his estates in his father's time had been corrected. It gave him great satisfaction – satisfaction that he really should not indulge in – to realise that he was now, in no way whatsoever, dependent upon his miserable brother. Alfred would be livid. He would have no leverage left, to use to try to make Lord Geoffrey behave *as my heir should*.

Hopefully, Raphael would be at Charlton's wedding – Geoffrey couldn't imagine him missing it, but who knew, with the sea, when ships would come in.
~~~~~

If Raphael was there, then it should be possible to get him to stay at Witherwood Chase a few days, to see the remarkable collection, and put in place a plan for its sale to the right buyers. There were, actually, a few pieces that Lord Geoffrey might keep – amongst the ugly paintings there were a small number of attractive ones – ones that Lady Harriet had expressed admiration for. Perhaps he would gift them to her.

With the wedding only a few days away, the pace of final organisation at Pendholm Hall was intense. When Charlton had decided to be married at Pendholm Hall, rather than in the crush of London as the Season began, Lord Geoffrey had been relieved.

Not only would he be able to continue his mission with less interruption, but he would not have to face the fluttering sea of hopeful young ladies seeking a wealthy war hero, who was heir to a Marquessate, to marry. Nor, whispered that part of his mind that he chose not to listen to, would Lady Harriet be surrounded by the sea of young fops who sought an heiress to marry.

The approaching wedding had, perforce, caused work to stop on the painting assessment, to a large extent. The last few rooms worth, carted down from the attics, would have to wait a week or so.

Lady Harriet and Miss Carpenter were required at the Hall to assist with the preparations, so Lord Geoffrey had asked Mr Featherstonehaugh to review his work so far and confirm his valuations as listed in the ledgers , adding some notes on which pieces he felt might sell fastest, and which pieces he believed he knew of specific potential buyers for.

With typical generosity, Lady Sylvia, upon hearing that Mr
Featherstonehaugh would still be in residence, had invited him
to the wedding as well.

After a hurried consultation with Peterson, Lord Geoffrey
had solved the issue of how to limit the activities of their two
suspect conspirators, whilst they were at the wedding, by
volunteering the men to Lady Sylvia as extra help, to assist with
the influx of horses, carriages and guests which would descend
upon Pendholm Hall. Putting aside his annoyance with the
stubbornness of his house, in not giving up its secrets, Lord
Geoffrey chose, instead, to spend some time in sword work.

The weapons from the attic were fast becoming old friends,
to the extent that the two swords he liked best now graced the
wall of his study, in easy reach whenever he felt the need to
work off his frustration.

Chapter Seven

As Lord Geoffrey dressed for the wedding, standing obediently still for Hurst to force his cravat into a complex style with military precision, her wondered what it would feel like, to want a woman so much, that you chose to marry her, and commit for life. He had seen, in both Hunter and Charlton's faces, the certainty that they had made the right choice, that happiness would be the outcome. Yet still, when he thought of the concept, what came to his mind was the image of his brother, bickering with his wife, both of them always miserable, trapped with each other forever. He shuddered.

Maybe happiness was possible – but for him? He wasn't sure. Perhaps his family was cursed. His parent's marriage had been no better than his brother's.

~~~~~

The wedding ceremony was done, and the day was drawing to a close.
~~~~~

Lady Sylvia and Lady Farnsworth had settled onto two chairs in the corner of the ballroom at Pendholm Hall, for a well-deserved rest. As they sat, watching the younger people dance, they discussed the events of the day.

The wedding had been wonderful, the celebration a success, and now Charlton and Odette were waltzing together, so obviously in love that it quite lit up the room. But wait, there, beyond them – Harriet was waltzing with Lord Geoffrey – the little minx, so she had finally persuaded him to at least look at her as a young woman. All that persistence with trudging through dusty rooms and taking notes about ugly old paintings must have achieved something for her. Lady Sylvia had to admire her daughter's sheer willpower. She was definitely beginning to think that Harriet's fascination with Lord Geoffrey had gone beyond mere infatuation, for surely, after a year, a simple infatuation would have faded.

Lady Sylvia still wasn't sure that she approved – after all, he was considerably older than Harriet, and a rather serious man – still, who knew what might come of it? He had proven himself, over this last few months, to be a man of integrity, a man who cared for his tenants, and stuck to his word. Perhaps that serious, caring nature was just what was needed as a foil to Harriet's bright volatility.

Turning further, she saw Mr Raphael Morton, the only one of the Hounds that she had not met before today. He had arrived just in time for the wedding, apparently having come almost straight from his ship, and been greeted with great joy by his fellow Hounds. She thought he looked pensive, sad, as if something troubled him, but his eyes followed Charlton and Odette wistfully. She wondered what that was about.

Lady Sylvia had liked him immediately, no matter his lack of title and the fact that he was a merchant. Any man who was a close friend of her son was welcome in her home. He was, she believed, planning to stay with Lord Geoffrey for the next few days – something to do with arranging the sale of all of those ugly paintings that Harriet had been helping to catalogue.

Her eyes found Harriet and Lord Geoffrey again, as they swirled past her on the dance floor. Harriet gazed into his eyes with that adoration which had, from the day that she had first met him, as the hero of the hour, never faded. And, most interestingly, Lord Geoffrey appeared to be gazing back into Harriet's eyes with an expression of wonder, as if he had only just discovered something new about her.

Lady Sylvia smiled to herself, well pleased with the day, all over again.

$$\sim\sim\sim\sim\sim$$

Lady Harriet had planned her campaign carefully. She had tracked, as subtly as she could, Lord Geoffrey's movements in the room, and made quite certain that she was close to him, when the orchestra struck up a waltz. As he looked around, apparently considering escaping the room, she had simply stepped in front of him, smiling, and waited. He had gulped, glanced around, and apparently, having now known her for some time, concluded that she had, yet again, trapped him neatly. He had offered her his hand, raised an enquiring eyebrow, and, at her nod of acceptance, swept her on to the floor.

She looked stunning. Her gown of a vibrant rich green (a colour officially unsuited to so young a woman, according to the disapproving old biddies of the *ton*) made her eyes shine, and made their green even brighter. Her rich dark gold hair was swept up into a pile of artful curls, which tumbled to the side, drawing the eye to her shoulders and the creamy expanse of her décolletage. His eyes were most happy to be led there.

As he took her into his arms, her unique scent surrounded him, a scent which he found arousing, yet the scent of safety, of home, of childhood delight. After the long day, and a glass or two of celebratory wine, she was intoxicating to his tired senses. He wanted to kiss her. He had known, for so long now, that should he take her into his arms, he would want to do just that. He forced himself to remain a gentleman, guiding her through the flow of dancers, letting the swirling steps of the waltz carry them smoothly around the room. She was light on her feet and sure, seeming made to fit against him, somehow perfectly matched, even though he was large and tall, and she was quite petite of height, and slim.

She was gazing into his eyes, her face full of that adoration that he found so alarming, however flattering it might be to be regarded as a hero. He found himself gazing back, and the room faded away around them, until it seemed it was only them, and the music. Her eyes, seen close up like this, were a mixture of shades of green, like sunlight through leaves in spring, and they shone with her pleasure in the moment. He was lost in their depths. How had he ever thought her a child? Once, that might have been the case, but no more. The woman he held in his arms was well shaped and grown, and well aware of her own desires.

In that moment, even the fact that what she desired was him, suddenly seemed less frightening. But, cold reason insinuated itself into the moment, she was still Charlton's little sister! He should not be looking at her like this, with eyes that heated with desire, that traced her delectable lips and wished to kiss them. He needed to escape, or he would, of a certainty, do something he would forever regret. As soon as the waltz ended he would deliver her back to that companion of hers, and find Raphael.

As if the thought had magically caused her to appear, he saw Miss Carpenter. But she wasn't standing patiently on the sidelines, as was usually expected of a companion and chaperone. She was swirling past them on the floor, in the arms of none other than Mr Featherstonehaugh. Well, if that was the lay of the land, things might soon be most interesting!

~~~~~

Harriet had lost all sense of time and place. The feeling of being in Lord Geoffrey's arms was better, oh so much better, than anything she had imagined. She gazed into his dark storm grey eyes and simply soaked up the moment. She knew well that her heart was quite likely on her face, her feelings spelled out for anyone to see, and she didn't care one whit. So long as he saw and did not instantly abandon her, she could cope.

His eyes connected with hers, and the warmth, and... was that desire?... that she saw in them made her heart race and her breathing come short. She had no idea how long the music played, only a wish for it to never end.
~~~~~

But, of course, it did.

He had appeared as caught up in the moment as she, but as the music stopped, he swirled her to the side, and quickly delivered her to Miss Carpenter's company, before bowing elegantly.

"Thank you, Lady Harriet. If you will excuse me, I must have a word with Mr Morton."

He turned, leaving her feeling somewhat lost and bereft, and walked away from her rapidly, as if escaping some terrible fate. Her mouth fell open in shock a moment, before she forced her best bright smile back onto her face. How could he? How mortifying! She had thought, for a little there that he... but no, obviously not.

She was still determined. There was hope. She would not give up. There was no-one else for her. She would convince him yet.

Chapter Eight

Three months! He had been searching through the entirety of the damn house for three whole months now! It had delivered him enormous riches in artworks, antique furniture, tapestries and trinkets. It had provided a magnificent collection of weapons. It had delivered him a new perspective on the world, and a new sense of self-worth, as he restored farmers' lives, as well as their cottages. It had delivered him the delicious torture of seeing Lady Harriet nearly every day. But the one thing it had not delivered him was the papers that Baron Setford required him to find.

And now he was at wits end. He could not imagine where else to look, yet he had not found the secret passageways or any other hidden spaces. And today, Mr Featherstonehaugh had finished the last of his assessment. In a few scant minutes, he, Peterson and the Ladies would appear in this very room to report the final discoveries.

What was he to do once that was done?

Raphael had been amazed at the paintings and other objects, and had readily agreed to arrange sale of the items. The first shipment was packed, and would be collected tomorrow, or the following day, by a specialist carrier that Raphael had engaged to transport it to his London warehouse.

Raphael had raised an eyebrow at Lady Harriet's involvement in the search and assessment of the contents of the house, but Lord Geoffrey had studiously ignored the implied question. Raphael let him be, but went away looking very thoughtful. So everything was in order. Everything except the reason that he was here in the first place, the reason that he had been given the place. The place that he had now made his home. What was he to do?

Barnstable chose that moment to knock, and ushered Mr Featherstonehaugh and the Ladies into the room, closely followed by a maid with the tea tray. Barnstable was becoming remarkably attuned to his habits, and he nodded his gratitude to the man as he quietly left the room.

"Lord Geoffrey. Today has been a quite marvellous conclusion to this work." The man's voice vibrated with excitement, despite his surprisingly bedraggled appearance. Obviously, he had managed to discover one of the last remaining caches of dust and mouse droppings in the house!

"We discovered another twenty paintings, in a tiny store room near the entry to the servant's stairs, just down the hallway here. And they are magnificent. I believe at least two to be by renowned masters, pieces thought lost to the world, now recovered! They alone may be worth nearly as much as all of the others together."

If Lord Geoffrey had been stunned by the wealth found so far, this statement tipped him into a state of total incomprehension of the numbers involved.

Then, quite spoiling the effect of his pronouncement, Mr Featherstonehaugh sneezed – violently and repeatedly. Miss Carpenter rushed to his side, concern writ large on her face. She proffered a dainty handkerchief, which he gratefully took.

"I must apologize – the dust you see – in my excitement I managed to pull the entire dust sheet down on me, from the largest canvas. I fear my attire is not at its best, nor are my nasal passages. If you will excuse me, I will go and change." He took himself from the room, Miss Carpenter fussing at his side.

Lord Geoffrey found himself alone with Lady Harriet, and a short but difficult silence ensued. Dragging her eyes from his, she spun away, looking for whatever distraction was available. There, right in front of her, across the room, was a large faded tapestry.

Why had she never noticed it before? They had certainly not yet listed it on their inventory. Stepping forward, she examined it closely. It was certainly old, but appeared to be of exquisite workmanship. The threads were unfrayed, the edges mostly firm.

It seemed, to her untrained eye, to be simply in need of a careful cleaning. There was so much dirt on it that, in parts, the picture was hard to make out. Stepping forward again she lifted one side of it, studying the only spot that she could see where the edge did seem a little frayed – as if that spot had been touched more than any other part of it.

As she stepped, her foot caught on the edge of the rug, and she stumbled against the wall, one hand tugging on the tapestry, and the other slamming into the whorl of carving on the top of the wainscoting beside it.

Except that the wall seemed to have suddenly become insubstantial, for she kept tumbling forward. Lady Harriet gasped and righted herself, just as Lord Geoffrey reached her and took firm grip on her shoulders to stop her fall.

Even in her moment of shock, she felt the warmth of his touch and a little burst of joy ran through her. He cared enough to catch her!

At the same second, they both realised what had happened, what they saw before them. For the wall had opened. The tug on the tapestry had caused it to slide to one side, and the hit on the whorl of carving had somehow opened a door – a door which swung inwards to a narrow passage. Their eyes met, and his lit with such joy that she knew there was something important about the opening wall, some secret.

But, when he whooped, and swept her into his arms to spin her around in an exuberant display of delight, she quite forgot about anything else but his touch, at least until he put her down again.

"Uhh, I apologize, that was uncalled for, but... I have been looking for something like this – I was so sure that the house had secrets yet to show us, and I was right! And you, most cleverly, have found it!"

He pulled her to him again for a moment, and kissed her full on the lips. She melted against him, heat flooding through her body.

If this was how he reacted to secret doorways, she would endeavour to discover one every day! Then he released her and stepped back, seeming suddenly embarrassed by his actions.

Lord Geoffrey looked into her flushed face, and wanted to kiss her again. He did not – what he had already done was unforgiveable, no matter how much he wanted to repeat it. She was not for him. Quickly, he turned to the matter in hand – the door in the wall. Grabbing a small decorative stone urn off a side table, he used it to ensure that the hidden door could not close, before stepping inside the space.

"Perhaps a lantern… or at least a candle… would be useful? Lady Harriet's voice penetrated his excited contemplation of what he saw. She was correct. He turned, to find her already offering him a lit taper. Resourceful as always.

The light showed that the space within the walls was not large. It appeared to be a small room, not a passage at all. He felt a moment of crushing disappointment – he had been sure it would be more than this! Perhaps it was. He set to examining it minutely. One end of the space appeared to be a cabinet built into the wall – that was the side towards the windowed wall – which made sense, for there was nowhere in that direction for a passage to fit.

The cabinet door was, as could be expected, locked. He huffed his disappointment again, turning to examine the rest of the small space. Nothing of significance that he could see. Lady Harriet peered in through the door.

"Oh, a cabinet. Is it locked?"

"Yes, unfortunately, it appears to be quite solidly locked – and no sign of a key."

She nodded, and squeezed in beside him. His body tightened at the press of hers against him and he gasped. She crouched, putting her face at a level with the lock (and also, alarmingly for his peace of mind, at a level with certain parts of his anatomy, which were very aware of her presence). She pulled a hairpin from her tangled locks as she did so.

"Hold the light down here please."

Shocked, he did as requested, and watched in open admiration as she swiftly picked the lock.

"How... Where... did you learn to do that?"

She looked back at him, flushing, perhaps embarrassed?

"I... when I was a child, Michael – my horrible, now deceased elder brother, you remember? Michael used to lock away anything I treasured, just to be mean – he was like that. So I learned to pick locks to get my things back. Jimmy taught me. He was our stable boy in London. I think he'd been a thief before we took him on. But he never stole from us."

"Lady Harriet, I am doubly indebted to you. And impressed by your resourcefulness."

She flushed again, definitely embarrassed this time, at receiving praise from him, and squeezed her way back out of the space to allow him to investigate the contents of the cabinet.

The brush of her body against him brought a new rush of desire, but he pushed it aside. Right now, the contents of that cabinet were his first priority.

She took the candle from his fingers, and held it for him, so that his hands were free to pull forth the roll of pages within. Shaking, he unrolled it. And, for a few moments, was hit hard by disappointment again. Not a set of incriminating letters or lists. Just a collection of maps or diagrams.

And then his brain caught up with what he was seeing. In his hands was a full set of maps of his house – every floor, of every wing, and the attics, and the cellars. Neatly drawn, well noted with names of rooms, and with some odd symbols in various places. Most importantly, these maps showed a large number of passages and rooms that were not part of the normally accessible parts of the house. It appeared that he held a full set of maps showing the hidden passages and rooms in the house, and under it.

This was a prize indeed. He stepped back out into the study, and allowed the hidden door to close, after carefully studying the mechanism. Then he opened it again, to be sure that he could, closed it, and took the maps to his desk.

Lady Harriet followed, her face alight with curiosity.

In that instant he realised – there was no going back now, no keeping her out of it – she had found the secret, opened the door, unlocked the cabinet – she knew that the maps existed. After all that, she had a right to see them. But what could he tell her, without revealing the detail of his mission?

Thinking carefully about that very pertinent question, he spread the maps out on the desk. They were old, and appeared to have been added to and annotated at various times over many years. He wondered who had first drawn them. Whoever they were, he owed them a debt of gratitude.

Lady Harriet stood close and peered over his shoulder to better see the detail. The brush of her body against him, the touch of a tendril of hair against his cheek, made him nearly groan aloud. He forced his mind back to the drawings in front of him. The longer he looked, the more excited he became.

There were, it seemed, secret passages and rooms on every floor except the ground floor. After some thought he concluded that one of the symbols used indicated the locations of doors into the passages. He was not entirely sure about some of the other symbols, but perhaps they might indicate the locations of peepholes, which would permit a person lurking in the walls to spy on the occupants of the normal rooms? It was a likely possibility.

By far the most fascinating thing was the drawing of the cellars. For, not only was there a sheet for the level of the cellars he knew of, where root vegetables and wines and other comestibles were stored, but there was another sheet, which appeared to show not just one, but two further levels of cellars below that. At this rate, he would be spending the next few weeks exploring secret rooms and passages, and still be lucky to get through all of them!

And... if the conspirators knew of these, if, as Peterson had surmised, they had hidden the treasonously incriminating papers somewhere in this warren of hidden passages, what action might they feel forced to take, once they realised that he was exploring them??

Chapter Nine

With a start, Lady Harriet pulled back, removing the contact between her, and Lord Geoffrey. She could still feel the heat of him, as if they yet touched. What she truly wished was to throw herself into his arms, to regain that moment when he had kissed her. Instead, she stepped back, considering the maps of the house, and what they had just revealed. She wondered how the mechanisms for the other doors worked.

The thought of exploring the passages was beyond exciting – who knew what they might find within, given what had been there to find in the open parts of the house!

"When will we…"

"No-one must know of…"

They both spoke at the same instant, and stopped at the same instant, startled. He was the first to recover his composure.

"No-one must know of this. It must be kept between us for now."

"Why?"

And here was the moment. The moment that he was still not truly prepared for. What could he say? Could he trust her with the truth? Or would that simply endanger her more than this knowledge already did? Her bright green eyes watched him, waiting.

He gulped for air, his throat suddenly tight, and made an impetuous decision, perhaps an unwise one, yet it seemed, in the moment, the only decision to make.

"Because, my dear Lady Harriet, these hidden rooms and passages may, nay, almost certainly do, contain evidence of treason against the crown, perpetrated by the previous owner of this house, and an unknown number of other conspirators. Some of whom are, I believe, still here in the house, in my employ. If they were to realise that we have discovered this, they might choose to act precipitously. Speaking of this would be to endanger your life."

Her face had paled as he spoke, and she stared at him in some shock. But her eyes shone with intelligence, and it seemed that she was thinking, rather than about to faint away in a ladylike swoon. Minutes passed, while she absently twirled a tendril of hair around her finger, and thought, then she spoke.

"I see. If that is the case, then we will simply have to take the utmost care as we explore them. For surely, whatever is hidden there is what you have been seeking this last three months. This information makes sense of your insistence on seeing every crevice of the house – am I correct in my deduction?"

She showed no sign of fear, and her usual enthusiasm for life was undimmed – before him, what he saw was excitement.

She was quite a remarkable woman.

In that instant, he realised that she had just, neatly, trapped him again – for he had no choice but to allow her assistance, if he wished to ever complete his mission. She would get what she wanted, in this, at least.

"Yes, you are correct. That is what I have searched for, and yes, I must reluctantly allow you to assist me in searching these hidden passages. I have already stepped beyond the bounds of what I should reveal to you, and, if Charlton knew of this, he would never forgive me for involving you, but I see that I have little choice. For now, I must lock these away in my own safe, before anyone sees them. Miss Carpenter is sure to soon realise that she has left you scandalously unchaperoned, and return in a fluster!"

He stood, and went to a small cabinet near the desk, opening compartments and locks to secure the plans. Lady Harriet had, until then, quite completely forgotten about Miss Carpenter, and prayed that her *tendre* for Mr Featherstonehaugh would keep her distracted a little longer.

"Then how will you explain to me what we must do? How will we plan, if we are never to be alone?"

It was an excellent question, to which Lord Geoffrey was sadly lacking an answer. All manner of thoughts flooded his mind, in the context of being alone with Lady Harriet.

None of them had the least to do with his mission.

He forced the inappropriate thoughts aside and considered.

"Perhaps, tomorrow, you should ride here, rather than take the carriage. I could then take a little time out from ugly paintings and dust to show you around the property – I believe that you have yet to see the extent of the grounds in the direction away from Pendholm Hall?"

She nodded, waiting for him to continue.

"Of course, Miss Carpenter would accompany us, for reasons of propriety. It would, I am sure, not prevent her chaperonage from being effective, even if her lamentable riding abilities meant that we were well ahead of her most of the time – not out of sight, but certainly out of earshot."

Lady Harriet's face lit with delight and amusement. So, he had noticed her rather naughty tendency to make poor Miss Carpenter struggle to keep up with her when riding! It was a very clever solution, especially as she loved to ride, and, now that the weather was warming, she would enjoy a chance to see the grounds. It would be the perfect way to talk privately. And Moonbeam needed the exercise after the last few months when Harriet had sadly neglected her to spend her time at Witherwood Chase.

"What a brilliant idea!" She clapped her hands together, and spun across the room, all energy and impatience for the morrow. At that precise instant, Miss Carpenter, looking flushed, embarrassed and guilty, all at once, entered the room. Finding Lord Geoffrey and Lady Harriet on opposite sides of the room, and most obviously not engaged in anything scandalous, she breathed a sigh of relief, and chose to say nothing. Lady Harriet smiled, and her eyes lit with devilment.

"Miss Carpenter! We are to have a treat tomorrow. Lord Geoffrey has most kindly invited us to ride over, and he will ride with us to show us the farthest reaches of the Witherwood Chase grounds. Is that not most delightful, after all of these days amongst dusty paintings?"

Miss Carpenter paled, then squared her shoulders with a long-suffering sigh.

"Delightful indeed, Lady Harriet." Her tone was dry, and Lord Geoffrey looked at her in surprise. Perhaps the companion was not so mousy as he had supposed.

~~~~~

All around, the ride was a great success. Miss Carpenter, whilst not exactly happy about it, managed to cope quite well, and was just slow and sedate enough to allow them the perfect opportunity to talk. Lord Geoffrey discovered himself having fun, even whilst discussing a topic of such a serious nature.

Lady Harriet rode extraordinarily well, and Lord Geoffrey thrilled to the chance to ride with a woman who could not only keep up with him, but potentially even outride him. He explained, in as minimalist a way as possible, that he was working secretly for a representative of the crown, to find and neutralise the last of the treasonous conspirators. That he was searching for a cache of incriminating papers, and possibly other items, and that Ashley and Jobs seemed the only possible guilty parties amongst the staff that had come with the house.
~~~~~

He also explained that Peterson, Walters and Hurst were to be trusted absolutely, but that everyone else was not. The difficulty was going to be finding a way that Lady Harriet might assist in the search, whilst staying within the bounds of propriety. The only possible option seemed to be taking Miss Carpenter into their confidence. A step that Lord Geoffrey was loath to take, for every extra person who knew was another person at risk.

In the end, they agreed to think on that for a few days, whilst Lord Geoffrey studied the maps, and began to identify the places in the rooms and corridors, which corresponded to the points on the map marked with the symbol which they believed to represent doors. For they had to find those locations, before they could work out how to open the doors.

Lady Harriet prayed that all of the doors would have similar mechanisms, for if they did not, the search would be slow and difficult.

Chapter Ten

Three days later, Lord Geoffrey was ready to start opening doors – if he could work out how. He was fairly certain that he had discovered the doors, less certain of the mechanisms controlling them. Lady Harriet, unable to bear the thought of missing out on exploring, approached Miss Carpenter carefully.

Fifteen minutes later, a combination of appealing to Miss Carpenter's patriotic nature (which was not difficult, as her father and brother had both perished as soldiers in the war) and threatening to tell Lady Sylvia of her *tendre* for Mr Featherstonehaugh, and the hour that she had spent in his company, leaving Lady Harriet unchaperoned, had persuaded Miss Carpenter to co-operate.

Once convinced, Miss Carpenter was surprisingly enthusiastic about the project, for which Lady Harriet was immensely grateful. The plan was simple, and still rather risky, but it was the best they could do. Miss Carpenter would continue to work with Mr Featherstonehaugh, sequestered in the library, working through his final notes.

They would all pretend that Lady Harriet was also working with them, and, if asked by a servant, or anyone else, Miss Carpenter would report that Lady Harriet had simply left the room to use the necessary. Miss Carpenter was quite confident that Mr Featherstonehaugh would, because she asked it of him, also ask no awkward questions.

Meanwhile, Lady Harriet and Lord Geoffrey would be exploring the passages. The doors, between the map allowing them to be found, and the fact that the mechanisms were all very similar – in each case there was a whorl of carving of some sort to push, and a drape, tapestry of painting to pull on, at the same time – proved remarkably easy to open. Lord Geoffrey felt rather foolish that he and Peterson had not found even one of them in those three long months of searching – they seemed so obvious now that he knew what to look for!.

~~~~~

Over the next two sennights, Lord Geoffrey and Lady Harriet discovered two things – that lurking in corridors and poking at walls, then disappearing through them, was remarkably difficult to do without drawing the notice of servants, and that hidden passages contained even greater amounts of dust and mouse droppings than long unused rooms. What they did not discover, was the cache of incriminating treasonous documents which they sought.

It also became, as they worked at checking the passages and tiny hidden rooms, at first together, and then separately, obvious that there were more passages than those shown on the maps.
~~~~~

Which depressing fact just made the work harder. There were moments of amusement, and moments of great surprise, as they discovered yet more paintings and other minor valuables, long forgotten in recesses in the hidden rooms and passages, or looked through peepholes to discover which rooms they allowed one to spy on.

Lady Harriet took especial delight in discovering a peephole which let her spy on Miss Carpenter and Mr Featherstonehaugh. They were studiously working away, whilst each casting surreptitious longing glances at the other, when they though the other wasn't looking. It took enormous effort for Lady Harriet not to burst into a fit of the giggles watching them. More seriously, she took note of all of the rooms for which she found peepholes, and they compared them to the symbols on the maps. It seemed that they had guessed the symbol correctly.

Each day provided another chance for Lady Harriet to be as close to Lord Geoffrey as she could manage, without actually throwing herself at him. Which was what, if she was honest, she truly wished to do. Now, more than ever, he took her breath away. Not only was he heroic by his actions, but also by his nature. His steadfast refusal to take advantage of their scandalous proximity, even whilst his storm grey eyes followed her and, in unguarded moments, revealed what she dared to hope was desire for her, was demonstration of his honourable character.

She found his dedication to his mission, and his willingness to suffer months of dirt, dust and tedium impressive, and worthy of respect. Especially when compared to the town fops who had clung to her side this Season past.

Still, for both of them, the lack of result for their efforts was wearing, as was the continual subterfuge required to keep their actions secret. By the end of the second sennight, the novelty of peepholes and hidden passages had quite worn off, and frustration had set in.

~~~~~

As it happened, their explorations had not gone entirely unnoticed. Late one evening, after Lady Harriet and Miss Carpenter had returned to Pendholm Hall, and Lord Geoffrey had locked himself away in his study, with the maps, and a glass of good brandy, two figures slid quietly through the shadows at the back of the house. They made no sound until they reached the run down shepherd's cottage at the edge of the boundary woods.

Once inside, by the light of an only partially unshuttered lantern, Ashley and Jobs looked at each other with fear on their faces.

"What'll we do Ash? He's found the passages – least some of 'em anyway. The dust's all disturbed and some of them old pictures in there's been moved." Jobs' voice quavered as he spoke.

"We'll move them things from up top down with the rest tomorrow – one way or t'other - we can't wait any longer. I don't think he's found the hidden door down the bottom – even if'n he has, he won't find the second one." Ashley put as much confidence as he could into the statement, but, in truth, he wasn't sure it was true.
~~~~~

"What if he does? What if'n we runs inta him in the passages?"

"Then we'll deal with it. Whatever it takes. If he catches us, we're dead – we'll hang or worse for those papers. If'n he finds us, he'll have an 'accident' – I'll make sure of it."

"I dunno about that. I nivver signed up fer no killin. But... if'n it's his neck or mine..."

"Exactly Jobs, exactly. I'll send a message ter Nobby first thing. Have him ready to cart off whatever might need to be... removed, if'n ye take me meaning."

"Aye, that be best then. Nobby won't be askin' any questions, 'n if'n he's not needed, no-one'll know."

They talked for a while longer, about the best way to get from the top passages to the very bottom, without being seen, or making any noises in the wrong places.

Finally, satisfied that they'd done all they could to prepare, they disappeared back into the night.

~~~~~

Lord Geoffrey locked the maps away again, satisfied with the day's work. There were only two areas of the upper floors hidden passages left to search – even allowing for possible extra bits that weren't marked on the maps. Tomorrow Lady Harriet would take the top floor, just below the attics, and he would take the one below. Surely they would find the papers in one of those two places.
~~~~~

If not, they would move on to the cellars. Which would be more difficult, for access to those meant moving into the servant's' domain, and staying unnoticed would be nigh on impossible. He prayed that would not be necessary. Every day of this work was more fraught with the risk of discovery.

His admiration for Lady Harriet's resourcefulness, determination and persistence had grown with every day of the search. Had she truly been still the tantrum prone child that Charlton had described to him so often, she would have long ago lost patience with the whole thing. But she had not. She had stayed true to her commitment to helping him, and applied her keen intelligence to searching, and to their efforts to update the maps as they did so.

And every day he spent in her company, especially when they had searched together in the tight confines of the passageways, it became harder and harder to convince himself that he should not be attracted to her.

She was like no other woman he had ever met. When she gathered up Miss Carpenter and went home at the end of each day, he found himself oddly bereft. The house felt infinitely emptier without her bright presence. He pushed those thoughts away, for the thousandth time, and went back to considering what he would do when they did, finally, find the damn papers.

It startled him to realise that he had no idea exactly what those papers would contain. No doubt Setford had a very clear idea. Which was all that mattered. Lord Geoffrey couldn't wait to find the things, pass them to Setford, along with his traitorous employees, and be done with the mission.

He had come to like Witherwood Chase, to feel at home there, in a way that he had not felt at home anywhere since he was a boy of eight or ten, and his parents and grandmother had still been alive.

He wanted the dark stain of treason gone from the place, to make it completely his.

He wanted that done before the rest of the Hounds, and their families, came to stay at Eastertide, so that it might be a time of joyous celebration of the bonds they shared, with no shadow hanging over it.

ARIETTA RICHMOND, CATHERINE WINDSOR, ISABELLA THORNE, KATHERINE KEATS, KELLY ANNE BRUCE

82

Chapter Eleven

Lady Harriet was determined. This was the day when she would find what they sought, and bring this tedious process to an end. *'But'*, whispered the stubborn small voice in her mind *'how will you then find cause to see Lord Geoffrey?'* She ignored it. That was a problem for another day. For now, Lord Geoffrey desired to find those papers, so searching for them was her first priority.

She stood in a small parlour on the upper floor, with windows which overlooked the herb and scent garden in the rear courtyard area of the house. This wing was one of the oldest parts of the house, and, along this side of the floor, the rooms all opened into each other, in the manner of centuries past, with the doors close to the windows in each case. The centre of the floor contained servants' corridors, but also secret passages, accessed through the apparently blank walls which faced the windows in each room. At the far end of the floor, there was an area which was not clearly explained by the maps.

Lad Harriet held high hopes for what that area might contain. Once certain that no-one was near, she stepped to the rear of the room and, with careful coordination, shoved hard on a carved leaf at the edge of the mantle above the fireplace, whilst also pulling on a shelf of the adjoining bookcase. The shelves pivoted out to her pull, and she stepped into the dark passageway revealed, partially unshuttered her small lantern, and pulled the door closed behind her, taking careful note of the placement of the lever which would allow her to open it later.

She worked her way down the passage, looking through peepholes, poking into crevices, seeking any evidence of other doors, of cabinets skilfully laid into the walls, or of any other possible hiding places. For a long distance, there was nothing of interest beyond the peepholes. Eventually, she reached what appeared to be an end to the passage. Frowning, she retraced her steps to the last peephole. Looking through it confirmed her suspicions – the passage should continue, for the room she saw was the second to last room on the floor, not the last.

Returning to the blank wall, she ran her fingers over its surface, and traced its edges, as well as the walls to either side. Finally, when she was beginning to think that she might be wrong, that the passage might simply end, her gloved fingers caught on an uneven area of the side wall. A few moments poking and pushing at it experimentally, and the blank end of the passage shifted slightly, with a soft click. She pulled it open and slipped through, impatiently pulling at an errant tendril of hair as it caught on the door frame.

~~~~~

Jobs had come into the kitchen for a quick bite of food, taking advantage of the left-overs from the nobility's luncheon. He turned away, as if about to return to the stables, catching Ashley's eye as he did so. At Ashley's quick nod, Jobs stepped out of the kitchen, but, when sure that there were no eyes upon him, went quickly up the servants' stairs, rather than out the side door to the stables. Not long after, Ashley also quit the kitchens and casually took the same path.

One floor up, they took separate ways, Jobs slipping into the walls as soon as possible, but Ashley continuing in the servants' corridors, looking for all the world just like any footman might, going about his appointed business. Closer to the end of the old wing, he also slipped into the walls, finding Jobs waiting. In careful silence, they climbed up another two floors of narrow hidden stairs.

They emerged into a dusty room, tucked right at the end of the wing, close below the attics. Unlike most of the hidden spaces, this had a tiny amount of natural light from a narrow strip of dusty window.

From outside the house, it seemed just another window in the row along that floor, a bit smaller for being right at the end, but nothing unusual. From the inside, it let in just enough light, past the aged velvet drape that hung over it, to show a tiny table, a single chair, a rough pallet on the floor and a small crate in one corner. On the crate stood a pitcher of water, and some battered cups, just below an odd looking tap on the wall.
~~~~~

The room was just below the rainwater cistern – as a bolt hole, it had the superior advantage of a water supply. Incongruously, beside the crate stood a largish basket full of dirty looking dust sheets, topped by a tangle of old ropes or curtain pulls.

"Right then, let's be about it." Ashley strode across the room and lifted the rough timber tray with the pitcher and cups. Setting it on the small table, he turned back to the crate. A few minutes work, and the apparently nailed together crate was in two pieces, revealing a smallish strongbox nestled at its core. The box was old, of ebony or some similar wood, banded in iron. It was locked, and heavy.

Jobs had pulled half the dust sheets from the basket, and Ashley carefully settled the box in amongst the remaining ones, and set to reassembling the crate, whilst Jobs reached for the dust sheets to cover the box. A sound shocked them to stillness. Their eyes met, with fear their uppermost emotion.

The other entry to the room – a secret door, behind a secret door, at the far end of a hidden passage, a door that no-one else should be able to find, opened, and Lady Harriet stepped through. The dim light from the window was enough to momentarily blind her after the deep darkness of the passageway, and she stood, blinking in confusion at the sight of the two men before her.

Ashley recovered from his shock first, and, just as Lady Harriet's eyes fell upon the box, and lit with startled comprehension of its importance, Ashley grabbed her, clamping one hand across her mouth, and the other around her body, trapping her arms against her sides. He hauled her back against him.

"Jobs!" Ashley's voice broke Jobs from his shock, and he leapt forward to grab Lady Harriet's legs before she could try to get away. Five minutes later, Ashley and Jobs bore bruises and scratches from Lady Harriet's failed attempts to escape.

They stood back, breathing hard from the effort, whilst Lady Harriet lay on the pallet, bound and gagged, her dress a little torn, and her eyes blazing her anger at them as clearly as if she could speak. If looks were daggers, they would both have been dead.

"Guess we'll be needin' Nobby then." Ashley's voice was flat, but not displeased. Rather be found by this little piece than by his Lordship with his bloody swords or a pistol. This way, they'd turn a nice profit too. Nobby had contacts. There'd be a few competing to buy something this pretty, if he wasn't mistaken. The high class houses of pleasure had a taste for quality fresh goods like her. They'd just have to be sure they got her out and gone tonight, and kept it so no-one suspected them.

But who would? She must have found the entry to this room by blind luck — and if she was alone, that meant no-one else knew where she was. For now, she could stay right there on the pallet, while they got the other valuables stowed away in the deep.

"Let's be getting this down t' the deep then. Once tis stored away with t'other, we c'n worrit about mileddy here."

Jobs piled the scattered dust sheets over the box, throwing aside the few pieces of old rope which had not been used in binding Lady Harriet, and Ashley lifted the basket. He looked at Lady Harriet, a touch regretfully.

"We'll be a seein' you later mileddy. Tis a pity we'll get a better price for ye untouched, or I'd be a tastin' the wares before we ship em, if'n ye understands me."

~~~~~

Lady Harriet watched as they exited the room, through a tiny door near the window. She'd think about the meaning of those words later. For now, once she was sure that they were gone, she would concentrate on trying to escape.

Lying still, she listened carefully. Their steps receded – it sounded as if there were stairs beyond that door. And then there was silence. Drifts of disturbed dust floated in the air, turned to sparkling gold by the faint rays of afternoon sun coming through the tiny window. She would have thought it pretty, were her situation not so dire.

Once their footsteps faded into the silence, she let herself move. She pulled and twisted her hands and feet, but only succeeded in abrading her wrists and ankles on the rough bits of rope that they had bound her with. She panted for breath, revolted by the taste of the dusty cloth that filled her mouth. She refused to think about what that taste might be caused by. She would especially not contemplate any thought whatsoever of mouse droppings. Definitely not.

Shouting was impossible, and anyway, it was extremely unlikely that anyone would be near enough to hear – for this was the furthest end of the least used wing of the house, and behind three layers of secret doors as well.
~~~~~

She could but hope that Lord Geoffrey would become alarmed when she did not return for their late afternoon discussion of the day's achievements, and would come seeking her. The hours between now and then loomed ahead of her, an interminable opportunity for despair.

Resting before another attempt at loosening the ropes, she finally allowed herself to consider the import of the footman's parting words. Try as she might to discover another, she could only find one possible meaning in what he'd said.

She might be physically an innocent, but she was certainly not ignorant about what men did with women, or of the existence of places expressly for allowing men to satisfy those needs. Her deceased elder brother, terrible man that he had been, had made quite certain of that by his actions. When her mother had, after his death, rescued the girls that he had abused and left with child, Lady Harriet had discovered many things that she might have wished not to know.

She loved Mary, Polly and Sally, and their children, just as much as she would have had they been legitimate, and so did her mother, for her brother's behaviour had certainly not been the fault of the girls. But, being of curious mind, she had asked them, once they trusted her, about their experiences. Their answers had been quite an education.

And, applying the understanding gained from those conversations to the footman's words, she was left with a single stark conclusion. Those men were going to take her somewhere, and sell her to a house of pleasure, to be used by men, against her will. The thought terrified her.

She well knew that, if there was love, or even respect, between a man and woman, as was the case with Charlton and Odette, and had been the case with her mother and father, when he still lived, then the physical activities carried out between men and women could be acceptable, or even pleasant.

But she also knew, from what her terrible brother had done to the girls, that it could be very unpleasant indeed.

She lay there shaking, exhausted by her struggles and close to tears. But she refused to give up hope. After all, this room was at the top of the house. They still had to get her out unseen – which would mean late at night.

So, there was time. Time for her to think, time for her to keep working at the ropes, and, she fervently prayed, time for Lord Geoffrey to find her. He was a hero. He was the most capable man she knew. Surely he would save her. She had to believe, and to keep trying to escape her bonds.

~~~~~

Lord Geoffrey was irritated and dispirited. It was late afternoon when he slipped carefully from the hidden passages into his dressing room, and allowed Hurst to assist him with a change from clothing which was much the worse for wear from his explorations, for the last passages on this floor had been, it turned out, quite the filthiest of all of the areas that he had yet explored. Thank God that Hurst was one of the men provided by Setford, and knew of the mission.
~~~~~

The mission. The mission that was still incomplete. For he had found nothing but filth this afternoon. Exploring the hidden parts of the cellars was looking inevitable. Cleaner, but no happier, he went down to his study to await Lady Harriet's return, praying that her search had been more fruitful, and less filth-encrusted than his.

Settled into his favourite chair, with a warming glass of brandy in hand, he wondered what his days would be like, once this mission was finally done with. What would he do with his time, when the search was complete? *'What would he do, when he no longer had a reason to see Lady Harriet every day…?'*

He would wait until she was here to pull out the maps, for them to update any of the detail of the passages they had explored today. For now, he would simply rest, and try to improve his mood.

He took down the beautiful old swords from the wall, and ran his fingers along the blade. It was now not only clean and polished, but sharp, as it should be. The balance was wonderful, and, had he not been waiting for Lady Harriet, he would have been tempted to take the blades straight to the drawing room which he had cleared of furniture to use as a *salle*. A little sword work always cleared his thoughts of any frustration – weapons required a clear and focused mind.

An hour later, he began to be concerned. Surely she should have returned by now? Even if she had found another unmapped section, surely it would not have taken this long? Generally, she and Miss Carpenter departed by dusk at the latest, and it was past that hour now. The darkness was closing in.

What if something had happened to her? He would never forgive himself should she be hurt. It was one thing to talk of the risk involved in this mission, and to speak of accepting it – it was quite another to meet that danger head on.

In that instant, he saw his own feelings for her clearly. No matter how much he might have been denying it, he did care for her, with an intensity that was almost frightening. The thought of any harm coming to her was like a blade to his heart. How could he have allowed her to place herself at risk? How could he have been so selfish, wanting her company and the success of his mission above her safety?

At that moment, there was a tap on his door. He breathed a sigh of relief – but his relief was short-lived. The door opened to admit Miss Carpenter and Mr Featherstonehaugh – who looked surprised, and then concerned, when it became apparent that Lady Harriet was not in the room.

"She hasn't returned." Lord Geoffrey broke the silence.

"What shall we do?" Miss Carpenter's voice was soft, and she twisted her hands together as she spoke.

"I am going to look for her. Miss Carpenter, please get Walters to take a message to Pendholm Hall – tell them that I have invited you, and Lady Harriet to stay for dinner. Let us not concern her family unduly. Should I not return by the time dinner is called, please, eat, and assure the staff that I am simply busy."

He strode out the door, and, seeing Peterson on duty in the hallway, called him to follow.

It was only when Peterson looked enquiringly at the sword in his hand that he realised he still held it. Well and good then. A weapon in hand was not a bad thing, should there be trouble.

They began on the top floor, searching through each room, then moving into the hidden passages.

Some hours later, they had covered every inch of the place twice over, and found nothing. Outside the walls, dinner had come and gone.

The candle in their lantern was burnt down to a nub, casting little effective light, and Lord Geoffrey had reached a state of internal turmoil unlike anything he had ever felt before. The fear of losing Lady Harriet forever ate at him. Not knowing where she was, or what she might be suffering was torture of the worst kind.

He slumped back against the passage wall, close against the blank wall where it simply ended. Peterson lifted the lantern, to better see Lord Geoffrey's face, and opened his mouth to speak. Lord Geoffrey's hand whipped out to arrest the motion of the lantern.

"I thought so! Look, Peterson – just there, caught at the edge of that piece of wall."

Peterson peered at the spot Lord Geoffrey pointed to, at first seeing nothing. Then he reached out a careful hand, and touched the dark gold hair that had glinted in the lantern light. He tugged on it gently, but it seemed trapped – trapped between the blank wall and the side wall that Lord Geoffrey leant on.

"Her hair!" Lord Geoffrey's voice was rough with emotion. "But… how is it trapped? What is it caught on?"

"I think, my Lord, that this wall is not a wall. It must be another door, for the hair appears to go into the crack along its edge…"

Without a word, Lord Geoffrey pushed away from the wall and began to push and prod at every part of the surrounding surfaces.

Chapter Twelve

Lady Harriet had worn her wrists and ankles raw, but had not succeeded in loosening the ropes enough to slip out of them.

The light was fading from the tiny window, and, with full darkness, she knew that it would not be long before they came for her. But unless she could somehow escape the ropes, there was nothing she could do but pray that Lord Geoffrey found her, before she was beyond his reach forever. She wished, most fervently, that she had, at every opportunity, thrown herself into his arms, propriety be damned.

She remembered that one kiss, and wished for more. If she was never to see him again, she wished for more to remember. She had known, for more than a year now, that he was the man for her. These last few months had simply deepened that feeling, deepened her love for him. Did he realise? Did he know how much she felt for him? Did he care for her in return? Or were those momentary flashes of desire she had seen in his eyes only that – desire, not anything deeper?

Her thoughts were interrupted eventually, long after the window had gone dark, by the sound that she had been anticipating with dread. The sound of feet upon the hidden stairs. As the door opened, she abandoned the last of her hope. It was too late. Lord Geoffrey could not save her now, they were here to take her away, to a life too horrible to contemplate.

"Had a comfortable afternoon, have you mileddy?" Ashley, the footman, smiled at her as he spoke. It was not a pleasant smile.

"Let's get movin Ash, the quicker she's off and gone, the happier I'll be." Jobs stepped towards her, then paused. "How's we gonna carry her Ash? Them stairs is narrow and steep. If'n she wriggles too much, we could all end up at the bottom with broken bones."

"Carefully – we's carryin her carefully. We wants to protect our investment here, doesn't we? And you, mileddy, you'll a be keeping still for us, won't ye? Cause I'm thinkin ye've no more wish than us to fall, have ye?"

Lady Harriet shook her head. She most definitely didn't want to fall – alive and unhurt, there might still be a chance to escape – injured there would be none.

"Right then. I'll get her by the legs, and you be liftin under her arms. I'll go down them steps first, backwards and slow, and you'll keep pace wiv me, wiv her between us."

Ashley bent to lift her legs. Jobs looked at the door to the stairs uncertainly, then shrugged and shoved his hands under her upper body, hindered by her hands tied behind her.

She flinched at the feel of their uncaring hands on her, but did not fight. She chose, instead, to be as limp and heavy as possible. With two older brothers, she had learnt, long ago, that limp and heavy was much harder to lift and carry than wriggling and screaming.

The men grunted and hauled her up awkwardly, making so much noise that she did not, at first, notice any other sound. But she did notice something else. The air in the room had moved, stirred like a light breeze across her face, drifting a fine tendril of her hair into her eyes. She gave no sign of anything having changed, but inwardly she prayed. *'Please, let that touch of moving air mean what I think it might.'*

And then she heard it – definitely a sound. A sound she was deliriously happy to hear – the sound of the other door moving, ever so slowly. Let it be him, let it be Lord Geoffrey come to save her. The men started to cart her towards the door to the stairs, and for a moment she thought that she must have been mistaken.

~~~~~

Lord Geoffrey was ready to give up poking about and simply batter at the door, when his fingers found an odd bump, low down on the wall. A bit of pushing at it, and the wall popped open, just a crack, releasing a gentle puff of air that sent Lady Harriet's golden hair drifting to the floor.

"Finally!"

He pulled it open, and stepped through into another dark and empty passage. A short passage. With no visible exit.
~~~~~

Geoffrey groaned aloud, then began the process all over again. There had to be another way out. She had come in here, so she had to have gone out of here. He just had to find it. The walls were rougher here – more possible bumps and lumps to push and prod at. He worked along the passage on one side, whilst Peterson took the other. Just as they reached the apparent end of the short length of passage, he stopped, and froze in place, touching Peterson to make him stop too.

There was a sound, he was sure of it. From the other side of the wall. Creeping forward, he pressed his ear to the rough plaster and listened. Men's voices. Two, he thought. He couldn't make out what they said. Then a thump and a bump, as if they were moving something heavy about, and bumped into a chair or similar, then a muttered curse – he might not be able to hear the exact words, but the tone and emotion in it were clear enough.

As he pressed harder against the wall, desperate to hear more, his fingers caught on a simple latch. He lifted it, and the door shifted gently. The disturbed air carried a scent to him from within the space on the other side of the door. A scent he would recognise anywhere. Lady Harriet's perfume, that unique mix of rose, daphne and lemon. He closed his eyes, as much from horror as relief.

She was here – but she was in the hands of the traitors – was she hurt? Why was she silent? He could not imagine Lady Harriet going anywhere quietly, if it was against her will. He eased the door open a little, and peered into the room. Ashley and Jobs were struggling to lift a completely limp Lady Harriet, moving awkwardly towards a door on the other side of the small room.

His fear for her drove him to immediate action. He could not, as much as he wished it, simply drive his sword through Jobs' back, even though it was presented nicely before him – for the sword could just as easily penetrate the man and harm Harriet, limp in his arms, as well. He leapt forward and drove the hilt of the sword towards Jobs head, hoping to knock him out with one blow.

But as the blow landed, Jobs staggered under Lady Harriet's weight, and what should have been a solid collision with the man's head became a glancing blow instead. Jobs dropped her and spun, roaring in anger. Ashley, after one look at Lord Geoffrey, sword in hand and eyes wild, with Peterson behind him, somehow hauled Lady Harriet up and over his shoulder, then staggered to the stairs. For one second, before Jobs rushed him, fists windmilling in panicked attack, Lord Geoffrey found himself looking straight into Harriet's beseeching eyes.

Then she was gone, and he heard a bolt shot into place on the other side of the door, as Ashley carried her away. Desperation drove him. He would not lose her now! He would not let her down – that look had told him she believed in him – that she had the utmost faith in his ability to save her. To her, as always, he was a hero. Well – it was time he lived up to that then, though he had never sought it.

Then all thought disappeared, as battle reflexes honed at war cut in. He became a coldly focused fighting machine. A minute or two later, Jobs found himself flat on the floor, Lord Geoffrey's sword at his throat, as Peterson used some of the remaining scatter of old rope on the floor to bind him tightly.

"Where is he taking her?"

The sword still hovered at Jobs' throat, and Lord Geoffrey's voice made it clear that anything but the truth would result in pain or death. Jobs gulped, flinching as the movement of his throat caused the sword point to break his skin. Stammering from fear, he spoke, with a last spark of defiance.

"You'll be too late. He'll have her out and away afore ye can get down t'ground. Once she's in the cart, ye'll nivver see her agin."

Lord Geoffrey looked at Peterson, and they reached a silent agreement. Geoffrey ran to the now bolted door that Ashley had carried Harriet through, and began to batter it, using anything to hand. The bolt might not break – but the wood was old – batter it enough, and surely it would splinter.

Peterson spun and ran back the way they had come, through the hidden passages and out into the main part of the house. He flung himself down the stairs, yelling to Walters, who was stationed in the foyer, to get Hurst and follow, then charged out into the night. Where was the nearest lane to the estate? Where might a cart be hidden?

Meanwhile, the door had finally shattered under Lord Geoffrey's onslaught. Geoffrey slid down the narrow stairs, perilously close to falling, uncaring of his own safety in the desperate need to get to Harriet in time. Unregarded, in the room above, Jobs muttered pathetically about being abandoned, bound hand and foot. He was quite unaware of the appropriateness of him being left exactly as he had left Lady Harriet all day. He did, however, realise after a while that, unless he could escape now, he was dead – for he would surely hang for treason. He began to struggle against the ropes.

Reaching the ground floor, Lord Geoffrey sprinted through the servants' corridor. Shoving a startled maid aside, he charged out the door towards the stables, sword still in hand, silver in the moonlight. Skidding to a halt, he looked around. Where had Ashley gone with her?

Then he saw it – a moment's glint of moonlight on the gold of her hair. Near the edge of the trees, across the wide lawn. He had to be heading for the rutted lane that led to the old shepherd's cottage.

Geoffrey ran, ran as he had never run before in his life, glad that he heard Peterson's footsteps on the gravel behind him, before he hit the smooth grass of the lawn. In that instant, he blessed his gardeners – they would all be getting an increase in their wages, for the immaculate lawn made it easier to run. And he, a fit, large man, trained to fight, could run considerably faster than an older, somewhat unfit footman carrying a full grown woman.

He was gaining on them, but they were still ahead, and nearly at the small stone wall that marked his boundary. When Ashley reached the stile over the wall, another man leapt up onto it from the other side, reaching for Harriet.

"No! no, no, no, no!" The words were muttered, for all his breath was spent on running. But his heart's agony was in every one of them. As other hands lifted Harriet away, Lord Geoffrey swung his sword at Ashley's lower leg, waiting only a second to see him fall screaming, before leaving him for Peterson to deal with. He vaulted the stile and launched himself onto the back of the cart as it lurched into motion in response to the driver's desperate whipping of the horses.

He paused a second to touch a finger to Harriet's face, where she lay tumbled in the bed of the cart, and realised, as he did, that the driver had thought the shudder of the cart as he landed on it to be simply part of the violent lurch into motion. The man didn't know he was there!

Moving with infinite care, he felt his way down Harriet's arm and used the sword edge to cut the ropes that bound her. She bit down on the gag at the pain of returning circulation, but made no sound. He eased down to trace her leg to her ankles, silently wishing he was doing so in any circumstances but these, and sliced the ropes from her ankles too. As he did so, she was already pulling the gag from her mouth.

He crept up past her, pausing only long enough to press a kiss to her lips, and edged towards the front of the cart. He felt, rather than heard, Harriet easing her way after him. He turned to look at her, and her green eyes sparkled in the moonlight. She motioned towards the man, then to Geoffrey. Then she pointed at herself, and mimed her hands holding reins and driving.

His heart bursting with love and pride, he nodded once, and turned back to his task. She edged to one side, close against him, but not enough to prevent his movement. He tapped her hand three times, and launched himself. His arm went around the driver's throat, cutting off his air, and the sword came around to hang before the man's face, the threat obvious.

The driver squirmed desperately, the ribbons falling unregarded from his fingers, then froze in place when he saw the sword.

As he dropped the ribbons, Harriet launched herself from the back of the cart onto the seat, snatching the falling ribbons of leather from the air, a fraction of a second before they fell into the gap between cart and horses.

She teetered a moment on the brink of falling herself, and Geoffrey felt his heart stop in his chest, then she grabbed the seat with one hand and hauled herself back, already beginning to bring the racing horses under control. She was, it seemed, as good at driving them as riding them.

"That thrice damned bastard's name is Nobby. He had a deal with them, to sell me to a house of pleasure, and split the profits. I'd happily see you skewer him now, but I suspect we'd better turn him over to the law."

Her voice was a little shaky, but not, he realised from fear. It was anger he heard, pure and simple. She was, quite simply, magnificent.

"Oh. That wasn't very ladylike language was it? I am sorry, but in this case, I rather think I'm entitled to swear."

He laughed, a shaky, almost hysterical edge to it.

"I believe you're right."

He kept the sword to Nobby's throat, while Harriet brought the straining horses back to a walk, then turned them carefully in a wider bit of the lane, before driving them back toward Witherwood Chase at a smart clip.

By the time they reached the stile again, Peterson had bound the bleeding Ashley, and Walters and Hurst were ready with ropes to bind Nobby. They hauled the screaming Ashley on to the back of the cart, and Harriet drove them all back around through the gates and up the drive to the stables.

Once the horses were held by the grooms, Lord Geoffrey slipped from the seat, supervising the traitors' removal from the cart, and the field dressing of Ashley's wound. He didn't want the man dying on him from an infection, before he'd had time to tell him where the papers were. Satisfied that things were under control, he turned back to the cart.

Lady Harriet was simply sitting there, staring ahead. She was, he realised, shaking, quivering like a leaf in the wind. He knew this reaction – he had seen it after battles, when the aftershock of action set in. Gently, he stepped up as close to the cart as he could, and, reaching out, slid her into his arms and lifted her down. She came willingly, sliding her arms around his neck, and burying her face against his shoulder. He thought she whispered something, but it was so faint he wasn't sure. It had sounded suspiciously like *'My hero'*.

He carried her into the house.

Chapter Thirteen

Lord Geoffrey settled Lady Harriet onto a chaise in the parlour, rang for tea, and brandy, and sat quietly beside her. She said nothing, but simply reached out and twined her fingers with his.

When the maid brought the tea and brandy, it was obvious that the staff were agog to know what was happening. They would have to wait. He shooed the maid out and poured a cup of tea, adding a generous drop of brandy. Harriet accepted it gratefully, and sipped.

Peterson knocked and entered when bidden, reporting that the traitors were bound and locked up in a secure room in the stables, with Walters guarding them. Lord Geoffrey nodded his thanks. Peterson turned to go, when Lady Harriet spoke.

"Please stay, Peterson. For you should hear what I have to tell, given your part in this mission."

Peterson hesitated, and, at Lord Geoffrey's confirmatory nod, stepped back into the room.

Her voice hesitant at first, then growing stronger as she spoke, and the brandy took effect, Lady Harriet described the events of the day. When she spoke of the box that she had seen, just before Ashley and Jobs had bound and gagged her, Lord Geoffrey sprang to his feet, pacing about the room. Could it really be over? Was that box the end to this mission? But where had they taken it? He broke in on her tale.

"Was there anything in what they said to indicate where they took the box?" She stared at him a moment, face blank, and he castigated himself for behaving in such an inconsiderate way - here he was, expecting her to have taken detailed note of what the men were saying, when she had just been roughly set upon, bound, gagged and threatened!

"I am so sorry! That is completely unreasonable of me to ask."

Lady Harriet looked up at him and smiled. His heart turned over at what he saw in her eyes.

"Ah, but I did listen to them. I was so utterly, blazingly angry, it hadn't yet occurred to me to be truly afraid. That came later. Just before they left the room, Ashley said something about taking it down to *'the deep'* and putting it with *'the other'*. It was just a single comment, before they left me there. They had put the box in a basket of dirty linens and covered it up. Probably so that they could take it down into the cellars somewhere, and be thought to be just adding a basket to the laundry pile. But beyond down in the cellars, which seems logical, I've no idea where *'the deep'* might be."

Frustration laced her voice. They might have the conspirators, but they didn't yet have the evidence.

Lord Geoffrey thought a moment, pacing about the room, then spun back towards her.

"Wait – they spoke of 'another' something?"

"Yes – they definitely were going to put the box with *'the other'*."

"But that's wonderful! Forgive me, I know that sounds terrible of me, but had today's events not happened, we would never have known of this second thing that is hidden. If we had found this box when they were not there, we would most certainly have believed that we had found all that there was to find."

Lord Geoffrey fell to his knees beside her, and pulled her into his arms, pressing a kiss to her lips as he did so. She clung to him, a little puzzled but delighted by his actions. Peterson met her eyes over Lord Geoffrey's shoulder and smiled. Lord Geoffrey pulled back and gazed at her.

"Oh Harriet, you are truly wonderful! Whilst I would never wish for you to have suffered what you have today, I am beyond grateful for what you have discovered. Your courage and resourcefulness never cease to amaze me. When any society miss might be expected to have fainted dead away, you were alert enough to listen and take note. And then on the cart! You are magnificent, magnificent!"

He had spoken her name! Without the 'Lady' in front of it! Her heart suddenly beat harder, the intimacy of her unadorned name on his lips leaving her even more flushed than the kiss.

Peterson cleared his throat, whilst feigning great interest in a book which had been left lying on a side table.

Lord Geoffrey, who had, for those moments, completely forgotten Peterson's presence, dropped Harriet's hands and leapt to his feet, a flush of embarrassment on his face.

"Ah, Peterson, it seems that we will need to interrogate our prisoners. I am sure that one of them can be convinced to tell us where the box is hidden. That would be considerably quicker than searching every hidden part of the cellars that the maps show, and probably parts that exist, but aren't on the maps."

Lord Geoffrey shuddered internally, even as he spoke. He hated interrogations. A good clean fight was one thing, but the process of drawing information forth was a dirty thing. Gerry had always been the one amongst the Hounds who dealt with that – expertly and efficiently. They were all beyond grateful that he had done that dirty work for them. Tonight, Geoffrey would have to deal with it himself.

"Yes, my Lord, I will arrange that – tonight – the less time they have to think about it, the more likely they are to tell us. Will you wish to be present?"

Lord Geoffrey took a deep steadying breath.

"Yes, it is my duty to do so."

Peterson nodded, having expected nothing less.

"And, my Lord, shall I arrange for Lady Harriet and Miss Carpenter to be conveyed home? And what message do you wish delivered to Viscount Pendholm to explain all of this?"

Harriet paled. The thought of explaining all of this to her brother and mother did not appeal at all.

They were reasonable people, and Charlton, she knew, had dealt with traitors before, but neither of them would be happy about her involvement in this mission, especially when they heard the details of today's events. But hear they would, for it was now past any reasonable time for her to be returning, even after a supposed dinner.

"I think that, before we consider returning Lady Harriet to her home, we must first call for some ointment for her poor wrists and ankles, which are, I now see, worn quite raw from her struggles. I do apologise, Lady Harriet, for not having that attended to sooner. Also, I suspect that some food would not go amiss, as you have had nothing since breaking your fast this morning."

Harriet looked positively enthusiastic at the suggestion of food. It was, at least in part, because that would delay facing her family, but the embarrassingly loud growl of her stomach was a pointed reminder of her actual need to eat.

"Whilst those matters are addressed, let us deal with our prisoners. Once that is done, I will personally escort Lady Harriet and Miss Carpenter to Pendholm Hall."

Harriet met his eyes, her gratitude and relief showing clearly.

"Thank you, Lord Geoffrey, your escort will be most appreciated."

~~~~~

The three prisoners, when asked questions separately, demonstrated rather different reactions.
~~~~~

Nobby refused to say anything, knowing full well that there was enough wrongdoing in his past to deliver him to the hangman's noose no matter what he said now. Lord Geoffrey let him be – for he had, as far as they could tell, no knowledge of what had gone on inside the house.

Ashley and Jobs were another matter. Threats of immediate violence had little effect on Ashley, but Jobs was quickly persuaded that cooperation might, perhaps, save him from the hangman's noose. Compared to death, transportation seemed a far better option. Lord Geoffrey gave his word that, if Jobs provided them a guide to the location of the hidden box, he would do his best to ensure that transportation was the sentence. But only once they had recovered the box – if Jobs gave them falsehoods, he would make certain the sentence was death.

"Jus' one other thing, milord. If'n I tells ye, don' ye be putting me back near Ash. If'n he knows I've ratted him out, I'm a goner for sure."

"That can be arranged. Now speak."

Peterson took careful notes as Jobs described the path to the secret doors in the cellars, and the exact location of the hidden boxes. Lord Geoffrey was startled to hear that below the cellars, there was not only a priesthole, dating back to the time of Cromwell, but below even that, a secret chapel with an ancient altar. The boxes were, sacrilegiously, it seemed, hidden in a cavity within the altar itself. Finally, when Lord Geoffrey was satisfied that they had all of the information needed to recover the boxes, Jobs was locked away separately, still securely bound.

But confirming the truth of his words would need to wait for the morning. For now, he must face Lady Harriet's family, and admit to the terrible danger he had placed her in, by allowing her to assist him. He would understand should they forbid him from ever seeing her again. At least his mind would. His heart was not so sanguine about that possibility. The ache in his chest at the very thought suggested that such a possibility would leave him empty forever.

~~~~~

Harriet perched on the edge of the carriage seat, desperately wishing that she could lean against Lord Geoffrey's temptingly close shoulder. But fear of the coming conversation kept her from moving. Miss Carpenter had exclaimed over her poor wrists and ankles, and tutted about the battered state of her dress, but said nothing further. Harriet knew that she would honour their agreement and support her.

When they alighted before Pendholm Hall, Lord Geoffrey graciously offered her his arm, and led her inside. The warmth of the strong muscle beneath her hand reached her, even through the layers of his shirt and coat, making her feel safe and protected somehow, as she had felt in his arms when he had lifted her down from the cart.

Lord Geoffrey, at that moment, was feeling quite as nervous as she was, if not more so, although he strove to keep his manner steady and calm, for her. Her scent wrapped about him, bringing, as it always did, that sense of safety and care. They would manage this conversation, together.
~~~~~

When they were admitted to the house, they were shown to Lady Sylvia's private parlour. As was their habit, Charlton and his mother had settled for a late evening coze, to talk through the events of their day. Lady Odette had already retired, happy to allow Charlton this time with his mother, knowing that he would not stay away from her long.

Charlton took one look at Lord Geoffrey's face, and his sister's dirtied and torn morning dress, and leapt to his feet. Miss Carpenter followed them into the room, and the door closed behind her.

"What has happened?"

"Oh my poor child – your wrists – what has happened to you?"

Charlton's voice tangled with Lady Sylvia's as they both spoke at once.

"It is rather a long story, I am afraid, but it must be told now, despite the late hour." Lord Geoffrey sounded more nervous than Charlton had ever heard him. Geoff didn't do nervous – in all their years at war, he had always been cool and steady, no matter what happened. This would be most interesting.

"Do sit then, and I'll call for some tea." Lady Sylvia was as practical as ever. In that moment, Harriet thanked God for her mother's nature. They sat, Geoffrey and Harriet instinctively staying together, sinking gratefully onto a comfortable chaise. Miss Carpenter settled on a small chair in one corner of the room, and tried hard to be invisible.

A somewhat strained silence ensued.

Once a maid had delivered the tea, and left them with it, Charlton's patience failed him.

"Out with it Geoff – I can see that there is a lot to tell, so please get on with it – or… is it Harriet's story to tell?" He looked at Harriet, waiting. Harriet looked at Lord Geoffrey, and some unspoken communication passed between them, which Lady Sylvia observed with great interest, then Geoffrey spoke.

"I'll start at the beginning. Charlton, you know I've been working for Setford. Lady Sylvia, I'll repeat this part for your benefit. You already know that I received ownership of Witherwood Chase as reward for services to the crown during last year. What you don't know, but Charlton is at least a little aware of, is that along with the property, I received a mission. The previous owner of Witherwood Chase was part of a treasonous plot. When it was discovered, he was dispossessed of all his belongings and incarcerated with many of his conspirators. But not, Setford suspected, all of them. So the price of me receiving the property was to ferret out any evidence still hidden there, and the remaining conspirators."

He paused for a sip of tea, feeling a little better now that he had begun.

"Hence my obsessive poking into every corner of the house, and taking inventory of everything I found. Which, I must say, has proved a capital idea. One which is set to make me a remarkably wealthy man, when all of those ugly paintings are sold. When Lady Harriet volunteered…"

At this description, Charlton snorted, and Lady Sylvia smiled in amusement. Geoffrey fixed them with a baleful look.

"As I said, when Lady Harriet volunteered to assist, I was most grateful. For, whilst she and Miss Carpenter trailed around with Mr Featherstonehaugh, taking interminable notes about the obvious contents of the house, I was free to search for hidden things. Things which I conclusively failed to find."

"Ah," Charlton broke in, "which was when you sought our suggestions at Meltonbrook Chase, about ways in which hidden rooms or passages might be concealed, and how to find them."

"Correct. Shortly after that, accidentally, Lady Harriet stumbled, quite literally, on a secret door, and opened it. Only I was present at that moment. Inside the room revealed, we discovered detailed maps of the entire house, showing most of the secret passages and rooms as well. We initially kept it between ourselves, but then found ourselves forced to draw Miss Carpenter and Mr Featherstonehaugh into our confidence to some degree."

At mention of her name, Miss Carpenter squirmed uncomfortably on her chair. So much for not being noticed….

"The last few weeks we have searched, usually separately, through every hidden passage we could. And found nothing but more dust and mouse droppings. This morning, we moved into the last two sections of the passages, except for the cellars. I admit, I was not hopeful, and searching the cellars, with access through the servants' areas was not a task I looked forward to."

Lady Sylvia nodded, listening to Lord Geoffrey, but watching Harriet's face.

"By late afternoon, I had finished searching my allocated section of the passages, with no better luck than on any previous day. I waited in my study for Lady Harriet's return. But today, she did not appear at the expected time. I waited, thinking that perhaps she had found some extra passages, and it was taking longer. But then I realised that it was far too late. I sent you that message – I do wholeheartedly apologise for the subterfuge – so as not to worry you unnecessarily, and set out to search for her."

Lady Sylvia had gone very pale, and was looking, again, at Harriet, and her bandaged wrists. Geoffrey continued, telling the tale of his frustrated and increasingly fearful search, the discovery of Harriet's hair trapped in the passage, and his reaching the room where she was held. When he spoke of noticing the hair and thus finding the door, Harriet gazed at him with open adoration.

At that point, Harriet spoke up, taking over the telling of the tale, describing her day, how she had stumbled upon the secret doors, and walked in on the conspirators, only to be captured and bound. When she spoke of the plans they had made for her, Charlton's face went hard as stone. When she reached the point in the story where Geoffrey had arrived at the room, he joined her in the telling of the rest, their voices interweaving as they shifted from one part to the next, instinctively finishing each other's sentences until the tale was complete.

Lord Geoffrey spoke of her heroic capture of the ribbons and controlling the horses, Harriet spoke of Lord Geoffrey's heroic disabling of Ashley, his leap to the cart, and the capture of Nobby.

To Charlton and Lady Sylvia, watching them, it was very obvious that the bond between them was extraordinary, and that something remarkable had been forged that day, beyond the achievement of capturing the villains. Lady Sylvia wondered if Harriet and Geoffrey had admitted their feelings to each other yet.

"So there you have it. A sordid and distressing tale. I can only most humbly beg your forgiveness for ever placing Lady Harriet in such danger. I will never forgive myself. At that moment when she teetered on the cart, I knew that my life would not be worth living if I had lost her. Now, to complete this damnable mission, all that remains is to go into the cellars tomorrow morning, and retrieve the hidden boxes, confirm that their contents are what Setford seeks, and allow him to carry off the conspirators and the papers."

"I insist on being the one to open that altar and remove the boxes. After all of this, I think I'm entitled to that." Harriet's voice was strong, and her bright cheerful manner was returning, even after all the shocks of the day.

Geoffrey looked at her a moment, then nodded.

"Charlton, would you do me the honour of being there as well? I would like another witness to this, one that Setford knows and trusts."

"Certainly, I wouldn't miss it!"

"You're not leaving me out of this either! After what my daughter has been through for those boxes, I want to see them with my own eyes."

Lord Geoffrey, seeing a glint in Lady Sylvia's eyes that was a rather clear echo of her daughter in a determined mood, inclined his head in acknowledgement. She smiled.

"Good, we are agreed then. We will bring Harriet to Witherwood Chase in the morning, and see this thing complete. And Lord Geoffrey – of course I forgive you – I am fully aware of how difficult it is to prevent my daughter from doing anything that she truly wishes to do. I do not blame you in the least. But I am overwhelmingly glad that you were there to save her – as you saved us all last year."

Lord Geoffrey flushed at Lady Sylvia's words.

"You are most gracious my Lady. I will look forward to your arrival on the morrow."

He turned to Lady Harriet, took her hand a moment, and bent to kiss it, before standing and bowing to the others, then took his leave.

~~~~~

In the carriage, he allowed himself to relax, and discovered, to his chagrin, that he was shaking. He had been so afraid that they might blame him, might cast him from their house, that he might never see Harriet again.

The relief was overwhelming. He could not bear to never see her. He loved her, he wanted to…

What! What had he just thought? He rewound the thoughts and there it was. He loved her. It was a startling idea, yet it seemed utterly right.
~~~~~

But... how did she really feel about him? What if her affection really was just the infatuation he had always thought it? What would he do?

Chapter Fourteen

Harriet had barely slept, between the aching in her arms and legs from the long hours bound in awkward positions, and the exertion afterwards on the cart, and the feverish dreams of Lord Geoffrey's arms about her, and his lips on hers, all mixed in with more terrible dreams of being bound in the darkness.

She tried to sit patiently whilst her maid dressed the wounds on her wrists and ankles again, wincing a little at the pressure on the sensitive flesh, then found herself still ravenous after the exertions of the previous day. Lady Sylvia was happy to see that Harriet's appetite was undiminished by her adventures.

Once in the carriage, she fidgeted, anxious to see Lord Geoffrey again, desperate to finally see the papers that had brought them all so much trouble, and, at the same time, afraid of what would follow. The days ahead looked bleak and empty if she should no longer have an excuse to spend them in Lord Geoffrey's company.

She had thought, last night, when he had cared for her, held her, that she saw something in his eyes, in his manner, that she had longed for, this year past and more. In the grey morning light, she was no longer sure. Did he care for her, truly, or was it just her wishes making her see what wasn't there? If he did not care for her, what would she do? For she loved him. She had from almost the first time she had met him. That would not change. She had known that he was the man she wanted, been quite certain of her feelings from the start – but how would she live if he never returned her love, or even affection?

As Witherwood Chase came into sight, she pushed those thoughts aside – first, the cellars, and the boxes of papers.

They were shown into the study and Lord Geoffrey greeted them a little seriously, although his eyes locked with Harriet's the moment she stepped into the room. That moment seemed to last forever, and to be gone too fast. He dragged his eyes away, and, showing them to seats placed near the desk, he brought forth the maps of the house.

Peterson had been busy, and had marked, on the map of the cellars, the places described by Jobs. Once they were all clear on the path before them, Lord Geoffrey rose.

"Shall we get this over with?"

"By all means. I would like to see these papers that are so precious as to be, apparently, worth my life and more." Lady Harriet rose from her seat. Lord Geoffrey led her from the room, followed by the others. The servants were shocked at the procession that entered their domain, and scurried aside.

At the back of the root cellar, Peterson led them to a section where sacks of various vegetables hung on hooks, and larger barrels of potatoes and onions stood below. Once the barrels were shifted aside, a push and pull on two of the hooks at once caused the panel to open, exposing dark steps beyond, steep and uneven. Lantern in hand, he led them downwards.

The steps turned, and finally deposited them in a small room carved out of the earth. Nooks carved into the wall served as shelves, and a space for a narrow bed. A trickle of water fell from a small hole in the rocks to one side, no doubt fed from the rain water cisterns above, and pooled in an old earthenware bowl, before overflowing to trickle out again through a crack in one corner of the floor. It was well constructed as a place in which a man could hide for a long time, given a supply of food. Harriet shuddered at the thought of priests being forced to hide in such places, those many years ago.

Turning, they studied the space. Where was the secret entry to the chapel, which Jobs had described? Lord Geoffrey, eyes narrowed, strode forward and swept the mouldering blanket from the boards that covered the earth in the nook designed as a bed. Grasping the boards, he lifted, and revealed, not the beaten earth that was to be expected, but a small space and more stairs leading down into inky darkness.

Again, Peterson took the lead, checking the steps for safety, and holding the lantern, as best he might, to allow them to see where they stepped. Lord Geoffrey assisted Lady Harriet, and Charlton assisted Lady Sylvia, who grimaced a little at the smears of earth now decorating their clothes.

When they reached the bottom, they gasped in awe. Whoever had built this had spent much effort and care. They stood in a small chapel, the walls lined with stone, plastered and decorated with paintings – religious imagery in a style many centuries gone, the colours still beautiful, only lightly touched with mould in a few places. Small gems embedded in parts of the pictures glinted in the lantern light, and silver candlesticks shone in nooks and on either end of the plain altar.

The altar was built of stone and wood, carved with elegant simplicity. Harriet stepped forward, and walked around it, wondering exactly where it opened.

"On the end, my Lady. The two floral pieces to either side of the cross in the carving. According to Jobs, they must both be pressed at once, and the timber panel on the end will open. In these old altars, they made these cavities to store relics – often the bones of saints, I believe." Lord Geoffrey's voice was muted. This might be long unused, but they all felt the sense of the intended sanctity of the place.

Harriet, praying that no bones of a saint graced this altar, sharing their housing with sacrilegious boxes of traitorous information, did as instructed. The panel popped out as they had been told it would, and she lifted it aside. Reaching in, she pulled out two boxes – one that she had seen upstairs, one which was larger and heavier, and passed them to Peterson, who sat them on the single simple pew.

They looked so insignificant, yet, for what these contained, men had been willing to destroy her life. Charlton tested each box.

"Locked. As was to be expected. How do we plan to open them."

"I have no key, and Jobs didn't know of the key's location either, but…" Lord Geoffrey had turned towards Lady Harriet, with a hopeful expression. He smiled when he saw that she was already pulling a pin from her soft gold hair.

She pushed past her brother and sank down onto the pew.

"Peterson, the light, if you would."

Peterson brought the lantern close and both Charlton and Lady Sylvia watched in some astonishment as Lady Harriet carefully picked the locks on both boxes. With a satisfied expression, she replaced the pin in her hair and turned shining eyes to Lord Geoffrey.

"There my Lord. If you would open them now, we may at last see what all of this fuss has been for."

Lord Geoffrey was watching Lady Harriet with unfeigned admiration. He bowed elegantly to her, with a flourish worthy of Mr Featherstonehaugh, and stepped forward.

The boxes proved to contain, as Baron Setford had expected, a collection of papers detailing meetings, conspirators' names, plans, and other deeply damning evidence of treason. They also contained a few small bags of coinage, and of gemstones, which was not expected. In the larger box, a small ledger listed payments made – a source of information that would delight Setford and no doubt lead his men to many of those who had supported the plot, however peripherally.

Papers. So innocent looking, and yet enough to send many men to their deaths. Lady Harriet shuddered, and gently closed the lids.

"Let us be out of this place. That so many should have plotted against our country leaves me feeling sickened." No-one disagreed.

~~~~~

Urgent messages were sent, and, three days later, Baron Setford arrived. He brought a second carriage, with barred windows and armed men to guard it. The prisoners were handed over to his guards, and the carriage departed, taking them to their fate. Lord Geoffrey, true to his word, told Setford of his promise to Jobs, and the Baron agreed that, under the circumstances, he would most likely be able to get the man transported, rather than hung.

Late in the evening, Lord Geoffrey, Charlton and Baron Setford took their ease in Geoffrey's study. Brandy in their glasses, and the boxes resting on the desk in front of them, they went over the events of the last few days again, for Setford's benefit.

He listened intently as Lord Geoffrey told the tale, leaving nothing out. He examined the contents of the boxes, and nodded, pleased. This would leave no loose ends. This matter would finally be done, and he could now report it as such to the Prince Regent. He hefted the bags of coin and gems, his shrewd grey eyes considering. Then he turned, and dropped them into Lord Geoffrey's hands.
~~~~~

"Excellent work. How convenient that these boxes contained only the papers we sought, and all of the papers we sought. And, from your description, I am most impressed with young Lady Harriet. She would, I suspect, have the talent to make an excellent contribution to our work. I don't suppose you'd consider recruiting her?"

"No!"

"Definitely not!"

Charlton and Geoffrey spoke at once, both glaring at Setford, who laughed.

"That's what I thought you'd say. But you can't blame me for asking – it's not often we find a woman with courage, and useful skills like lock picking!"

"True. It's not a talent I was aware my sister had, until today."

Charlton looked chagrined at admitting this.

"Apparently," Lord Geoffrey contributed, "she learnt that skill as a child, to recover her prized possessions when your nasty piece of a brother had locked them away. I am not surprised that she has kept it secret. It's not exactly a socially approved 'suitable skill for a Lady'."

Charlton looked thoughtful, wondering just how it was that Geoffrey knew more about his sister than he did.

Setford finished his brandy and reached out to close the lids of the boxes.

"Please lock these away for tonight."

As Geoffrey did so, Setford continued.

"I'll be away tomorrow with these, and set things in motion. I will keep you apprised of the outcomes. But it may take a month before I have much news for you."

"In that case, let me invite you to partake of my hospitality again – the Hounds and their families intend to gather here for Eastertide, and we would be delighted if you would join us."

Setford stilled, and, for the first time ever, Geoffrey saw something in his pale grey eyes that looked alarmingly like uncertainty. Then he nodded, as if coming to a decision.

"I'd be delighted m'boy. Catching up with all of you at once will be a pleasure. But now, let's to our rest. I, at least, have a long day ahead of me tomorrow."

Chapter Fifteen

To Harriet, the week after they had descended into the hidden chapel, and recovered the evidence against the traitors, passed in an odd dream like way. The whole thing, after months of searching, and the drama of her almost abduction, seemed monumentally anticlimactic. Her abraded wrists and ankles healed, but her heart ached.

She wanted to see Lord Geoffrey, missed him dreadfully, in fact, after so long seeing him almost every day. She had hoped, at first, that he might come to visit her. He did not. Charlton told her that he had been very busy with Baron Setford, seeing off the prisoners and handing over the boxes. She supposed that was reasonable – but that did not make her heart ache any less.

Lord Geoffrey, once Setford was gone, found himself at a loose end, unable to settle to anything. The funds from the sale of the first batch of paintings had been deposited to his bank, and Raphael had sent him a quick letter, telling him so, and informing him of the astounding sum involved.

Mr Featherstonehaugh, who seemed equally a little out of sorts and lost, was working at finalising the inventory and packing of the next two shipments of goods to be sold. These would not be sent to Raphael until after Easter, for Raphael had also written to advise that he would be away again for some weeks. He neglected to mention why.

Which left Lord Geoffrey with absolutely nothing to do. Except think. About Lady Harriet, to be precise. All the time. He felt like a lovesick boy. He busied himself with simple things - visits to the tenant farmers, and meetings with each and every remaining member of his staff. He wanted them to know that they were not under suspicion, that he valued their work.

Universally, they greeted that news with relief, and a cautious warming of their attitude to him. Mrs Chester even went so far as to confide that 'she'd never held with them strange types the old master went about with'. Whilst it all needed to be done, none of it really distracted him. Thoughts of Lady Harriet were ever present in the back of his mind. He wanted to see her. Truth be told, he wanted much more than to just see her. He wanted to hold her, to kiss her, to be near her every day.

But the only way he could do that would be to... he shied away from the thought. He sent no message, for he had no idea what he could say. And the longer he was away from her, the more doubts he felt. What if she hated him for having endangered her, now that she'd had time to recover and think about it? If he didn't see her, there was still hope.

So it went for a week or more, until an invitation arrived.

Lady Sylvia would be delighted if he would join them for dinner on the morrow. His heart leapt, with hope and fear at once. He would see her. But what if she did not wish to see him? Still, cursing himself for having been a coward, when that had never been his way, he accepted the invitation. The hours until that dinner lasted longer than any other day of his life.

~~~~~

Lady Sylvia had watched her daughter with some concern. Where was her bright, volatile child? This moody drifting girl was not her Harriet! How had it come to a point where Harriet, who had determinedly pursued Lord Geoffrey's company at any opportunity, for over a year now, was limply fretting rather than acting?

In the end, with that sense of mischief which was part of her (and which she had passed on to Harriet), she could not resist interfering, just a little. She invited Lord Geoffrey to dinner, only informing Harriet, Charlton and Odette after she had sent the invitation.

Harriet's face lit up at her words, then clouded with some fretting concern. Charlton watched the emotions chase across Harriet's face, raised an enquiring eyebrow at his mother, then smiled.

"An excellent idea, mother."

Lady Odette happily agreed.
~~~~~

Odette was still adjusting to becoming mistress of a large household, and was more comfortable deferring to Lady Sylvia's judgement as yet.

Lady Sylvia went on her way to discuss menus with Cook, and Harriet, suspecting that Charlton would ask her about her expression, developed a sudden desire to go and ride Moonbeam, as she had been rather shamefully neglecting the mare of late. Charlton wisely let her go – Harriet would work out whatever was worrying her, all in good time.

~~~~~

When John led out Moonbeam for her, Harriet smiled and thanked him as he boosted her into the saddle.

"I know you'll follow me John, but please, give me at least the illusion of being alone. I need some time to think."

The groom bowed in acknowledgement.

"As you wish, my Lady."

The mare was fresh, and keen to run, so Harriet let her do so, enjoying the feel of the wind on her face, and the scent of the first spring grass as it was crushed beneath Moonbeam's hooves. When they reached the river's edge, she slowed the mare to a walk for a while, until she reached her favourite spot.

Slipping down, she tethered Moonbeam and settled on the large fallen log that afforded a view to the bend of the river. She had told the truth when she said she needed to think.
~~~~~

This evening, she would see Lord Geoffrey again. What would she do? How would he react?

She was quite certain that, as soon as she saw him, she would have the completely inappropriate urge to throw herself into his arms. Which she could not allow herself to do. For, before she completely embarrassed herself, she needed some indication of his feelings. Did he truly care for her? Or was she deluding herself. And how was she to discover the truth?

The afternoon flowed away with the river, and she was no closer to having answers to those questions. Soon, she would need to return, to dress for dinner, and prepare for the moment when he walked into the room. Just a few minutes more. As she stared into the distance, a sound came to her – quiet at first, then getting louder. Hoofbeats.

~~~~~

Lord Geoffrey could no longer stand the slow creep of the minutes. He had to do something to fill the hours before the dinner at Pendholm Hall. He stared out of the window at the gardens, where the approach of spring was bringing new leaves and the first buds of flowers, and decided to ride.

He could take Rajah out for a good gallop, take a turn past the furthest tenant farmers' cottages, and then make his way to the lower ford, cross, and go to Pendholm Hall along their side of the river. He was sure that Lady Sylvia would forgive his appearing for dinner in riding clothes rather than full evening attire. Decided, he called for Hurst, and went to dress.
~~~~~

Half an hour later, he sped across the fields, feeling freer than he had in months.

The tenant farmers were glad to see him, and he noted with pleasure that they, and their families, looked in much better health than they had when he first came to Witherwood Chase. Good shelter and enough food through the winter had made a difference. A difference that was sure to also result in better crops this summer, and in the years to follow.

The river was high with the last of the snow melt from the hills, but the ford was still easily passable. He slowed Rajah and simply soaked in the beauty of his surroundings, deeply appreciative of land not touched by war. Even after more than a year back in England, he could not forget the destruction of the land that the war had wrought, in France, and in Spain.

Coming closer to Pendholm Hall, he rounded a corner of the path and saw ahead of him a horse standing quietly, and beyond it a person, perched on a fallen log. Immediately he recognised the horse as Moonbeam, and the dappled sunlight glinting off Lady Harriet's hair made her identity unmistakable.

His mind froze. Rajah continued along the path at a steady walk, unconcerned with the turmoil of his master's mind.

What would he do? He could not give in to his first impulse, which was to rush to her, fling himself from the horse and gather her into his arms. What if she did not wish him to do so? What if she bitterly resented the danger that he had placed her in? He had no answers. Rajah reached the small clearing, and stopped, whickering a greeting to Moonbeam as he did so.

Lady Harriet turned, her green eyes wide, and a hesitant smile touched her face.

He drank in the sight of her.

Well, not hate then, if she was smiling – that was good.

Time seemed to slow, and he slid from the horse, his eyes never leaving hers. They each stepped forward, until they stood mere inches apart, neither sure what to say, how to breach the gap that had somehow appeared between them.

His voice came out a whisper.

"Harriet…"

She watched his storm grey eyes, and saw the message in them, that he struggled for words to express. She sighed, and a tightness left her posture, which she had not even realised was there.

Of its own accord, her hand reached for him, as surely as her words.

"Geoffrey… I…."

He took her hand, pulling her into his arms, and swept her words away with his lips, kissing her as he had so often dreamed of doing, as she wrapped her arms around his neck and pressed herself to him. Long minutes later, they pulled away from each other a little, still unsure of what to say, but each certain of their feelings. Keeping her fingers twined in his, Geoffrey took a deep steadying breath.

Now was the time to speak, no matter how much the words were hard to find.

"Harriet... I... I have missed you abominably this past week. Can you forgive me for not calling? I am ashamed to admit that I was afraid – afraid that you would not wish to see me, that you might hate me for having put you in such danger."

Harriet put her finger to his lips, arresting his words.

"Never think such a thing! I could never hate you. You have always been a hero to me, and the events of last week have only made that more so."

He lifted her hand, and pressed a kiss to her fingers.

"Then... if you cannot hate me, can I dare to hope that you might be able to love me? For I have discovered that I love you, beyond any sense or reason. When I saw you come so close to falling from that cart, I knew that I could never live without you. Harriet, my wonderful brave and clever Harriet, will you marry me?"

His breathing stopped, and he stood, utterly still, waiting for her response. She tipped her head to one side, and her green eyes sparkled, then she laughed with delight.

"Yes, oh yes, of course I will marry you. How could you think otherwise? I have loved you from the moment I saw you!"

He swept her into his arms again, spinning her around, her feet in the air, as she laughed with joy. When he set her feet to the ground again, she clung to him, dizzy with happiness.

For some time they simply stood that way, safe in each other's' arms, until the lengthening shadows reminded them that it was time to go.

Harriet, in that moment, suddenly realised that John must have seen, from a distance, the whole thing. And he had done nothing. How wonderful! She must thank him later.

Geoffrey boosted her onto Moonbeam, then mounted Rajah, and they set off along the path to Pendholm Hall.

"As soon as we arrive, I shall speak to Charlton. Er, how do you think he will react? Will he approve? Will your mother approve?"

Harriet looked at him like he was quite mad.

"Of course they will approve. And, if they seem to have any doubts, I will convince them."

This was the Harriet he loved – strong minded, determined, bright and beautiful.

~~~~~

Charlton laughed at the worried look on Geoffrey's face.

"Of course I approve! I shall be proud to call you brother-in-law, as well as brother-in-arms. I never thought to see this day, yet I should have known. My sister has always had a knack for getting what she wants – and she made no bones about wanting you."

Geoffrey's face lit with a grin to match Charlton's.

"I thought that we might have the wedding at Witherwood Chase, at Easter, when everyone will be here. That's just more than the necessary month needed for the banns. And I doubt Harriet wants to wait longer, any more than I do."
~~~~~

Geoffrey actually blushed as he spoke, and Charlton laughed again, clapping him on the shoulder.

"Come then, let's go and tell mother the news. I suspect if we take any longer to come out of this room, Harriet will come bursting in, ready to force me to agree!"

Lady Sylvia embraced Geoffrey, smiling with tears in her eyes.

"At first I was not so sure that you were right for her, you know. But the more I saw you with her, the more right it seemed. I cannot imagine a better man for my wild child of a daughter!"

At that moment, Harriet burst into the room, Charlton captured her before she had taken more than two steps, and spun her around, laughing at her expression.

"Harriet, I approve, and so does mother. You've no need to demand our agreement."

She stopped, and had the grace to flush, before looking up defiantly and reaching for Geoffrey's hand.

Epilogue

Their Easter gathering was full of life and happiness, of friends become family and lifelong bonds made. It was made more joyous by the occasion of Harriet and Geoffrey's wedding, the arrangements for which had been taken in hand by Lady Sylvia. Geoffrey had never realised just how much organisation went into a wedding!

Finally the day dawned.

The small village church was full, with the Hounds and their families, including Odette's aunt, Lady Farnsworth, plus Baron Setford, as well as all of the staff of both Pendholm Hall and Witherwood Chase, and most of the villagers and tenant farmers.   Even Geoffrey's brother Alfred and his wife had deigned to attend. Geoffrey was darkly amused to discover that his new status as a man of wealth with substantial property appeared to have made him a more acceptable person in his brother's eyes.

As if any of those things mattered to him. Harriet was what mattered.

It was a day full of laughter and joy, with Harriet having chosen to wear a gown of spring green which set off her eyes, and Geoffrey looking elegant in simple black and white attire.

When the words had been said, and they walked from the church as man and wife, they were met with a cloud of rose petals to rival those that Geoffrey had arranged for Charlton's wedding. There was a very happy purveyor of hothouse flowers somewhere!

The only slight sad note in the day was Raphael's absence. It seemed that he had not yet returned from his latest travels. Geoffrey hoped that he might still arrive, before everyone departed in a week's time, as the Easter season ended.

They all returned to Witherwood Chase, to be served a sumptuous feast and dance in the newly renovated ballroom. Lady Sylvia had settled contentedly in a quiet corner, and was watching the festivities with great satisfaction.

Both of her children wed within a few months of each other, and both so happy – what more could a mother ask for?

At least Geoffrey and Harriet had not been forced to wait, as had Charlton and Odette, by the mourning period for Odette's father. She was not sure that Harriet's quicksilver temperament could have produced the patience to wait a year to wed!

She watched the people around her, noting who danced with who (waltzes were so revealing of people's feelings…), and whose eyes followed who. There were some interesting possibilities before her – she wouldn't be at all surprised to see more weddings in the near future.

She was particularly delighted to see Lady Farnsworth dancing with Baron Setford. She rather thought that Lady Farnsworth's acerbic wit would appeal to Setford, and Lady Farnsworth deserved some companionship.

Also pleasing was seeing Miss Carpenter dancing with Mr Featherstonehaugh, who was cheerful and dapper as usual.

Miss Carpenter had been a patiently long suffering shadow to Harriet for so many years now that Lady Sylvia had been concerned for her future, once Harriet was wed. Perhaps there was nothing to worry about after all.

Setford's wedding gift to Harriet and Geoffrey had been a quietly delivered missive from the Prince Regent, which thanked them both for their recent actions to protect crown and country, and added a further grant of lands to Geoffrey's holdings.

He had confirmed that the remaining conspirators had been found and taken, that Jobs had been transported, and that the other two were held in Newgate, awaiting the hangman's pleasure.

The waltz ended, and Geoffrey swept Harriet out onto the terrace, where the sweet smell of the herbs in the scent garden drifted on the breeze as the Eastertide brought the growth of spring to the world. They stood, watching the stars, his arm holding her close to his side.

His voice was quiet, for her ears only.

"No more missions, no more searching. We can take life as we wish, go anywhere you wish. What do you wish, my darling Harriet?"

She stayed silent, thinking, at peace with the world. When, after some time, she spoke, it was a whisper, but her words were more powerful than a shout.

"It doesn't matter where we go, or what we do, so long as I can do it with you. Whatever may come, you will always be my hero."

The End

(You'll find a taste of book 5, "Enchanting the Duke" just after the 'About the Author' section in this book!)

Arietta Richmond
Regency Historical Romance

ARIETTA RICHMOND, CATHERINE WINDSOR, ISABELLA THORNE, KATHERINE KEATS, KELLY ANNE BRUCE

About the Author

Arietta Richmond has been a compulsive reader and writer all her life. Whilst her reading has covered an enormous range of topics, history has always fascinated her, and historical novels been amongst her favourite reading.

She has written a wide range of work, from business articles and other non-fiction works (published under a pen name) but fiction has always been a major part of her life. Now, her Regency Historical Romance books are finally being released. The Derbyshire Set is comprised of 10 shorter novels (6 released so far). The 'His Majesty's Hounds' series is comprised of 7 novels, with the second having just been released.

She also has a standalone longer novel shortly to be released, and two other series of novels in development.

She lives in Australia, and when not reading or writing, likes to travel, and to see in person the places where history happened.

Be the first to know about it when Arietta's next book is released!

Sign up to Arietta's newsletter at

http://www.ariettarichmond.com

When you do, you will receive a free copy of the <u>subscriber exclusive</u> novella **'A Gift of Love',** a prequel to the Derbyshire Set series, which ends on the day that 'The Earl's Unexpected Bride' begins

This story is not for sale anywhere – it is absolutely exclusive to newsletter subscribers!

ARIETTA RICHMOND, CATHERINE WINDSOR, ISABELLA THORNE, KATHERINE KEATS, KELLY ANNE BRUCE

Here is your preview of

Enchanting the Duke

His Majesty's Hounds – Book 5
Sweet and Clean Regency Romance

Arietta Richmond

Chapter 1

The County of Berkshire, England – March 1814

The cold, spring air carried the last frosts of winter across the bleak countryside and nipped the exposed cheeks of the burly coach driver who steered the stately coach carefully through the wide wrought iron gates and into the grounds of Casterfield Grange. Frost-covered poplars lined the gravelled driveway and groundsmen in warm, long, woollen coats touched their hats in respect as the coach rolled by, wheels clattering on the small pebbles and steam swirling from the backs of the tired horses.

"Finally," whispered Lady Cordelia Branley, the elder daughter of the Baron whose family had held the noble title of Tillingford for nearly eight hundred years. She pushed her hands deeper into the fox-fur muff that kept her hands protected from the bitter cold and smiled.

"Home at last and we have arrived whilst it is still daylight."

Her companion (once her governess) tried to smile, but looked tired from the journey. Miss Millpost was a strict and severe spinster of some fifty summers, a woman whose main responsibility was to chaperone the pretty, dark haired sixteen-year old girl, teach her how to run a household as only a good and obedient wife should, and keep her out of mischief. The companion shifted her bony frame on the hard, leather-bound coach seat.

"How may we even know if the sun still exists beyond those dark clouds and the bitter cold? If I don't have warm tea to revive me, child, I fear I shall expire from the ague!"

Lady Cordelia tried not to laugh, for she knew that Miss Millpost would sooner revive her spirits with a glass or two of her father's excellent Madeira. She sighed. It felt good to be home once more, and she was more than excited to see her loving father again and her beautiful younger sister, Georgiana.

Ever since their dear mama had died, in a cholera epidemic when Georgiana was only five, Cordelia had tried to assume the role of mother, and she naturally felt deeply protective of her sister. The younger girl often behaved more like a boy and had seemed to prefer playing in the garden and getting herself covered in mud and leaves rather than learning to embroider and excel at the feminine arts. But their father loved them both dearly and indulged them in whatever ways might make them happy.

Despite the constant shadow of their mother's tragic death, it was still a happy household and a wonderful place to grow up.

Georgiana's insatiable curiosity had even prompted her father to consider appointing a tutor for his younger daughter and he was weighing the issue in his comfortable library with a pipe of fine Virginia tobacco and glass of good cognac when he heard the carriage wheels and the horses' hooves approaching the house.

Clouds of hot breath surrounded the horses as they pulled the carriage across the frozen ground and finally slowed to a welcome halt outside the grand entrance portico of Baron Tillingford's elegant home. Servants hurried to open the carriage door and unfold the steps so that the passengers could alight. They were smiling as Cordelia stepped down, obviously pleased to see her Ladyship safely returned from her journey. They fussed around her, almost ignoring the companion as she struggled to step down without lifting the hem of her heavy skirt and revealing her bony ankles. It was important to observe the correct proprieties at all times, she felt. Especially in front of the servants.

"Papa!" Cordelia cried as she caught sight of her father at the top of the steps. She raced up the broad stone stairs and hugged the Baron, who could barely contain his tears of joy as he held his lovely daughter in his arms and gave thanks for her safe return.

"You look so much like your beloved mama, my dear. How can I look upon you and not see the radiance of her grace and beauty? It warms my heart and cheers my soul!"

The companion coughed loudly behind Cordelia's back to announce her presence. "Miss Millpost. Well met and welcome back. You must join me in the library for a glass of light refreshment and tell me how went your visit to London."

Cordelia had not long celebrated her sixteenth birthday and the Baron had finally bowed to pressure from his precious elder daughter and allowed her to visit relatives in London. The Baron's cousin was influential and a well-known and popular guest in the salons and elegant drawing rooms of London's high society. The cousin and his wife would provide the perfect opportunity to introduce Cordelia to the nobility of the nation's capital.

At sixteen, the Baron was also aware that his daughter would soon be eligible for marriage and that it would do no harm for her pretty face and lovely smile to be seen in the discerning circles of the gentry. The hard fact was that the endless wars with Napoleon had taken far too many young men away from England's shores to offer their service in His Majesty's Army and Navy. And too few of them ever came back.

The result was that there simply were not so many young, eligible noblemen around who might come to Baron Tillingford and seek Cordelia's hand in marriage. Introducing the young woman into London society might possibly draw the attention of a noble young suitor, and then the ageing Baron could rest easier in the knowledge that at least one of his daughters had made a good match. It was all he wanted for his girls. To see them happily married and presiding over a great and noble household.

For, as he sadly had no son to follow him, the Barony, and its entailed estates, would pass to someone else, probably some extremely distant relative, or someone chosen by the King, as he had, to his knowledge, no male relatives to succeed him.

That made it all the more important that his girls be well placed with suitable husbands. He could leave them Casterfield Grange, for it was not entailed, nor were a few other properties he held, so their beloved home would still be theirs when he was no longer here to care for them. Still, he wished to see them happy, and married to men of suitable wealth and breeding, as soon as possible.

It wasn't too much to ask for, but the Baron was aware of his age and his growing infirmity. Time, he felt, was not on his side.

ARIETTA RICHMOND, CATHERINE WINDSOR, ISABELLA THORNE, KATHERINE KEATS, KELLY ANNE BRUCE

Chapter 2

London had been a revelation for the young Lady Cordelia Branley. She'd been thrilled to see the well-dressed young bucks in their expensively-tailored attire, seated around card tables and wagering loudly on the outcome of every hand. Whilst the card rooms at Balls were more commonly frequented by men, and a few of the older ladies, only, Cordelia had begged her hostess for a chance to see what went on.

The games had been exciting to watch and, when one of the young nobles had spied Cordelia and nodded his head at her with a courteous smile, it was all that she could do to contain herself. She'd blushed and the young man had laughed, his carefully-oiled mass of dark curls set off with a black silk ribbon tied in a bow at the back. He'd looked back at the table and roared with delight as he turned the final card and gathered up his winnings. His companions had groaned as they threw their cards on the table and Cordelia had turned to her hostess and asked who the young man might be.

"That is Lord Edward FitzHugh, second son of the Earl of Bolton, my dear, a fine young man who should be alongside his father in the King's uniform, fighting the French in Spain. But he prefers to spend his days slug-a-bed and his nights gambling at the card tables and carousing."

Her hostess' voice had been severe, quite disapproving, but she refused to say more on the matter.

With her heart beating and her pretty eyes widening, Cordelia was utterly convinced that he was by far the most handsome young man she had ever seen.

Ever.

During the following days, Cordelia had conspired with her hostess to attend as many social functions as possible, overtly to meet as many noble ladies and gentlemen as possible but secretly with the hope that she might catch sight once more of the dashing Lord FitzHugh. Her hopes were not in vain.

Many of the great salons offered cards and the sport of wagering on the outcome, a pursuit that might have been reserved for the candlelit interiors of the gentlemen's clubs, but was widely accepted as a fashionable way to offer entertainment and draw the young bucks into the well-lit reception rooms where eligible young ladies might be viewed and appreciated for their potential as future brides.

Lord Edward was considered to be a most fortunate card player for he displayed remarkable skill at the gaming tables. He always smiled and offered his fellow players a warm handshake when the games were done and he was filling his purse with his prize of gold coins.

On the final night of Cordelia's stay in London, she was sipping her glass of punch and watching the other guests in the elegant ballroom, when someone touched her bare shoulder and gently moved an artfully trailing curl of lovely auburn hair aside. She turned and stared into the pale grey eyes of Edward, Lord FitzHugh, and her heart nearly stopped beating.

He bowed to her, and when he looked up again he was smiling.

"Your servant, my Lady."

Miss Millpost, standing beside Cordelia, seemed on the verge of apoplexy when she noticed that the young Lord was being far too familiar with her charge, and without a formal introduction!

Cordelia, well used to Miss Millpost, was aware of her disapproval, and ignored it. Miss Millpost would, no doubt, berate her soundly later. She was more interested in what Lord Edward had to say, than in Miss Millpost's opinion at that moment.

He looked into Cordelia's eyes and she found the intensity of his attention flattering, if almost unnerving.

"Pray, my Lady, would you grant me the boon of your favour and let me hear from your lips the sound of your name? For 'tis a perfect misery to my heart to behold your loveliness and not know how to address you."

At this rather overly dramatic pronouncement, Miss Millpost coughed so loudly that people in the vicinity turned to see if she were having a spasm, or a fit of the vapours.

"Sir!" she finally spoke with a steely edge to her voice. "You may address that question to me, for I am sure that you have not been formally introduced to the young lady and that you presume too much by speaking to her!"

The young lord laughed.

"The fault is entirely mine for forgetting my manners in the presence of such beauty. I was bewitched and enchanted by the lady's smile and I no longer know what I do."

Cordelia nearly clapped her hands in delight at his poetic manner, but managed to restrain herself beneath the watchful gaze of the disapproving Miss Millpost, who continued to speak to him firmly.

"Sirrah, I will have none of your poetry and nonsense! This is the elder daughter of the Baron Tillingford whose estates lie but two days ride from London and whose name and family are well known to His Majesty the King! Who might you be, to presume so rudely to speak to her?"

FitzHugh bowed deeply before Cordelia, with a dramatic sweep of his arm that brought his forefinger to almost touching the marble floor at the young lady's feet, before drawing himself up to his full height and declaring, "And I am Lord Edward FitzHugh, my Lady, and I am at your service."

Cordelia almost stuttered in the presence of the young lord, so swept away by his looks and manner did she feel, but she made an attempt at appropriate behaviour, nonetheless.

"I am not at all certain, my Lord, that this represents a suitable introduction, to allow me to speak with you, within the bounds of propriety."

"Those foolish conventions apply only to the lesser mortals who strut but briefly upon this globe of dust and dreams. But you are divine, my Lady, a goddess, Venus herself come down from lofty Olympus to earth to torment the hearts of mere men and you have stolen both my wits and my heart, which I give to thee most gladly!"

Cordelia began to suspect that her heart would burst out of her chest as her face lit up with undisguised joy.

"I am Lady Cordelia, my Lord," she said, as she curtsied, "and I pray that I do not intrude too heavily upon your sensibilities."

"The intrusion is an oasis of perfect delight in this warren of the mediocre. Does a goddess require refreshment? More punch perhaps?"

Miss Millpost chose that moment to step purposefully between the couple.

"You have a way with words, Sirrah, and a pretty turn of phrase. Perhaps we should all go to the punch bowl to seek refreshment and ensure that the lady's honour and reputation remain as pure and unsullied as they were when first we arrived."

With that, Miss Millpost took a firm grip on Cordelia's elbow and guided her in the direction of the long, white damasked refreshment table. She barely acknowledged the young Lord's presence, speaking only to Cordelia as they walked.

"It is insufferably warm in here and I believe a glass of punch would be most welcome to my poor dry throat."

Lord Edward took up station on the other side of Cordelia as the trio walked towards the crystal punch bowl. He waved away the servant with a brush of his hand.

"Dearest Lady, permit me."

He filled a glass with a small measure of the bright red liquid and offered it to Cordelia. As she took it in her lace-gloved hands, Edward filled a second glass to the brim and handed it to her companion.

"Your good health, Madame," he nodded at Miss Millpost as he raised his own glass in a simple toast, "and here's to your happiness and the loveliness of your eyes, Lady Cordelia."

He noticed how quickly Miss Millpost downed her punch, and quickly offered her a second.

"Thank you, Sir. I had not realised quite how thirsty one may become on these grand occasions."

By the time Miss Millpost had consumed her third measure of punch, she was beginning to feel a little dizzy and a little unsteady on her feet.

"Pray, child, but the heat is becoming too much for me and I fear I must sit." Cordelia helped her to an elegantly embroidered couch and eased her onto the seat where Miss Millpost promptly closed her eyes and fell soundly, but not noiselessly, asleep. Cordelia placed a cushion beneath her head for comfort and support, and the older lady began to snore softly. A small chuckle caught her attention.

When she turned her head, she discovered that Lord Edward was standing behind her.

"My dear Lady. It would appear that the kind hand of Fate has cast us adrift without the restraining anchor of your companion." He smiled broadly at the young woman. "Perhaps you would care to accompany me for a while and enthral me with tales of life on your father's estate?"

They spent the next half hour standing in front of a wide fireplace, chatting to each other as the split logs crackled and the dancing flames lent their warmth and gaiety to the room. Lord Edward proved to be a most attentive listener and smiled at every nuance and detail that Cordelia shared with him.

For his part, he said very little, preferring to listen to the young heiress and cleverly eluding her questions with humour and evasive replies, implying that, despite his wealth and titles, he really didn't take himself too seriously. He seemed effortlessly charming, an open book, a man of wealth and position who only played cards for the fun of the sport, a man who enjoyed seeing his wealthy young friends squeal with horror whenever they lost. Which seemed to happen a lot.

A sudden and dramatic cough interrupted the young couple as Miss Millpost approached with a bleary eye and a slight waver in her gait.

"Ah! There you are, Lady Cordelia. I was resting my eyes for a moment and when I opened them again, you were gone."

Cordelia tried not to laugh.

"Yes, Miss Millpost, I saw that you were resting and I could not bring myself to disturb you. So I waited for you here by the warmth of the hearth and Lord Edward kindly volunteered to keep me company until you felt refreshed."

The companion cast a critical eye over Lord FitzHugh and nodded her head.

"I see. Very thoughtful of the gentleman. Very thoughtful indeed. Well, we must be away. It is already late. I shall summon our carriage, for you will need your rest, if you are to be fresh for tomorrow's activities."

She turned on her heel and went to find a footman. Lord Edward murmured in Cordelia's ear, so close that she could feel the warmth of his breath upon her skin.

"She could probably outdrink half the men under service in His Majesty's Navy!" Cordelia laughed at his words, even as she felt a tingling warmth flow through her when the young Lord touched the tips of her fingers with his own. "And I would see you again, if you would permit me, sweet Lady Cordelia."

She smiled as she looked into his pale eyes.

"We leave for my home tomorrow morning, but I am sure that you would always be welcome to visit," she hesitated for a heartbeat, "for I would always be pleased to see you, Lord Edward."

Miss Millpost stepped back into the room and immediately seized the hand that she saw was far too close to the young Lord's fingertips. "Time to go, Lady Cordelia, time to go. Lord Edward, it was a pleasure meeting you. We shall take our leave and be on our way now."

"Farewell, Lord Edward," Cordelia spoke as she was half coaxed, half pulled from the room, "'til we meet again."

He bowed his head and blew a gentle kiss to her that she could've sworn had sailed across the widening gap that was opening between them and brushed against the smoothness of her beautiful cheek. She raised a gloved hand to her face in an attempt to hold the impression of the kiss upon her face for the rest of eternity.

Lady Cordelia Branley, Baron Tillingford's beautiful elder daughter, was hopelessly in love.

....

Read the rest as soon as it's released.......

Get

"Enchanting the Duke"

as soon as it's released – go to
http://www.ariettarichmond.com

and make sure that you are signed up for news and release notices !

Books in the 'His Majesty's Hounds' Series

Redeeming the Marquess (coming
soon)

Healing Lord Barton (coming soon)

Winning the Merchant Earl (coming soon)

Loving the Bitter Baron (coming soon)

Rescuing the Countess (coming soon)

Attracting the Spymaster (coming soon)

Books in 'The Derbyshire Set'

Available at all good book stores and for ebook readers too!

Coming Soon!

Regency Collections with Other Authors

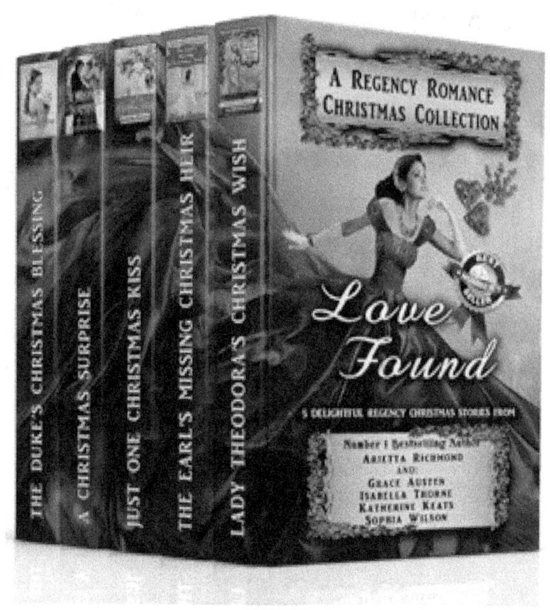

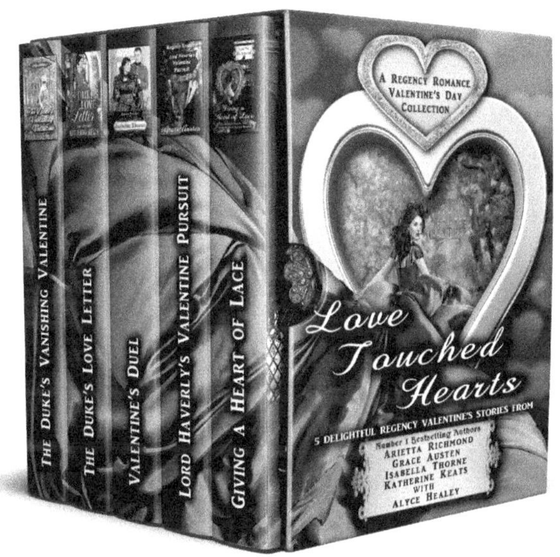
A REGENCY ROMANCE
VALENTINE'S DAY
COLLECTION

THE DUKE'S VANISHING VALENTINE
THE DUKE'S LOVE LETTER
VALENTINE'S DUEL
LORD HAVERLY'S VALENTINE PURSUIT
GIVING A HEART OF LACE

Love
Touched
Hearts

5 DELIGHTFUL REGENCY VALENTINE'S STORIES FROM
Number 1 Bestselling Authors
ARIETTA RICHMOND
GRACE AUSTEN
ISABELLA THORNE
KATHERINE KEATS
WITH
ALYCE HEALEY

ARIETTA RICHMOND, CATHERINE WINDSOR, ISABELLA THORNE, KATHERINE KEATS, KELLY ANNE BRUCE

Clean Regency Romance

Trusting the Earl

Catherine Windsor.

168

Chapter One

Wiltshire, England

Arabella used her hip to push open the kitchen door, stepping inside and greeting Mrs. Buttons with a tired smile.

"I'm back."

"I can see that dearie. I've just about got supper ready. It's not much, but it will fill your stomach."

Mrs. Buttons continued stirring the soup, grateful for the chunks of potato and carrots that would provide the bone-weary Arabella some much needed nourishment.

"Why don't you go sit down and rest your feet for a wee bit?"

Arabella nodded her head and sighed.

"Thank you, I might do just that. The children were rather out of sorts today. This incessant rain has kept them inside for the better part of a week now, and they are anxious to get outdoors again. I look forward to the springtime."

The children she spoke about were wards of the local orphanage. The dozen children had all come to the orphanage by different means, and from different backgrounds, but they all shared one trait. They all lacked parents.

Being the only daughter of the local vicar, Arabella felt it was her duty to try to bring some kind of happiness to their lives, even if it was nothing more than a paltry puppet show with hand puppets which she and Mrs. Buttons had fashioned from cast-off clothing. Her father had passed away months earlier, but Arabella had continued to visit the elderly and the sick, teach the children their lessons, and carry on her parents' legacy to the best of her ability.

Arabella's father, the former vicar of Wiltshire, had been a gentle man whose compassion and wisdom had been sorely missed in the small village where he'd served the people for more than twenty years. He'd done his best for the people of the village, and caring for the orphans had been a large part of that. After Arabella's mother had passed away, years earlier when she was just fourteen years old, Arabella had taken over the care of the children who lived up the hill, and was still doing so today.

"The rain will stop soon enough and then we'll be praying for it to start again. 'Tis the way it is." Mrs. Buttons had been with Arabella and her father for as long as she could remember, helping with the vicarage, and she felt blessed to have the older woman's companionship.

It had been six months since Arabella's father had passed away, leaving Arabella to carry on until a new vicar could be found. Arabella smiled, sinking down into the chair by the hearth.

The cottage used as the vicarage only contained one large room, a loft, and a single bedroom. Her father had used the loft as both a study and sleeping quarters, and as Arabella tilted her head back, she felt sadness as she surveyed the bookshelves that lined the upper walls.

Her father had been her best friend and she missed him terribly. He'd been the victim of a highwayman on his way back from visiting a neighbouring village. His death hadn't been discovered until the following morning and the entire village had mourned his passing.

Arabella closed her eyes and tried to focus on the changes that were coming her way. She'd received word, three weeks earlier, that a new vicar and his family would be arriving at the end of the month. Because she still occupied the vicarage, she would have to find alternative lodging. The problem was that she had limited funds with which to do so.

Mrs. Buttons approached her with a bowl of soup and a crust of bread.

"Here you are, dear. You just sit there and relax while you eat."

Arabella took the offering and asked, "Will you join me?"

"I'd be delighted to."

Mrs. Buttons retrieved a bowl of soup for herself and took a seat opposite Arabella. They ate in silence for a while, each lost in their own thoughts. Eventually, Mrs. Buttons asked the question Arabella had known was coming.

"Did you post the letter?"

Arabella nodded, "Yes. It should reach London sometime tomorrow. The coachman promised to see that it was delivered, in person, to Lady Marianne, so by this time tomorrow, she will know that I've accepted her kind invitation to come and stay. I only wish I knew how my mother's cousin is going to react when she sees me. She mentioned wanting to introduce me to society. I'm not sure how I feel about that."

Arabella was actually Lady Arabella, the only daughter of Lady Diana, who in turn was the only child of Charles Worthington, the Earl of Compton. Her father also came of noble blood, but had chosen the church, and serving his parishioners, over London society, and been estranged from his family.

"You'll be an instant success." Mrs. Buttons smiled as she reached across the table to pat Arabella's hand.

Arabella gave her a rueful grin.

"Or an embarrassment that forces the entire family to hide away in the country."

Mrs. Buttons shook her head, "Never!"

"Thank you for your confidence, but I remember the stories my mother told me about her days as a young girl entering society. It truly does not sound like a place I want to be. I've no wish to attend dances for the sole purpose of snaring a husband."

"You may enjoy having someone take care of you for a change. You take on too much."

Arabella smiled, "If I do not, who will? I will continue to do what I can, and pray that the new vicar will be so inclined. I know my father would never have wanted me to abandon the children."

"You are a good daughter and a compassionate young lady. Those children are lucky to have you on their side. If things don't work out in London… well, I've told ye before, you are more than welcome to come live with Mr. Buttons and myself. Until you figure out what comes next."

Arabella smiled at the woman, "Mrs. Buttons, I appreciate your kindness and friendship more than you can possibly imagine, but it is time I meet my only remaining relatives. My cousin has graciously invited me to stay with her in London, and I am hoping that, after a suitable period of getting to know one another, she might be inclined to pen me a reference. With a reference from someone of her stature, I will look for a governess position."

"Oh miss, your parents would not want that for you," Mrs. Buttons said. "You are so accomplished and could do anything you set your mind to."

Arabella had been taught a variety of subjects normally reserved for males, her father having only one child and a wealth of knowledge to impart. Of course, she'd been taught, by her dearly beloved mother, to play the pianoforte, to paint with watercolours, and to stitch a straight seam. In addition, her father had taught her numbers, history, a love of literature, and philosophy.

A little science had been thrown in from time to time as well as a variety of languages. Arabella had proven, at a very young age, to be adept at learning things. Had she been born a male, she might have been offered a spot at Eton or even Oxford. Instead, she'd been raised a vicar's daughter.

Arabella gave the housekeeper a sad smile, "I know, but I really don't have any other options. Even after I sell the horse, and what little jewellery my mother left me, I would barely be able to survive a month in town." *If that. Living in town was very expensive.* Or so she'd been told. She'd never been to London and was looking at her upcoming journey as a Grand Adventure.

"I shall be fine. Tomorrow, I will sort through father's books and take out the ones I wish to keep. The bookseller will be arriving after lunch to take the rest. I have arranged with the coachman to ride back with him in three days' time."

"I will miss you, Bella," Mrs. Buttons said, her eyes moist with unshed tears.

"And I will miss you as well. I promise to write often."

Arabella broke off as tears clogged her throat. She'd never known anything other than the village where she'd been born and raised. She was actually terrified of the changes that were about to occur in her life, but she was also determined to try to make amends with her late mother's family. If possible, she even hoped to meet her elusive grandfather. This was her future and no matter how scary it seemed, she was going to move forward.

London

Lord Lucas Stanthorpe, Earl of Rothglen, watched the crowded ballroom with a cynical eye and a firmness to his lips, which only those who knew him well would be able to interpret. He was bored! Not just marginally so, he was completely bored with London and everything that went with it.

A fortnight earlier he'd been summoned to London to take his rightful place in the House of Lords, the seat now his in consequence of the title he held. His father, the late Earl of Rothglen, had died last year from sheer orneriness and old age, leaving his only surviving heir the title and everything that went with it.

Not that Lucas actually wanted any of it. He'd been pleasantly enjoying life at the summer estate of his mother, Lady Charlotte. She'd been living at the northern estate for the last fifteen years and Lucas much preferred staying in the north, most especially during the Season.

The endless parties, Balls and the expectations of a member of the *ton* such as he were more than he was prepared to deal with. He was considered, by the matrons of the *ton,* the most elusive and most eligible bachelor of the Season. At the age of twenty-four, he was doomed to be hounded until his unmarried status was corrected.

He turned his gaze towards the line of debutantes, their mothers eagerly trying to gain his attention from across the room. *Blast my father's eternal need to control everything!*

His father had been furious when Lucas had retired to the country, only coming to town once or twice a year, and choosing to spend the rest of his time on his friends' estates or with his mother. His father had seen that as a deliberate defection, which it was, and rather than allowing Lucas to live his life in peace, he'd done everything possible to try to lure his son back into his control.

He hadn't succeeded in life, but in his death, he'd done a remarkable job of it. In his Will, he'd demanded that Lucas marry within a year of his passing, or all of his wealth and unencumbered properties would go to his snivelling cousin, Herbert Paxton.

Without the money and income-producing properties his father had held, he would be hard pressed to finance the entailed family properties. He would end up a titled pauper while his witless cousin squandered everything!

Lucas would not allow that to happen. Herbert hadn't the common sense given a goat, and cared only for the latest fashions and being seen at the right events. That and his many mistresses.

Herbert had inherited a substantial sum from his mother, yet if rumours were correct, he would be nearing financial ruin before this Season was complete. His stepfather was a Baron whose title would pass to his own son. There was no money backing that title anyway, the Baron having married Herbert's mother for her wealth, now nearly exhausted by both men.

Lucas couldn't stand the thought of the imbecile doing the same with the Rothglen Estates, or the many other properties which his father had held. Hundreds of lives were at stake, in the form of the tenants who worked the fields and farms, not to mention the household staff who would be put out onto the street should Herbert be given a chance to ruin things.

Therefore, to meet the terms of his late father's Will, he needed a bride. And not just any bride. He needed a bride who at least equalled him in rank. His father had been afraid that Lucas would use a common doxy, with the promise of a large purse for her troubles, to meet the terms of the Will. He'd stipulated that Lucas must marry within a year of his death, and to a member of the *ton* who was equal to, or higher ranked than, his own titles. The second part of his decree was that the marriage would result in the birth of an heir within one year of the matrimonial state being entered. His father had efficiently found a way to control his son for the better part of two years!

Sighing, he returned his attention to the occupants of the other side of the ballroom. Quickly cataloguing the debutantes present at tonight's event, he realized that not a one of them could boast such a rank. There were several daughters of Barons and Viscounts who were unaware of his restrictions and had so far stopped at nothing to gain his attention.

But the selection of eligible females, this Season, who also met his father's rank requirements, was very limited – there were only two young ladies, both of whom had already been spoken for by classmates of his from Eton.

The arrival of a new young Lady caught his attention and he cringed as he surveyed the newcomer. She was dressed horribly, in a mustard yellow gown that did nothing to conceal her rather large size. She laughed at something and Lucas grimaced at the piercing sound as it echoed around the room.

"Who is that?" he inquired of his closest friend, Byron, the fifth Earl of Denby.

"That, my friend, is your only eligible bride this Season. Lady Margaret Chiltenham."

Byron was fully aware of Lucas' father's Will and, while he normally teased his friend mercilessly about his dilemma, the idea of Lucas being stuck with Lady Margaret was even too frightening for him to contemplate.

Lucas watched the portly Lady saunter around the ballroom, her bearing and demeanour as outlandish as her attire, her hideous cackling laughter drowning out even the music.

"There is no way I am going to marry her!"

Byron chuckled, "I can't say I blame you, but with only two months left to find a bride, you are quickly running out of options."

Lucas turned to his friend and gave him a determined look.

"I will not marry Lady Margaret. Yet somehow, I will be married by Easter, because Cousin Herbert is not getting his hands on my properties. Or my father's money."

"Spoken like a true aristocrat," Byron told him, slapping him good-naturedly on the shoulder as another piercing shriek cut through the music and they both repressed the desire to press their fingers to their ears and grimace.

"An aristocrat with few options," said a soft voice behind him.

Lucas turned, just as an elegant woman reached her hand out to stop his retreat. Elizabeth, Marchioness of Vale, was one of the *ton's* most influential women. Her husband, the Marquis of Vale, was elderly, reclusive and never attended these events. His much younger second wife, however, never missed an opportunity to do so.

She was in her mid-thirties and had taken the *ton* by storm, arriving out of nowhere, ten years earlier. As a woman with significant standing in society, she did and said what she wanted, ignoring the whispers behind her back about her husband, no one completely sure which rumours about him were true or not.

"Marchioness," Lucas inclined his head in greeting. "You seem to find my… er, shall we say… predicament, of some amusement? I am all ears to your opinion."

Lady Elizabeth slipped her arm through his and commanded, "Walk with me. I may have a solution to what you refer to as your predicament."

The familiar action was likely to draw raised brows from the dowagers who had nothing better to do than cast aspersions on the younger members of the *ton,* but given Lady Elizabeth's status, they would keep their opinions to themselves.

She looked at Byron and waved him off, "Your presence is not needed for this conversation."

Lucas inclined his head and motioned for his friend to give them some privacy, "I'll catch up with you later at the club."

"Very good."

Lord Byron bowed to Elizabeth, turned on his heel and strolled across the room in search of a lively dance partner.

Lucas turned his attention back to the lady on his arm, "So, do tell. You perhaps know of another eligible young lady, to whom I might be married, who meets the terms of my father's will?"

Elizabeth smiled, "As a matter of fact, I do. Join me in the gardens and I will tell you a story."

Lucas led her out of the stuffy ballroom, listening with interest as she told a story about love and the consequences that followed.

Chapter Three

Wiltshire

Arabella tried not to cry as the bookseller packed up the last of her father's books. She'd kept only a few of her favourites, and several of the study tomes he had written copious notes in. The rest had been sold for mere pennies, but the sum was enough to ensure that she would be able to travel to London by coach.

The journey to London would take at least two days. The coachman had promised to save her a seat two days from now, and she turned her attention to finishing the task of packing her belongings.

"Mrs. Buttons?" she called out, needing help to lift the valise containing the books she had kept down to the floor. "Mrs. Buttons?"

When she received no answer, Arabella dusted her hands off, on the apron tied around her waist, and climbed down the ladder, looking around for the woman.

She stepped into the kitchen, finding no one, when the distant sound of an arriving coach captured her attention.

"What now?" she sighed as she headed for the front door. She pulled it open, caught off guard when a black-leather encased fist, raised and ready to knock on the door, greeted her blue gaze. She jumped and stepped back, watching as the gloved hand dropped down to the side of the most handsome man she had ever laid eyes on.

"I beg your pardon," his deep voice washed over her as he bowed slightly at the waist. "I am seeking Lady Arabella."

She blinked at him and then, clearing her throat, found her voice. "It's just Arabella."

She stood mesmerized as she scanned his presence from head to toe, then eventually became aware of the impropriety of her gaze. It was several long moments and a knowing smirk upon his lips that brought her attention to the fact that she had been gawking at him like a smitten debutante.

When his own eyes took a similar inventory of her, she couldn't contain the blush that rose to her cheeks. Straightening her spine, she asked, "How may I assist you?"

The gentleman's eyes travelled back up to her own, and then he offered her another slight bow, "Lucas Stanthorpe, Earl of Rothglen, at your service."

Wondering why a Lord was standing on the front step of the vicarage, Arabella asked, "Lord Rothglen. Are you lost?"

He straightened, "No, my lady." His lips curled upwards as he explained. "Lady Marianne bid me to collect you and see that you are brought safely to London."

"Lady Marianne sent you?" Arabella asked, surprised that her mother's cousin would send a man to escort her all the way to London.

She stepped forward, relieved when she saw a handsome carriage, drawn by a matched pair, and complete with driver and a footman waiting with the vehicle. A shiny black stallion stamped the ground beside the carriage as a groom struggled to hold onto the reins of the impatient thoroughbred while his rider spoke to Arabella.

The sound of the man's voice brought her eyes back to his own.

"Your cousin was unable to make the journey herself, but she asked if I would escort you to her home. Since I fancied some fresh air and was happy to escape the city, I was pleased to agree to her request."

Arabella was stunned into speechlessness. Only the arrival of Mrs. Buttons nudged her from her silence. She stammered, "Mrs. Buttons, this is the Earl of Rothglen. He has come to escort me to London."

"Oh my! Well, don't keep him standing in the doorway, dearie. I'll see about making some tea, and I think there are some scones left from breakfast." The older woman scurried to the sideboard and started gathering cups, saucers and plates.

"Mrs. Buttons, do not put yourself out on my account. I simply wanted to make Lady Arabella's acquaintance and to inquire at what time tomorrow she would be ready to travel." Lucas remained in the doorway and made no attempt to enter the cottage.

Arabella raised an eyebrow.

"Tomorrow? I had not planned to travel until the day after." After a moment's silence, she stated more firmly, "I simply cannot leave tomorrow."

Lucas paused, trying to not to display impatience at the impertinence of her statement, then inquired politely, "May I know why? Is there a problem that I can help you attend to? I assure you, whatever is needed to help you complete your preparations can be easily remedied."

Arabella shook her head, "No. And this is not a problem, but an obligation."

The children at the orphanage had planned a small going away party for her, to take place tomorrow afternoon, and Arabella wouldn't disappoint them.

"I appreciate my cousin's kindness, but I simply cannot travel until the day after next. If the delay interferes with your schedule, I will continue with my original plans and take the post coach. Now, I believe Mrs. Buttons mentioned tea."

She stepped back and gestured with her hand for him to enter the small cottage.

Lucas shook his head, "No, that would not be appropriate. Single young ladies do not travel by coach unescorted. I will return the day after tomorrow at first light to collect you and whatever belongings you wish to take with you. Please be ready as we have a long way to go."

He offered her a bow, and then nodded to Mrs. Buttons, who still lingered behind her.

"Good day."

Arabella watched him mount the massive stallion, which the groom was still struggling to control, and ride out of the small yard. He was an impressive figure atop the black horse, and she watched him until he disappeared from sight.

She shut the door then and turned to Mrs. Buttons.

"Why do you think my cousin sent such a man to be my escort?"

Mrs. Buttons smiled at her and gave her a conspiratorial wink, "Who cares why he has come. He is most handsome. Maybe you won't have to worry about getting that reference after all. You'll be getting a husband instead."

Arabella stared at Mrs. Buttons, then laughed.

"A husband? Surely not. I'm sure he is just a friend doing another friend a favour."

Mrs. Buttons smiled indulgently.

"Believe what you will. Time will tell. I'll get that tea for us. You should finish packing. We have a full day with the children tomorrow, and I do believe that the gentleman means to be here before the sun rises the day after. You wouldn't want to keep a man such as he waiting."

Mrs. Buttons giggled to herself as she set about making tea and Arabella shook her head at the foolish notions in her companion's head.

Arabella finished packing the books she had decided to keep, along with her few clothes, her mind drifting often to the imposing man who would come to take her to London.

She had never met a man such as he, and she only hoped that all of the fine young men in London did not look like him. Otherwise, she'd have a hard time concentrating on anything else but finding the husband Mrs. Buttons seemed to think she required.

Arabella wasn't opposed to the matrimonial state, but if she was going to marry, she wanted a marriage based on love, like the marriage her parents had enjoyed. She was a romantic and not willing to settle for anything less. Although she certainly hoped that her future husband would also be as handsome as the Earl of Rothglen. She felt her cheeks become warm as she pondered that thought. No, she would marry for love, or not at all.

Chapter Four

"Bella! Bella!"

The sound of children chanting a shortened version of her name caused Arabella to smile in delight, a mistake since she was currently trying to keep from falling down after spinning herself around the requisite ten times.

The children were always coming up with new ways to play, and tag was one of their favourites. They'd come up with a clever way to even out the odds, whenever the older children or adults were playing with them. They had to spin around ten times before attempting to catch the younger players.

Arabella stopped spinning, laughing as the world spun around her crazily. She could see the children taunting her, managing to keep just out of her reach, and she staggered across the meadow grass towards them, her hands outstretched as she attempted to tag one of them.

Mrs. Pickerly, the widow tasked with watching over the orphans, stood nearby, an indulgent smile upon her face.

When Tommy, a precocious child who was the most recent resident of the orphanage, stepped up behind Arabella and poked her with the stick in his hand, her smile faded away and she scolded him sternly.

"Tommy! That is inappropriate. You may sit out the rest of this game."

The sound of her stern voice and the sight of Tommy's crestfallen face stole the fun from the game for Arabella and she stopped chasing the children and quietly called a halt to the game. She looked at the little faces she was going to sorely miss and sent them to see Mrs. Buttons. She and the housekeeper had stayed up late the night before making honey cakes for the children, one of their favourite treats.

Tommy had joined Mrs. Pickerly and Arabella walked towards them. The sound of horses in the distance didn't distract her as she concentrated on the little boy who was obviously fighting back tears.

"I'm sorry, Mrs. Pickerly. I didn't mean to hurt her."

"That is not the point, Tommy. Young men do not poke others with sticks!"

"Mrs. Pickerly, I don't believe Tommy meant me any harm. May I speak with him?"

Mrs. Pickerly smiled and nodded her head, "Of course, miss. I'll just go and help Mrs. Buttons serve the treats."

Arabella waited until the older woman had moved away before she squatted down so that she and Tommy were eye-level with one another.

"Tommy?"

His bottom lip quivered and then he launched himself into her arms, sending her sprawling backwards into the dirt in a flurry of skirts and dust.

"Hey there!" a masculine voice called out from behind her.

Arabella tried to turn her head but Tommy had wrapped his little arms around her neck. She was still trying to untangle their limbs when Tommy's weight was suddenly lifted from her amidst his cry of fright.

"Don't hurt me, sir. Please. Don't hurt me. I didn't mean to knock her over."

"Hush!"

Arabella had managed to straighten out her skirts and now looked up from the dirt to see Lord Rothglen holding a very scared looking Tommy by the back of his shirt, his feet dangling off the ground.

She scrambled to her feet, demanding, "Put that child down! What do you mean by coming here and accosting him?"

"Me, accosting him? I saw him knock you over," Lord Lucas told her incredulously.

Arabella reached out and pulled Tommy from his hands, "Let him go!"

Lucas stepped forward, retaining his hold on the child, and bringing himself within inches of the very alluring young Lady, who seemed to care not that her skirts were covered in dust, or that her hair pins were beginning to come loose.

When Tommy tried to kick at him, accidentally kicking Arabella instead, Lucas had reached the end of his patience. He hauled the child up and quietly told him, "Apologize. Now."

Tommy gulped and turned to look at Arabella over his shoulder, "I'm sorry, miss."

Arabella finally managed to pull Tommy away from Lord Rothglen and hugged the young boy close for a moment, "'Twas an accident. I'm fine, but please, do me a favour?"

Tommy bobbed his head in acquiescence, his wide blue eyes watching her in admiration and no small measure of infatuation.

She smiled at him.

"Let's leave the sticks on the ground where they belong. If one of the little ones decided to play with those sticks, someone could become seriously hurt."

Tommy nodded his head, "I won't let them play with sticks. I'll make sure they don't."

"Thank you. Now, I believe Mrs. Buttons is keeping some honey cakes just for you."

Tommy's eyes lit up and he launched himself at her waist once again, but this time she was ready for him. She absorbed the impact from his body, returning his hug even as tears stung her eyes. She was going to miss all of the children, but Tommy most especially.

He had come to the orphanage half-starved and filthy dirty. As far as everyone could determine, the child had not had a proper bath in months, and convincing him that the water would do him no harm had been quite a feat.

Arabella had finally intervened, taking him by the hand and marching him down to the nearby stream. She'd then surprised them all by walking right into the water with him. His first bath had commenced with his clothes on, and their lips turning blue from the chilliness of the water. He'd quickly realized that taking a bath indoors and with water heated over the coals was much preferred.

Arabella watched the children for another minute before turning her attention to Lord Lucas and the other gentleman who had ridden into the meadow with him. She remembered her manners and inclined her head, "My lord, may I inquire why you are here today? I thought we were traveling to London tomorrow."

Lord Rothglen raised a brow.

"Rescuing you from the clutches of over exuberant children, it would seem." He ended his statement with a smile and then turned to watch the children, "Where are their parents?"

"They have no parents. Those children are residents of the orphanage." *And I'm going to miss them most of all.* Part of her reason for traveling to London was to obtain a good position somewhere, in the hopes that she would have excess funds to send back for the children's care. The vicarage had been funding the orphanage since Arabella could remember, but it wasn't required.

Mrs. Pickerly had expressed her fears that the new vicar would not be so inclined. Arabella shared her fear, especially since the new vicar had not one, but seven children of his own.

The sound of Lord Rothglen clearing his throat pulled her thoughts back to the present.

"Thank you for your assistance, but as you can see, it was unnecessary. I enjoy the children's energy and do not at all mind a little dust. Seeing them happy is more important than a clean dress."

Lucas was becoming more intrigued by the minute by this young woman, who was not in the least cowed by his presence.

"Who cares for these children?" Lucas enquired, counting an even dozen children, ranging in age from three to ten.

"Mrs. Pickerly is the house mother, and I have been teaching them and making sure that there are adequate supplies. But now… I…," she paused, not wanting to give voice to her concerns. Swallowing them back, she gave him a smile, "They will be fine. Was there something you required?"

Chapter Five

The other gentleman stepped forward at that point, and bowed to Arabella.

"I believe Lord Rothglen has forgotten his manners."

Lucas gritted his teeth, but made the requisite introduction. "Lady Arabella, may I introduce Lord Byron Wellmont, the Earl of Denby."

Arabella watched Lord Denby, a faint blush staining her cheeks when he took the hand she offered him, and kissed the back of her glove. Lucas rolled his eyes as Byron released her hand, chuckling softly.

Arabella seemed unaware of the hidden messages that were silently passing between the two men, "I'm pleased to meet you."

"The pleasure is all mine, I assure you." Byron backed away when Lucas sent him a glare, "I'll leave you to discuss our travel arrangements."

Arabella watched him retreat and then asked, "Travel arrangements? Is the Earl traveling to London with us?"

"Yes." Lucas answered her abruptly and without further explanation. "I thought you had obligations to fulfil and packing to complete, preventing you from traveling today. Yet you have time to play games with these children."

Arabella cocked her head to the side, ignoring the judgmental tone of his voice, and said, "I am already packed. And the obligation was this party. The children planned it for me before I leave for London. It is important to them, particularly as I shall miss the Easter festivities this year."

She could see Lord Lucas considering her explanation, unable to voice any further complaint about her delaying their departure.

"Would you care to join us?"

Lucas watched her cheeks turn pinker as she issued the invitation and he found himself intrigued. He turned towards the children who had all gathered around Byron's horse and were taking turns stroking its nose and feeding it crumbs from their honey cakes.

"It would seem I have little choice."

He gestured with his hand for her to precede him and he followed her, watching the sway of her skirts and liking what he saw. For the next hour or so, he watched her interact with the children and was amazed to see how easily she handled their questions with enthusiasm. The children soiled her skirts with their hands, and he noticed that the younger children had no qualms about coaxing her to lift them up.

She did so with a smile, and even when two of the older boys started arguing, she calmly dealt with it, hugging both boys after they apologized to one another.

She was an enigma and he found himself wondering how she would handle the ballrooms of London. Lady Marianne, her mother's cousin, had not even known of Lady Arabella's existence until several weeks prior.

Elizabeth, one of Marianne's closest friends, had been privy to the meek letter Lady Arabella had written, requesting permission to visit her mother's cousin and possibly meet her grandfather, the Earl of Compton.

Lady Diana, the only child of the Earl of Compton, had chosen to marry the second son of an Earl – a man who had chosen the church as his calling, and cast aside his family connections and wealth. She had disappeared from society two decades earlier. The Earl of Compton had washed his hands of his daughter, and broken off all lines of communication.

Lady Marianne had been shocked to receive a letter from her cousin's daughter, informing her that both of her parents had passed away, and requesting an opportunity to meet her other family members and try to rectify things with her grandfather.

Lucas had listened with interest as Elizabeth told him that the girl's plan was to meet her grandfather, and then to obtain a letter of reference in hopes of obtaining a governess position. The idea that the granddaughter of two Earls would even consider doing such a thing was preposterous.

Lady Marianne had invited Arabella to join her in London and then, at Elizabeth's prompting, began making her own arrangements for the girl's future. Not even knowing what Arabella looked like, nor her demeanour or manners, Elizabeth's head had begun to stir with an idea. Lady Arabella was the answer to Lucas's matrimonial crisis. When Elizabeth had shared this news with him, he'd agreed to travel to Wiltshire and make the young lady's acquaintance on the pretence of being her escort to London. That way he could get a look at her, away from the prying eyes of the *ton,* without her being aware of his situation.

He had promised to give Lady Elizabeth an answer, upon their arrival, as to whether or not he wished to pursue the young lady as a viable candidate for the position of his wife. After having met her yesterday, and watching her interact with both children and adults today, he couldn't wait to see how she handled the dragons of society. Her naiveté would be a breath of fresh air at the events that had become stale and lifeless in his eyes.

Lady Arabella was going to take the *ton* by storm. He just wasn't quite sure if it would be a gentle misting, or a torrential downpour. Either way, he planned to have a front row seat and at the end of the day, he planned to have her by his side. It was obvious that she knew nothing about how to be the wife of an Earl, but with Lady Elizabeth's promised support and Lady Marianne to give her instruction, she would learn all that was required of his future wife. And he would fulfil the requirements of his father's Will so that he could retain his birthright.

As the afternoon wore on and the children's energy began to fade, for the first time in years, he found himself actually looking forward to being in town during the height of the Season. Two months from now, he would be a married man. Now he just needed to convince the Lady he'd set his sights on that he was a much better option than becoming a governess. A feat that shouldn't pose any significant problem, from his point of view.

$$\sim\sim\sim\sim\sim$$

Arabella slid from the seat of the coach for the fourth time, her frustration with the travel experience marring her normally pleasant disposition. She righted herself and then grabbed the walking stick she'd discovered beneath the bench on her first tumble to the coach floor. She raised it up and pounded it against the roof of the coach in a desperate attempt to get the coachman to stop the conveyance. She just needed a few moments respite or she was in serious danger of losing the contents of her stomach!

She listened as the driver called to the horses, bringing the coach to a stop a few minutes later, once again sending Arabella scrambling to remain seated. The door was opened a moment later by a scowling footman, "Yes Miss? What's the problem?"

"Sir, I believe that answering that particular question will only result in hurting your feelings, so I shall refrain from doing so. Could you please put the steps down so that I may step out?"

The footman did so, offering his hand as she gingerly stepped down. Her relief at having her feet on solid ground, that wasn't lurching to and fro, was immediate.

"Miss, the road is better just up ahead. With the recent rains, this section of the road is quite rutted and difficult."

She gave the coachman a smile, "I understand, but I still require a few moments before we continue."

The footman inclined his head and stepped back, as the coachman dropped down to check on the horses. She took a few hesitant steps, and once she was sure that she had gained her equilibrium, she walked a short distance away, looking out between the trees at the rolling fields beyond.

Turning back to the two men who were impatiently waiting on her, she asked, "Where are we?"

"About fifteen miles from the outskirts of London." Lord Denby answered her query. "If you're looking for the city, you'll need to look behind you."

Arabella nodded and then walked around the coach, her eyes going wide as the open fields and trees seemed to become thinner. In the distance she could barely make out what looked like a sea of buildings and she found herself anxiously wanting to see more.

"That's London?"

"Yes, miss. Are you ready to continue?" the footman asked hopefully.

Arabella was somewhat relieved that they would not be trying to find lodging for the night, as she would have been required to do had she gone with her original plan.

When they had stopped for a midday meal, the inn had been shocking to her. Horses, carriages, peerage and servants, all milling around, not enough room for anyone to fully relax, and a myriad of voices creating a very hectic scene.

Arabella had eaten a crust of bread and some cheese, but the meat had not been properly cooked, and the room had been filled to overwhelming with other travellers.

Lord Rothglen, to his credit, had found the situation untenable and requested food be prepared for them to take as they continued on their journey.

"Helmsly, shall we proceed?" Lord Lucas called out, bringing his magnificent horse to a stop a short distance away. He looked her over carefully, before giving the coach the same thorough glance.

"Yes, my Lord. I trust that Lady Arabella is feeling better now?" The footman knew who his master was, but was nevertheless concerned about his female passenger.

Lord Rothglen turned his deep blue eyes on her, dismounting from his horse and striding towards her.

Arabella felt her face heat under his scrutiny and she backed away, "I am ready to continue."

"Why did you ask the coachman to stop?" he asked, following her as she made her way to the steps of the coach. "Are you ill?" he inquired softly, a look of concern on his face.

"No, I was simply tired of being jostled around like a sack of potatoes. The coachman assures me that the road is more passable up ahead."

"It is. I'm sorry for your discomfort, I will instruct the coachman to travel slower."

"Please do not. That would only prolong our journey. I will do my best to not slow us down again." With that, she lifted her skirt and entered the coach, arranging her skirts around her ankles and preparing for the rest of the journey. She turned her head to see Lord Rothglen watching her and offered him a pleasant smile.

"I'm ready to go."

He gave her another look and then closed the door. She heard him instruct the coachman to avoid the ruts as much as possible, and then a few minutes later, the coach began moving again. For the next three hours, the ride did become much smoother and she was able to close her eyes and rest a bit.

The sun began to set as the cry from the footman came up that they were entering London. Arabella came awake and leaned towards the window of the coach, her eyes wide as she got her first glimpse of the town. She was tired, dusty, and her body ached, and yet a strange excitement filled her. *This is my Grand Adventure.*

Chapter Six

Mayfair

Arabella looked up at the grand house as she stepped down from the coach and tried not to appear too out of place. She followed Lord Rothglen to the door, amazed when it was opened by a uniformed butler before he could even announce his arrival with a knock. Lord Denby had already left them, headed to his club.

"How did…?" Lucas smiled at her and she bit her lip, feeling completely out of her element. She shook her head, rather than finishing her question.

"Good evening, sir. Lady Templeton will join you shortly."

"Very good, Wills. Is Lord Templeton in this evening?"

"No, sir. I believe he is at his club."

"I will see him later then. Wills, this is Lady Arabella. Please ask Mrs. Cummings if she could have a light supper sent to the sitting room."

"Right away, sir. Welcome to London, my Lady."

Arabella nodded her head as she looked around her, taking in the elegant furnishings, chandelier and highly polished wood. The house was breathtaking and she realized that her mother's cousin had, indeed, married well.

"This way," the butler said, leading them down a short hallway, where he opened two doors and gestured for them to enter the room. Arabella stood in the centre of the room, taking it all in. A pianoforte stood on the far side of the room, situated in front of large windows. Several couches were positioned in front of the oversize hearth, and a variety of historical pictures hung on the walls.

"Arabella, it's so good to finally meet you," an elegantly dressed woman said from the doorway.

Arabella turned to see a woman watching her. She was dressed in a gold brocade gown, her hair elegantly coifed atop her head, and a beautiful, warm smile upon her lips. She glided across the floor and took Arabella's hands in her own, "You are the image of your mother!"

Arabella allowed herself to be pulled in for a brief hug, "Lady Marianne?"

The woman smiled, "Yes, but please, just call me Marianne. We're family."

Arabella immediately felt an affinity with the woman. When she turned to Lord Rothglen, she watched as he bowed low over Marianne's hand and kissed the back of it as she said, "Thank you for escorting Lady Arabella to our home."

"It was my pleasure, my Lady. Now, I will leave you to get acquainted. I trust Lady Elizabeth and yourself were successful in your plans?"

"Yes. The seamstress will be here tomorrow morning at first light, and I've already obtained an invitation for Lady Arabella to attend Almack's this coming Wednesday. Will we see you there?" Lady Marianne inquired politely, with a twinkle in her eyes.

Lord Rothglen looked at Arabella as he answered, "Most certainly." He then bowed over her hand again before turning his attention back to Arabella. "I hope you will save the first dance for me?"

"Dance?" Arabella asked, stunned.

"She would be delighted to do so. Now, as we have much to do in the next five days, I would like to get to know my cousin a bit better."

"Ladies, I will see you five days from now."

Arabella blushed when he bowed low to her before striding from the room. She watched him until he was completely out of sight and then turned back to her hostess.

"I'm so glad you have arrived safely, and hopefully no worse for wear. Has your maid been shown to your rooms?"

Arabella looked at Lady Marianne, and her expression must have given away the truth.

"No maid! Oh dear! How very inappropriate of Rothglen to have brought you all this way with no maid. We will resolve that problem immediately. For now, Mary can see to your needs."

Overwhelmed, Arabella simply nodded. Lady Marianne, obviously used to organising things, looked please, and gestured her to a chair.

"Now, come, sit and eat and tell me everything."

"Everything?" Arabella asked thinly.

"Absolutely everything. I remember your mother from when we were little girls. I only wish I had enquired about her sooner. Her father can be very difficult to deal with."

"My grandfather?"

"Yes. My uncle. I'm afraid he's not well."

Arabella nodded her head and then asked, "Does he reside in London?"

"Yes, but he does not receive visitors. He is a bit eccentric and reclusive and has chosen to keep to himself."

"But how am I to see him if he doesn't receive visitors?" Arabella asked in dismay.

Marianne smiled at her, "Leave that to me. Now, I've instructed the maids to heat water and take it upstairs to your rooms. I haven't travelled any great distance by coach for a good while, but I remember how uncomfortable they can be on rutted roads. The dressmaker will be here first thing, and then we shall make a trip to Bond Street and procure everything else you might need for a proper Season."

"Oh no!" Arabella declared. "Lady Marianne, you've misunderstood my reason for coming to you. I have no desire to partake in the social whirl."

"Nonsense! Every young Lady looks forward to attending the soirees, parties and Balls that come with the Season. Being introduced at Almack's is the first step, and then the invitations shall start rolling in."

"But I don't even know how to dance. And I'm sure my attire is not up to par with what will be expected."

"That is why the seamstress is coming tomorrow morning," Marianne told her with a smile.

"Please, I appreciate you arranging things, but even if I wanted to partake, I'm afraid my funds are not sufficient."

Marianne smiled at her.

"It is my pleasure to sponsor you. It will be good practice for the future when my own daughter is ready to be presented to Society."

"You have children?"

Marianne placed a hand on her stomach, "Not born yet. I am due in the autumn. George says we will leave town after Easter, when it should be safe for me to travel, and retire to our country estate."

"Congratulations," Arabella told her. "But you must not tire yourself on my account. I truly only wrote to you because…"

"… you were hoping for a letter of reference," she finished Arabella's sentence for her. "I remember, dear. However, I believe we can do much better than that. After all, you are the granddaughter of an Earl."

"What does that matter?" Arabella asked.

Then worried that her question may appear rude, she added, "Forgive me, but I was not raised to be concerned with titles and do not understand how it should affect my ability to find a governess position."

Marianne poured the tea that Mrs. Cummings had delivered, as Arabella carefully selected several small sandwiches, now acutely aware of how hungry she had become during the journey.

"This year, eligible young ladies are in short supply. I believe we can find you a good husband by the time the Season ends, even though we are starting late."

Arabella's eyes widened.

"A husband? But, I truly hadn't considered such a thing."

"You just leave all of that to me," said Marianne.

Arabella went quiet, not wanting to seem ungrateful to her cousin who was being so kind to her. But then little Tommy's face came to mind and she found herself shaking her head. "I'm sorry, but I really need to find a position as a governess. There are children depending upon me."

"Children?!" Marianne asked in shock.

"The orphans. My father started an orphanage and the vicarage financed their upkeep, but now, the new vicar has seven children of his own and I fear he will no longer provide for them. I must find a paying position as soon as possible so that I can see to their welfare."

Marianne looked at her, shaking her head, "The orphans are surely not your responsibility."

Arabella felt tears sting her eyes, "But they are. I promised I would find a way." She stopped and gathered control of her emotions, "I truly do appreciate your wishing to help me find a husband, but I have no dowry, and my requirements for a husband would make me even less desirable."

Marianne raised a brow, "Your requirements?"

Arabella gave her a tired nod, "I will only marry for love. Like my parents. Nothing less. And now I would have to know that my husband was prepared to provide me the funds necessary to see that the orphans were well cared for. I doubt that is a desirable prospect for any gentleman."

Marianne looked at her and then gave her a secretive smile.

"Why don't you let the young men of the *ton* decide that? Give me a month, and if you haven't found a man you can love, and who will provide for the children of the orphanage, I will write you that letter of reference."

Arabella wrung her hands, overwhelmed by the suggestion but anguished over the delay. It would soon be Easter and she had hoped to be placed in a governess position in the country, not far from Wiltshire, before then.

She and Mrs. Buttons had dreamed of dying eggs, surprising the children with an egg roll, and sewing Easter bonnets for each of the girls, some of whom had never had a colourful bonnet in their entire lives.

"What have you got to lose? Wouldn't you rather be a wife and mother, than a governess?"

"Yes, er… no, er… I do not know," she broke off, no argument coming to her aide. Finally, she nodded her head, "One month. And then I shall have my reference?"

"Yes," Lady Marianne confirmed. Considering the subject closed, she led Arabella to the staircase.

"It's settled then. Now, let me show you your rooms. I suggest you have that bath and get some sleep. The next weeks are going to be very busy."

Chapter Seven

Arabella stepped through the doors of Almack's, her hands sweating inside her new gloves, the pale blue gown she was wearing highlighting her sparkling eyes. Music played, and Arabella followed Marianne as she was introduced to more people than she could ever hope to remember.

Everyone was polite, almost too much so, especially the ladies who had daughters and nieces with them. They smiled with their lips but not with their eyes. Arabella's nervousness only seemed to increase as they made their way towards the centre of the large ballroom.

"How are you doing, Bella?" Marianne asked, nodding as they passed two older women who had taken seats that afforded them a full view of the dance floor.

She'd confessed to Marianne that she missed hearing the shortened version of her name, and from there on, Marianne had begun to use the familiar sound that reminded Arabella of her parents.

"Everyone seems… how shall I put this… curious."

Marianne laughed lightly.

"That is one way of saying that they are all extremely jealous. You are the newcomer and are bound to have a full dance card this evening. That colour of blue matches your eyes, and you are a like a breath of fresh air compared to the rest of the women here tonight." She leaned in conspiratorially, "Remember, you promised the first dance to Lord Rothglen."

Bella remembered. In fact, as she'd allowed the maid to get her ready for this evening, she'd been able to think of nothing else. The last five days had been filled with trips to Bond Street, dress fittings, trips to the shoemakers, lessons in dancing and a whole variety of lessons about how to act amidst the *ton.*

Arabella had found it all very confusing and impossible to remember.

"What if I forget something?"

"I will try to help you remember everything. Oh, here comes Rothglen." Marianne subtly pointed over Arabella's shoulder and they both turned to watch as he and Lord Denby approached.

"Ladies," Lord Rothglen bowed to them both, followed by Lord Denby.

"Gentlemen, how nice to see you here tonight." Marianne said, perfectly comfortable in the presence of the men.

Lucas turned his attention to Arabella, "Lady Arabella, you look much more rested than when last I saw you."

"I am, thank you," she told him, blushing and unable to do anything to stop it.

"Your dance card." He held out a gloved hand. He didn't ask. And she didn't even think to deny him.

She fumbled with the card attached by a ribbon to her wrist and watched as he scribbled his name across not one, but the first two slots. She looked up in alarm, "My Lord?"

"One dance I fear will not be enough." He gave her a nod and a smile and then Lord Denby was taking her dance card and claiming the third dance. When he stepped back, Lord Rothglen addressed her again, "I will return for you in a few moments."

Arabella was stunned speechless and turned to Marianne after the men had left, questioning, "What just happened?"

Marianne was beaming, as was Lady Elizabeth who had joined them.

"I believe Rothglen just declared his intentions, at least where you are concerned. In a manner that will leave no question after tonight."

"But two dances? You told me that was frowned upon unless...," she broke off as she realized exactly what had just occurred. "But, we don't even know one another."

"Precisely why two dances are an excellent idea," Lady Elizabeth commented.

"He definitely means to pursue you. That is wonderful news, Bella. Oh, the musicians are getting ready to start. And here comes Rothglen. Have fun, my dear."

Arabella turned and watched Lord Rothglen approach her. He bowed to her and she curtsied back. He held his hand out and she placed her gloved hand upon his forearm.

He led her to the middle of the dance floor and they took up their positions as others did the same.

Lord Denby joined them with a lovely young lady who spent the entire dance batting her eyelashes at him and giggling loudly each time she missed a step. Lord Denby, to his credit, never allowed his smile to falter or his courtesy to slip, but Arabella was thankful they only joined them for one dance.

"Don't worry about her, you dance wonderfully."

Arabella glanced up into Lord Rothglen's dark blue eyes and smiled, "Thank you, my Lord. Before coming to London I had never danced with a partner."

"You never danced with the children?" he asked.

Arabella shook her head

"No. A lively game of chase was more our usual sort of activity."

She smiled as she thought of the children, and then she sighed.

She wished she knew how everyone was getting on, but the letter she'd sent three days ago hadn't yet been answered.

The first dance ended and she moved to leave the floor, only to find Lord Rothglen turning her back towards him with a slight touch of his hand on the small of her back. The physical contact brought a gasp from her throat as she looked up at him.

He immediately dropped his hand and nodded, "I believe the second dance is mine as well."

Arabella looked around at the dowagers and hopeful mothers standing on the sidelines with their eager daughters and inwardly cringed. Many of them were whispering behind their hands, while their eyes shot daggers in her direction.

"Are you sure this is a wise thing to do?" she whispered.

"I would be offended if you denied me now," he told her. "Come, they are dancing a reel this time. I trust you know the steps?"

Arabella nodded.

"Just barely. I've only just learned."

She turned to look at the other side of the room and then gasped at the blatant stares coming her way from the other bachelors who were in attendance.

"Everyone is staring at us!"

"They are simply jealous." Lucas smiled in amusement. "I, however, am not worried about their stares or their comments. You should not be concerned either."

"I shouldn't?" she asked, as the music started and he gently guided her to match his steps.

It was a much faster dance than the first and their conversation faded away as Bella concentrated on avoiding a misstep. By the time the musicians finished their song, she was out of breath and laughing softly.

"That was fun!"

Chapter Eight

Lucas looked at her and thoughts of changing anything about Lady Arabella's behaviour faded away. She was smiling freely and having a good time. She had the same look on her face as she'd had whilst playing with the children. A look he hoped to see more often.

Society could take their notions of how a young Lady was supposed to act and toss them out as far as he was concerned. He liked this carefree Arabella and couldn't imagine her trying to conform to the manner of the coy, quiet, calculating young Ladies he was used to.

He knew that she had made an agreement with her cousin. He'd been paid a visit by George, Marianne's husband, Lord Templeton, two nights previously, while playing cards at White's and the pair had discussed, at length, the requirements Lady Arabella had of her future husband. Funding the orphanage was of no consequence for Lucas, but it was her first requirement he found puzzling. *She would only marry for love.*

"George, no-one of our class marries for such a frivolous notion."

"I'm telling you she isn't even going to consider entering the matrimonial state unless there is love involved. Would it be so hard to develop some feelings for her?"

Lucas had shaken his head, ignoring the fact that he already had some rather unwanted feelings where the lovely Lady Arabella was concerned. Desire had been at the top of the list. And jealousy. Just the idea that she would be dancing with other gentlemen made him incredibly uncomfortable. That was why Byron had consented to claiming her third dance at his request.

By the fourth dance, he had planned to have her walking outside to keep her away from the other eligible Lords of the *ton*. He would use the pretence of getting some fresh air. A light supper would then be served, and there would only be a few dances left after that. He'd already spoken to several of his friends, all of whom had intentions towards other debutantes, and they had agreed to claim her remaining dances.

Now that he was convinced that she would be an appropriate wife, he planned to convince Viscount Barnsley, whose name filled the last slot on Arabella's dance card, to slip out early, feigning a headache. He would then boldly claim the last dance of the evening, shocking the dragons of society, while sealing Arabella's fate firmly in their minds. Two dances might be forgiven, but three? They would be expecting a betrothal before the end of the Season. And he aimed to do just that.

He escorted Lady Arabella back to Lady Marianne's side, bowing to her and nodding to Lord Denby as he arrived to claim his dance.

Lady Elizabeth was waiting for him, "So? Will she do?"

"She'll do. Did you know she expects her husband to fund the orphanage in Wiltshire?"

Elizabeth grinned, "I had heard that. I assume that would not be a problem for you?"

"It is a minor amount of money compared to the amount I would stand to lose if I do not marry appropriately." He paused and then asked, "Did you know about her other condition?"

Elizabeth laughed softly.

"Yes. I take it the notion of love doesn't appeal to you?"

Lucas was silent for several moments, watching Arabella laugh at something Byron had said to her.

She was beyond lovely, and a fierce sense of possessiveness overtook him.

"I've never given the emotion much thought to be honest. What really is love after all?" He continued to stare at Arabella as he spoke to Elizabeth. "Although I can't say that I find the concept objectionable."

Elizabeth smiled as she patted his arm and murmured, "That look in your eye is lust, not love. And I dare say you shall have to convince the Lady to love you as well, my dear Rothglen. I do not think she will be easily convinced. And she may need time. Time that you do not have."

Lucas did not even consider that he might be denied, or that he would be unable to win Arabella over in the short time needed if he was to fulfil his father's Will.

"I thought to take her driving the day after tomorrow. I intend to make my intentions clear at that time."

Elizabeth smiled.

"Excellent. I trust that Marianne is already aware that a wedding will be taking place before she leaves for the country?"

Lucas smiled.

"I'm not sure if she's come to that conclusion, but I trust that you will take great pleasure in divulging that information to her."

"Naturally."

"What is in this for you, Lady Elizabeth?"

Lucas was puzzled as to why Elizabeth was taking such an interest in his personal life. He was aware of her reputation for meddling in the lives of the *ton*, but she rarely played such an active role without an ulterior motive.

"I only wish to see two delightful young people happy, my Lord," she replied coyly, and quickly added, "Well, I shall take my leave before the dragons start to gossip about *us*." Elizabeth tossed her hair as she laughed at the notion that gossip would concern her.

"It appears that your intended is becoming a bit overheated. Maybe a short walk in the evening air would serve nicely?" she suggested.

"My thoughts exactly." He met Arabella as Byron took his leave and then addressed Marianne, "I believe Lady Arabella could do with a breath of fresh air."

"That seems like an excellent idea, Lord Rothglen. I will see you both during the supper." She smiled at Arabella and then walked away.

From the corner of his eye, Lucas saw several eligible bachelors headed their way and he took Arabella's elbow and steered her quickly towards the side door, "Come this way."

"Is this appropriate?" she whispered to him, glancing around to see if their departure was being noticed.

"As long as we are not gone too long and remain in full view. You look flushed."

"It is very warm in here."

"Yes it is. Come, we will walk in the gardens for a few minutes. I would like to speak to you further about a private matter, but it can wait until the day after tomorrow. I have appointments tomorrow that cannot be changed."

He pushed the doors open and escorted her out of the building and towards the manicured lawns and gardens. The sun had set, but the lanterns in the gardens had all been lit, and he made sure to steer Arabella away from the shadows.

"The day after tomorrow?" A flutter of butterflies stirred in Arabella's stomach and she was surprised to realize that she would be counting the hours until that time.

"Yes. I will take you driving in the park."

He didn't ask, he simply stated his intent, and only after the words left his mouth did he realize how overbearing he might sound.

"A drive? In your coach?" Arabella knew that she should not ride alone in a closed carriage with a single man.

"No. I have a new phaeton I thought to take out." Lucas walked beside her, ramrod straight with hands clasped behind his back.

"A phaeton?" she asked, excitement lacing her voice. "I saw one the other day and they look very grand. And possibly dangerous?"

"Never fear. I promise that no harm will come to you while in my company."

He could not help chuckling at her reaction.

Arabella smiled at him.

"I shall ask Lady Marianne's permission then." She lowered her eyes, aware that it was inappropriate for her to be making arrangements to spend the afternoon with Lord Rothglen without her guardian's consent.

"She will agree, I am sure," said Lucas confidently.

Arabella nodded, "I just don't want to embarrass her. She and her husband have been so kind to me."

Lucas nodded and led her to a bench surrounded by roses.

Arabella was exhausted but exhilarated as the dancing master called for the last dance of the evening. She looked at her dance card, and saw the name Viscount Barnsley printed on the line, but could not see the gentleman approaching her. She would not mind sitting this one out if they missed the start of the music.

Elizabeth reached her side and said, "You dance divinely, my dear. Is it true you only learned the steps this week?"

"Yes, it is. Lady Marianne insisted I spend many hours with the instructor." Arabella looked around the room in anticipation, then said to Lady Elizabeth, "I think my last dance partner cannot find me and I do not see him now. Do you know Viscount Barnsley?"

"Oh what a shame," Elizabeth said. "I fear that I saw the Viscount departing earlier. He was feeling quite poorly." Elizabeth's eyes left Arabella's as she peered over the younger woman's left shoulder. Her lips curled slightly upwards in expectation.

Arabella heard a soft voice behind her say, "My lady, would you do me the honour of joining me in the final dance of the evening? I understand your partner has been taken ill."

Lord Rothglen took her hand and guided her onto the dance floor as the first chord was struck, giving Arabella no opportunity to accept or refuse his invitation. Instinctively, she rested her gloved fingertips atop his forearm.

He inclined his head and leant ever so slightly towards her to whisper, "You look like a vision tonight."

Arabella had blushed and bitten the inside of her lip as butterflies took up a staccato rhythm in her stomach.

"Thank you." *You look very dashing yourself.* But she didn't say the words, feeling that something momentous was happening, that her life path was inexorably changed and she could do nothing to stop it.

They lined up and began to go through the elaborate steps, conversation halted for the time being. When the music ended, Lucas led her back to Lady and Lord Templeton for their carriage ride home. Arabella was still smiling as they threaded their way through the throng to reach the exit and be on their way in the cool night air. She ignored the looks sent her way, both by envious debutantes and disapproving dowagers. She hadn't cared what they thought of her before coming to London, and she truly didn't see any reason to care now.

As they moved through the London streets it was as if a spell had been broken and Arabella was jolted back to reality by every sway of the carriage. She had had a wonderful evening and Lord Rothglen was a handsome gentleman and a delightful dance partner. But Arabella had a goal and a path to get to it. She would stick to the agreement she'd made with Marianne and spend the month enjoying the social events of the Season. But once that month was up, she would have her referral and find a governess position. The orphans were depending upon her and she would not be dissuaded from taking care of them, one way or the other.

Chapter Nine

Arabella clasped her gloved hands in her lap and tried not to cringe, or to show any sign on her face of how truly awful the afternoon's entertainment was. She'd awakened the morning after her debut at Almack's to find a large stack of invitations waiting for her.

Marianne had been thrilled and together, over a cup of tea and some biscuits, they'd opened the invitations and separated them into three piles. The first had been the reject pile — invitations that no respectable young lady would ever consider accepting. Marianne had informed her that no reply was necessary for those.

The second pile was the one that concerned Arabella the most. The invitations to be accepted. A written note needed to be sent to each person, notifying them that Arabella and Marianne would be attending their dinner, or tea or dance. The number of events was staggering to Arabella, but Marianne had suggested that this was only the beginning and that, as she'd made such an impression the night before, she could expect twice as many the next day.

Arabella was completely overwhelmed, but she trusted Marianne's advice and simply gave in.

The first event was a musical soiree to be held at the Eversby House that same afternoon. Marianne had already been scheduled to attend, and after meeting Arabella at Almack's the previous evening, Beatrice Eversby had insisted that the newest member of society be brought along to hear her sing.

Marianne chose a day dress in a delicate mint green colour as the perfect attire for the afternoon's excursion and Arabella had allowed herself to be dressed and groomed by the maid once again.

As Beatrice Eversby strained to hit a note several steps above her range, Arabella tried not to cringe. The screeching voice had been going for almost an hour now and she surreptitiously glanced around to see everyone else in attendance trying to keep their composure as well. She breathed a momentary sigh of relief when this latest vocal disaster concluded, only to mentally groan when yet another piece was selected.

Arabella tried to remember what Marianne had told her about endurance and proper behaviour, but when Beatrice launched into a note that shook the walls and caused pain in her ears, she knew something had to be done to stop this torturous debacle. Using a distraction the orphans often employed, she surged to her feet, her chair clattering as it fell over while she clutched her throat, coughing and gagging in a most horrendous fit.

Gasps from everyone in the room ensued, and Marianne came to her aid, patting her lightly on the back and peering into her face to see where her source of distress was coming from. Beatrice even came over and patted her back a moment or two, exclaiming, "The poor dear, she was so overcome by the song."

Overcome with fright maybe. Arabella accepted their help, calming down only after she had watched the musician who'd previously been playing the pianoforte, leave the room.

She miraculously recovered and then asked to be placed where she could recover her composure in quiet before enjoying the rest of the recital.

"Oh, I wouldn't want you to become overwhelmed again," Beatrice informed her. "I think my voice needs a slight rest anyway." She turned to her other guests, "There are refreshments on the patio. Please enjoy yourselves."

Arabella dabbed at her forehead with a handkerchief while Marianne fussed over her, making sure that Beatrice knew she didn't need to stay and that she and Arabella would join the others in a few minutes.

Once Beatrice was gone, Marianne burst into laughter, "That was awful of you."

Arabella gave her an innocent look, "Whatever are you talking about? My ears were getting ready to bleed."

She could not contain a giggle, causing Marianne to join in again.

Turning serious, Marianne said, "There are times when I wish I could ignore certain invitations, but the Eversby family is not one to offend. Beatrice imagines herself singing on the London stage one day and has engaged a private tutor for two seasons now. I'm sad to say that her vocal talents have not improved with age."

A sound at the door caused both women to look up and smile.

"Elizabeth! I didn't know you would be attending."

"Fashionably late as usual," Elizabeth lowered her voice, and added, "have I managed to escape the performance?"

Arabella blushed as Marianne recounted the actions that had halted Beatrice's recital earlier than anticipated. When she was finished, Elizabeth smiled.

"Good for you. Why don't Arabella and I take a walk and meet you at the coach? You can let our hostess know we are taking her home to rest."

"Very good," Marianne smiled, pleased to see Elizabeth taking an interest in her cousin's well-being.

Elizabeth led Arabella out into the gardens.

"So I understand that Rothglen will be taking you driving tomorrow?"

Arabella nodded, "That is what he said. He wishes to speak with me."

"Yes, I imagine he does after last night's display."

"Display?" Arabella asked in confusion.

"Three dances in one night. What was that man thinking?" Elizabeth slipped Arabella's arm through her own and led her along a pathway lined with colourful flowers.

"Well, what's done is done. You and Lucas will do well together." Elizabeth didn't want Arabella to know that she was instrumental in setting up the entire plan. That was to be her and Lucas' little secret, at least for now.

"My Lady?" Arabella stopped walking and looked at Elizabeth, uncertain she understood the full meaning of her words.

"Rothglen is a tremendous catch. There are many young ladies hoping he might notice them, and he has chosen you. You have done well for yourself, and you've only just arrived," explained Elizabeth. "Now if you'll excuse me, I shall make my excuses to our hostess before joining you and Lady Marianne at the coach."

Arabella stood for a moment on the path, pondering what Elizabeth had implied. This was all moving so fast. All she wanted to do was prove herself to her mother's family so that she might receive a referral to be a governess, and earn enough money to take care of herself, with a little left over to help the children at the orphanage. How she did miss, them and wish that she could be with them now, not in the midst of London society, pretending to be something she was not.

She had no idea how she had so quickly become the potential marriage interest of an Earl, and one considered to be amongst the most eligible bachelors of the Season. She would have to try to slow things down with Lord Rothglen.

He was certainly attractive and enjoyable to be around, but she would need time to get to know him, to discover if there was a mutual attraction that could possibly become love. Marriage was not something to be decided within weeks of meeting.

As she paused before returning to the coach, she heard voices coming through the hedgerow on the other side of the path, no doubt some of the other guests clearing their heads from the dreadful performance.

Arabella was just walking away so as not to eavesdrop on the women when she stopped dead in her tracks at the mention of Lord Rothglen's name.

"I cannot believe he is back in London from the north already and did not call on me. I did not attend Almack's last night because I thought he would not be there." The petulant whine no doubt belonged to a younger woman.

"From what I heard, he was quite occupied last evening and would not have given you the time of day anyway," said the second woman, clearly an older, more haughty, voice.

"Nonsense! Whatever you heard, his attentions on one of the other debutantes can only be fleeting. It cannot last," said the young woman. "I happen to be aware of some very specific requirements Lord Rothglen has for his bride and I also know that I am the only one who can fulfil them. I was under the clear understanding that we would be betrothed before Easter."

The older woman clucked her tongue and spoke with unmistaken pleasure in her voice.

"Actually, Lady Margaret, rumour has it that the young woman who held Lord Rothglen's attention last night fulfils his requirements as well."

Arabella felt guilty for listening, but was transfixed to the spot. What did the women mean about Lord Rothglen's requirements? Who was Lady Margaret. Clearly she was someone who anticipated a betrothal from Lord Rothglen.

Arabella was now quite anxious to see Lord Rothglen the following day, but she was not going to join him for a drive in public as he had wanted. He may wish to speak to her, but she had questions of her own that she wanted answered.

ARIETTA RICHMOND, CATHERINE WINDSOR, ISABELLA THORNE, KATHERINE KEATS, KELLY ANNE BRUCE

Chapter Ten

Arabella awoke exhausted from a fitful night and with a dull headache. As she rubbed the sleep from her eyes, she recalled the odd conversation which she had overheard the previous day, about the requirements that Lord Rothglen had for a wife. Her apprehension came flooding back, and she knew that she would have to confront him before any more so-called rumours started swirling around the *ton*.

But she really had no right to question him about what she'd overheard. Perhaps she should ask Marianne or Elizabeth what to do. In the meantime, she would refuse any further activities where she could be seen in public with Lord Rothglen, until she got to the bottom of this.

~~~~~

Bella was enjoying a light morning tea with Marianne and was just building up her nerve to ask her about what she'd overheard in the garden the previous day when Wills announced the arrival of a visitor.
~~~~~

"Lord Denby to see Lady Arabella, my Lady," Wills announced to Lady Marianne.

Upon Marianne's approval, Lord Denby was shown into the drawing room. He bowed to the ladies.

"I do hope you've enjoyed your first days in London, Lady Arabella?".

Arabella smiled, "It's all so new, and exhausting, but yes I have. It feels so far away from my life in Wiltshire."

Lord Denby nodded in understanding.

"Actually, I am here to speak of Wiltshire. I will be traveling through there soon. I will be departing London tomorrow. Was there anything you forgot that you would like me to bring back for you?"

"You're headed to Wiltshire?" Arabella felt a tug at her heart at the thought.

Lord Denby nodded.

"Just beyond it actually, but I would be close enough to stop on my return journey should you require anything in the area."

"That is so kind." Arabella debated asking such a favour, but found the opportunity too compelling to let pass.

"Actually, do you remember the orphanage where you and Lord Rothglen found me? The day I met you for the first time?"

"Of course. Was there something you needed from there?"

"Just word that everyone is doing well."

Arabella saw Lord Denby's confusion and explained her concern.

"The manor house that is used for the orphanage was originally the vicarage. When my father was vicar, he saw no need for us to occupy such a large estate when there were children in need. So he declared it should be used as the orphanage while my parents and I lived in the cottage. The new vicar, who replaced my father, has seven children and I worry that he may have changed my father's directive. It is too soon to have had a response to any of my letters, but knowing that the vicar was due to arrive the day after my departure, I have been concerned while awaiting some news."

Lord Denby smiled and tilted his head as he considered the lovely young woman before him, envious of his friend who would very likely make her his wife.

"I would be happy to stop and check in on the children and their caretakers. I will be gone several weeks, but I will bring you word upon my return."

Arabella's eyes glistened and she smiled sincerely.

"Thank you so much, that is very kind. I feel better already and I hope that my worry is unfounded."

"I will make it my purpose to bring only good news upon my return then," Lord Denby told her, intent on fulfilling this charming creature's wishes.

"My Lady, Lord Rothglen has arrived."

She glanced up at the maid and gave her a wan smile, "Thank you. I'll be down shortly."

Lady Marianne had gone to tea with Lady Elizabeth and wasn't planning to return until late in the afternoon. That left her to deliver the news to Lord Rothglen that she was not feeling well enough to accompany him for a drive in his phaeton. She would take her leave as quickly as possible and avoid any further conversation with him until she'd had a chance to speak to Marianne about all that had transpired and her confusion about what it meant.

She went to the wash basin and splashed some of the water on her face, before taking the cloth and patting it dry. Her eyes looked tired, but she felt no desire to mask this from her visitor.

Bella descended the stairs and stepped into the drawing room, her eyes drawn to the man standing near the windows. He was tall, his shoulders were broad, and his legs strong beneath the material of his fawn breeches. His tall Hessian boots were polished perfectly, and the blue waist coat he wore almost matched the deep blue of his eyes.

He sensed her entrance and turned, a ready smile upon his lips. She swallowed and stepped forward, her excuse tumbling from her lips.

"I'm sorry but I'm unable to go driving with you today."

Lucas searched her face for a moment and then asked, "You are unwell?"

"I have a headache, nothing a day of rest won't cure."

That is, if I can forget what I overheard yesterday long enough to fall asleep.

"We do not have to drive today. Why don't we go and sit in the gardens for a while? I need to speak with you about a delicate matter."

Arabella raised a brow and considered refusing his request, opting instead to confront him.

"More delicate than the fact that you claimed three dances with me at Almack's so that I should become the centre of gossip and rumours within days of my arrival in London?"

Lucas grinned at her and then immediately tried to adopt a more serious expression, sensing the gravity of the situation for Arabella.

"What I wish to discuss involves that and more."

Arabella sighed.

"You acted deliberately that first night, knowing there would be consequences." It was a statement, not a question. In the short time she'd known Lord Rothglen, he'd not struck her as the type of man who acted impulsively. He'd known full well what dancing three times with her at Almack's would mean. Elizabeth had explained that should a wedding announcement not be made in the next few weeks, it would be her reputation that suffered. Not his.

"I should have known to refuse that last dance," Arabella murmured to herself, as she thought about ways to protect her tender heart and her reputation.

"Were you trying to test how well I had learned the rules of society? Did you wish to embarrass me?"

"Of course not, dear Arabella, if I may be so bold as to call you that? And I would not have let you refuse the last dance." He tried to coax a smile from her lips but to no avail. "Come, we'll sit in the gardens and discuss this where the servants cannot overhear."

Arabella, seeing that she had no other choice, inclined her head and led the way towards the back door and the gardens beyond.

The sun was shining, and she immediately went to a bench situated beneath a large tree. Because of her headache, the sun hurt her eyes and she sighed gratefully as she sat down in the shade.

Lucas sat down next to her, so close that mere inches separated their thighs. She tried to put more distance between them, but doing so put her in danger of falling off the narrow bench.

"You understand that by dancing with you three times that first night I have all but declared my intention to offer for your hand?"

"Yes, and you have placed me in a most delicate situation by doing so. Lord Rothglen, why would you do that? We hardly know one another?"

"Do you believe in fate, Lady Arabella?"

She considered his question for a moment, "Possibly. Why do you ask?"

"From the moment that I met you, I felt we were destined to become man and wife," he said. "You see, it is time that I marry and start a family. Now that my father has passed, I have a duty to carry on the family name and title."

"But why me?" she asked.

Lucas lowered his eyes sheepishly. "You may have noticed that many eligible debutantes have been vying for my attention." He glanced up at her but her expression gave nothing away. "But not one of them meets my requirements for marriage."

Arabella trembled. He was going to be honest with her. He was going to tell her about his requirements. Lady Margaret was right. But what could those requirements be that she would fulfil?

Lucas hesitated as he considered how much to reveal. He did care for her and he believed she would make a good wife, that they would grow to love one another in time. But he did not want to offend her, or frighten her away.

"In a society where marriages are arranged primarily based on convenience," he began, "I have decided that this is not enough for me. My requirement is that I will only marry for love."

Arabella gasped. Her heart was pounding so hard in her chest that she felt dizzy. Was Lord Rothglen actually telling her that he loved her. She knew she had feelings for him, desires that frightened her. But could they actually feel real love for each other, having only just met?

Lord Rothglen gazed intently into Arabella's eyes and took her hand.

"What do you say, my lady? Would you do me the honour of becoming my wife?"

Arabella returned his stare for a long moment before responding. She slipped her hand from his and said, "I have my own requirements for marriage, my lord. I have a moral obligation to the children of the orphanage. If I cannot work as a governess to earn money to take care of their needs, then I will require my husband to do so."

"Done," he said simply. "Is that all?"

Her eyes widened and he laughed.

"You really mean it? You will provide funding for the orphanage?" she said in delight.

"Yes, my dear, I will. Whatever makes you happy." He took her hands again, guided her from the bench and twirled her around in the garden.

Arabella looked coyly at the man who would imminently be declared her fiancé. "I'm sorry if this sounds forward of me, but I am quite concerned for the well-being of the children since the new vicar may have taken over the manor house already. Could we please see to their care immediately?"

"Yes, of course we can." Lord Lucas said. "Do not think of it again. I will have my man of affairs take care of it at once. You will have enough to take care of to plan a wedding. I would propose we wed before Lady Marianne retires to the country for her confinement. We should just have time for the bans to be read."

Chapter Eleven

The engagement of the Earl of Rothglen and Lady Arabella Compton-Worth was announced at a grand evening at the home of Lord and Lady Templeton. Lady Marianne and Lady Elizabeth had assisted Arabella with choosing an emerald green gown and instructed that her dark hair be woven with gold threads before being placed atop her head.

Arabella was breathtaking and Lucas could not take his eyes off his betrothed. With Arabella's parents and Lucas' father deceased, and his mother unable to travel, Lucas preferred to keep the party small and for close friends only. He was disappointed that Lord Denby had not yet returned from his journey, but was certain that he'd be forgiven for not awaiting his closest friend's return before making the announcement.

Although Lucas preferred not to invite him, his cousin Herbert was also in attendance as excluding him would have been quite beyond the pale, and have caused yet more unpleasant gossip amongst the *ton*.

Herbert sneered in Lucas' direction as he spoke to Lady Elizabeth, who was observing the room from a corner, visibly pleased with herself for her matchmaking prowess.

"I know you had something to do with his," he said to her through clenched teeth. "I will find a way to make you pay if it is the last thing I do."

"You can no longer harm me, you snivelling imbecile," she said, being sure to fix a stiff smile on her face for the entire time that they spoke, lest any of the other guests look in their direction.

~~~~~

Arabella was radiant and relaxed as she accepted congratulations from the many guests. While she had finally learned to enjoy the parties and dances and whirl of activities in London somewhat, even looking forward to donning the beautiful gowns and dancing, she was relieved to know that such frivolous pursuits would not necessarily be required of her in her new life as the Countess of Rothglen.

Shortly after accepting his proposal, Lord Rothglen had surprised Arabella by asking her if she would mind terribly if they spent most of their time living at his country estate.

"I spend as little time in London as I can. I prefer the quiet and wide open fields of the country, my horses, the gardens," he explained. "I hate to deprive you of the lifestyle you deserve as a Countess, but would you be willing to spend most of our time in the country?"
~~~~~

Arabella couldn't help the smile that formed on her face.

"I don't know how people do this for months on end." She said, visibly relieved. "Do you know how long it takes to get dressed and have my hair done for an evening out? Longer than the evening itself. I do so miss the simple life in the country."

If there was any doubt in Lucas' mind that he was marrying for love, it had been quashed by the kind, generous and caring nature of his Arabella. Each day he grew more and more fond of her, not to mention his growing desire for her. Perhaps he understood what love was after all.

~~~~~

Marianne sent the maid to bed after the long day and told her she would help Arabella undress after the party. She wanted to hear how Arabella was holding up after the whirlwind of activity and attention that she had received.

She was now the most famous and envied lady of the Season, having become engaged to Lord Rothglen.

Arabella threw her arms around her cousin and held her in a warm embrace.

"Thank you, my dear cousin, for everything you have done for me," she said. "I never would have believed that in such short time my life would change so, and that I could be happy again."

"And I am happy for you, Bella," said Marianne.
~~~~~

"Lord Lucas will make a fine husband. And I trust he meets your requirements?"

Marianne winked at her impressionable charge as she stood behind her and brushed her long hair after taking the pins and gold threads from it.

"And I his." Bella blushed at this revelation.

"Oh!" Marianne said as she lowered the brush and looked at Bella in the mirror. "He has told you about his requirements and you are alright with them?"

"Why, of course," Bella said, confused as to why she would not be alright with her fiancé expressing his desire to marry for love, just as she. "Why would I not be?"

"I know you have had a hard time with the ways of London society and the notion that for most of the peers, a marriage of convenience trumps any other reason," she explained. "But I am sure that Lord Rothglen will be a good husband and grow to care fondly for you as time goes by. My marriage to George was arranged and I hardly knew him when we wed, but we grew quite fond of one another. It does not matter one wit that Lord Rothglen has to marry quickly to meet the terms of his father's Will."

Arabella turned on her stool and stared at Marianne, forcing her to stop brushing her hair.

"Wha... what are you saying?"

Marianne realized at once that something was amiss and that Lord Rothglen had not revealed the whole truth to Arabella.

"Oh, Bella, do not be concerned. He cares for you, I know it. I can see it in his eyes."

Arabella's eyes widened in horror as she became aware that her fiancé was not the man she thought he was.

"Tell me the truth, Marianne. I want to know everything."

After Marianne told Arabella the full extent of the terms of the previous Earl of Rothglen's Will, Bella dove face down onto her bed and wept in anguish.

"He lied to me! He does not love me. I will not marry him!"

"Arabella, it is too late to turn back now," said Marianne. "You would never survive a broken engagement. You will be ostracized."

"I do not care," she wailed. "I did not want to marry in the first place. Please, you must give me the referral you promised. I shall be a governess and return to the children of the orphanage. I shall never marry."

Marianne sat beside her and stroked her hair.

"'Tis not so simple, my dear," she said. "Do you not understand? The granddaughter of an Earl is not so easily placed as a governess."

"I am not the granddaughter of an Earl," Bella sniffed. "He has not even acknowledged me."

"Get some sleep," said Marianne. "Things will not seem so grim in the morning. At least Lord Rothglen agreed to fund the orphanage. He does care for you, Bella, you will see."

Marianne extinguished the candle and closed the door softly behind her as she exited Arabella's room, devastated to hear the sobs as she retreated to her own chamber.

Chapter Twelve

The early spring day was unseasonably warm, causing Lady Marianne and Lady Arabella to choose to walk to Belgravia for tea at Lady Elizabeth's town home, rather than take the carriage. The sun was bright in the sky and trees were greening quickly following the rains of the previous days, the air refreshing as they strolled along the edge of Hyde Park, their maids trailing at a suitable distance behind them.

The nuptials of Arabella and Lord Rothglen were only days away and Arabella was still stinging from his deception, despite his attempts to convince her that his feelings were true. He had sent flowers to her every day after the confrontation she'd had with him following Marianne's revelation on the evening that they announced their betrothal.

"My Lady, I protest, I did not lie to you," he insisted. "I am sorry that I did not reveal all of the details of my father's Will, but I did not think it relevant any longer. My feelings for you far exceeded any further thoughts of marrying only to comply with the requirements of his directive."

Arabella did not believe him but also realized that her options were limited. Lady Elizabeth had implored her to heed the warnings of Lady Marianne and proceed with the wedding. Part of today's visit for tea was so that Elizabeth could convince her that love came in many forms and was expressed in a variety of ways.

Upon their arrival, the butler showed Arabella and Marianne through to the day room, which was near the back of the town home, with large windows overlooking the garden. Arabella noticed a gentleman sitting on a bench with a blanket over his knees, but before she had a chance to ask Marianne about him, Elizabeth greeted them.

"My dear Ladies." She embraced first Marianne then Arabella, taking the younger woman's hands in her own. "The big day is near, how are you feeling?"

"I'm fine," said Arabella, although her meek voice betrayed her, as did her gaze that looked downward.

"Before we sit down to tea, I hoped you would say hello to my husband. He is well enough today to sit in the garden and has been anxious to meet you," Elizabeth said.

"The Marquis?" Arabella inquired. She had heard so many different rumours about the Marquis of Vale that she was immediately apprehensive about the unexpected meeting. Politeness would not allow her to refuse, however, and she allowed Elizabeth to guide her through the French doors to the garden. Arabella turned around to look at Marianne imploringly, but her cousin encouraged her to proceed without an audience.

"Darling," Elizabeth spoke gently to the Marquis, a grey-haired, shrivelled man who was at least twice her age and looked older. "Our dear Arabella has come to meet you." She drew Arabella closer so that she stood directly in front of the pale old man as he slowly raised his head.

Arabella curtsied tentatively and said, "My Lord, it is an honour to meet you."

"Lady Arabella." The Marquis of Vale slurred her name, one side of his face and mouth drooping lower than the other, as he met her eyes.

Arabella started as she looked directly into the eyes of Elizabeth's husband. A vague sense of recognition tingled in her breast. She knew these eyes. These were the eyes of her mother. Arabella stared for a moment, speechless, and then turned to Elizabeth with a questioning look.

Elizabeth smiled and nodded. "Yes, Bella, this is your grandfather."

At that moment, Marianne joined them and, after a reassuring squeeze of Arabella's shoulders, crouched down in front of the Marquis.

"Uncle, you look well today."

"Hmm, the sun helps," he said. "Elizabeth has told me of your kindness to Arabella. Thank you for taking care of my granddaughter."

The housekeeper interrupted discreetly to tell Lady Elizabeth that the tea had been served.

The Marquis chose to stay in the garden, but Bella promised to return after tea and sit with him for a while. The ladies retreated indoors to partake, leaving the Marquis to sit peacefully in the sunshine.

Over tea, Marianne and Elizabeth explained to Bella how her grandfather had come to be the Marquis of Vale and Elizabeth's husband

~~~~~

As they sipped tea, Elizabeth told Arabella the fascinating story of how she had become the Marchioness of Vale.

Ten years earlier, Elizabeth was a commoner, a governess in the home of James Paxton, Baron Hartford, none other than the stepfather of Herbert, Lord Rothglen's cousin. Elizabeth was a beauty and was forever fighting off the advances of her employer. She did her best to ensure that she never was alone with Baron Hartford, yet he would touch her inappropriately at every opportunity. His repulsive threats, whispered in her ear whenever he pressed himself against her, promised that he would soon have her exactly where and how he desired. She lived in constant fear of being caught alone and unable to retreat from his overtures.

One day she entered his private study to collect the stuffed toy of her charge, who would not settle down to sleep without her favourite cuddle toy, carefully ensuring that the room was vacant before doing so. As she retrieved the toy she heard the voices of Baron Hartford and Herbert approaching, so she slipped behind the drapery to avoid detection.
~~~~~

"This is excellent, Herbert," said the Baron. "I do believe your idea will work. We only need to falsify one document to change the rightful heir to the Marquis of Vale so that I should gain the title on his death. You will be well rewarded for your efforts in this matter."

"Thank you, stepfather," said Herbert. "The Earl of Compton does not deserve to inherit the Marquisate. He is a miserable shell of a man, not fitting to hold such a title and high honour. Also, he will not stand in our way, because he is totally unaware of his standing in the line of inheritance and I understand that he keeps to himself, not mixing in society at all since his wife's death."

Elizabeth continued to listen as Baron Hartford and his stepson, Herbert, detailed their plans to steal the inheritance and title from the the Earl of Compton, an elderly gentleman who she'd heard, from some of the servants, was a sometimes disagreeable soul, but one who'd had a rather tragic life.

He had disowned his only daughter when she married an impoverished younger son, a vicar dedicated to his flock - a decision which his wife never forgave, but which he was, alas, too stubborn to reverse. His beloved wife had subsequently died and he had become a joyless, reclusive man. According to his few servants, the Earl was actually very kind to them and they protected him and served him with pleasure, but the peers of society found him distasteful, no doubt because he did not comply with their expectations of his position.

After Elizabeth heard their voices cease and footsteps recede, she slid out from behind the heavy velvet drapes and was preparing to leave the study, when she collided with Herbert returning to the room.

"Hmph! What the… ," he started.

"Excuse me, my Lord," said Elizabeth, trying to recover. "Jane wanted her stuffed toy or she would not be able to sleep."

"Where were you just now?" He demanded.

"I've just come now to collect the toy," she repeated.

"You did not just arrive, I would have seen you," he said. "You were eavesdropping, you ungrateful tart."

He grabbed her wrist and twisted it.

"No, sir, I swear I only wanted the toy," she sobbed.

"You were here for my stepfather, admit it. I see the way he looks at you. You've been giving him favours and disgracing my mother."

Herbert yanked her arm behind her and held her tighter, pulling her into him so that she could feel his hot breath on her neck.

"I want some of what you've been giving him."

"No!"

He slackened his grip on her as he reached down to release himself from his britches and in a single swift move, she raised her knee sharply between his legs, twisted away and ran from the room while Herbert doubled over in pain, groaning.

"I'll make you pay!" She heard his shout as she retreated up the staircase to Jane's room, out of breath as she reached the top.

The coming weeks were unbearable for Elizabeth as she now had two men to avoid. She also feared that Herbert would tell his stepfather that he'd caught her eavesdropping in his study. Luckily, he seemed to have forgotten all about it when she heard of the death of the then Marquis of Vale. Baron Hartford's household was immediately thrown into a frenzy of preparation as the family and servants alike started speaking of the Baron's forthcoming title.

Elizabeth could not bear to hear of the deception by these two conniving men, who she felt were not worthy of such a title. Although she knew that she would be fired from her position as governess, and be out on the streets for doing so, and having no idea how she would be received, she went directly to the Earl of Compton's town home and asked to see the Earl about a vitally important matter. To her surprise, after being left to wait for ten minutes in the foyer, the butler returned and led her through to meet the Earl.

She soon learned that her apprehension was unfounded and that the Earl was a kind and gentle man, although the mistakes of his tragic past weighed heavily on him and he was painfully unhappy. At first he had no interest in challenging Baron Hartford for the title of Marquis, which was rightfully his, but he was smitten with the young woman who seemed to only want what was fair and right for him, with no concern for how it may adversely affect her.

By the end of the month, the the Earl of Compton had acquired the title of the Marquis of Vale, along with several grand properties, and Elizabeth had become his wife.

Herbert had initially tried to ruin her by announcing to anyone who would listen that she was a commoner who had tricked the Marquis into marriage for his money and titles. But the new Marquis made sure that Baron Hartford and Herbert would never speak ill of her, and in exchange, he would not expose the deception they had tried to perpetrate.

In the years that followed, Elizabeth doted on her elderly husband whom she truly grew to love. After he had suffered an apoplexy, she cared for him night and day, insisting on serving him his meals herself and walking with him in the garden when he felt able to. Although he remained somewhat reclusive and never fully recovered from the apoplexy, nor his heartbreak over the death of his first wife and the loss of his daughter, he credited Elizabeth with making his twilight years comfortable and enjoyable.

Elizabeth and Marianne had become fast friends during Marianne's weekly visits to her uncle, given that the Marquis' niece and wife were similar in age. When Arabella wrote to Marianne and asked for a reference to get on her feet following the death of her father, Elizabeth gently told her husband about his granddaughter. She vowed to do whatever she could to protect the girl and see that she would be taken care of.

~~~~~

Arabella could barely drink her tea as she absorbed the extraordinary story. Occasionally, she would gaze through the window to look at her grandfather, expecting him to disappear at any moment.
~~~~~

But there he was, sitting with the blanket over his lap, sometimes dozing with his eyes closed and head bowed, then alternately raising his head to the sun to feel the warmth on his skin, cocking his head as if to listen for the sound of some forgotten voice in the distance.

"We should be getting home, Bella," said Marianne. "Would you like to tell your grandfather that you are leaving?"

During her recitation of events over the past hours, Elizabeth had explained that the Marquis was fully aware of Bella's betrothal, as well as her misgivings and concerns about the reasons for Lord Rothglen's proposal. In fact, since Arabella's parents were both deceased, Lord Rothglen had asked the Marquis for permission to marry her.

As Arabella said her final goodbyes and the Marquis wished her well on her wedding day, which he said he did not feel fit to attend, he sensed the lingering doubts behind her sombre eyes. He reached for her hands and urged her to sit beside him.

"My dear granddaughter," he began. "I am an old fool and do not expect you to believe anything that I say, because my mistakes have likely caused you much pain during your life. But there is one thing of which I am sure." He started to cough, and as a cool breeze fluttered through the garden he pulled the blanket closer around his knees.

"When your Lord Rothglen asked my permission to marry you, there was only one reason I gave him my consent," he said.

"What was that, grandfather?" Arabella asked.

"The look of love in his eyes," said the Marquis simply. "I recognized the same look in Lord Rothglen's eyes that I saw in the eyes of your father more than twenty years ago when he asked my permission to marry your mother, and I denied him. I denied him because I did not think he was good enough to be her husband. And I was so wrong."

Arabella's eyes teared as she thought of her parents whom she missed terribly. "They were happy, grandfather."

"I know. And I have regretted my actions for all of these years. Neither you nor Lord Rothglen need my permission to marry. You must make your own decision. But he loves you, Bella, of that I am certain. Be happy."

Elizabeth had come into the garden as she sensed that the coolness of the air was starting to distress her husband.

"Now I must go indoors and rest, my dear," he said softly.

Chapter Thirteen

"Lady Arabella, you were a beautiful bride," Lady Elizabeth told her as she made her way from the church. She and Lucas had been married just a few moments earlier, and the number of well-wishers that had come to show their support for the couple was extraordinary.

"Why are there so many people in attendance?" Arabella whispered to Lucas as they went to the waiting coach.

"Everyone wanted to see the bride that captured my heart." Lucas was beaming, only too happy to let the world see his beautiful Bella.

"Ahoy!"

Lucas turned his head toward the cry and was thrilled to spot Lord Denby in the crowd, making his way forward to congratulate the couple.

"About time you made your way back to London, my good man!" called Lucas.

Arabella was even more anxious to see Lord Denby than Lucas. She did not waste any time on greetings, nor to accept his good wishes on their nuptials.

"Have you any news of the orphanage?" she asked. Lucas had been evasive during the past week when she'd tried to ask him what progress he'd made in seeing to the orphans welfare, only telling her that his man of affairs would deal with it and she would be advised as soon as a solution was found.

Lord Denby's smile faded, as did his hope that he could avoid the delicate subject with Arabella on today, of all days.

He bowed his head before breaking the news to her.

"I'm afraid I come with bad news. I stopped at the manor house, but the orphans were no longer there."

He glanced at Lucas who shot daggers at him with his eyes for delivering such distressing news to his bride on their wedding day.

"What?" Arabella tried unsuccessfully to control a sob. She wrung her hands and asked, "Did you locate the vicar and ask where they went?"

Lord Denby nodded, "A most uncooperative and sour fellow I've yet to meet. He was not at all inclined to speak with me regarding the orphans or their whereabouts. I was simply informed that they had left the manor some weeks earlier, as he and his family had need of the entire manor house. He said that he did not know where they planned to relocate."

"He kicked them out! Oh, I was afraid that might happen..."

"I am so sorry, my Lady. My own travels were delayed and I fear that I reached Wiltshire later than I had anticipated. Perhaps if I had passed by sooner…" he said.

"No, it is not your fault," she said, turning her gaze to her husband. "You promised me more than a month ago that you would take care of them immediately! I trusted you."

Arabella tried to control her emotions, considering that several of the wedding onlookers were still within earshot.

"Bella, I promised you that I would provide for the orphans and that is exactly what I shall do. I am certain that my man of affairs will be able to inquire with the other villagers and locate them," Lord Lucas said.

"The poor darlings. And what of Mrs. Buttons and Mrs. Pickerly? Their well-being is just as dependent on there being a funded orphanage as the children. Their life's work has been in caring for those children. My father would be so disappointed in me to know that I have not protected all of them."

She could no longer hold back the sob.

~~~~~

Despite her distress and concern for the orphans, it was impossible for Arabella to stay angry with her husband. As the carriage drove them from the wedding chapel to their London town home and she snuggled against him, they spoke quietly about how unfortunate the timing had been that both Lord Denby and Lucas' man of affairs must have just missed reaching the children and their caretakers before they had to move on.
~~~~~

They spent their wedding night in the London town home where Lucas was charming, flirtatious and gentle and Bella was unable to hide her desire for her husband, or resist the touch that sent shivers up her spine. Lucas felt like the luckiest man in the world.

Even with little sleep, they were both anxious to be on the road first thing the following morning, to reach his country estate before Easter. Lucas had vowed to Arabella that his first order of business when they reached the country was to send ten men, if needed, to find the orphans. Arabella believed her husband and trusted that he would not let her down again.

She watched the various houses and buildings pass by and found herself smiling. How different this journey was to the one she had taken only a short time earlier, when she knew not what the future would hold for her. She was now a married woman, a Countess, she had met her grandfather and she was very likely to have a child of her own within the year.

~~~~~

They arrived at the Rothglen estate after dark and Lucas immediately ushered Arabella up the stairs and down the hallway to his suite of rooms. He turned to address his butler, who waited just inside the ante room, "Please have cook prepare a light supper and send it up. You may retire after that."

Lucas lit an oil lamp and took a short stroll through the grounds with his estate manager. He was pleased to see the grounds in good order and the outlying buildings exactly as he had requested.
~~~~~

"Bella," he called softly to her when he returned to their bed chamber. He smiled as he saw that she had fallen asleep. It had been a long day and she must have been exhausted. He would take her on a tour of the grounds in the morning, after breakfast, and hope that they met with her approval.

~~~~

In the morning, Arabella dressed in a simple country frock, pleased to inhale the fresh air after the smoky air of London. She entered the morning room as Lucas was dismissing the housekeeper with a list of instructions.

"Good morning, my dear, I trust that you slept well.".

Actually, she still felt slightly woozy from the carriage ride but was happy and hungry.

Lucas spoke again, "I hope it will be alright with you if I show you around the estate before we have breakfast. It is Easter in only a few days and I hoped you would agree that we plan an egg roll for the village children on the grounds."

Arabella felt as though she'd been kicked in the stomach. She and Mrs. Buttons had spoken of their plans for Easter with the children. She did not want to seem ungrateful for the beautiful home she would now be sharing with her wonderful husband, but she could not ease the pang of guilt that gripped her as she thought of the orphans.

"Yes, of course, my Lord," she answered, a bit too formally and in a voice rather lacking in enthusiasm.
~~~~

Lucas, seeming not to notice her unenthusiastic response, took her hand and slipped it into the crook of his arm, leading her from the room.

"I would like to give you a wedding gift." He continued to walk, leading her outside into the crisp morning air and across the dewy grass. He was certain that she would forgive him if the hem of her dress became damp with the dew.

Arabella looked around and tried to take in the vast estate and rolling hills. It was beautiful and seemed to go on for miles. After a stroll of perhaps five minutes, they reached a stone building with a wooden staircase leading to a large open veranda.

"What is this building," she asked, feigning interest although she was more than ready to return to their home for breakfast.

At that moment, the front door was flung open and, before Arabella could grasp what was happening, a sea of smiling faces squeezed out of the door, ran down the stairs and raced to her. Within seconds, she was surrounded by children, arms wrapped around her legs and faces buried in her skirts.

"Bella, Bella, we missed you!" chorused the children. She looked up to see Mr. and Mrs. Buttons and Mrs. Pickerly on the porch, the two women unable to contain their tears.

Chapter Fourteen

Easter weekend was a flurry of activity. Mrs. Buttons made Arabella's favourite Easter buns on Good Friday, after which they showed all of the children how to dye the eggs and decorate them for the egg roll the following day. In addition to the orphans, the village children would attend the egg roll at the estate and Bella was looking forward to hearing the giggles and laughter of children once again. She had missed that in London.

Arabella had forgiven Lucas for keeping secret from her that he had been the one to move the orphans from the vicarage. He had wanted it to be a delightful wedding surprise and had not anticipated that Lord Denby would report to Bella that they were missing.

Mrs. Pickerly reminded Arabella that eggs were associated with rebirth and fertility and new beginnings. She winked at Lady Arabella Stanthorpe, the Countess of Rothglen, who blushed at the suggestion the widow was implying.

Once the children had settled down for the evening, the three women sewed pastel-coloured bonnets for all of the girls to wear on Easter morning. By the time they had finished, Arabella was exhausted.

~~~~~

"I thought you'd never come to bed," Lucas said, pouting to his bride. "I fear I shall have to compete for your attention now."

"Never fear, my love," she said. "I will always have time for you. In fact, don't we have another order of business if we are to fully comply with your father's Will?"

She smiled as she wrapped her arms around her husband's neck and kissed him deeply. Lucas slipped one arm under her legs and easily lifted her up and carried her to the bed.

~~~~~

The leaves were changing from green to vibrant shades of yellow, orange and red. Lucas was anxious to return to Arabella following a trip to London to deal with business. She had not joined him, because she had been feeling tired and nauseous for several days before his departure. He was hoping it was actually a foreshadowing of good news.

He had news from London for her. Lady Elizabeth had reported that Lady Marianne had been delivered of a healthy baby boy a few weeks earlier.

Elizabeth was going to go to the country to keep her company and assist her for the coming months.

Arabella's grandfather, the Marquis of Vale, had passed quietly in his sleep the night that Marianne was delivered of her child. Lucas had just visited him and reported that Bella was thriving and looking forward to a London visit in the spring. He knew that she would be saddened to learn that she would not see her grandfather again. Lady Elizabeth assured him that her husband had died peacefully and happy, knowing that his granddaughter was happy, healthy and loved.

The End.

If you enjoyed 'Trusting the Earl'

I'm sure that you'll enjoy my other books

You'll find a taste of "The Earl's Desire" just after the 'About the Author' section in this book!

About the Author

Catherine Windsor was born in Cambridge, England and raised in upstate New York. She enjoys reading both historical and contemporary romance and has written short stories and novellas for her own enjoyment for years. Encouraged by her teenage daughter, she now publishes her Regency romance for the enjoyment of fans of the genre

Catherine, with her husband and daughter, lives on an acreage which is reminiscent of her native England. In addition to writing fiction, she loves to cook with fresh herbs and vegetables from her own garden.

Other Books by Catherine Windsor

ARIETTA RICHMOND, CATHERINE WINDSOR, ISABELLA THORNE, KATHERINE
KEATS, KELLY ANNE BRUCE

Regency Romance

Here is Your Preview of

The Earl's Desire

Catherine Windsor

Prologue

"You can't catch me! Not with those big feet!"

Thirteen year old Isabel Wyndham ran along the path, dodging roots that stuck out from the trees as she attempted to be as surefooted as possible. Alexander's footsteps grew louder behind her, gaining on her, and she thought for a moment about teasing him further. Normally, he was faster, beating her to the tree fort they had secretly fashioned, on his father's property, deep in the woods. But, today, she had managed to trick him and had gained an advantage.

As the fort came into sight, she slowed her pace, reaching out to touch the rough bark that signalled she was victorious. Alexander arrived mere moments later, his breath harsh to her ears.

"You beat me." He exhaled loudly and filled his lungs with a gasping breath.

She turned to see him red faced, despite the coolness of the morning air, and she offered him a satisfied grin.

"I did, and I will do it again tomorrow!"

The moment the words were out of her mouth she wanted to force them back in, pain immediately filling her chest at the reality of what the following day would bring. After her entire thirteen years of having Alexander only a short walk away, he would not be there tomorrow.

"Tis fine," Alexander replied, leaning up against the tree with a huff. "I have been reminded all morning that I am to depart for Eton as soon as the sun rises. I should just run away tonight so that they are unable to find me in the morning."

"Oh, posh, Alexander," Isabel replied, swallowing hard at the thought of her best friend not being there with her in the morning, or any morning afterward for quite some time. She and Alexander, Viscount St. John, only son of the Earl of Hertford, had been friends since the cradle. Their families' estates bordered each other. With neither having any other siblings to play with, it seemed natural that they had forged a bond. But now, that bond was about to be broken and Isabel could almost not bear it. Who would she spend her days with now? And Alexander? He would meet new and exciting friends at Eton and forget all about her. She met his gaze and tried to hide the sadness that had crept in.

"You are positively dreadful for leaving me," she finally said, her lower lip jutting forward in a pout, while knowing that it truthfully wasn't his fault.

"I find no pleasure in leaving," he admitted in a huff. "I do not wish to receive a *gentleman's education*, as my father calls it. I want to learn the land, ride my horse, sail the seas, and—"

"Spend time with me?" Isabel finished with a smile.

Alexander grinned and nudged her lightly on the shoulder. "Of course, silly. Who else would I spend time with? You are the only one who I can talk to."

Isabel walked around the tree, noting the makeshift fort where they had played for years. Her own mother had started to discuss the need to send Isabel to finishing school, so that she could learn to be a lady and not run around in the woods with a boy. Isabel detested the thought of having to learn to dance or how to curtsey properly. She had no need for that.

"Perhaps I shall run away as well," she announced, coming full circle around the tree to once more stand beside Alexander, who was still leaning against the tree. "I shall run away to London and become a courtesan to the royal court."

"That is preposterous, Isabel, and you know it," Alexander answered with a laugh. "You would never shame your family by doing such a thing."

Isabel sighed, knowing that Alexander was right. She would never do something so rash, but the thought of being able to control her own destiny was so alluring. They both wished to do different things from what their parents had laid out for them. Why must they follow in those footsteps? Why couldn't they do something completely unorthodox?

"Besides," Alexander continued, pulling a leaf from a nearby tree branch and busying his hands by tearing it into little pieces. "I have no other option but to journey to Eton and become the gentleman my father expects me to be. You will learn to be a lady while I am away and when I return, we shall marry. You shall be my Countess."

"Marry?" Isabel asked, surprise in her voice. Certainly, she held a great affection for Alexander, but she hadn't thought about marriage between the two of them... until now. He was her best friend, the one person who knew her better than anyone on earth. Thus, upon her thinking of it, it did seem only natural that they marry. "Is that your desire?"

"Of course," he replied, pushing away from the tree and brushing his hands together, the pieces of the leaf falling to the ground. "We enjoy each other's company and I can tolerate you longer than any boy in the village. Besides, I know all of your favourite things."

She pushed at him, knowing it would illicit his smirk.

"You will be lost without me, Alexander, admit as much."

He reached out and grabbed her hand, pulling her toward him. Isabel squeaked as her free hand collided with his chest. She'd never been so close to him, close enough to feel his heartbeat under her fingertips. It was beating erratically and she was suddenly unsure of what to think or say.

"I have always wanted to be a Countess," she said. Her lips turned up at the edges in a sly smile as she curtsied and announced, "Lady Isabel, Countess of Hertford." Her voice was wistful as she twirled in front of the future Earl.

"So that is all I am to you? A title?" Alexander's hurt expression almost tricked Isabel into thinking that she had truly wounded her friend, when he broke into a broad smile.

"You are correct, Isabel. I shall be lost without you," he said softly, his eyes searching hers. "So you will become my wife." Without warning, Alexander's lips touched hers gently.

Isabel's mind barely registered that Alexander was kissing her before he pulled away, his cheeks stained red. She brought her fingers up to her lips and looked at him, her own cheeks flushing with surprise.

"Oh," she gasped.

A sly grin formed on his lips and he shrugged before he turned, taking off down the path.

"I will also beat you back!" he called, as he disappeared around the bend. Isabel straightened, the feel of Alexander's kiss still on her lips, the brief contact still tingling on her skin. She had been kissed. Her first kiss and it was from Alexander. There was no other boy that she would want to kiss her. With a soft sigh, she smiled and started down the path, intent on catching him before he reached the house.

Continue reading at

https://www.amazon.com/dp/B01LVY4DH2/

ARIETTA RICHMOND, CATHERINE WINDSOR, ISABELLA THORNE, KATHERINE KEATS, KELLY ANNE BRUCE

Regency Romance

Love Springs Anew

Isabella Thorne

Chapter One

It was a cold grey day in the beginning of March and Philippa Dunn, the only daughter of the Baron of Montclair, sat in the parlour, near the window where the light was best, with a book open upon her lap. She ran a skinny finger down the page line by line, to help keep her dark hazel eyes focused on the scintillating text. Her father would not approve of the racy French novel, but her father didn't know of its existence. It was unlikely he would visit to find out what Philippa's reading material consisted of - why would he? He didn't notice her for any other reason

Philippa's maid, Lydia, had procured the novel from the widow Sinclair's maid, with some difficulty and the utmost secrecy. It was doubtful that anything which happened in Philippa's books would ever happen to her in real life, but that didn't stop her from imagining it.

Philippa was an argumentative woman with sharp features and a sharper tongue, a spinster, unlikely ever to marry. Her father had apprised her of this fact often enough.

Philippa was unlikely to forget just how unattractive she was. She was thin-boned and sickly, her bosom slight as a boy's, her hips too narrow for childbearing and her feet overly large. Her eyes were her most appealing feature, according to Lydia; they were dark brown with flecks of green, and long lashed, but that was not enough to make up for her other insufficiencies. Cow eyes her father called them, but no matter if her eyes were beautiful, or at least lovely enough for bovine appreciation, they could not make up for her frail nature or her shrewish disposition.

Her hair was dark and long, always looped in intricate styles, done by Lydia, the same maid who procured her clandestine books. When she wasn't reading, Philippa was sitting in her chamber, in front of a rounded mirror which hung on the wall, while Lydia arranged her curls. Philippa couldn't see why the style of her hair mattered. She didn't go anywhere for anyone to see her. She could leave it in long braids or a rat's nest for that matter. She told herself that it was for Lydia's practice, not her own beauty.

Philippa liked Lydia but she was not a friend. Lydia was her maid, and Philippa's father made sure that she remembered the difference in their class, lest Philippa find herself a companion in her serious bookish maid. No. Philippa had no friends. Her father saw to that fact, but Philippa herself was the reason she had no suitors.

Philippa was six and twenty, but felt older. Most of those her age thought she was a dour sort. Only she was not dour; she was weary; a heavy sense of melancholy settled upon her shoulders each morning and rarely dissipated.

This was especially so as the cold grey days of winter melted into a soggy grey spring. It seemed as if the coldness seeped into Philippa's soul and indeed some members of the *Ton,* those who deigned to speak of her at all, called her the Ice Lady, and remembered her shrewish nature from an incident when she had lost her temper in public, and screamed obscenities at her intended. After that day the freezing then came from without.

Truly, she had little to raise her spirits. She was, after all, firmly a spinster, which was quite the reason for melancholy. No one would want a skinny bird of a woman with a bad temper. Her father told her often enough. Philippa knew he had regretted marrying her mother, who was also slight of body and had died giving birth to one sickly daughter. Often Philippa wondered if her mother would have felt differently than her father about her existence – if her mother had lived.

Her father was a busy man. Robert Dunn, The Right Honourable Lord Montclair; was very hands-on with the running of his estate. Although, for a long time, it had just been the two of them, as often as not Philippa would go for days without seeing her father, which meant, of course, that she did not have permission to leave the manor. As busy as he was, Philippa was sure that he sometimes avoided her, due to embarrassment, or a simple sense of uncomfortableness - she could not be sure. And so, for almost a decade her companions were mostly the staff, first her nurse, then her governess, and then a tutor and now, finally, her maid, Lydia.

Her father had let her study her books, saying that at least she would be of some use doing calculations for him.

He brought her his accounts to look over, and she found several mistakes his clerk had missed, but he gave her no word of praise. He said it was unnatural that a woman should be so bookish. It didn't really matter. No one would look at her whether she was a blue-stocking or not. She was a woman grown and scrawny as a twelve-year-old. Certainly no one would offer for her.

As she grew older, she did not seek the company of others. She was more than happy alone with her books. Instead, she sat in her room, reading and making up all matter of elaborate games, where the men were strong and virile and the women were small, spirited and beautiful. Books had such heroes in them, but Philippa had never seen a real hero. She doubted that they actually existed. No, actual men were quite like her father in that regard; more likely to be absent or abusive, and she preferred the former.

Then her solitary life changed overnight. Her Lord father had once had a younger brother who had passed away several years ago, along with his wife, when a terrible fever had swept through the countryside just outside of London. Her uncle also had a daughter, Charlotte, and her father The Right Honourable Lord Montclair, was nothing if not honourable. He did not hesitate to bring the child into his home and raise her as his own, which meant that he paid for her keep and promptly forgot about her existence, leaving both Philippa and her young cousin to their own devices.

Though Philippa had not ever said it, having the girl nearby had made her happy. She had never been lucky enough to have a sister, or even a brother.

She had been on her own since her mother had died. Now her cousin, Charlotte, was by herself as well -she too was an only child in a world of siblings.

Charlotte was beautiful. She came to the manor tall and gangly, but four years later she was beginning to blossom into a striking young woman, with golden hair that shone as bright as her personality. Her breasts were full and round and Philippa couldn't help but notice that they were larger than her own, although Charlotte was nine years her junior. The small girl had a curve to her hips and pouty lips. She was everything that Philippa was not, which might have ignited a cold stab of jealousy, but did not. Philippa loved the girl dearly. And the attention Charlotte was getting from men as she matured was fascinating to Philippa

Charlotte had missed her parents dreadfully and cried almost non-stop for the first month. Philippa consoled her, wondering if she would even miss her father if he died. She doubted that she would cry at all. Crying, she had learned early, did not improve one's lot in life. It only made one's face red and blotchy and more ugly than usual, but still, she held the young girl while she cried. She rubbed circles on her back and gave her a handkerchief to wipe her tears.

Charlotte's face remained prettily flushed, instead of going blotchy. Philippa found herself going to the kitchen to ask cook to prepare special delicacies which would raise Charlotte's spirits. Philippa wondered if this was what it was like to be a mother, and have another soul cling to her like her life depended upon it. If it was like this, she thought she would not mind so much being a mother.

In time, Charlotte became adjusted to her new life and her naturally optimistic spirit took hold once again. She was like a bright ray of sunshine upon the rainy day of Philippa's life. She was always laughing and, as sour as Philippa's own mood so often was, she found Charlotte could always lighten it.

When Philippa looked up from her current book, she saw that Charlotte was staring at her with half a smile. She often did this, and it was maddening. Her long looks always left Philippa wondering if she had dirt on her nose or a piece of spinach between her teeth.

"Yes?" Philippa asked.

"I didn't speak," Charlotte said, while kicking her feet in front of her slightly, a childlike quality she had yet to shed.

"But you are staring at me," Philippa replied. "It is very rude."

"I may be," Charlotte said, "However, I did not mean to stare."

"You did not mean to be looking at me?"

"No, I am just thinking," Charlotte said with a small giggle which escaped past her full lips. She tossed her golden curls. She was naturally the coquette.

"About?" Philippa asked, letting the question hang in the air.

"You," Charlotte said, and then she couldn't help but laugh.

"What?"

"I was wondering why you never married. Surely some man would offer for an heiress even if she had a less than genteel temperament."

"You are doing your best to make me feel uncomfortable," Philippa complained sharply. "Or at least it seems to be the case to me."

"I am sorry, sweet Philippa," the younger woman said with a twinkle in her eye.

Philippa chuckled. She was not sweet. Everyone said so.

"I was looking at you, that much is true," Charlotte said, "And I was thinking of you, that too is true. I was thinking how happy I was, at that very moment, to be sitting with you, reading quietly, and simply enjoying your company. Why would a man not enjoy your company too?"

"I am not good company," Philippa replied.

"Oh posh! That is not true. I do not know what I would have done without you – after mother and father died."

"You would have survived," Philippa said coolly, but she could not hide a smile, and something softened within her. "I often feel the same," she said. "I love you like a sister."

~~~~~

A knock from the front door echoed in the parlour. Philippa did not look up from her book: she was at a particularly good part, and often shut out the sounds of the world when she read. Whoever it was, it was not for her.
~~~~~

It would be someone from the bank for her father, most likely, a solicitor or business man, come to talk of lands and taxes for the Regent. Charlotte was in the parlour as well, sitting across from her older cousin, a book in her lap still unopened. Instead her soft blue eyes were focused out of a nearby window, which overlooked the garden where the dormant sticks of the rose bushes dripped with the spring rain.

Their old butler, Jackson, came to the door of the room.

"There is a visitor for Miss Charlotte."

Charlotte was up in a flash, moving like a rabbit startled from the underbrush.

"Charlotte," she cautioned.

"Yes?"

Charlotte flashed Philippa a smile as she left, but the older woman did not return it.

"Remember your decorum," she said. "And it is Lent," Philippa called, as Charlotte continued towards the door. "There shall be no frivolity."

Charlotte gave a quick mocking curtsey to her cousin and rushed to follow the butler. Philippa quickly scanned the next two paragraphs of her book and then closed it, marking her place, and carried the book with her. She walked more sedately behind her cousin, not eager to be her chaperone, but also unwilling to leave her without one.

Of course Charlotte had a visitor. More and more suitors were stopping by each week.

The season had begun after Christmas, and the gentlemen would soon return to town for Parliament and the Easter Balls, even though father did not hold with Balls and such to-dos. Philippa had been overseeing Charlotte's coming out as best she could, considering that squeezing money out of her father for the dresses needed was like plying juice from a turnip.

The truth was, she was not quite sure what to do with Charlotte, having never actually had a season herself. Father had said the mass of ball gowns would be a waste of money and since she didn't have an older female companion, the whole ordeal of a season would be difficult. However Philippa knew that, unlike herself, Charlotte would not be long in search of a husband. There were several eligible young men who were flitting around her like bees about a flower, and the young girl would have a proposal before long, even without a formal coming out.

"My company is quickly forgotten when a suitor comes knocking," Philippa said to the girl's back, knowing well that she would not hear her. She was already at the door, and with thoughts of love in her heart. Philippa cast down the envy in her mood. She would not deny Charlotte her suitors. Without them the bright girl would wither and die. Philippa herself was made of sterner stuff.

Philippa seated herself in a corner, unobtrusively, while Charlotte ordered toast and tea from the servants. Philippa opened her book and stared at it unseeing as she thought back to her own lack of a coming out. She'd had suitors as well. She was not pretty or soft spoken then, but her father had money and a minor title, The Baron of Montclair.

She had fallen for a man quickly.

He was dashing and personable, the younger son of Henry Goldthwaite, the Earl of Stone, a tall and barrel chested man named Simon. When he smiled at her, her heart fluttered and it felt as if the sun came out. The Goldthwaite home was beautiful, and twice the size of her father's. An expansive manse located atop a hill, which overlooked a small village of quaint houses and a curving path that wound along one side of the valley.

Simon Goldthwaite was dashing, and kissed her on the lips. She was quite sure that meant marriage. She'd had his entire house redecorated in her mind. It had truly been a whirlwind romance, but it had ended when Philippa discovered Simon kissing another woman when he returned from a fox hunt. The woman was a Lady of some substance, both monetarily and physically. Philippa could see in an instant all that her rival had, that she, Philippa did not.

In a fit of passion Philippa had screamed at them both, calling them vile names. She had cursed him quite publicly with vulgar words from her secret novels, words no gentlewoman should know, much less say. She flung his grandmother's heirloom ring into the bushes outside, thus necessitating the aid of the footman to crawl around on his hands and knees in the dirt to find the expensive bauble for his master.

The Lady in question, of course, was ruined, and had to marry Simon, but perhaps that was what she had wanted, helped in her quest for his hand by Philippa's ire. Supposedly, she was engaged to some stuffy nobleman. Philippa did not know the lady or the nobleman, as both were above her circle.

She did not care to know them... any of them. Philippa had called her own carriage and rushed home unchaperoned. She had barricaded herself into her room to cry. Father was right. No man would want a skinny bird of a woman, who was all bones and angles, when he could have a buxom lass with softness to spare and money besides.

Philippa had realized, for the first time, that the only reason Simon had noticed her at all was her father's money. She was available and rich. The thought disgusted her. Lydia comforted her with hot chocolate, and when Philippa was done crying, she buried herself in a book that Lydia had procured for her. There in the fiction, she could imagine herself with a body with all of the attributes that young men wanted. At least she could imagine what if felt like to be sought after, and loved by her hero. In her imagination she did not need money. Instead her hero loved her for herself. She gave her husband a strong son, whom they both loved, but of course, it was all a fantasy.

Philippa was now labelled a shrew and firmly on the shelf. At least that was what everyone thought. Even Philippa had to ask, what gentleman would tolerate such behaviour? She had merely lost her temper, but she certainly had not acted with decorum, which would have been calm and discrete.

She had not acted as a gentlewoman, who would never know such words, much less utter them. Her eyes stinging with tears, her body and mind exhausted form crying, in one day, with a single incident, she had gained a reputation as a shrew among the *Haut Ton*.

Her own father had called her a senseless woman, and took her into the country in the hopes that her suitors would forget. They did not forget. Her already sparse suitors had fled quickly. She had been eighteen. Now at twenty-six, she was sure she would never marry. The more she thought about that, the more she tried to convince herself that she was fine with that fact. Of course, that was a lie. Her sour mood was enough to betray the idea that she might find the prospect of being an old maid preferable to anything else.

Money would not be an issue for Philippa. With his younger brother dead her father had no one else to leave his fortune to. She was an heiress, and she would be fine monetarily. But money and land and a beautiful home were not the only things a woman needed. She needed companionship. She needed love. She told herself the love and friendship of her almost sister, Charlotte, was enough. Then just when she had almost convinced herself of that fact, a suitor would take Charlotte away from her and she would have to re-examine her wishes. And Lydia, who knew her mistress so well, would bring her another book to devour.

Philippa glanced up at Charlotte now, laughing with her latest suitor. Would this one be the one to marry her? Philippa wondered. It would be sad to lose her friend, but she did want Charlotte to be happy. Charlotte grinned at her over a cup of tea, and Philippa went back to reading her book.

Charlotte and her suitor were whispering with their heads together and giggling like two school children. Philippa smiled. Perhaps she would give them just a moment of privacy.

She remembered Simon's secret kisses in the garden with bittersweet fondness. She caught Charlotte's eye and said, "Would you like to walk a bit in the garden? The rain has stopped."

"We will accompany you, Miss Dunn," her suitor said picking up on Philippa's cue. It was easy to lose one another among the vegetation even though the summer foliage was not in full bloom.

Philippa took one path and as expected, Charlotte and her suitor — what was his name — William perhaps — took another. Philippa frowned. She should keep track of these things, but it seemed a different man called every day, and until Charlotte settled on one of them, Philippa couldn't think that it mattered.

ARIETTA RICHMOND, CATHERINE WINDSOR, ISABELLA THORNE, KATHERINE KEATS, KELLY ANNE BRUCE

Chapter Two

Philippa eyed one of the benches in the near garden. It was wet from the rain, and sitting would spoil her dress, so she tucked her novel under her arm and made her way for the covered gazebo. It was peaceful there, with the slacking rain dripping on the window sills and from the leaves of the trees which ran along the edge.

She tilted her head up towards the sky. The sun was peeking out, fat and orange above her, sending down warmth. It had been a week of thunderstorms, and this was the first time it hadn't poured all morning for some time. The world felt washed fresh and dripping. She was glad for the sun on her face and the fresh smell of the rain drenched earth.

Something was amiss however, there was something else there, in the garden, and it took Philippa a minute, and a few steps forward, away from the manor, before she located it.

Smoke. Someone was out in the garden. A man, and her father did not smoke a pipe. Could it be Charlotte's suitor? That would be horribly rude, she thought.

Philippa paused, her heart pounding within the confines of her chest. It was not uncommon for her father to have guests; of course, he was an important man after all, with many acquaintances, both purely social and from his work. Was her father out here in the garden? She thought not, but she may be wrong. Perhaps her father's guest wanted a bit of air. Philippa went out of her way to avoid people, for they always seemed to know her, and always seemed keen to speak about her behind her back, whether she was actually out of earshot did not seem to matter.

"I'm sorry Miss, allow me to put my out my pipe," a voice called. Philippa turned her head and saw him. He was simply right there, perched upon a bench that was only partially out of sight beside a bush, which had several pale green shoots just beginning to make themselves known. He stood at her appearance, as a gentleman should.

The soft sound of conversation told her that Charlotte and her suitor were not far behind, but right now, she could not think of chaperoning. She could only think of the man in front of her.

"No," Philippa said, shaking her head. "Please do not put it out on my account. I like the smell of it. Cherry, is it not?"

"It is," the man said, tapping out the tobacco beside the stone bench and then slipping the pipe into his breast pocket regardless. "But the smell permeates everything. It invades my hair and my clothing. Even my small clothes," he added, his voice dipping as though his words had traversed too far, across some invisible line drawn through the centre of good taste.

Perhaps he had crossed that line, but Philippa was no young girl at her coming out. She would not blush and giggle, or raise her hand to her lips or dab at her forehead in a show of feeling faint. She was not that girl, not any longer at least, if she ever had been. The man was expecting some reaction from her, perhaps he had been hoping for one, but she would not give it to him. She turned to face him long enough to make him an apology, and then she planned to retire, but he said nothing. He only looked at her.

"I am sorry for intruding," she said.

"Don't be," the man replied. "The garden is yours, Miss Dunn." He bent over her hand and kissed it. "It is I, who am intruding."

He held her hand longer than was polite, the smile refusing to fade from his face.

Philippa was very aware that she was not wearing gloves, sitting as she was previously. Gloves made turning the pages of her books difficult. His hands were inordinately warm as he squeezed her hand lightly with both of his.

"It is fortunate that you happened upon me Miss Dunn; it has been so long. I have not seen you in town."

Philippa hoped her own face contorted into something that could at least be mistaken for something resembling civility, though she couldn't be sure. She wasn't sure how she felt, with this man holding her hand, pressing his lips upon her bare skin. Apparently, he thought she should know him.

Philippa couldn't help but note how handsome he was. Tall and broad shouldered, he looked particularly striking. His jaw was strong and he wore a closely trimmed beard, the brunette hair on his chin matching that upon his head, but the later was streaked with grey. Like two white stripes, perfectly matched along both sides of his face, which reached from his temples through his sideburns.

There was something about the man that was undeniably familiar to her, but she could not place him. Blast, this was embarrassing.

"But I am invading the privacy of your stroll," he said with a bow and a smile.

"Yes," she said frowning as she tried to place his face from her brief time coming out time, before everything fell apart. "I mean, no. I don't mind. I am only chaperoning my young cousin and her suitor who are walking in the garden. I do not mind company."

Who was he? She felt certain she should know.

And he apparently, was familiar with her too, although he had the advantage, knowing whose house and garden he had frequented.

"Is the bench not wet?" she inquired gesturing where he had sat.

"No longer," he said with a smile and a gesture. "I have cleaned it for you with my trousers, if you will sit with me, or walk if you will."

"Oh," she said sitting.

"Miss Dunn," the man said, the handsome face beneath his beard breaking into a broad smile. "You do not remember me."

His eyes were green and shone like the sea at dawn as he sat beside her. He had caught her out, and she was mortified. It was only then that Philippa remembered the man, and her embarrassment escalated.

"Your Grace," she said standing immediately and slipping into a hasty curtsey. He was The Duke of Chesney, she remembered in a rush. His given name was Gregory Burrowes; he was quite a few years Philippa's senior, and he had been her former fiancé's best friend in childhood. Perhaps it was former best friend now, she thought with a bit of scorn.

The woman Simon had quite thoroughly kissed in that, oh so public, scandal years ago had been the heiress who was expected to marry The Duke of Chesney. The very man that stood in front of her!

It dawned on Philippa that finding one's best friend in a compromising embrace kissing your own intended bride may be bit more of a jolt than finding your friend kissing some nameless tart. She doubted that The Duke remained friends with Simon after such a scandal. She suddenly felt sorry for The Duke. It was a feeling she was unused to.

He chuckled at her discomfiture and then apologized.

"Oh do sit. It did not occur to me that you would not remember me. After all, we shared an acquaintance or two... and the embarrassment they caused.

"Yes," she said, as she sank back down, bonelessly, onto the bench. He did not bring up the embarrassment she had caused, and for that she was grateful. Hadn't he married not long after that dreadful affair? She could not remember.

Charlotte would know. She kept up with all the news of the *ton*, but Philippa let it slip by her. She felt completely adrift. Why could she remember figures on paper and characters in a play, but such gossip eluded her, even when it pertained to her.

Perhaps she had purposely forgotten the whole ordeal and all involved.

The Duke was still talking easily.

"I had business with your father this morning, and then snuck off for a pipe," the man said, sitting beside Philippa on the bench. He noticed the book in her lap, and asked, "What are you reading?"

"Oh," she said attempting to hide the offending volume in the inadequate folds of her skirt. It was too late. He saw.

"*The Memoirs of Emma Courtney*," he read. "Do you not find Mary Hays a bit... onerous for a maid?" he asked.

Onerous was not the word she would have chosen.

"I do not think my reading material is any of your business, Your Grace." She said, raising her chin a little.

"So your father is aware that you are reading about forbidden embraces during a thunderstorm?"

His teasing attitude annoyed her.

"The book is far more than that! Emma is an amazing woman who has overcome much. She does not let the fact that she is a woman stop her," she snapped, and then realized that she was digging herself in deeper. "You are no gentleman to tease me so. But, how would you…. Pray, how do you know the plot?"

"My wife was taken with such novels," he said. "Miss Hays, Maria Edgeworth and more. All filled with such passion — adultery, abortion, murder and madness."

"Your wife," she repeated stupidly. "The Duchess of Chesney, your wife."

The Duke smiled softly and shook his head to the side. "Yes. She loved them so. She died over two years ago; a fever."

"My condolences," Philippa said, her cheeks burning. "I did not know."

"And how could you have?" The Duke asked, attempting to drive the conversation away from his dead wife.

"You met with my father?" Philippa asked. She still had enough social sense in her head to remember how to tactfully allow a conversation to be steered from one subject to the next. Neither his dead wife, nor her choice of reading material, were subjects which she wanted to pursue.

"I did," the man said. "Always a pleasure to experience the sharp mind of Lord Montclair.

"It is regrettable that you no doubt had to experience my father's sharp tongue as well," Philippa said, and The Duke laughed.

"Your own tongue, Miss Dunn, is as sharp as ever," he said
to her. "I'd best be wary so as to not cut myself upon it.

"I suppose, then, you must keep yourself out of my mouth,"
she said without a thought.

He blinked at her as if startled and then laughed, his voice
booming and echoing off the stone pathway and tall bushes.

It was only then that Philippa realized how very
inappropriate her words had been, but after all, she had a
reputation to keep up, and he already knew the sort of novels
she was reading. There was no going back now. She met his eyes
baldly and refused to blush or look down, much like Emma, her
favourite heroine, who positively stalked the man she wished to
wed.

"I'm so glad to have seen you," The Duke said when he had
regained his general demeanour. "I would be grateful if you
would sup with me at my country home."

Philippa paused for a moment - as sharp as her tongue was,
she was not used to requests for her company.

"Surely you have someone you'd rather dine with," she said
softly.

"I do not," The Duke insisted. "I am in residence at my
country home, and the servants have nothing to do."

"That is surely an untruth," she said.

"I am hosting Lord Grafton; his father The Earl of Taftwater
passed recently, and I have offered my support to an old friend.
Well, that said, I do suppose James is The Lord Taftwater now.
It ill suits him."

The Duke shook his head.

"James is despondent. He and his father were very close. I'm sure some feminine company will cheer him."

Philippa had never thought of herself as cheering company.

"I had heard of The Lord Taftwater's passing," Philippa said. "Surely a kinder man has not walked this world."

"He was a blustery arse and we both know it, but it is good to see that closing yourself up in your library here has not entirely dulled your sense of civility."

"I would not speak ill of the dead," she said.

"Only the living." The Duke said lightly.

"Well, they are so much more able to return the favour." Philippa returned.

He chuckled again.

"I am so glad to have drawn you out of your library, Miss Dunn. You are a treat."

"My library?"

"I may have peeked into the parlour as I passed. The smoke was a way to steel myself to speak with you," the man said.

"Surely I'm not so repellent?"

"You don't understand," The Duke of Chesney said, shaking his head and taking up Philippa's naked hand once more. His own hands were soft, the fingers blunt and manicured, with only the barest of callouses along the palm, horse's reins, she surmised.

She remembered now that he was an avid horseman. She knew almost nothing else about him, except that he quite obviously liked novels as well as she. She blushed at the thought. She drew her musings from the touch of his fingers and back to the conversation at hand. He was speaking.

"You are quite the opposite of repellent, so much so that it made me nervous to speak to you as soon as I saw that you have not lost a drop of your radiance in the years since I last saw you."

"Radiance? Oh, you flatter me," Philippa said, and she felt her cheeks burn red. A blushing child, that's what this man had turned her into, with just a sentence. "Tell me, true," she said. "Did you even remember me before you spied me in the parlour?"

"I most certainly knew that Lord Montclair had a daughter."

"And you remembered my radiance?" she persisted. "Or perhaps my wit?"

"I did not," he said. "It was a pleasant surprise, but that does not make it less true."

"Flatterer," she accused.

"I hope I flatter you, Miss Dunn, enough that you will accept my invitation. I am sure that I can convince my young friend James to join us. The new Lord Taftwater would truly benefit from someone of your father's ward's temperament to cheer him."

"Ah, I see," Philippa said finally understanding "The invitation is for my cousin Charlotte then." It was expected but her heart sunk nonetheless.

"And for your radiant self," he said quickly as if sensing her melancholy. "I would rather no one else be to be my fellow... chaperone for the youngsters."

The Duke favoured her with a wry smile and Philippa smiled in spite of herself.

"We shall join you then, Your Grace" Philippa said, before she was aware of what she was saying, and before she could manage to stop herself. Afterwards she told herself it was because she could not deny Charlotte's chance at securing an Earl for her betrothed, and as for William... Williams... there were two of them she thought, both entirely too boorish for her radiant cousin. Yes, Charlotte was the one who was radiant.

ARIETTA RICHMOND, CATHERINE WINDSOR, ISABELLA THORNE, KATHERINE KEATS, KELLY ANNE BRUCE

Chapter Three

Supper was a simple if elegant affair, devoid of many rich creamy dishes due to the fasting season of Lent. There were still several small dishes of vegetables and seafood set on the table before them by a number of the servants. The Duke's country home was called Gladwell, and it sat on expansive grounds with a large lake near the rear, and the dining room had a large window which looked out at the water, showing the sun shining atop the still, glass-like surface.

"It is quite beautiful here, Your Grace," Philippa said, as the gentlemen re-joined the ladies after the meal. She looked out the window, admiring the view, while Charlotte, half a room away, tittered at Lord Taftwater.

"That it is," The Duke agreed with Philippa. He followed her gaze out to the lake. "I remember playing in that lake as a boy, the mud between my toes. There are a lot of good memories here. Have you ever visited previously?"

"Twice if I remember correctly. I was quite young."

When Philippa did not elaborate, the Duke changed the subject of conversation. He felt that speaking with Philippa was the same as being a ship's Captain steering between rocks rising from the water. You had to be swift and tactful to keep from running up onto the shoals.

"What have you been doing as of late?" The Duke asked as he sipped from his glass. "Have you been to the theatre? There is nothing but oratories there now, of course. Or have you seen the gardens at Vauxhall?"

"I should love to go to Vauxhall," Charlotte said as she and Lord Taftwater came near. "They say that the gardens are spectacular, decorated in a Chinese theme with pavilions and waterfalls, and oh, can you really see the fireworks from the cast iron bridge?"

"Perhaps when you are in Town," Lord Taftwater said. "We can take a boat over from Westminster."

"I am sure that there will be fireworks after Easter," the Duke added.

Charlotte clapped her hands delightedly. "I would love that."

"The gardens are in Kensington, on the south bank of the Thames," Taftwater explained, "and the boat ride is lovely. That is the best place to watch fireworks. We shall make a day of it, if your chaperone agrees."

"What say you, Miss Dunn?" the Duke inquired of Philippa.

"I do love gardens," she said. "I dare say, you saw my primary pastime when you met me again, Your Grace," Philippa said.

"I read mostly, and spend time in our own garden when strange men aren't there smoking."

Her smile took the edge off her words and he found himself smiling in return.

"Surely I do not qualify as a strange man," the Duke said.

"I suppose that much is true," Philippa allowed.

"Do you not go into Town?" James asked. "It is much the same as you will remember, I'm sure."

Philippa took a moment to answer. "I go to London only as often as it is necessary," she said finally. "More so now with Charlotte."

The young Earl did not push her further, and instead, pulled Charlotte aside to speak with her.

"What about the village," The Duke said at last. "I saw that the bakery was no longer there, in the square," he tried.

"It burnt down," Philippa said. "Two summers ago I think."

"That is horrible. I trust no one was hurt?"

"The baker's son died, but the whole town smelled of baking rolls for a week after, so it lessened the sting."

The corner of Philippa's devilish mouth curled upwards, and the Duke found himself fighting off his own smile, and when he couldn't he attempted to at least hold it there and allow it no further, a laugh at such a remark would surely be in poor taste.

"Surely not," the Duke said at last.

"No," she agreed. "He was pretty badly burnt and the townsfolk made jokes that he was too fat to remove the dough from the oven, but that was all. People are cruel are they not? The whole family moved to an uncle's place several towns over, and I think they still bake."

"I remember going there for the cinnamon rolls they made for breakfast. When we were not yet quite men, Simon and I bought them out. I think we ate close to twenty that morning."

The name of Philippa's one time fiancé, so carelessly thrown about in her presence, caused her to seize up. It felt as though she wasn't able to breathe, and her heart was nothing more than a lump of stone in her chest.

"I'm sorry," the Duke said quickly, realizing his mistake. He and Simon had been close friends for most of their childhood. His own intended was Simon's bride, the woman Philippa had seen him kissing. She wondered if the Duke felt any sense of loss from the woman Simon took from him, or if only his pride was hurt. The Duke stayed silent after that, knowing he had been foolish to mention Simon, but Philippa would not let it bother her. She forced herself to smile at him, and sipped her wine.

He watched her with tense eyes, his heart beating as though it were in his throat, instead of behind his breastbone. He was waiting for the explosion, waiting for her to rise from her chair, to yell, to cry as the *ton* had said she would.

She did none of those things. She simply patted her lips with her napkin and asked, "Did you remain friends with him?" They both knew she spoke of Simon.

"No," the Duke said without embellishment. "You?"

Philippa burst into laughter.

"No," she said, at last, "Gads, no," amazed that she was now able to laugh at Simon's betrayal.

Time truly did heal, if not all wounds, at least some of them. She smiled at the Duke.

"We've had a lovely time, Your Grace, but Charlotte and I must be going. I promised my father that we would not be late."

He nodded and called a servant. "Have the carriage brought around," he ordered.

"We will take you both home, and I hope that we will see you in Town."

"Oh Philippa, say yes," Charlotte urged as Lord Taftwater settled her cloak about her shoulders.

"I do not know," Philippa said. "My father abhors the extravagance of Town."

"With you chaperoning Miss Charlotte, need he come?" The Duke asked.

"Actually what he abhors is the expense of Town." Philippa explained.

"There will be nothing elaborate until after Easter," the Duke said. "Perhaps, in addition to Vauxhall, we can go to a mummer play? There are several."

"I don't think so," Philippa said. "Father only attends those invitations which he feels he cannot forgo without giving offence."

"I suppose I must host a Ball after Easter, then," The Duke said with a smile and Philippa felt her heart melting, "You may inform Lord Montclair that I will be very offended if he does not allow you and your sweet cousin to attend."

~~~~~

When the Duke returned home, he sat for a long time at the table, well after the food had been cleared away, but with a glass of wine brought at his request. He held the stem in his fingers, his eyes on the nearly black water outside. The moon reflected in the surface. Now and again a small turtle head would break the surface near the middle of the lake, sending circular rings of disturbance through the water.

Gregory finished his wine and then stood. He wondered how he could have been so foolish. He had meant nothing by mentioning Simon of course, he had simply been remembering a fond story, and Simon was in so many of his fond memories.

But Miss Dunn surely had no fond memories of Simon. She had made them of course, but he knew full well that she did not retain them. He needed to make things right. And he would do so.

Even after James had returned to his own home, Gregory could not keep his mind from Miss Dunn. She was different, enchanting in a strange way. Her wit was immeasurably quick and her company amusing. She was pretty, like a fragile bird, but at the same time, he sensed a wiry strength in her. He had to believe that she was kind, once you got beneath the chilly demeanour she presented to the world.
~~~~~

It seemed that she had covered herself in ice to insulate against hurt. He could certainly understand that, the *ton* could be cruel, and it would be harder still if she had once loved Simon. It seemed unlikely. Her father had, no doubt, arranged the match, like his own father had arranged his. He had not given Lady Margaret a second thought when he released her to Simon, other than that surely she could have broken the engagement without making such a scene.

Miss Philippa Dunn, on the other hand, had unfortunately succeeded in making much gossip. She had vulgarly shouted down her erstwhile fiancé. There was no greater sign of a hysterical woman, was there? She had discovered a grand betrayal, that much was true. He knew the feeling of betrayal himself.

He had had words with Simon too, though not quite so publicly. But for a woman to lose her composure so completely: Surely that was not the kind of woman the Duke needed concern himself with. Although, when he had mentioned Simon after dinner, while flustered, Philippa had acted with decorum, certainly not in the way that the *ton* gossip suggested she would. Honestly, he found that he rather enjoyed her wit, and her tendency to say whatever came to her mind.

He found himself thinking of her novels. He remembered sitting up in bed with his late wife, Janet, reading and giggling like two school children over the impossibilities of such books. He had never thought to recreate that feeling, and yet was it fair to even consider it? Philippa was a different woman. She was not Margaret. She was certainly not Janet.

Since his Janet had died, The Duke had thought of women little. He had the same urges that all men had, of course, but that was not enough to shake him from his dreary days and nights.

After Margaret's betrayal, his mind had been singularly centred upon marrying and producing an heir. Then he had found Janet. She had been sweetness itself - a friend and easy companion. He and Janet had enjoyed only a few short years together, before he lost her too. When she died, he threw himself into his work at home, in Parliament, and here in the country. He had much to keep his mind busy, but the truth was that he still needed an heir. Now, the thought of taking a girl of Charlotte's age to his bed was distasteful. She, like so many of the debutantes available, was barely more than a child. What could he do? Marry a widow? All of those women who were available held no interest for him.

Until that day in the garden, when Miss Philippa Dunn had come swooping back into his life, supplying him with a taste of yearning that he had not felt in some time. Yes, he realized, the thought of making an heir with the irascible Miss Dunn was something that he could consider as not just a duty. No; when he considered Miss Dunn a rush of desire shot through him.

His blood ran hot at the thought of it. He had once believed Margaret had wrung all such notions of passion out of him with her betrayal. Then, when Janet died, he had sworn that he would not give his heart again. At least, he thought, Miss Dunn would not betray him. No she'd had a taste of that bitterness, along with himself, through Margaret and Simon. Philippa would speak her mind. She may be sharp, but she would not betray him.

He called to his butler. "Pen a letter."

"Of course, Your Grace. To whom?" The man replied

"To Berkley, at the London house. Tell him I am planning a Ball, just after Easter. Make preparations."

"Very good, Sir"

"And now, I am to bed."

"Are you to return to London on the morrow, Sir?"

He hesitated. There was Parliament. He should return. Yet he didn't want to leave.

"On the day after," he said. He would spend one more day with Miss Dunn and her father, Lord Montclair. He should, of course, warn the man that he expected his family at the Easter Ball.

~~~~~

Two weeks later, James, and the Duke were playing cards at one of the gaming clubs in London. The clientele was sparse at this time of the night.

"What is going through your mind, pray tell?" the new Earl of Taftwater asked his friend.

The Duke just smiled and shook his head.

James set his cards face down, waiting for a reply.

Gregory sighed.

"Miss Philippa Dunn," he said, finally.
~~~~~

"That one?" James asked, his lips already parting in a smile. "The chaperone?"

"She is more than that."

"And you're thinking of her still?" James chuckled.

"If I am, it is no reason for your mirth," the Duke replied dryly.

"But it is indeed," James countered. "She is… hysterical. She dressed down Simon Goldthwaite like a sailor. Everyone remembers, although I think even some of the matrons would have had to research her words." He sipped his wine, grinning at the memory. "I was surprised that her father chose to allow her to chaperone her young cousin. In fact I'm surprised her father did not send her to bedlam."

"Bedlam?" The Duke asked, incredulous. "Surely you jest, Grafton… Blast… Taftwater. I shall never get used to calling you so."

"Don't act so surprised, and don't change the subject. You cannot argue that she is touched. Why for any Lady to speak so…"

"I've spoken so. So have you."

"But it is not in the temperament of a Lady to even know such words, much less to speak them aloud. It is unnatural."

The Duke smiled down into his drink, thinking that the young Earl had much to learn about women.

"You are attracted to her," James said, disbelieving. "She is terribly dull. She hardly ever leaves her home."

"And you think that makes her dull?"

"Doesn't it?"

The Duke shrugged.

"No doubt she stays private because of the ridicule of the *ton* and black mark upon her. I would imagine it pains her," Gregory sipped his brandy and tossed his hand of cards aside.

"True enough," James said. "I am just grateful that she haunts her own manor and not mine."

"And yet you met her cousin," the Duke said. "It appeared you got on rather well with the chit."

James laughed as he took another card.

"The cousin is not the chaperone."

"And the chaperone may not be the chaperone," the Duke replied.

"What on earth do you mean?"

"I mean that she is more than meets the eye, my friend"

"I would never have guessed."

"Guessed at what?"

"That a hysterical woman would be the one to take your interest once more. You do know how to choose them."

James shook his head.

"She is not hysterical," the Duke replied coolly.

"This hand is awful," James complained as he threw it in and leaned back in his chair, "another drink?"

Gregory raised his glass, indicating the barely touched brandy and shook his head. James took another drink from a servant and looked at his friend, the card game forgotten.

"How long has it been since your wife passed?"

"Over two years," the Duke replied.

"A tragedy that was," James said, nodding.

Gregory nodded in agreement. He had heard such things often and agreed with them each time. They meant nothing, just courtesy. Janet had been a woman like no other: beautiful and smart – loving and strong. She had made his life better by decades, though she was only in it for a short time. She was not his one true love – Gregory was not even sure he believed in such things – but she was more than his wife. She had been his friend.

They had met later in life than most couples, he had been nearly thirty, and she was twenty-two. She had been promised to a man before him, but the man had fallen from his horse during a hunt and broken his neck. She had refused to marry another, and her father, who doted on his only daughter, had refused to make her.

That had changed when she met Gregory. They struck up a friendship, more than a year after the horrible ordeal with Simon and Margaret. Strangely, she was Margaret's friend, and she had helped him to understand what before he had called 'the unfathomable foibles of women'.

He remembered their first conversation, where she drank alongside him and beat him at cards.

She had reminded him that Margaret had never loved him. Never cared for him at all, or even thought of him as a person. He understood that now. They were only betrothed because of their lands and titles. They weren't even friends, and when it became clear that Margaret loved another, it seemed natural, to him at least, to break off the engagement.

"Why did she not just break the engagement quietly," he had said. "She could have done that."

"Her father would not think so," Janet had said, and he had, at last, understood the predicament in which Lady Margaret must have found herself. He wished that she could have come to him, to explain. She need not have publically embarrassed him, but he also finally understood that Simon and Margaret loved one another. Both men and women do foolish things for love, he thought. Had Philippa loved Simon, he wondered? If so, he understood her fury and forgave her the outburst of so long ago.

He and Janet had continued their friendship, and they were married within a year of their first meeting. They had hoped for an heir before their first anniversary, surely by their second. But it was not to be, and by their third, Janet was dead.

Her death had crushed Gregory, not because he loved her desperately, although he supposed he did love her after a fashion. She was the only person in his life who did not take him too seriously. She did not let him intimidate her. She did not back down to his occasional gruffness. Instead, she told him when he was being thoughtless, and supported him when he needed her. She let him be himself.

She was a good woman, and he just could not make himself take to wife a silly ninny who didn't have the sense of a gnat.

"I don't mean to jest about Miss Dunn," James went on. "Anything to get you interested in courtship is good. You are too serious my friend. You need some frivolity."

"That's not what this is," The Duke replied, shaking his head softly.

"Is it not?" James asked.

Gregory had no answer. He found himself comparing Janet and Philippa and that was not fair to the living woman. He needed to learn about who Philippa was, without thinking of Janet.

Miss Dunn was her own self – without comparison.

<center>~~~~~</center>

Chapter Four

For her part, Philippa Dunn had spent a lot of the previous evenings thinking of the Duke of Chesney. It was with a mixture of pain, sorrow, and interest that she thought of the man, even as she lay in bed, staring at the hanging curtains that surrounded it.

In the morning she woke with a start and a gasp. A nightmare had gripped her in her slumber, but as she tried to recall what exactly she had been dreaming of, the memory left her, dissipating as it fell from her mind like water from an overturned jug. She knew Simon had been involved. When her dreams turned sour, he almost always was.

She swung her legs over the side of her bed and sat like that for a moment, before calling for a bath to be drawn. She soaked in the steaming water from some time, and then she washed. Once the water had cooled, while Lydia helped her tie her corset, there was a knock at her door.

"Enter," she called.

Philippa knew it could only be one person, for her father never visited her in her chamber, but Charlotte often did. And indeed, her young cousin opened the door and strode in moments later, bringing in a draft of cool air before shutting the door behind her.

"I wanted to speak with you after dinner last night, but you had retired early," the girl said, as she settled herself on the settee in the dressing room, ready for a long talk.

"I did," Philippa said, lifting her arms above her head as Lydia pulled a gown of soft blue with white trim and lace over her head. "I did not feel well."

"Dorothy told me that the Duke has called," Charlotte said, with a smile plastered across her face.

"Dorothy should best learn to hold her tongue, lest she find herself out of work," Philippa replied sharply.

Dorothy was an old woman who worked very little, in truth, but her father had employed her for many years. Both Charlotte and Philippa herself knew that the man would never see her go. As much as he paid little attention to his daughter and niece, he was attentive to the servants, especially the women.

"Are you going to see him?" Charlotte asked.

"Who?"

"Do not be dense, cousin - the Duke, of course."

"I have seen him," Philippa said cryptically, and ended at that. Charlotte did not push further, though it was evident that she wanted to. Still, she bit her tongue, and Philippa was happy for that.

"I had the most wonderful morning," Charlotte said, without being prompted. Philippa came and sat on the small chair in front of her dressing table, watching Charlotte pull her heeled boots on through the mirror.

"Ah, so that is why you spoke of Dorothy," Philippa teased. "Did she sleep in the chair and give you a measure of privacy?"

"Dorothy was a perfect peach," Charlotte said with a smile.

"And which of your charming suitors came by to collect you this morning? Frederick, whose sister is Evelyn, correct?"

"Yes. Frederick," the young girl said.

"He is the one with ginger hair?"

"No, that is Shelby. Fredrick has brown hair."

"With green eyes?"

Charlotte sighed dramatically.

"No, that is William. One of the Williams."

"I see."

"Frederick came and took me to the lake. He rowed us out to that island there, and we picnicked. He is so sadly short of funds."

"I see."

"He seemed most anxious to get back to London."

"I see."

"And he doesn't seem to get on well with his sister," Charlotte mused. "She is somewhat of a shrew."

Philippa gave her a look.

"Oh not as shrewish as you, dear cousin," she teased. "You have the honour of holding that title for all time, or at least the foreseeable future."

"I see," Philippa said dryly.

"Is that all you can say?" Charlotte pouted. "I see? I see this, I see that."

"I see," Philippa taunted."

Charlotte sighed and stood up.

"I won't bore you with the details of my day any longer."

Philippa felt bad; a stinging regret that Charlotte so often caused to rear up within her.

"I'm sorry my sweet girl, please tell me all about Fredrick and his shrewish sister and this island."

Charlotte couldn't tell if Philippa was being genuine, so she stood for a moment, searching the woman's eyes and face for signs of another joke, but when she found none, she sat once more and shared the recollection of her day.

"And tomorrow is... William?" Philippa inquired.

"Shelby."

"Oh, pray tell me we are not going to eat," Philippa said in a long suffering voice. "He has the worst table manners. The servants were cleaning up what fell from his lips for days."

"If I married him I should have to get a lap dog, like a French girl, to eat the scraps," Charlotte mused.

"Perish the thought. You should strike Shelby from your list."

"But he is ever so rich," Charlotte said.

"So is the Earl," Philippa prompted.

"James?" Charlotte said.

"The very same."

"I like him," Charlotte said. "But he is so sad. I cannot bear it."

"His father passed away recently. Do you not remember the rivers of tears you cried for your dear parents? He will get past his sadness. It is only natural. It shows that he loves deeply and true. Has he called?"

Charlotte shook her head.

"No. He has not."

~~~~~

The next morning, Philippa broke her fast with Charlotte and her father, and afterwards retired to the garden with a book. She sat with her back to the great stone fountain, and held the book open with one hand in her lap.

The early morning spring air was a bit chilly. She pulled her shawl close as a breeze caused her to shiver.

"There is going to be a bit of rain," a voice called, "Perhaps a thunderstorm."
~~~~~

Philippa started as she looked up from her reading to see The Duke of Chesney approaching. She stood quickly, tucked her book under her arm and curtseyed to him, before replying. "Certainly not, Your Grace."

"You do not think we are in for a thunderstorm?"

"No. It will pass," she said with confidence. "See, the wind is blowing away the clouds." She gestured as the sun peeked through the clouds.

"I will bow to your expertise," he said after kissing her hand. "Another book?"

"Indeed," Philippa said.

"Poetry?"

Philippa grinned and held the book up. "Mathematics."

"Mathematics?" the Duke laughed. He shook his head slowly from side to side. "You are surprising."

"I cannot be interested in maths?"

"You can certainly. Most women are not."

"Most women are rattle-brained ninnies," Philippa said. "Now, to what do I owe the pleasure?"

"I was thinking about you, and I wanted to know if you would like to accompany me today, to my holdings."

"Your holdings."

"It is really but a farm. The true lands are north of London."

"You have a farm nearby?"

"Of sorts - a small property which my mother owned, and which is now mine. I don't do much with it day to day, I have a good man who lives there. He sees it through."

"What do you grow?"

The Duke laughed.

"I don't know."

"You don't know what you grow on your own farm?"

"It's been close to five years since I've been there. There is a stable there as well, I was intending on riding for the afternoon, not helping with the current crop."

"I love to ride," Philippa said.

"Do you?"

"I do."

"Then you must join me," the man requested. Philippa gave it a little thought, and then nodded.

"I shall then," she said.

She considered asking Charlotte to come, or perhaps Lydia, but neither were very fond of horses and riding. Of course, she could coerce either of them into chaperoning her, but she was Charlotte's chaperone, not the other way around. Her father was not at home to object, though she doubted that he would raise an eyebrow at her going with the Duke, no matter how irregular it was, even were he here. Anyway, he was concerned with Charlotte, not with her. She was no blushing flower. Surely she did not need a chaperone, when she was one herself!

It was a longer trip than she expected, and by the time the carriage stopped at the end of a long path, just outside a large white farmhouse, Philippa's derriere was sore from the coach jostling over the rutted road. The Duke helped her down from the carriage, and led her to the farmhouse. Inside, she was introduced to Mr. Stephens, who served them water with slices of lemon dropped into the glass, and a brief repast; then led them out to the stables, situated at the rear of the house and some distance away.

Mr. Stephens handed them off to a young man named Theodore, the head groom. He had already been working on saddling up two horses, and he helped Philippa to mount hers. She settled on to the side-saddle on a young mare, who had large kind eyes. She was a dark chocolate brown. The only other colour on the horse was a snip of white at the tip of her nose. Solid black booted her legs and her mane and tail were also glossy black.

"I bought her for Janet," The Duke said as he mounted his own bay. "I hope you don't mind. The side-saddle fits her best, and she's a gentle thing."

"Not at all," Philippa said.

The Duke led the way from the stables, thanking the boy as he went. They started at a leisurely pace, the animals stepping lightly side by side.

"It is beautiful here," Philippa said, as they made their way through a field of sprouting greenery, heading towards a coppice of trees.

"It is," the Duke agreed as they followed the path. "I should come here more often."

"You should," Philippa said with a smile.

The Duke didn't reply to that, he found himself wondering, once again, just what the woman meant to him. He couldn't quite put a finger on how she made him feel. He was nervous around her, but simultaneously at ease. It was a strange feeling, his emotions at odds with nothing but themselves.

"My father taught me to ride," the Duke said, turning in the saddle to look at her, "he always loved horses."

"My father does not ride," Philippa said. "Well, not horses at any rate," she continued under her breath.

"Not horses? Pray tell, what does he ride otherwise?"

"That is between him and the female members of the staff," Philippa teased, always ready with a bawdy comment, no matter who was listening. She chuckled when she saw the Duke let his mouth fall open. "Are you shocked?" she asked. "I thought I was well past shocking anyone."

"Riding with you is like being at the card table with my male friends," he said.

"Do you then see me as a male, Your Grace?" she asked, as he reined in where the trail widened to allow her to walk her horse side by side with his.

Must she always put him off balance?

"Of course not," he said quickly

"Am I your friend then?" She asked with another teasing smile.

"Does a man have friends like you?"

"Like me?"

"A woman."

"A man can do what he wants, and have what he wants, unlike us poor women, who must suffer under every man's whim."

"I wouldn't go that far," The Duke said with a shrug. He led into a narrow trail through a bit of vegetation.

"A Duke at least may have his way," Philippa said.

Gregory laughed.

"I am fortunate," he said. "But I find that even being a Duke does not mean I have all I desire."

"What is it that the Duke desires?"

He pulled his horse abreast with hers again and considered, looking at her with intense scrutiny. At last he looked away and sighed. After another long moment he spoke.

"What about mathematics? Did your father provide that love?"

Philippa nodded and let him change the subject.

"He is good with numbers, but I dare say I surpassed his expertise when I was quite a young woman."

"You are wholly singular then," the Duke remarked.

"Am I?"

The Duke laughed as he brought his horse to a stop. They were at a crossroads, where the path widened again.

Philippa urged her horse into a trot, and started up the hill ahead of him. Her mare was anxious to go, so she let her. When the Duke brought his horse to her side, she gave her mare her head, and the willing girl pushed onward, into the long comfortable strides of a ground covering canter, anxious to make it to the top of the rise. Once atop the knoll, Philippa pulled her mare up and paused to wait for the Duke.

Philippa had watched as he brought his horse level with hers. She had noticed several nasty scars on his horse, which was obviously older than her own mount. The horse looked as if he had been beaten, and the Duke certainly did not seem the type of man to abuse his mounts.

"The poor creature. Was he injured?"

The Duke looked to her, patting the horse's neck absent mindedly. He nodded finally. "Yes," he said simply.

Philippa was intrigued, and no matter what etiquette said, she found herself curious.

"How? He has so many scars."

She was afraid that he wouldn't answer, but he did not seem offended."

"The stupidity of others," he said with a grim smile, and that smile alone was enough to make Philippa think twice about continuing her inquiry. She let the matter drop and enjoyed the ride. The sun was filtering through the scattered trees, casting shadows, as the breeze blew lightly.

"It seems the stupidity of others is often the cause of distress," she said.

"Yes," he agreed

They had entered the forest by then, the sparse shade of the springtime trees working wonders against the warm air. They came to a brook swollen from the northern thaw and followed alongside, small silver fish in the shallow stream darting in and out of the sunlight and shadows which fell upon the water. A bush nearby rustled, and a pheasant flew up into the path of the horses. Her mare startled, but his gelding stayed solid. It took Philippa a moment to regain control of the mare and she was nearly unseated, but the Duke was there beside her, settling the animal.

"A bit further," the Duke said, surprising Philippa, who had no idea that he had a specific destination in mind.

The brook curved and so did their path, and then they were out of the forest and Philippa smiled. The brook broadened just then, and they stopped their horses. There was a sandy ring next to the water, a minute beach made up of tiny smooth pebbles. The Duke helped Philippa to the ground and tethered their horses. He sat down slowly, and then pulled the boot from his right foot and then his left. "Your turn," he said.

"To?"

"Take your shoes off. Let's wade in the water."

"You expect me to take off my stockings. Are you mad?"

"And here I thought you were adventurous."

"There is a difference between adventure and fool-hardiness."

"Emma took off her stockings," he said.

Philippa blushed crimson. She remembered the scene in the book he was speaking of, and it did not include a stream. "She did not!"

"Maybe it was one of Clair Tomalin's heroines," he said thoughtfully.

"I do not know of her."

"Ah, I see a prospect of a gift."

"You cannot tell my father," she said.

"My lips are sealed," he said, which drew her eyes to his lips. She stood quite still, thinking that this ride may not have been the best idea. She licked her lips. "Clair Tomalin?" she questioned.

"Ah, she did things that spoke of much more impropriety."

"Than showing her ankles? The hoyden!"

"Truly."

Her heart was racing. It was one thing to read of scandalous acts and quite another to be involved in one.

"I am not Emma," she said softly, hoping that she had not misled him. She was suddenly aware of their complete privacy and his very maleness. Perhaps she should have brought a chaperone after all.

"Tell me, do you not imagine yourself as Emma? She was such a strong woman — like you, Philippa."

Her name rolled off of his tongue. It sounded so perfect there.

"I have not given your permission to use my given name," she whispered, thinking that, positively, she did need a chaperone.

"Very well, Miss Dunn," he said. "Will you come wading in the water with me?" he held out a hand. She blushed and looked at the water. She considered what it would take to bare her legs to the ankles and shook her head. "I fear, I must abstain," she said.

"It is Sunday, a day of more relaxed rules, even in Lent"

"But there are... things in the water," Philippa said, her voice alarmed.

"Only fish. Fish are allowed." He said with a laugh

She shook her head.

"Don't tell me you are afraid of fish."

"Not afraid," Philippa corrected. "Disgusted by."

Gregory laughed.

"Have you never eaten fish?"

"When I eat fish they do not nibble on my skin."

"These fish don't nibble on your skin," the Duke laughed again. "You are creating scenarios in your mind that simply will not happen."

"What will not happen?" she asked.

"Nibbling," he said.

She turned away, blushing again.

"When you get nibbled, please do not come to me for sympathy."

"I don't think I would come to you for sympathy no matter what," The Duke said, instantly regretting it as soon as he had spoken, hoping that the remark was not as biting as it sounded to his own ear. If Philippa was offended, she played it off well, smiling as she spoke.

"That is for the best, I would imagine. I am not a sympathetic woman."

"No. But you are an adventurous one I think," the Duke said, with a wry smile.

Philippa did not answer right away. She thought about all that he had said on the ride out. She thought on all that she knew of this man. He was not a cruel man. He was caring and honest. In fact, he came the closest she had ever known to the heroes of her novels. Had she not wished, in her mind, to be adventurous like the heroines?

She took her boots off, but she made him turn away so that she could peel down her stockings. Philippa held her skirts up in her hand as she waded into the cool water after The Duke of Chesney, and he gained a glimpse of her pretty bare feet.

She gasped as the cold water shocked her.

"Oh, the rocks are slippery," she said as he steadied her.

"They do nibble at you!" Philippa shrieked as she felt the tiny silver fish brush at her ankles.

The Duke of Chesney laughed and held her hand.

"I am undoubtedly more delectable than you are, so perhaps if I stand close to you they will feast upon me instead," the man said moving closer.

Philippa felt her heart pound in her chest. Her head felt light, dizzy. The Duke was standing so near to her, that she could reach out and wrap her arms around him if she wanted to.

She could smell the spiced scent of him. Cherry pipe tobacco and something else, musky and sweet, that distinctive male scent that was just him. The warmth of his hand in hers was intoxicating. She closed her eyes for a moment, and thought about what it would be like to wrap her arms fully around him, to pull him close.

She could close her eyes, he would close his. He would kiss her. She would allow him. If he attempted to do more... what would she do? A shaft of heat rushed through her at the thought and she realized, once again, that she should not have gone riding with him, but the time was oh, so sweet.

She opened her eyes and looked at him. He smiled. He was so close. He leaned in and pressed his lips to hers and she kissed him back, her eyes fluttering closed again. His body pressed against hers, his one hand still on her hip, the other pressing near her shoulder, tantalizingly close to the top of her breasts.

She gripped her skirts tightly to keep them from the water, or perhaps it was because she was at a loss for what to do with her hands. She wanted to touch him.

The Duke broke the kiss.

The taste of him was still in her mouth. She wanted more. She wanted to have what she had imagined. She stared at him open mouthed and dewy eyed.

"I'm sorry," he told her. "I forgot myself."

"No," Philippa said simply. She looked to him, and could see the conflict in his eyes. She thought that she knew what he was thinking. Her breath came in little gasps and she was very aware of the heat of his hands contrasting with the cold water at her feet.

"We should go back," he said.

She nodded. The Duke opened his mouth as if to say something more, but then he shut it. He turned from Philippa and made his way back to the shore, leaving her, in a most ungentlemanly way, to make her way along the slippery rocks by herself.

He busied himself with pulling his boots on, keeping his back turned as she followed and did the same. They rode back in silence, and when they reached the stable, he was all that was proper as he handed her into the carriage.

~~~~~
~~~~~

ARIETTA RICHMOND, CATHERINE WINDSOR, ISABELLA THORNE, KATHERINE KEATS, KELLY ANNE BRUCE

Chapter Five

"I think I love her," the Duke said to his friend, as they sat at the breakfast table.

Taftwater made a rude sound as he choked upon the steaming coffee he had been sipping.

"No, please..." he began.

"Stop it," the Duke commanded, and his voice was so stern that James knew it was not the time for jesting.

"You love Miss Philippa Dunn, the shrew extraordinaire?" he asked in disbelief.

"She takes up the majority of my thoughts, and has since I spoke with her in her garden. Then last week when we went riding ..." the Duke's voice trailed off as he remembered.

"I thought that was over?" James asked. "After the trip to your farm, you haven't seen her, have you?"

"I kissed her there. Standing bare-footed in the stream."

"You kissed her?"

Gregory sighed and set his own coffee cup down upon the saucer.

"Please don't merely repeat what I tell you; the conversation will be more taxing than I can deal with if you do not deign to hold up your end of it."

"I'm just surprised," James countered. "So you kissed her?"

"I wanted to make love to her, there on the bank of that stream," Gregory confessed.

"No one is beating down the door to marry her," James replied. "And her father is only a minor noble who does not care two figs for her. You can set her up in Town..."

The Duke shook his head.

"No. I will not take her as my mistress."

"Why not?"

"I kissed her, and... it felt like... a betrayal."

"Of your late wife?"

"No. Of Philippa herself, because I keep comparing her to Janet."

"The Duchess is..." James said, unsure of how to finish the thought in words.

"Dead," Gregory said simply. "I know it."

"Miss Dunn is... alive," James said.

Gregory laughed. "Is that the only kind word you can think to say about the woman? She is alive."

"What would you have me say?" James shook his head. "Have you forgotten how cruel the *ton* can be?'

"I only think, she has become dear to me," Gregory said.

"She is hysterical. She is a known shrew. She is strange; she reads mathematics books…"

"That is not all she reads," the Duke interrupted.

But James continued undaunted.

"She is a bluestocking. She is crass, and rude, and forsakes society."

"All true," the Duke agreed.

"Well then, you do know what the *ton* thinks and says," James joked, and both men took the opportunity to laugh.

"I have never given much thought to what others think." He smiled at his friend. "She makes me happy."

"Then be with her, my friend."

"It's not that simple," Gregory said.

"It seems as though it could be," James replied.

The Duke fell silent, and they finished breakfast like that. He wondered if that was true. He wondered if it could all be so simple.

"None of that matters," James said finally, after lowering his gaze and finding the words in his coffee cup.

"What?" The Duke asked.

"What Miss Dunn is and what she not. Life is fleeting. Do not waste your happiness. If she makes you feel… better. Then have her."

"Are we talking about me or you?" Gregory asked. "What of Miss Charlotte?"

James shrugged.

"She is surrounded by other men."

"Do you want her?"

"I do, Chesney, but it is so soon after my father's death. She will be snapped up and betrothed before I am ready."

"Tell her so. You are an Earl. You are rich. You are worth waiting for."

"Shelby Eglinton is also rich."

"Eglinton is a pig," The Duke said. "And he has no title. She will have you before him."

"Thank you for your vote of confidence," James said. "I am better than Eglinton."

"You are."

"I do not know if she is right. Yes, Charlotte makes me happy, but she is so young."

"You are young," Gregory protested.

"That is not what I mean. She sees the world with such joy. I fear that I am just looking for a diversion to distract me from my father's death. And Charlotte is no diversion. She is a true Lady."

"And what about your mother? What does she say?"

"She hasn't met Charlotte."

"Perhaps she should," the Duke offered. "You mother is a sensible woman."

James snorted into his cup.

$$\sim\sim\sim\sim\sim$$

After breakfast the Duke had the carriage prepared and went to the Montclair manor. When he arrived, he asked to speak to Lord Montclair, all the while finding his courage waning and his mind racing for an alternative reason for being there.

He shook off the feeling. He was a Duke asking for leave to call upon the man's daughter. Montclair should be ecstatic. He had no cause for nerves. He was not a green lad as he had been the last time he had made such a request. A manservant alerted the Duke to the fact that Lord Montclair had gone to London, and was not due back for some days.

"I see," Gregory said. "Another time then."

"Very well, Your Grace" the servant said. Gregory had turned to leave when he heard her voice.

"Your Grace", she said simply, and he turned back as she curtseyed. She was standing in the doorway, looking like a fragile flower in a gown of light yellow. Her hair was elegantly piled upon her head and her dress floated about her, like petals in the sun.

"You look magnificent," the Duke of Chesney said. All he could think of was her standing in the stream, her lips parted under his.

"My thanks," she said. "I thought perhaps you had gone back to your main estate," she added.

"Not as of yet," The Duke said. "I would not leave without saying goodbye."

"I thought you had," the woman said, her voice icy.

"You are going out?"

"I am chaperoning my sweet cousin as she attends a soiree today."

"And who is chaperoning you?" Gregory asked, quick on his feet.

"Are you offering?"

"I am."

"Then the job is yours. Otherwise I would sit silently, as those of the *ton* who come into contact with me think me more a leper than a person."

Gregory smiled at her directness.

"Whose soiree?" he asked, thinking back to the stack of cards and announcements that invited him to various events, even during Lent.

"Wickham's," Philippa said. "I am sure that they would be honoured by your presence, Your Grace. They are but merchants in the town and would not presume upon your time."

~~~~~

When Charlotte entered the room, the Duke was momentarily cowed by the young woman's beauty. He could see why his friend James was taken with her. She was golden haired with a somewhat fairy quality in her crème dress. He bowed and kissed her hand, feeling that he was holding a bit of a moonbeam. She was the complete opposite of her earthy cousin. He helped both women into the carriage. They exchanged pleasantries as they travelled.

Philippa made him feel at ease, The Duke reflected on the fact that he had married the last woman to make him feel so comfortable. Spending time with Janet had done the same to him. He was a strong man, well born, and important. He went into almost every situation proud and sure of himself, but Philippa made him feel so much more – both stronger and weaker at the same time. He was not just attracted to her; he really was in love with her.

There were a number of tables set up in the Wickham's beautiful garden. The soiree was well populated and the Duke stood with the two women, and the young man who was paying court to Miss Charlotte, a son of a prominent business man in town. A Mr. William Durky, who didn't even have a minor title, but was a businessman of some account, or at least his father was. Miss Charlotte played her role well, laughing at any middling joke the man told, and listening to the stories of his father's numbingly dull business with apparent interest and rapt attention, as the guests and the musicians entered.
~~~~~

The Duke thought that his friend James would have been much better company for the woman and used every opportunity to tell her so. Besides, if James was courting Miss Charlotte it would be so much easier for him to visit Philippa.

The Duke watched as others filtered into the musicale, realizing that some were to be left standing in the entrance hall, so great was the crush. He had no idea that there were so many social upstarts in the area. The Cavish family then arrived at Wickham House, and the Duke found himself in the company of Lady Cavish, an elderly Baroness who was interested in telling The Duke all about her daughter Penelope. Presently, Miss Penelope was introduced, along with Miss Barrott, Miss Tolfish, and Miss Lovejoy, all equally unremarkable.

Miss Caro edged in, pushed by her chaperone, and was rather insistent upon telling him how she loved pianoforte pieces and how the current head musician was simply superb. She had heard him play in London, she explained, as she leaned in close to the Duke.

"Then perhaps we should listen to them play," Philippa said rather tartly.

The Duke smiled at her.

As Miss Caro continued her ceaseless stream of conversation about the musicians, Philippa sighed and thought. It was perhaps not the best idea to have arrived at the soiree with a member of the Peerage. The man seemed to have outshone the musicians and the repast. To find herself in such a place of prominence made Philippa feel ill at ease.

She much preferred to blend into the background, but that was not possible beside the Duke. Even as Charlotte's chaperone, with the Duke at her side, she was clearly the centre of attention.

Glancing right, she recognized their hostess, Mrs. Wickham who was staring at her, or perhaps she was staring at the Duke. At any rate, Philippa's heart rate inexplicably picked up. She hoped that she would manage to speak to the woman without causing some new gaffe. At that moment, Miss Caro seemed to come to the end of her treatise on the musicians, and the Duke caught Philippa's hand and placed it on his arm, expertly excusing them with the comment that they must greet their hostess.

He gave Miss Caro a quick smile as he began to lead Philippa towards Mrs. Wickham, and another group of acquaintances.

"Good evening, Mrs. Wickham," Philippa said, with a smile and a curtsey. "What a lovely gathering."

"Thank you for inviting us," Charlotte added, while Mrs. Wickham tittered over the Duke.

After much too long a time for pleasant conversation, the musicians struck up their piece and the crowd settled to listen. Philippa was never an accomplished pianist, but even she could appreciate the beauty of the music, and of course, the Duke's arm beneath her hand.

After the Duke saw the two women back to their home at the end of the soiree, he found himself still not ready to part company with Philippa.

"We could go for a walk," he said, motioning to the gardens around them. Evening was coming on, and the horizon was streaked with purple and pink clouds, darkening the sky.

"We could," Philippa nodded, and turned to Charlotte, who tactfully thanked the Duke for accompanying them, while he bowed to her and kissed her hand. She then politely managed to say her goodnight and slip inside, leaving Philippa alone with the Duke.

The Duke offered Philippa his arm, which she took. They went around the side of the manor and through the grounds.

"When will you be going back to London?" Philippa asked.

"I do not know when I shall leave, but I won't do so without saying goodbye," The Duke said.

"I'm glad."

They walked for a moment or two longer.

"Did you enjoy the soiree?" he asked.

"I did. I would like to visit the stream again," Philippa said abruptly. "It was beautiful." She felt a hot blush colour her face.

"You are beautiful."

"I'm not," she insisted.

"Who has convinced you that you are not beautiful?" The Duke asked. "He should surely be whipped."

"My father says that I am not what gentlemen want in a woman."

"He is wrong," the Duke insisted. He turned her to face him. "Do you believe me?"

"Perhaps he meant that I am not what men want in a wife."

"Again, he is wrong."

They walked along in silence for several moments.

"It is not always about what the man wants," the Duke said at last. "You should consider what you want, Miss Dunn. You are a bright woman. I can see that. What do you want?"

She stopped and looked at him for a moment, and then smiled. He had asked… "I would like it very much if you would kiss me again," she said, rather forwardly.

"I would like it as well, but I am not sure that it is the best course of action," the Duke said truthfully.

"And why would it not be?"

"Because… you are not Emma," the Duke said softly.

"This makes me think very highly of you," she retorted.

"I think highly of you as well," the Duke said with all seriousness.

"Do you?" she asked.

"I do." the Duke confirmed, his eyes soft upon her. They had stopped walking and stood suspended. With the pause in the conversation, Gregory thought that he ought to kiss her again.

However, her face was so screwed up with a frown, he was sure that he had vexed the woman, perhaps he should not kiss her after all. When she spoke, her voice was even and unemotional.

"I am fond of you," she said.

"And I you," The Duke nodded, studying her face.

"And Charlotte approves. I am glad of it. Father will approve. Of course how could he not approve. You are a Duke." She stopped and looked at him then. "I shan't care if father approves though. Do you think that makes me a horrible daughter?"

"Nothing could make me think you horrible," he promised.

"What does your friend, Lord Taftwater say about me? Surely men gossip like women do?"

The Duke laughed in the cool dusk air.

"I like your friend," she said. "And if he is to marry Charlotte, we must get on, you know. She is my best friend, and we are more like sisters than cousins. It would be so horrid if she were to marry someone I could not abide."

"I was not aware that Taftwater had offered for Miss Charlotte," the Duke said.

"Oh he will."

"I shall be sure to inform him." the Duke said dryly.

"Oh, you must not!" she said, suddenly aware that the conversation had spun out of her control.

"I am sorry," she said, placing a gloved hand to her mouth. "I misspoke. Charlotte cautions me that I speak before I think. She will be so vexed with me if she thinks I have ruined her chances."

"So she is not taken with Shelby Eglinton?"

Philippa groaned.

"I understand," The Duke said. "I will not speak of it. In fact, Taftwater cautions me in most aspects of my life."

"He cautions you about me?"

"He does. But as I said, he cautions me about a great many things. Wine. Fox hunting. Gambling. He is a careful man full of careful thoughts. I do not share in his carefulness; I think you can be assured of that."

"He cautions you of me because he fears that I am some hysterical woman, who does not know how to conduct herself in polite society?" Philippa asked. "I do know how to conduct myself - I just cannot bring myself to care what they think."

The Duke nodded.

"I do not concern myself with the gossips."

"It was not so bad as the gossips make it out to be. Mr. Goldthwaite was prone to exaggeration."

The Duke was unsure of what to say. It was the first time she had voluntarily mentioned Simon. He was unsure of whether or not he believed what she had said. She went on.

"I am glad it happened in a way. If it had not, I would be married to Goldthwaite and you to... what was her name?"

"Lady Margaret," he supplied.

"You would not have had your time with the Duchess," she whispered.

"I loved her," he said.

"I know."

"Janet, not Margaret. Once I thought I loved Margaret..."

"She was not worth a farthing," Philippa said, surprised at her vehemence.

If he expected that to sour the walk he was surprised when she let the matter drop, and they continued their circuit around the grounds.

"Did you love Simon Goldthwaite?" he asked at last.

"No," she said. "I don't think I did. I was hurt, of course. My pride was devastated, but I did not love him."

Philippa hadn't known it then, but she knew it now, because at last she was really in love... with the Duke of Chesney.

He caught her hand and held it. When they returned to the front door the sky was nearly dark, and the Duke bid Miss Dunn a good night. He kissed her cheek, and she touched his face. "I'm glad that you loved her," she said. "It means that you have the capacity to love, Your Grace. Many men do not." She turned and went inside, leaving him thoughtful.

Chapter Six

"What is wrong sweet cousin?" Charlotte said then, placing a hand on Philippa's back. She had not heard her come in.

Philippa sat up.

"I am a nervous ninny," she said.

"The Duke of Chesney has left?"

"He has."

"He cares for you."

"I hope he does," Philippa said.

Charlotte laughed.

"Then what is the problem, my dear Philippa?"

"I am just not good at conversation, dear cousin. I may have ruined your chances with Lord Taftwater. I am so sorry."

"What happened?"

"I misspoke. I mentioned that it would be grand if he married you and …"

"You said no such thing!" Charlotte chastised her.

"I'm sure it will be fine. The Duke only laughed and said that he would not tell Taftwater that he should offer for you, but I am sure that he will. The conversation just keeps running over and over in my head. I keep thinking of things that I should have said instead… It all works out so much better in my head, Charlotte. I am a fool. I nearly ruined things for you, and I am deluding myself."

"Poppycock," Charlotte exclaimed. She sat across from Philippa, and with the wisdom of a woman who was seemingly much older than her few years, she calmed her cousin.

"If you think like that, such fantasies will float in your head forever. You are wrong. No matter what that man may say or do, if you love him, and he loves you, then that is enough. Or it should be. If you refuse to let it be, then you are forcing yourself to a life of sadness and loneliness, which you do not have to experience. I do declare, Philippa, I think that you find ways to be sad, even when life offers you happiness."

"I do not. Truly." She doubted her own denial.

Philippa smiled weakly at her young cousin, knowing that Charlotte was right, but the words could not penetrate the bitter core she had built up over the years. Philippa was a being made up of hurt, confusion and yearning. It had been too long since she had known anything else.

She had fallen for the man; there was no doubt about it, but she could not let herself hope. She wanted to see him again, but she would not hope.

~~~~~

Two days after their last walk around the grounds, Philippa and the Duke sat in the parlour, sipping tea.

"I wanted to see more of you," the Duke said simply.

"And here you are."

"No, I mean…. I am thinking of spending more time here. I tire of my time in London.

"What about Parliament?"

"Well, obviously, I will always have that obligation, but I want to return here, to home, to relax. And I want you to be here too. I want to see more of you."

"You plan to set up residence here, Your Grace?"

"Yes."

"And do what? Ride around on your horses all day?" She blushed as she thought of their last ride.

"Would that be so burdensome?" he asked. "Would you ride with me?"

He looked at her searchingly and she felt that she couldn't breathe.

"I would court you," he said.

"Court me? I am not courtable, if you would listen to your friend, or countless others here. The things that they say, those whispers at my back when they think I cannot hear. They will say similar things about you if you let them."
~~~~~

"I am a Duke," he said.

"It does not make you immune to gossip."

"I don't care what they say," The Duke said sharply, then stood, obviously agitated. Before Philippa could stop herself she stood as well, putting a hand on his arm to calm him.

He took her into his arms. Their lips met. He tasted of the tea, and of passion. She closed her eyes. He pressed his body to hers. Her heart beat frantically beneath the swell of her small bosom pressed against his hard chest.

He looked at her for a long moment and then kissed her again, softly.

"Forget the courting," he said. "I am not a young man and you are not a young woman. I am impatient." He took a slow breath, and then asked, "Will you become my wife, my darling Philippa?"

"You jest," she said.

"I do not." He snapped.

She realized that he was offended. Dare she hope that he was speaking truthfully?

"You want to marry me?" she blurted.

"I think you have some fondness for me," he said. "I have not yet undertaken the task, but I will speak with your father..."

She touched his lips. They were so very warm.

"I do have a fondness for you, Your Grace,"

"Gregory," he corrected.

"I do have a fondness for you…, Gregory," Philippa whispered. "But we cannot announce wedding plans. It is Lent."

"I don't care. Just say that you are mine. I do not expect love. I know these things take time, but I think that we have a good companionship. We both like our novels, and I will enjoy your taking my accountant to task with your skills in mathematics." He grinned at her, looking almost boyish as he did so. "We both enjoy riding," he said. "And I can see many a day down by the stream, when you will not be so shy with your stockings."

"Your Grace!" she said, embarrassed.

"You are no child, and you must know that my mother grows anxious that I do not yet have an heir. I think that the task would not be unpleasant…" He kissed her again then, and when he let her come up for breath, she realized that the thought of bearing his children, and all that entailed, struck a fire in her soul.

"Gregory!" Philippa said, forgoing his title. "I do love you." She continued breathless. "I don't know how it happened; I never thought that I would love anyone. I tried not to; I kept to myself. After Simon, I was so unwilling to feel that pain once more, that stinging hurt of betrayal. I did not want to be hurt."

"I will not hurt you," the Duke promised.

"I believe you. Despite everything; despite myself; I love you. I love reading with you and riding with you and talking about the gossips. I do. There is nowhere I would rather be than beside you."

"You will marry me then?" the Duke asked, "Just say yes, everything else can wait, as long as you say yes."

"Yes," she breathed at last, and he kissed her again.

The End

If you liked this story, please be sure to go back to Amazon and leave a review.

Isabella loves to hear from her fans and can be contacted at www.isabellathorne.com. To be notified when the next book by Isabella Thorne is available, please go to www.isabellathorne.com and sign up for her newsletter. When you do, you will also receive a FREE STORY from Isabella!

Continue reading for a SNEAK PEEK of the next book by: Isabella Thorne –

Promise Me a Handful of Horses

Book 1 in The Duke's Wicked Wager Series

About the Author

Isabella Thorne is an author of Regency and Georgian Romance. The first grown-up books she read were historical, authored by Georgette Heyer, Victoria Holt and Anna Seton. Unfortunately, for her own daughters, the beauty and hallmark of Regency Romance, witty dialogue and the manners of the time, have been over-shadowed by explicit books instead of true Regency Romance.

With a return to romance, Isabella Thorne hopes you will enjoy her light, fun books. You can share them with your daughters with the guarantee that, although there is romance aplenty, and a bit of sexual tension and a kiss, there is nothing explicit in her books.

They are clean and wholesome reads with lots of humour and upbeat "fun poking" at the English mannerisms of the time.

Because Isabella loves the pageantry of the period, she loves to include true events or set stories during a war -- the English were involved in so many of them at this time! You will find bits of history scattered through the books and an occasional historical figure, but these books are FICTION and not intended to be a definitive history.

None of the Peerage mentioned in them, of any land, actually existed. Isabella hopes that all the British and the die-hard historical readers will please forgive this passionate American if she makes any mistakes, and, if you find one, send an email off to isabellathorne58@yahoo.com so that she can make corrections.

Stop by her website, www.isabellathorne.com for a free story and a notification of special sales.

If you love her books, PLEASE REVIEW and SHARE, so that others can come to love them too!

Please Like Isabella Thorne on Facebook

https://www.facebook.com/Isabella-Thorne-Author-1737782389810565/

Share or comment on an Isabella Thorne Facebook post for a chance to WIN an AMAZON GIFT CARD

Other Books by Isabella Thorne

The Duke's Wicked Wager Series

Promise Me A Handful of Horses

Promise Me Daring

Promise Me This Dance

Promise Me Your Heart

Mischief, Mayhem and Murder: A Marquis of Evermont Regency Romance

The Georgette Quinby Series

The Mad Heiress Meets the Duke

The Mad Heiress and the Search for a Spy

The Mad Heiress Visits Vauxhall

The Mad Heiress and the Rose Room Rout

The Mad Heiress' Cousin and the Hunt

Georgette Quinby Boxed Set

Other Books by Isabella Thorne

Colonial Cressida and the Secret Duke

Mistletoe and Masquerade.

Just One Christmas Kiss

New Year's Masquerade

Mistletoe and Masquerade Collection

To find more Regency Romance stories, please visit my website - www.isabellathorne.com

Regency Romance
Isabella Thorne

Here is Your Preview of

Promise Me a Handful of Horses

Regency Romance

Isabella Thorne

Evelyn did not mean to eavesdrop — well maybe she did. It was hard not to. The door was cracked open and the voices inside were too loud to ignore. One of the voices belonged to her brother. If he'd had a quieter way of speaking, she would never have heard the conversation. In the hallway, she crept closer and pressed her ear against the doorframe, holding the somewhat frayed ruffled hem of her mauve dress back so that it would not be seen.

"She will not like this plan, Frederic." That was the Duke of Pemberton's voice. He was her brother's friend, acquired during their mutual pursuit of mischief.

"And yet, she will have no choice in the matter," Evelyn's brother, the Marquis of Evermont, said, "it is her duty to marry, and she will do it."

"Have you no kindness for your sister? She is an odd one, true, but she does not seem to be a shrew or a nag. It would not be a bother to find her a husband she could grow to love. She does have a certain... grit."

There was a long pause, filled only by the just-audible inhales and exhales of cigar smoke. She could smell the earthy plumes of it wafting into the hall.

"It is marriage in a hurry or ruin for our family name, George."

"And this has naught to do with your latest flame, dear Adele? That pretty little actress is costing you a fortune to keep."

Frederic snorted a laugh.

The clink of crystal was followed by the sound of liquid pouring, and Evelyn could imagine the amber drink flowing from the decanter into their glasses.

"But Adele is worth every penny, my dear George, for when I have done something to please her she will do her damnedest to please me." Frederic's smug smile was evident from his tone. "Isn't that the entire purpose of the gentler sex?"

Evelyn's cheeks burned at the rude talk and she spun away from the door. Servants edged out of her way, pressing back against the wallpaper to let her pass in a flurry of lace and ruffles. The house was not as staffed as it had been, only a year ago, when her father still lived. They had been forced to let go some of the maids and footmen, but they managed. It was quieter without them, and without her father's booming laughter.

Her lip trembled as she stepped out of the house and made her way to the stable. It was some distance from the house, an immense, quadrangular structure that had, at its prime, housed sixty horses. Only a handful remained, but they were the twenty finest horses Evermont had ever boasted. Still, it was a sad state of affairs, and the beautiful white-stone complex seemed wasted for want of activity.

One of the grooms worked Valiant in the yard, putting the blood-bay through his paces. The stallion was retired from his racing days, but his elegant body still rippled with muscle beneath the shining coat, and he sired the finest foals in all of Norfolk. She paused a moment to watch him kick up the sand beneath his hooves. His shoes caught the sunlight and glinted.

Her father had purchased Valiant when she was only a child, but she could still remember the day that the stallion had come home, all fire, calming only under her father's touch. He had been a master horseman, and a wonderful father. She missed him so. She brushed back the tears, determined not to cry again.

"A fine day for a ride, Lady Evermont," said the stable master, Stanton, coming up beside her where she stood at the rail. "Shall I have Bellona saddled for you?"

Evelyn was tempted by the offer, smiling at the thought of the beautiful grey filly, but she was not dressed in her riding habit and that would require going back into the house near her brother.

"No, thank you, Stanton."

He reminded Evelyn of her father, though whether it was the similarity in their appearance or only that the two men had spent most of their days together and thus adopted similar mannerisms, she could not be certain. Regardless, his presence soothed her, as her father's had.

"An inspection of the mares in foal, then?" he asked, gesturing toward the stable. At her nod, Stanton led the way out of the dusty yard and into the coolness of the stone building.

The empty stalls dampened her spirits. They were swept clean, but Evelyn could picture every horse that should be there — horses that had already been sold, although their presence still filled her heart.

Not ghosts, quite, but something like them filled the space now, as her father's memory did the house, a presence felt, but never seen. She could close her eyes and picture them, so many born right here at Evermont.

Modeste, a chestnut mare with an obscenely bulging belly, nickered at their approach. She was a placid, sweet-tempered thing, even in foal. Evelyn offered her palm to the mare and she pressed her white blazed nose there, snuffling for treats. Evelyn smiled at the feel of her velvet nose on her hand.

"Expectin' the birth this week now," Stanton said, reaching up to scratch the mare's neck. "An old pro, she is, should be no trouble at all."

"Let us hope for a colt. We cannot expect Valiant to live forever, though if any horse shall manage, it will be him." Evelyn patted Modeste in farewell, and checked in on the other two pregnant mares.

They were not so far along as Modeste, but in the next few months they would have three new additions to the stable, if all went well. Two would need to be sold just after weaning, and potential buyers had already made offers. It pained Evelyn to part with any of Valiant's get. His line belonged at Evermont, but those were the ways of the past. She fingered the amethyst bracelet at her wrist, nodding as she half-listened to Stanton as he talked about the mares. A mark of her mourning, the bracelet felt as heavy as the burden of her grief.

She had lost not only her father, but her betrothed as well. It had been a dark year at Evermont. Her fiancé had been killed in battle, a noble death for an officer, but one that had left her in shock.

Their love had been a quiet one, of friendship rather than passion. He had been eight years her senior, but a kind, gentle man and she held him still in the greatest affection. Evelyn's father had made the match, selecting for her a husband with a love for horses and an open mind, a man who would not temper Evelyn's spirited ways. She had lost them both within a month of each other. What else could fate throw at her?

"Lady Evermont?" Stanton was eyeing Evelyn with concern.

"Your pardon, Stanton, my mind was elsewhere. May I see the ledgers?" She had already looked at them *ad nauseam*. They did not change. There was nowhere else to save a farthing. If only her brother was not so loose with his cash.

The stable master's office was tidy and austere. A simple desk stood in the middle of the room and a window looked out over the pasture, where a few horses were grazing on the yellowed grass. Stanton offered her a chair, and pulled a thick stack of papers from a drawer in his desk. Despite its innocuous look, the ledger was an evil thing, listing out the shortcomings of Evermont's accounts in neat black figures. Evelyn schooled her features into a neutral expression as she went over the numbers with Stanton, but her emotions were a storm just beneath the placid surface.

Her brother sat somewhere in the manor, wasting his time discussing frivolous affairs over expensive brandy and expensive cigars, while the horses were meted out rations like soldiers on a long march. He planned to have her betrothed while she was still in mourning for her fiancée and father, only so that his insatiable lust for tawdry women would not need to be tempered by restraint. Her blood boiled at the thought.

At the bottom of it all was the Duke of Pemberton, a rake if she had ever known one. The ruin of Evermont lay at his feet, dragging her brother after him with his expensive ways.

"I cannot see any way around it. We shall have to sell another coach. Let the coachman select one, he will know best which one will fetch the highest sum. If it happens to be Frederic's favourite, well, that would be a shame."

Her mouth was in a tight line.

"Of course, Lady Evermont." Stanton said. "I will see to it this afternoon."

Evelyn closed the ledger and pushed the chair back from the desk. She stood at the window and watched the horses for a moment, marvelling at their grace as they took off in a sudden burst of speed, kicking up their hind legs and squealing.

"They are like children with their joy, are they not?"

Continue reading about Lady Evelyn in

Promise Me a Handful of Horses

Book 1 in

The Duke's Wicked Wager Series

4 BOOK BOX SET

NOW ONLY $2.99

READ FREE ON KINDLE UNLIMITED

Or

Continue reading the single volume of

Promise Me a Handful of Horses

Only $0.99

FREE on Kindle Unlimited

Please don't forget to Review if you liked the story.

ARIETTA RICHMOND, CATHERINE WINDSOR, ISABELLA THORNE, KATHERINE KEATS, KELLY ANNE BRUCE

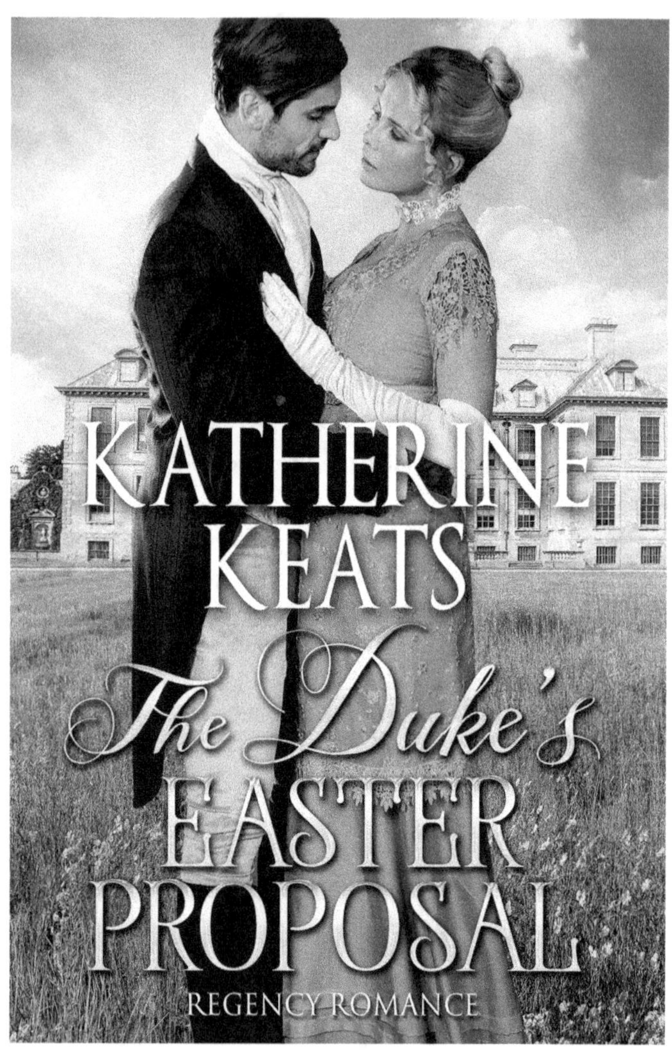

Regency Romance

The Duke's Easter Proposal

Katherine Keats

Chapter One

It was busy. Every table was taken, every chair claimed. For some parties, the gentlemen were forced to stand by their wives, occasionally eyeing with jealous disdain those more fortunate than themselves, who had been able to steal a seat. It was loud and spirits were high. Today was a day for indulgence and excess.

The great and the good gorged themselves determinedly on the cakes and sweet fancies put in front of them, seeming not to care how they might look to their neighbour. Women, who on any other day would take care to eat only the minutest portion of a cake and with a very delicate fork, were eating with their hands. The most intrepid of all the assembled mass of gluttons ate with jaws that seemed to distend to almost inhuman lengths when grappling with the challenge of eating a tall piece of round cake.

Only two were not set on the business of eating, Both women. The older of the two rushed about the tables, clearing away empty plates and topping up the cups of those who had finished their coffee.

This woman, Mrs Fairway, was, to all intents and purposes, the proprietor of this rather spacious London coffee house. To look on her was to gaze on a picture of perfect practicality and sense. The woman did not waste a single movement of her body, nor an ounce of her strength. Though most of her customers were too busy enjoying themselves to notice, one man amongst them was always impressed by the widow's constant ability to be two steps ahead of her ever mounting and changing list of chores and responsibilities.

Joshua Goodrich, Duke of Falmouth, looked to the ever-moving shape of Mrs Fairway. He admired the woman. As much as she reminded him very much of a squirrel always running about in search of food for the winter, her tenacity and verve was commendable. As he watched her comings and goings, two green eyes looked on him, the eyebrows above them displaying their discontent.

"Your Grace, are your thoughts elsewhere?"

The Duke blinked and Lady Primrose came back into focus. He felt a blush rise to his cheeks as he endured her pursed lips and stern expression. Here was a woman who did not like a man's attention to be on anything other than herself.

"I am sorry; I was just musing on how animated and jovial everyone appears this day. It is wondrous what silly little rituals we create for ourselves to shake up the norm of our humdrum lives. On almost any other day, you would never see so many piling in here to sample the delicious delicacies Mrs Fairway and her daughter create."

He smiled, eyes flicking again to where Mrs Fairway continued her constant motion.

"Still, as soon as Shrove Tuesday comes around and ministers at the pulpit tell us to abstain from every possible good thing there is in the world, then we see everyone out in force to gorge themselves whilst they still have the chance."

Lady Primrose looked about her. The blank expression on her face showed either a lack of comprehension, or a lack of caring about how the others around them behaved. As if to drive home the point that she was nothing like these others, she turned her attention to the slice of round cake she had in front of her.

She trimmed off the thinnest sliver imaginable for herself. For such a small morsel, she took a good deal of time in swallowing the bite down and added to the silence by taking a measured sip from her coffee too.

"I am to take it then, that you are not a believer in abstinence and fasting over the Lenten period?" Her eyes narrowed, studying the Duke carefully. She was evaluating him and the Duke was sure that he would find his answer marked after giving it.

"I am in favour of men appreciating the almighty in the way that suits them best. If a man finds he can be closer to God by lying out in the fields of his creation on a warm Sunday morning, let him do that instead of forcing him into a dark dingy chapel. If, likewise, a man finds that he can appreciate the Lord's blessings by indulging in the sweet foods or other pleasures he has given us for our enjoyment, then let the man do so. There is very little, to my mind, to be gained by long periods of abstinence. It only puts people in worse moods and leaves them perpetually short on energy and vitality."

Lady Primrose nodded, taking a moment to consider her response.

"And yet, some say that absence makes the heart grow fonder. I believe they were talking about people, but might the same be said of things we must give up over Lent?"

The Duke nodded. "Hmm, a good saying, though I worry about it in part. I can only speak for the human side of things, but I think that there is an even chance of hearts being made colder by absence as well as fonder."

The woman smiled, her thin lips making the smile seem more perfunctory and forced.

"Well then, Your Grace, I suppose I must be sure to make the most of the time we still have together in London. Otherwise, it seems that I am in danger of you forgetting me like yesterday's newspaper."

The Duke leaned forward, his own smile more playful and unstudied.

"I look forward to being the centre of such attention. Though, please do not fear the ending of the London season, not when it is only just beginning. We have plenty of time yet to know one another better."

"Yes, but every other woman will no doubt be trying to get to know you too. I must stay on my toes if I am to ensure I have the best chance of your remembering me after you return to your country estate."

The Duke continued to smile. He was not sure what to make of Lady Primrose. Like so many others before her, she seemed very invested in trying to garner his good approval.

Unlike the others, Lady Primrose didn't seem to shy away from stating her objective and intentions to him. It certainly added an attractive quality to the lady, though it was yet to be seen if this would be enough to convince him, at last, to settle down.

Draining the last of his coffee, the Duke looked to the time and frowned. There was nowhere in particular that he needed to be at this hour, but he was keen to have some time to himself. He did not want to encourage too much gossip by being seen out with Lady Primrose for too long a stretch. London being what it was, it was highly inadvisable to spend more than two to three hours with a woman in public - any more, and you subjected yourself to rumours of a forthcoming engagement.

"Well, my lady, perhaps we should consider taking a slow meander back to your father's home. I am sure he will want you returned home before the hour gets outrageously late."

Lady Primrose pouted, her cheeks puffing up like some little rodent.

"I suppose it is for the best," she conceded.

"If you'd like to wait outside for me, with your maid, I'll just settle with the proprietor."

This was an important part of his ritual when coming to this particular coffee house. For, while the squirrel-like Mrs Fairway was always on the move and keeping busy with a constant stream of chores, she managed always to keep an eye on her customers and an ear open to their words.

Walking to the small doorway, which the owner had just entered with a large pile of fresh dishes for washing, the Duke waited for the ideal moment to catch her.

"So, what did you make of this one?" his voice was a conspiratorial whisper, but loud enough to catch Mrs Fairway's attention as she re-entered the room.

The woman jumped then let out an exhausted breath.

"My goodness, Your Grace. You have an awful habit of lingering in the sides of one's vision like a common sneak thief. It is not very becoming of a Duke."

"It's not very becoming for the proprietor of a coffee house to so insult a Duke by comparing him to thief."

Mrs. Fairway gave a wry smile and tilted her head, a sign that the Duke should follow her as she continued working.

"I liked this one well enough I suppose. I will grant that she's a beauty and very good with her fashion too. That black choker about her neck... exquisite."

The Duke smiled and leaned on a counter as he watched Mrs Fairway restock her shelves with clean plates.

"I am sensing the word 'however' approaching."

Mrs Fairway didn't bother facing him as she worked.

"If you think you already know what I am going to say then why do you persist in having me say anything at all?"

"Because I like to hear you say it." The Duke waited for the line Mrs Fairway always gave whenever called to give a verdict on a woman he had brought in to her establishment.

"Well, I don't mean to compare, but my Bridget would never be as brazen as that woman."

There it was, the comparison that Mrs Fairway used every time she considered a woman that the Duke was courting.

"This one you've brought in is too sure of herself - far too confident and conceited in her looks. I'm not saying that this is altogether a bad thing. I do not approve of pretty girls saying that they are plain in order to appear humble. Still, I think this lady knows, all too well, her strengths, and I think she plays them far too well... almost makes me wonder if she has had a lot of practice courting the attentions of other men before now."

"Oh? You think she might be less ladylike than she lets on?"

The Duke leaned closer, his smile wide.

"Of course, sometimes you seem like no true gentleman yourself, so maybe there is something in this match after all."

The Duke laughed and put his money down on the table to pay the bill.

"You know, if it were not for the delicious cakes your daughter makes, I would not so easily forgive the insults you cast at me. I do wonder when I will see this elusive creature, who is the benchmark against whom you set all women I bring here."

Mrs Fairway laughed and waved a heavy spoon in the Duke's direction.

"With your smooth words and roguish manner, I should like very much to make sure that you never do meet her. My daughter is a good girl, an unspoiled girl, and I will not be having you corrupting her."

A call from a patron in need of more coffee drew Mrs. Fairway away and the Duke walked out, whistling a jaunty tune.

Chapter Two

For those unaware of her situation, the period of Lent would appear to be a dream for Bridget Fairway. As the most skilled cook in the family, it was her ability to bake and produce perfect cakes of all kinds that put the Fairway's little Coffeehouse on the map. Nearly all of the regulars who made habitual stops at the place did so because there just happened to be some way that she made the cakes which could not be found reproduced anywhere else in the city.

Owing to this fame, it was often impossible for Bridget to spend more than a handful of hours each day away from the kitchen. She would bake and decorate cakes every waking moment the coffee house was open, only pausing when her mother would come through with dishes for her to wash. Even these interruptions only went so far, however, as she would invariably plan her new creations for the patrons' tables as she cleaned and dried.

Lent was the one time of year where Bridget was permitted to take a period of rest.

While the rest of the nation took to hard fasting, Bridget took to catching up on lost sleep and catching up with the few friends she kept. While Lent was a time of penance for many, it had always felt to her like a time of reward. At least, this had had been so in the past.

Standing in the kitchen, Bridget tried to identify something useful she could be doing. She could think of nothing. For those who did come through with a sweet tooth and no regard for observing religious fasts, there were a few simple cakes ready to be served. She had already baked enough bread to see her, and her mother, through for several days, and the work counters and cooking equipment had all been cleaned so as to look almost brand new.

If there was something she had missed, some chore or task she had forgotten about, she could not think of it now. For the first time since Lent had begun, Bridget had to confront the irritating fact that there seemed to be nothing for her to do.

Stepping up the small flight of steps into the main coffee house, she looked about at the empty chairs and tables. Her mother was engaged in polishing silverware and the two shared bored sighs in greeting.

"It will pick up in a few days. Everyone is more fervent in their desire to observe the Lenten fast in the first week. Once we are into the second week and people's bellies begin to crave better fare than bread and water, then we'll see people coming back to us."

Bridget offered a smile, determined not to show any hint of worry to her mother. Worrying about how this season of low trade might affect their finances was a fruitless endeavour.

No amount of fretting would put an extra penny into their pockets.

"As it is so quiet, would you like me to take over out front? You could go out and do some shopping, or even go and see a friend?"

Mrs Fairway laughed.

"My goodness, I don't think I've had a friend in nigh on five years. Your father was about the only friend I had, aside from you and this dear old place."

Bridget managed to keep her smile on her face. Her mother never liked to be viewed with sympathy by others.

"Well, you could just take a walk then. It is only fair. Yesterday you shooed me away from the kitchens for a day to rest up in bed. It is only fair that I return the favour for you now. After all, you need to take the occasional break too... I think I can handle keeping the place in order. Even if you take just an hour, I doubt we will have more than one customer."

Bridget fidgeted with her hands, playing with a loose cuticle as she watched her mother hopefully.

Mrs Fairway brushed down her apron and looked to the clock. Bridget could tell that her mother was uneasy and not at all eager to consider being bound to a period of inactivity.

"Are you sure that you would not prefer to go out and enjoy the good weather instead? It is honestly no trouble for me."

Bridget pursed her lips, determined to have her own way on this.

"Mother, I can't even remember the last time you went outside and just took a moment for yourself. I do not need a break right now; I need to keep occupied. You go out for an hour and let me worry about the place."

Mrs Fairway shook her head and began to untie her apron with a deliberate slowness.

"I suppose an hour couldn't hurt me. I promise I will not be a second longer though."

Bridget believed her. When given the choice, neither of them would accept rest over work.

It took a full ten minutes to shoo her mother out of the shop door and into the streets. Before she left, Mrs Fairway tried to contrive any number of reasons to stay, and then, when that failed, she insisted on devising a list of items that they were short on and which would be worth fetching while she was out. When at last she did leave, Bridget took over the polishing of the silverware, relieved to have escaped the possibility of doing nothing for a spell of time.

Despite her confident belief that no customers would come in, at the early hour of eleven on the third day of Lent, Bridget was surprised to hear the gentle jingle of the bell that hung above the door. She had only just settled into a rhythm with the polishing, but she felt a shiver of excitement at the prospect of serving a customer. She had, of course, served in the past, but only when it was exceptionally busy, and never without her mother being nearby.

Looking at the man who had entered, Bridget realised at once who she was serving.

"Oh, Your Grace… am I correct? You are the Duke that my mother keeps boasting of entertaining?"

Bridget's eyes wandered over his exceptionally fine tail coat. It was midnight blue and looked incredibly soft to touch. The man's waistcoat was a similar colour and decorated with silver trim, worked to look like vine leaves from some hanging ivy. By his clothes alone, she felt certain that her guess was the right one.

The man smiled broadly, revealing a set of well-kept teeth. Taking off his hat, he walked forward, seeming to put aside the matter of his identity as he studied the woman before him. His eyes were the colour of moss and flecked with areas of brown: a soft colour, though his gaze was piercing.

"Well, I shall take a guess that you are the elusive Miss Bridget Fairway."

Bridget smiled, finding it hard to meet the man's stare which persisted unrepentantly.

"I am indeed."

She found her right hand moving to her long brown hair and playing with one of the ringlet curls that framed the side of her face.

"I thought you were a myth your mother had created."

The man took a seat and brought it over to the counter. He did not seem at all fazed to be talking to a complete stranger and had an easy way about him.

Bridget giggled and put down the piece of silver she was half way through polishing.

"Well, I do not think I am a myth. Although, I have heard that my cakes are somewhat legendary amongst the clientele here." Her smile quavered a little, unsure if her joke would be well received or come across as a little arrogant. "You did not actually answer me though. Are you the Duke my mother keeps telling me comes in here?"

The man nodded, his eyes seeming to study her all the more rigorously. Perhaps he was looking for her reaction to his station. Was there some special etiquette needed for this moment. Uncertain, Bridget curtseyed.

"Well, Your Grace, it is an honour to serve you. Can I get you anything particular?"

"Coffee and whatever you think is the best cake you have right now. Normally, your mother has them out on display."

The Duke looked down the empty counter top with some disappointment.

"Ah, well on account of Lent, we do not want to be responsible for tempting our customers who might be fasting. It is a hard thing to do and we do not wish to make it harder by dangling forbidden fruit in front of them."

"Why not? God didn't seem to have any qualms putting forbidden fruit in front of Adam to tease him with."

Bridget bit her lip, trying not to laugh at that. This man was turning out to be quite a bit more than her mother had let on. She had said that the Duke was quite an animated character, but Bridget had not expected him to make sport of the season's solemn religious observance. She could also feel a blush rising to her cheeks, which she tried to will away.

"Well, I am sure that the minister of the local parish would have a keen discussion with you on that score. For my part, I will leave temptation for the devil to deal in."

The Duke leaned forward and rested his chin on his hands as he pouted.

"So, does this mean that you don't, in fact, have any cake available right now?"

Bridget found herself unable to stifle her laughter any further. She had never heard someone wrap theology around food before, or seem so determined to ensure that they had something sweet to eat.

"I shall go out at once and see what we have. Honestly, it will be good to see someone eat what we have and not see them grow stale."

"So, I can take it as read that I can expect a rather large slice? Excellent!"

The Duke clapped his hands in approval and watched Bridget as she retreated to the kitchens.

As soon as the door was closed, Bridget felt something like relief washing over her, and she allowed herself to slump against the door for a moment. While she attempted to collect her frayed and confused thoughts she was left with one very real and slightly concerning thought: the Duke was far more handsome than her mother had indicated.

There had been several occasions where Bridget had tried to find out about the mysterious nobleman who chose to frequent their humble establishment.

She had, more than once, crept to look out of an ajar door, to try and spy the man amongst their clientele. This was always a fruitless endeavour, as Mrs Fairway never alerted her to when the Duke was in. Now, Bridget understood why her mother had acted as she did. She was concerned that her only daughter might develop some liking for the well moneyed and handsome Duke.

The realisation that she was meant to be bringing her customer some cake brought Bridget back to action and she looked through the few items she had baked that morning, trying to decide which would be most pleasing on the Duke's tongue. It was no mean feat. Each of her creations was a testament to her skills as a cook, and Bridget was proud of all of her work. It was rare, though, for her to have the opportunity to hear her work praised first-hand and so she wanted to make sure that she had chosen perfectly for the Duke.

There were some almond tarts which she had made just a few hours ago. These had come out very well: not too overbaked, or over chewy. They were sweet too, and probably just right, if she had guessed the Duke's palate correctly. Settling on these, Bridget put six on a plate for the man.

He likely didn't need, or want, so many. Still, since customers were currently in short supply, she felt it best to see as much of her labour as possible enjoyed, rather than left to go stale. Once she had these, Bridget found her body tensing at the thought of returning to the shopfront and the Duke's company. She bit her bottom lip and tried to remind herself that he was just a man.

"Sorry for keeping you waiting, Your Grace. It took me awhile to decide what you might like best. I hope almond tarts are to your liking."

The Duke sat at perfect ease, not seeming at all perturbed by the emptiness and silence that surrounded him. He shot her a smile that reassured her at once.

"I am sure that, if you have made them, they will be delicious. Better yet, I can see that you've supplied enough to tide my stomach over 'til evening."

Bridget hurried to put the plate in front of him and went to make the coffee.

"I just hope that I can make the coffee properly. I am not as proficient as my mother and always end up spilling a few grounds into the cup."

The Duke's smile persisted.

"I consider myself warned."

He watched her as she poured the black liquid carefully into the cup, nervously holding the hot pot far from herself in case she burned herself. In her awkward pouring, a little splashed over the rim of the cup and she looked to the Duke with a blush on her cheek.

"Do not worry about a spillage, he assured her." He took the cup gratefully and took a sip, enjoying the bitter taste.

"Is it to your liking?" Bridget asked the question with eagerness, barely giving the Duke a chance to properly taste it.

"Yes, there are no grounds at all in this cup, that I can taste."

He put down the cup and turned his attention to the plate of tarts. Taking the smallest, he brought it to his lips, taking a moment to savour the smell of the almond before taking a bite.

Bridget seemed to stop breathing at that moment, her body leaning across the counter as she studied his face.

"Absolutely perfect."

"Do you really think so?"

Bridget's smile at that moment was broad and infectious, and the Duke found himself returning it in kind.

"I swear. Have you not had one yet yourself?"

The Duke pushed the plate to her in offering.

"Oh no, I couldn't. These are for you of course."

Bridget looked at the plate, uncertain if it was polite to turn down a Duke's offer.

"Well, as I am paying for them, I think I can be permitted to decide who does and doesn't get to eat them. So, go on. I don't think I am going to manage all six by myself."

Bridget beamed and took one of the tarts, nervously nibbling the corner. She nodded, happy to find them to her liking.

Before long Bridget found herself sitting opposite the Duke, drinking her own cup of coffee and helping him work through the plate she had set out. They talked on a number of topics, Bridget finding the man's gregarious and kindly nature much to her liking.

"So just how does it happen that this charming little place finds itself so barren and empty at this time of year? I know it is Lent, but I am sure the other coffee houses around do not suffer as terrible a trade as you and your mother seem to have about now."

Bridget lowered her gaze. "I sometimes think it is my fault that we are unusually held up over Lent. My late father built our coffeehouse's reputation on the fact that we served sweet cakes and good food; not just the bottomless cup for a penny that the other houses do. For much of the year, this does a lot for our business. However, it also means that we are seen as a haven of sweet food and excess. So, when it comes time for fasting, I think most of our customers steer clear, just to avoid the temptation. The other coffee houses gladly take them in and they return to us after Easter Sunday."

The Duke nodded. He took a deep breath and Bridget found herself staring at his chest as it expanded and contracted.

"I am sorry your customers are so fickle. You shouldn't feel like it is your fault though."

Bridget nodded, pursing her lips. She had been told this before by her mother, but it was hard for her not to feel responsible. "I know that our parson is also a contributing factor. He is a fierce orator and very good at reminding us to take these religious observances seriously. He makes a habit of coming around to the houses to check on the flock and will, from time to time, press his head to the window of establishments such as ours just to ensure that no-one has strayed."

The Duke shook his head and began to tap the countertop with his finger.

"He sounds like quite a personality. I imagine fire and brimstone are particular favourite topics for his sermons."

Bridget laughed.

"You are not far wrong."

She watched as the Duke drained the last of his cup. It was a purposeful action that signalled he would be leaving, and she found herself disappointed by the prospect of his departure.

"Well, it has been a real pleasure to find you to be a real person, Miss Fairway. I hope that, in future, your mother will see fit not to keep you locked behind that kitchen door every time I visit."

Bridget frowned.

"I wasn't aware that I was being kept locked away. I will certainly be sure to listen out for you though, if you will be returning during Lent."

"You can count on it," the Duke assured her.

Chapter Three

Bridget had been waiting. Since receiving the Duke's promise that he would return, Bridget had found herself lingering nearer to the front of the coffee house at all hours. When she could, she would invent reasons to help her mother with polishing, cleaning down table tops and tackling long hidden stains in the main part of the house.

She had, by necessity informed her mother of the Duke's visit. It was not a thing she could keep secret, when money lay quietly behind the counter. She had noted the way that her mother seemed ill at ease when she spoke of the meeting, and Bridget found herself subjected to a great many questions about the man and what she had thought of him.

Though normally honest about her feelings, Bridget chose to keep her admiration and liking for the Duke to herself. Something in her mother's questioning gave Bridget pause. She remembered the Duke saying that her mother seemed to keep her locked in the kitchens when he was about. Could it be that she disapproved of the Duke in some way and was working to ensure that Bridget never grew to know him?

It was very plausible. Many mothers were fearful of their daughters being abused by rakish and charming gentlemen. Every Season, some girl found herself taken in by a suave and sophisticated nobleman, only to be left broken hearted and with a swollen belly. Across London, there were probably dozens of illegitimate children being raised in poverty which belied a noble heritage.

Six days of waiting had seen Bridget's expectations wane. She did not look out the front as often as she had on previous days. Her hopeful optimism was gradually being supplanted by cynicism which assured her that the Duke was just as unreliable as any other customer who wandered in. He likely had only promised to return out of politeness and would probably not give her, or the coffeehouse, another thought until he next happened to passing by.

It was a perfectly natural way to behave and Bridget berated herself for having thought that the promise was something special. As she chastised herself for her own naivety, she reflected that maybe her mother was right to try and keep her away from the Duke. His charm and good looks were a potent combination which seemed made to overpower a woman's reason.

Her mind returning to the present, Bridget whacked the half-kneaded dough. How long had she been standing over the counter, staring aimlessly through the bread mixture which she ought to already have put in the oven? She hastened to finish her work, setting the loaf hurriedly into the oven before wandering away to see if her mother needed anything else in particular done.

At that moment, she was so preoccupied with the task of not thinking about the Duke that it quite escaped her to consider the possibility that he might be in the café now.

Opening the door, Bridget noticed three patrons sitting at a table and talking over coffee. These people fell away to the periphery of her mind though as she noticed the man standing in conversation with her mother.

"Your Grace!" Bridget's voice was laden with surprise and loud enough that all eyes in the house turned to her, including those of the elegant looking lady who seemed to accompany the Duke.

Mrs Fairway gave her daughter a look, one which Bridget had learned to fear from infancy. It was that special kind of warning glare that had always made her quieten down and stand still, lest her actions lead to further reprisal.

Whether the Duke noticed the nonverbal exchange between mother and daughter was hard to say. He looked to Mrs. Fairway and then back to Bridget, a smile encroaching on his face after a moment.

"Incredibly good timing, Miss Fairway. I was just telling your mother here how delicious your almond tarts were last week."

Bridget smiled, but fell short of blushing. Her body was tense and she found that she could not relax in the Duke's presence as she had on their last encounter. Her mother's watchful eye prevented her from it.

"I am glad that they were to your liking. It is always good to hear my efforts in the kitchen are appreciated."

Knowing that there would be no chance for real conversation with the man, Bridget decided to press on with her reason for having left the kitchen.

"Sorry to interrupt Mama, I just wondered if you needed any help out here? I have put the bread in the oven. While it rises, I thought I might be of some use here."

Mrs. Fairway looked to the Duke and then back to her daughter. She had her hands placed on her hips and frustration was written all over her knotted brow.

"It is good you've come out in fact. It seems the Duke here has need of a cook for a party he is holding at his home this Sunday."

"It is a most dreadful bore, and I must apologise for inconveniencing you. However, I have had to let my own cook return to his family for a spell. He had some rather tragic news regarding his mother. It seems she passed away after a short illness, and I did not feel it right to deny him leave to return home. I have made do these last few days by prevailing on friends, but had quite forgotten I was going to host an evening meal for a party of six this Sunday. As I puzzled over what was to be done about the issue, well, I found myself thinking immediately of you, Miss Fairway, and decided to ask your mother if she might release you for an evening to cater."

The Duke fell silent, then added, "Of course, this will be paid. To make up for the trouble of asking so late and robbing you of time you doubtless need to bake, I am fully prepared to pay triple what my cook would make on such an evening."

The lady standing next to the Duke studied Bridget, eyes scanning over her, from head to feet, as she apparently made quiet mental notes. After a few seconds she looked to the Duke, her eyes still on Bridget.

"Do you not think you are going above and beyond here? I know that your guests will be disappointed to have the evening cancelled, none more so than I, but you would be forgiven for it readily if you just explained the reason behind it."

"I do not mind catering for you in the slightest, Your Grace." Bridget made her answer hurriedly, trying to avoid the looks her mother and the elegant lady gave her.

"Excellent. Well then, unless you have any further worries or concerns, can we consider the matter settled?"

Mrs Fairway looked to the Duke and then back to her daughter. Bridget tried not to appear too invested in her decision.

"I suppose I can let my daughter out for one night. But I would ask that she is returned at a reasonable hour."

"I give you my word on it. What's more, I will have her brought to my home and returned in my carriage so that you do not have to worry over her wandering the streets in the dark."

Mrs Fairway nodded, but Bridget could tell that her mother was not best pleased about the arrangement. Normally, she was far more bubbly and good humoured with her customers.

Indeed, in her accounts of her previous meetings with the Duke, Mrs Fairway had always implied that they shared friendly banter quite often. She was intrigued then, to see how her mother treated him now.

"That will put me a little more at ease. I will release Bridget to you after church on Sunday and would like her back by nine thirty if that is agreeable to you?"

"More than satisfactory."

If the Duke was put out at all by her mother's uncharacteristically frosty reception, he wasn't showing it.

"Will you be staying for coffee, Your Grace?"

Bridget asked the question hopefully, her eyes darting away from the Duke's when they met.

"Sadly not."

The Duke looked to the Lady at his side.

"While I am determined to make no observance of fasting for the season, Lady Primrose has been very good. I would hate to tease her by consuming more of your wonderful tarts alone, while she can only look on in envy."

Lady Primrose let out a laugh, delicate and well-rehearsed.

"Well, it is very good of you to consider my needs so. I must say, it makes a lady feel quite special. You will not abstain from the pleasures of the world for the Lord, but you will do so for me."

As the lady spoke, Bridget was left with the distinct impression that her words were not meant for the Duke's ears.

She was marking her territory and intentions, letting Bridget know just where she stood in the man's esteem.

The Duke sighed and looked to the three women in turn.

"I think it is time we let you get back to your customers. I shall see you on Sunday then, Miss Fairway."

Both Bridget and Mrs Fairway curtseyed, Bridget noting the way that Lady Primrose threaded her arm possessively through the Duke's as they departed. Only when they had left and the door had been shut did Mrs Fairway speak.

"You seem exceptionally eager to please the Duke. He must have made quite an impression on you the other week."

Bridget didn't know what to say. She felt that she should continue to try to downplay the encounter as a triviality. However, she felt a growing hunger and impatience to know just why her having met the Duke was so distasteful to her mother.

"He was perfectly charming, which is far more than can be said about you right now. I have never seen you treat a customer so coldly before. I always thought that you liked the man."

Mrs Fairway marched back to the counter and began preparing another pot of coffee to go on the fire.

"He is like quite a lot of the noblemen who frequent the lower class areas of town: thoroughly charming, agreeable, attentive..."

Mrs Fairway tailed off and she fixed her daughter with a serious look.

"He has all of the qualities necessary to make for good company, and I enjoy his banter and wit just fine. Still, he is not the kind of man I want you to be spending time around."

"Why ever not?"

Bridget asked the question with a note of hurt in her voice.

"Because that man comes in here every few weeks with a new Lady on his arm. Lady Primrose may be the smartest of the women he has brought in here, but she is not the first by any means. Men like the Duke have their pick of women and most will throw themselves at him for a chance of tasting his wealth."

"And you think that I will cheapen myself by throwing myself at him?"

Bridget was offended to think that her mother had so little faith in her.

"Of course not, dearest. Still, the Duke has a charm about him, and I do not want to see you hurt by him."

Bridget bit her lip as a new question came to the fore of her mind.

"Is this why you are always encouraging me to stay in the kitchens at all hours? Are you worried that I will have my heart broken by some man?"

"No, of course not. The Duke is just a very particular case."

Mrs. Fairway looked at her other patrons. All three had stopped their talking and were now listening in on the argument brewing between them.

"Let's not argue about this. You have met the Duke now, and I am allowing you to go unaccompanied to his home. That should be more than enough to prove that I trust you."

Bridget sighed and looked at the men who had been listening in. Her mother had made a good point. She was being trusted to handle herself and her affairs with proper sense and decorum.

"I had best go and check on the bread: don't want to see it burn."

ARIETTA RICHMOND, CATHERINE WINDSOR, ISABELLA THORNE, KATHERINE KEATS, KELLY ANNE BRUCE

Chapter Four

Nervousness had kept Bridget awake through much of the night and she found herself paying for it in church - as Pastor Michaels extoled the virtues of sacrifice, abstinence and spiritual cleansing, Bridget found herself fighting a losing battle with her eyelids. From time to time she felt her head drooping forward, as she fell into momentary bouts of slumber. She was vaguely aware of her mother sitting next to her.

Mrs. Fairway watched her daughter carefully and Bridget feared she might use her tiredness as an excuse to forbid her catering for the Duke that evening.

This fear was enough to give her the power to struggle against encroaching sleep and Bridget redoubled her efforts to stay awake, forcing her mind to concentrate on little things to help her stay conscious.

At the service's end, she fled quickly into the open air outside the chapel. Amongst the gravestones that dotted the chapel's grounds, she was able to find her mind reinvigorated by the cool breeze.

Winter had not quite given up its grip on the air and Bridget found herself grateful for it as she walked past the familiar stone monuments to the dead. There was one in particular that she wished to see before going to the Duke's home.

Mr. Fairway had a small grave in the farthest corner of the chapel grounds. He was buried right on the border of the parish property, his small tombstone looking away from the city and out towards the countryside. Better still, being so far from the chapel doors, Bridget was always assured of privacy when she went to visit her father.

"It's an interesting day, father."

Bridget ran her hand over the cold headstone and turned to look out on the hillside, imagining she was standing by her father's side.

"I'm going to cook for a Duke. I know you would be proud of me. You were always encouraging my cooking and baking. I remember how put out mother was when you declared me the superior cook and put me in charge of all our meals. You always made me feel so encouraged and proud of my work, and now I have a chance to really prove myself..."

She found her words failing her. Normally she didn't have any qualms talking to her father in this place. Her hesitation came from something else: the feeling that she was lying to him and to herself.

"Actually, I think I am more concerned about who I am cooking for than anything else. I think I have found myself inadvertently taking a fancy to the man. He's very unique and free spirited. You're probably laughing at me admitting to taking a fancy to a Duke: too far above my station, I know."

Bridget took a deep breath, listening to a bird singing in the nearby tree that shaded this part of the graveyard.

"I wish you were here right now. I could really have done with your advice on what I should do. Mother is behaving very oddly about it all. She tells me that I should steer clear of the man, yet I know she has spoken very highly of him in the past. I cannot figure her out at all."

As if summoned by her name, Mrs. Fairway rounded the corner at that moment and looked to her daughter. She did not approach the grave. Unlike Bridget, Mrs. Fairway did not like to visit her husband. She struggled even to stand in the vicinity of his burial site. Instead, she stood as far as she could from him, arms wrapped about herself as though cold. She did not speak, but it was obvious that she was waiting for Bridget. Not wishing to keep her waiting, Bridget gave her father's headstone a kiss before walking back to her mother's side.

"I am sorry; I just wanted a moment to talk to Papa before the day got underway."

Mrs. Fairway nodded, but was quick to shepherd her daughter away, only slowing her pace once they had turned a corner and Mr Fairway's grave was out of sight.

"I wish you'd tell me before you go off like that. I worry when I lose sight of you, and I really do not see what reassurance you were hoping to gain from a slab of stone."

Bridget let the comment pass. She did not want to get into a debate on the significance of visiting her father's grave, or the feeling that she had, that they were still being watched over by the man they had both loved.

There was no point adding to her anxieties for today by arguing with her mother. She simply marched in step with her as they walked home.

The Duke was as good as his word, and a smart black carriage was waiting for Bridget outside the entrance to their little coffeehouse and home. The driver loitered near their door, straightening up when he noticed the women approaching. Bridget felt a rush of excitement pass through her as she considered that she was about to take a ride in this elegant vehicle. It was not a thing many girls of her acquaintance could claim to have done, and would be a nice little bonus to the day's work. There would be a number of these it seemed. The Duke undoubtedly had a wonderful and expensive kitchen and Bridget looked forward to working in such a space.

Beyond this, she would get to see one of the finer houses in London. She tried to keep her mind centred on the work ahead and kept her expression as serious and business like as she could.

"I assume you have been sent for me... I'm Miss Fairway?"

"That's right Miss." The driver doffed his cap. "The master bade me to give you this, Mrs Fairway." The man reached into his jacket and produced an envelope which he handed over with reverence, only letting go when he was sure Mrs Fairway had a firm grasp of it.

Bridget looked at her mother as she ripped open the envelope and looked inside. She puzzled over the way her mother's eyes seemed to widen.

Mrs. Fariway took a long moment to study the thing and then pursed her lips as she looked at the driver with disdain.

"Is this some kind of joke? Might you perhaps have mixed up deliveries and some other man has the correct pay owed to us for this day's work?"

"No mistake, ma'am. The Duke even labelled the envelope if you'd care for verification."

Mrs Fairway turned the envelope over and shook her head. "What ridiculousness."

"What is it, Mama?"

Bridget asked, trying to fathom just what the Duke could have put in the envelope to inspire such a reaction.

"He must think we are some kind of a charity case."

She handed Bridget the envelope and began to pace on the spot in frustration.

Bridget looked inside and found her hand trembling as she realised just what she was holding.

"Ten pounds? For one cooked meal?"

"Exactly," Mrs Fairway said, snatching the thing back. "I would dearly love to know who the Duke thinks he is trying to impress with this gift. I would have him know our coffeehouse is surviving perfectly well without his generosity. If he wants to give money to keep us going as a business, then he can come in and pay a penny for a cup the way other men do."

"Mother!" Bridget could not be sure she had heard her mother aright and shot an apologetic look to the Duke's driver.

"I am sure that the Duke did not mean to slight us in any way with this generous gift. Most likely, he was simply trying to express his gratitude. I am at least certain that he did not intend for you to react like this."

The driver gave a slow and solemn nod.

"Quite right. He is a little extravagant but he does not mean to lord it over other men. Why else would he choose to frequent a common coffee house so often... no offence meant of course."

His words might have done as much harm to Mrs Fairway's mood as good and Bridget bit her lip, hoping this whole fracas wouldn't see the carriage shooed away.

"Come Mama, if you wish me to, I can take the money with me to the Duke and inform him that we do not require so much for one day's work. There is no point, however, in delaying like this over conjecture and assumption about the meaning of this generous sum."

"You are far too eager to attend the Duke at all. If I could work my will, I'd send this man back to his master empty handed."

Mrs Fairway took a deep breath, her chest swelling massively as she tried to achieve some inner calm. Finally, she continued in a deflated, but no less bitter tone, "I will not have myself made into the villain here. Go do your duty child, as we had agreed, and then tell His Grace that we expect be paid exactly as was agreed and not a penny over."

Bridget, was not going to argue and risk her mother changing her mind on the issue.

Gripping the envelope containing the needlessly contentious money, she walked over to the carriage in silence. The driver seemed equally eager to avoid further quarrel and opened the door at once.

"Remember to be home no later than nine thirty. A minute later and I swear I will look to sue the Duke for every penny he owns."

Bridget ignored the voice calling to her as the carriage began to trundle down the street. Just what had come over her mother she could not say. This new attitude was so unlike her. Had it always been there?

There was much Bridget did not understand and she tried to quiet the questions in her mind as she was driven towards the Duke's home in Grosvenor Square.

ARIETTA RICHMOND, CATHERINE WINDSOR, ISABELLA THORNE, KATHERINE KEATS, KELLY ANNE BRUCE

Chapter Five

Bridget had assumed that she would be taken into the Duke's home via the rear tradesman's entrance. When the carriage pulled up outside the main entrance, with the great and the good of London milling about her, Bridget felt a little overwhelmed and hesitant about leaving the carriage. Was the Duke really happy to be seen admitting a woman of her social standing into his home for all to see? She would appear more as a guest than one hired to perform the business of cooking.

Once again, this did not seem to be a thing that the Duke minded, as he actually came out onto the street to greet her. It brought a smile to Bridget's face as she considered that he must have been waiting for her, standing by a window for some time, in order to receive her.

"Miss Fairway, I am exceedingly glad you were able to come. Time always seems to slow to a crawl when one is waiting for something, but I swear it seems like an age since I sent my carriage for you. I was beginning to fear you might have been unable to make it today."

The Duke hurried down his front steps, opening the door of the carriage for her and extending a hand.

Bridget took his hand, revelling in the sensation of her small fingers being wrapped up in his strong ones. She stepped out of the carriage, noting a few stares from passers-by, who were eager to see who the Duke was so eagerly greeting.

"I am sorry to have kept you. There was a small issue with my mother, but perhaps it is best we discuss that inside."

Bridget gave a weak smile, regretting the unpleasant attitude her mother had taken with his driver.

The Duke gave her a curious look, and nodded.

"By all means, let me escort you inside. You will take a drink before you set to your work, will you not? The coffee I have here pales in comparison to what you and your mother sell, but it has its own charms."

Bridget laughed, feeling her cheeks glow as she once again found herself falling easily under the spell of the man's charming ways.

"I suppose a quick drink to revitalize me might be welcome, though it cannot be for long as I will need to acquaint myself with your kitchen before I set to cooking."

The Duke's abode was incredible to behold. The rich carpet and plush chairs were all of such vibrant and warm colours that Bridget felt she was having a detrimental effect on their value just by being there. When she went to sit down, she made sure to brush the folds of her dress with her hand in order to shoo off any dust or dirt she might have picked up over the day.

The thought that she might damage or stain the furnishings had her on edge. Even holding the cup of coffee she was given filled her with fear, lest she spill it.

"So, I believe there was something you needed to discuss with me? No second thoughts or fears about cooking for me I hope?"

"Nothing like that, but I must return you this, and I am so sorry if it offends you." Bridget bit her lip as she reluctantly revealed the crumpled envelope containing the Duke's ten pounds.

"I am confused… This was supposed to be your payment for today's work." The man ran his fingers over the envelope, flattening the creases as he looked to Bridget for an answer.

"I am sorry. It was a very kind gesture, but I am afraid my mother saw it rather differently to how you might have intended. I think she saw it as an attempt to give us charity. I have honestly never seen her so proud before. She demanded I return this money to you and ask that I accept only the amount that we agreed on originally."

Bridget studied the Duke as he absorbed her words. If his expression was anything to go by, he was mortified.

"I… I see. Well, if you could please relay my humblest apologies on to your mother. I did not wish her any offence in the slightest. The sum was only meant to reflect my gratitude for your filling in at short notice and proportionate to the value of your cooking."

Bridget laughed at that last point and shook her head.

"I do not know what quality of fare Princes and Dukes are accustomed to, but I do not think any chef's skill is worth that much for a single meal. Honestly, were I to accept that amount of money, I do not think I would ever be happy with what I would finally lay on the table before you."

"I am sorry." The Duke's head was turned slightly away from her, his eyes seemingly unable to meet hers. "I should have thought more instead of acting rashly. It is, one might say, a bad habit of mine."

Bridget took a deep breath and strove to meet the man's gaze, craning her neck slightly until she was able to catch his eye.

"Please do not be so hard on yourself. It was honestly a lovely thought. I am afraid that my mother has become rather unpredictable of late, but it is not your fault. Do not let yourself dwell on it. After all, you have guests arriving in the next few hours and I can think of nothing more off-putting than a sour host."

The Duke laughed and ran a hand through his short dark hair.

"I must look like a petulant child about now."

Bridget giggled. "Just a little. Still, I think it's better to be chastised for trying to commit an act of kindness, than for one of wickedness. I really, honestly, appreciate what you were trying to do with your gift. Perhaps you can still pay us the total sum over time. If you come by our coffeehouse each day for the next few years I am sure you will end up paying ten pounds eventually."

The Duke nodded and took a deep breath. His humour recovered, his eyes met her with a fresh confidence.

"It is a promise then, Miss Fairway. Every day for the next year."

Bridget laughed even more.

"What was it you were saying about acting rashly? Perhaps you shouldn't promise past Easter, lest chance or circumstance forces you to break your word on the issue."

Her eyes sparkled and she felt her breath catch as she realised that she was actually flirting with the man.

"Well then, I will promise until Easter and have to ensure that I purchase a lot of cake in that time, to try and smuggle this ten pounds into your mother's purse somehow."

The Duke put the envelope into his pocket, his humour seemingly returned.

"Try not to let yourself grow too rotund. I am not sure a full, fat belly would suit you."

"Shocking reply, Miss Fairway! Who knew you could be so judging of appearances."

Both laughed and Bridget found herself playing with one of the ringlet curls framing the side of her face.

"I wouldn't want you losing the good opinion of Lady Primrose now."

Those words ended the humorous banter and a silence took over the room. Once again, neither the Duke nor Bridget could look the other in the eye.

"Perhaps I should show you to the kitchen so that you can get yourself prepared. I am sure there is a lot you'll need to do and I do not wish to see you rushed."

Despite the difficulty of working in a largely unknown space, Bridget felt that she handled the task of cooking for the Duke exceedingly well. The various courses came out on time and everything was cooked to her satisfaction. However, she was anxious for some feedback and harassed the servants every time they came down, asking them to tell her how the Duke and his friends seemed to be reacting to the meal. Without exception, they all assured her that all in the party were perfectly pleased with the food she had provided for them, but this was not enough to satisfy her.

Since hearing the Duke first complimenting her baking skills at the coffee house, Bridget found that second hand praise was no longer adequate. She wanted an opinion straight from the Duke if she could have it, and she prayed that she might have an occasion to see the man once more, before she was returned home. As the hour approached nine though, and Bridget realised that the Duke's guests were not in any great hurry to leave, she accepted that she would likely not hear any report of how her food had been received.

Assured that the cleaning up of dishes and utensils could be left to the servants, Bridget began to collect up her things and bade one of the servants inform the Duke that she was ready to leave. Hopefully, he had remembered to have the carriage made ready for her, as well as the correct payment her mother had insisted on. It was not long before the same servant returned, bidding Bridget to go upstairs.

She expected to be led quietly to the door and maybe paid her dues on the way out. Instead, the servant led her up to the second floor, where the Duke and his guests were currently reclining in the drawing room.

Ushered into the room, Bridget could feel her face turning crimson as the assembled guests simultaneously began to applaud. She could swear that she felt hotter in this moment than she had earlier, slaving over the Duke's stove, and a part of her wished that she could retreat back into the corridor.

"My dear friends, might I present Miss Bridget Fairway, the saviour of our evening." The Duke walked to Bridget's side, hand pressing on her back as he encouraged her further into the room. "We have all been remarking on how excellent the meal was tonight. I could not let you return home until my guests had a chance to thank you personally for the contribution you have made to our evening."

"Well, that is very kind of you, Your Grace, my Lords and Ladies." Bridget gave a formal curtsy and turned her attention to the Duke. "I believe it is time I returned home, before my mother grows worried."

"You will not stay for a drink?"

One of the men in the company seemed somewhat disappointed by the revelation and a few other voices rose up to coerce the Duke into forcing her to stay awhile.

"I am sure that one drink would not hurt too terribly, would it, Miss Fairway? You might have it while my driver readies the carriage, and it will help to keep off the chill during your return home."

Bridget bit her lip and looked the Duke in the eyes. She found it so difficult to disagree with anything that he suggested, especially when it led to more time in his company. Only the lingering stare of Lady Primrose stood against her, but Bridget found herself prepared to ignore this.

"One drink only. I need hardly tell you that my mother will not stand for it if I am home any later than the agreed upon time."

Chapter Six

As it transpired, being home on time, and with the correct payment Mrs. Fairway wished to see, was not enough to please her. As soon as Bridget had stepped out of the carriage, her mother had smelt the alcohol on her breath and flew into a fit of temper. A barrage of questions were put to Bridget, some incredibly offensive to both her and the Duke equally. Most of these referred to the Duke's use of her time and checking that he had not tried to put a hand to her while she was 'inebriated'.

This was the term that Mrs. Fairway used, but it was far too overdramatic for the small glass of wine Bridget had taken at the Duke's home. Sent to bed after a barrage of harsh words and comment, Bridget feared just how her mother would be the next time the Duke happened to enter the coffeehouse. She remembered the promise he had made to visit every day over the rest of the Easter period. This could be a very dangerous thing for the man, now that her mother had so inexplicably taken against him.

As Monday morning came, Bridget could not help but feel a sense of trepidation as she went down into the kitchen, to begin the familiar work of baking for the day's clientele. There was much hanging on her heart it seemed. There was a real desire to see the Duke live up to his promise of returning to the coffeehouse, but added to this was the fear that her mother would find more fault with the man, and with her too. She had been warned against forming any kind of feeling for the Duke, but Bridget just couldn't help but do so.

In spite of his somewhat extravagant nature, he had a kind heart and seemed genuinely interested in her. What's more, he felt completely genuine in his praise of her craft. About the only thing not to like about the man was his tendency to come by the coffeehouse with a new woman every month. Perhaps it was this tendency in him which had her mother most concerned. Certainly, she reflected, she would not look forward to his being more often at the coffeehouse if it meant seeing him always in the company of someone like Lady Primrose.

As had become her custom, Bridget spent her free moments taking glances at the front of the coffeehouse from the kitchen door, eager to see if the Duke would keep his word to her. It was not like she could sit down and have a proper conversation should he come in, but it would be enough to know that he had kept his promise.

Customers were beginning to return to the coffeehouse. One by one, the most fickle and weak-willed found themselves giving up on their Lenten promises and coming back in search of coffee and a slice of something sweet to eat.

Of course, these types always tried to offset their guilt by begging Mrs Fairway to only cut them a small slice of whatever cake they happened to order. This, they hoped, would be enough to absolve them of the sin they were committing by breaking their fasts. Neighbours who would otherwise greet each other and share a table sat apart, tacitly ignoring each other as they all succumbed to their personal vices in quiet shame.

By one in the afternoon, there had been no sight of the Duke. Bridget had arrived at a routine of peering out into the front of house every half an hour or so, and was just about to do so again when she found the door leading from the kitchen to the main house floor to be locked. This came as a shock to her and she turned the handle a second time just to ensure that she had not imagined the resistance there.

She frowned as she stared at the wood for an answer. Why would her mother suddenly choose to lock the door into the kitchens? In the past, she had only done such a thing if patrons became rowdy for any reason. Still, she could hear no ruckus and so had to assume that all was in order out front.

She continued to stand by the door for some time, knocking once to see if her mother would come and unlock the door for her and give some reasonable explanation for her imprisonment. There was no answer and eventually Bridget was forced to return to the kitchen and wait until her mother came down to her.

"Do we have any more round cake ready, dearest?" Mrs Fairway came into the kitchen in a great hurry and with a smile on her face that Bridget could not account for.

It had been over an hour since she had discovered the kitchen door locked, and she watched her mother in confusion. She could not work out just why she looked so cheery and offered no explanation at all as to why she had been left locked in the kitchen for the last hour.

"I made some earlier this morning. Over there."

Bridget pointed dumbly to where the freshly baked cake was laid out on a large decorative stand.

"Very good. It looks wonderful. I am sure it will go down a treat with the customers upstairs."

Mrs Fairway grabbed the thing and seemed set to retreat in a hurry.

"Did you lock the door to the kitchen earlier? I tried knocking to get your attention but you didn't answer me."

Bridget stared at her mother, noting the way she seemed to be making an exorbitant show of studying the cake she held.

"Oh, I was just worried about two customers who were arguing over some trivial matter. It came to nothing, but I didn't want to risk it if a fight broke out."

"Strange, I didn't hear any raised voices."

Bridget inched closer to her mother as she tried to read her face for the truth.

"Well, as I said, it came to nothing. That kind of thing is just part of the trade."

Bridget took a deep breath and decided to ask the one question that she knew could ignite her mother's mood.

"I do not suppose the Duke happened to come by while I was in here, did he?"

"Not at all. It's rather absurd of you to think he would call by so often. I told you, I've had reason to worry about you ever meeting the young Duke. You're getting grand romantic ideas with absolutely no basis in reality."

Mrs. Fairway began to move back to the door, taking swift strides as though trying to outrun something. She mumbled something about not keeping the customers waiting as she made her escape.

Left alone once more, Bridget found herself, for the first time in her life, actually concerned about being in the kitchen. For years she had always accepted her place in the back of the shop and away from those who frequented their family's establishment. She had never thought of herself as having been imprisoned or kept away from others.

After all that had happened since she had met the Duke though, she could not help but wonder if her mother was, indeed, seeking to keep her locked away. She felt certain that the Duke had called when her mother had locked the door.

If he kept to his word, Bridget knew that he would return the next day and every day thereafter for the rest of Lent. There was no way on earth that her mother could keep her tucked away from view for that long with only paper thin excuses to shield herself.

ARIETTA RICHMOND, CATHERINE WINDSOR, ISABELLA THORNE, KATHERINE
KEATS, KELLY ANNE BRUCE

Chapter Seven

By the time the week revolved back around to Sunday, Bridget had found herself locked in the kitchen on five separate occasions. On the Friday, the door had been kept locked for a full three hours straight. As much as it dismayed her to know that her mother was purposefully trying to keep her in seclusion, it was incredibly pleasing to think that the Duke had kept to his word and come by the coffeehouse every day in the week.

His dedication to keeping his promise, even without Bridget coming out to thank him for it, touched her deeply. She pictured him drinking his coffee alone, no doubt asking questions about her, while her mother fed him lies or excuses as to why her daughter was indisposed.

With every day that had passed, Bridget had given her mother the opportunity to come clean and admit to having purposefully kept her from seeing the Duke. She did not want to have to accuse her only remaining parent of lying to her, and prayed that the Duke's persistence in visiting would eventually force her mother to reveal the truth.

However, now that a week had passed, it seemed that her mother was far more stubborn than Bridget had at first believed.

Throughout the morning service, Bridget found herself casting her mind back to when her father had still been alive. The loss was still relatively recent: three years in November. Before his untimely death, she remembered working hard, but not to the same extent she did now. In those days, her father had insisted on her having time to herself, to mingle with others and to have friends of her own.

After he passed away, Bridget had let herself become absorbed into the work of keeping the coffeehouse, his legacy, alive. Her mother had done much the same, throwing herself into the work with a zeal that bordered on the fanatic. Their cousin, who had inherited Mr Fairway's estate, had offered, on more than one occasion, to sell the coffeehouse for Mrs Fairway and give her the profits so that she might live elsewhere in relative idleness. It was an offer that Mrs Fairway always refused, citing that she needed to keep her husband's business going, that she was not prepared to see the life they had made together crumble apart, now that he had gone. As soon as the service was over, Bridget went to her mother with her simple request.

"Mother, I would like to go pay my respects to father, if you don't mind."

Mrs Fairway narrowed her eyes and her brow knotted as she looked at her child. Bridget wondered if she might actually refuse her request, but conversation with another woman had her momentarily preoccupied.

"Yes, I suppose that is fine. Just do not be too long about it. I would like to start for home in the next ten minutes, and do not wish to have to come down to that part of the graveyard in order to fetch you."

Bridget nodded.

"Of course, mother. I will not be too long."

She was not about to argue or whine. This was the first freedom she had been allowed all week and she was not going to risk losing the opportunity by trying to extend it.

Slipping quietly away through the large wooden doors, Bridget found herself taking in great lungfuls of air. It was far warmer today, but the fresh air was still welcoming to her. It felt as though this momentary escape from her mother's side was coming up from a long spell under water, and she savoured every breath she could take before the current of her life would invariably drag her down again.

As she began to walk hurriedly along the side path of the chapel, Bridget almost failed to notice the man standing near the front gate of the church. It was only as the figure moved in her direction, seemingly bent on pursuing her, that she turned around in surprise.

Standing before her was none other than the Duke, resplendent in his Sunday best. The man did not smile as he so often did. His face was a picture of concern and worry as he looked on her with questioning eyes.

"Miss Fairway, forgive me for descending on you so suddenly and on a Sunday."

Bridget felt a shiver pass through her body and looked towards the church door. She knew that, at any moment, her mother would emerge, giving them little time for a long colloquy.

"I am happy to see you, Your Grace. I feared I might not get the chance. Pray tell me, have you been honouring the promise you made me Sunday last, when I cooked at your estate?"

With time of the essence it was vital that she find her answers quickly. The Duke's confused look seemed to give her the answer.

"Of course I have, all this week in fact. Did... your mother did not tell you I have been calling, did she?"

Bridget shook her head.

"I have no idea why. She has been so resistant to your talking to me in any way. She says it is to protect me as she fears I might develop feelings for you..." Bridget trailed off, surprised at how candid she was being on the subject

"I see... I must confess I feared something like this might occur. The way that your mother has been with me over the past days had me worried about just what was going on. I could not help thinking that something was amiss. I remembered our first meeting when I joked that she must keep you under lock and key. The more I considered this, the more I let myself worry."

"I fear you were right to. I do not know what has happened to her of late. Since I met you, it is as though she has become an entirely different person, one I no longer recognise."

"Can I assist you at all Miss Fairway?" the Duke moved closer to her, reaching out to touch her arm.

"I do not know what there is to be done, Your Grace," Bridget admitted sadly.

"I could make you an offer," the Duke said in a hushed tone. He whispered something quietly in her ear. Bridget's eyes widened and she took a step back from the Duke.

"Marriage? You cannot be serious, Your Grace. We hardly know each other. I could not ask you to do such a thing just to aid me in escaping my mother."

The Duke nodded but took Bridget's hands in his.

"This is not just some whimsical proposal I am making in jest Miss Fairway. While the circumstances are not ideal, I have found myself pondering you often since our first meeting. There is an honesty and vitality to you that I have not found in other ladies of standing I have met over my Seasons here in town. While I would like to know you better, I will confess, I have entertained the thought of a future together. I hope that does not seem too forward of me to say."

"Not... not at all," Bridget admitted, feeling flustered by the frank admission the Duke had made. "But... what of Lady Primrose? I thought you and her were..."

"I have not seen Lady Primrose since Sunday last. She is a woman who aims, as so many do, to find a husband of wealth and means. I have no doubt she will recover quickly from losing me and move on to find another man of suitable wealth to meet her needs. I would much rather someone honest and real."

Bridget closed her eyes, trying to fight back tears that were born of equal parts happiness and disappointment.

"I would dearly love to accept you right now, but I cannot accept you, knowing that I am doing so in order to flee my mother. Even if we were to have a happy and blissful marriage, I would always feel regret, knowing that I had accepted you for some reason other than love."

Before either could speak further, a voice from the church door caught their attention.

"Bridget! I thought you said you were going to your father's…" Mrs Fairway's words caught in her throat as she recognised the person speaking to her daughter.

"Excuse me, Your Grace, I did not realise it was you. I am afraid my daughter and I have to be going. I am eager to return home to get started on preparing for the new week."

"We know you have been lying to us both Mama."

Bridget blurted out her confession, her voice strained with hurt at the deception her mother had perpetrated.

Mrs. Fairway looked back at some of the other parishioners who had stopped to witness the exchange.

"I am only trying to look out for you my dearest. I wish you could see it. This man will use you and discard you the moment he becomes bored with you."

"For your information, Mother, the Duke has just asked me to marry him. I hardly believe that to be the action of someone wanting only to use me, do you?"

Mrs. Fairway's expression turned to one of abject horror in that moment.

"Is this true, Your Grace?" She whispered the words, her body quaking as she looked at them both.

"Yes, it is true. I would have liked to have done things properly and courted your daughter as a proper gentleman should. However, your lies and deception have forced me to ask for her hand now, if only to protect her from whatever imprisonment you are holding her in."

"I am not holding her in a prison!"

"Yes, you are mother." Bridget interjected, with a fierce passion in her voice. "I never noticed it until I met the Duke, but you have kept me hidden away in that kitchen ever since father died. I thought, at first, that it was because we were always so busy managing the coffeehouse, but now I am convinced that there is something more to it. You've been locking me away whenever the Duke calls, hoping that I would not notice. To top it all off, you were perfectly happy to speak good things of the man until he came to know me. If you had a serious dislike of his character, I cannot believe you would have praised him to me, as you had done."

Mrs. Fairway was beginning to cry. Tears were forming in the corner of her eye and she seemed to struggle to form her words.

"I do not want to lose you, child! Is that such a crime? After losing your father, I felt my whole world being taken from me. I just wanted to keep us together as a family. I couldn't bear to lose you too."

Bridget's mouth fell open at her mother's confession.

"You mean that all of this was just to ensure that I never met a man I might marry? What did you think I would do Mama? Did you think I would marry and suddenly want nothing to do with you in the future?"

The Duke looked at Mrs Fairway, his face seeming to soften, and he spoke gently.

"I can see that there is far more going on here than meets the eye. I do not think it can do any good for anyone to have this aired publicly. Perhaps, if we can all retire to your home, we might get to the bottom of this matter."

Bridget looked at her mother, trying to resist the urge to feel sorry for her. It was never going to work. Whatever she had done, she was still her mother, and she could not bear to see her reduced to a crying mess in front of the entire parish.

"Yes. Mother, I think it is perhaps best we return home. I would ask you not to leave though, Your Grace. Even if some words have to be shared privately, I would feel better knowing you are close by."

The Duke nodded.

"I would prefer it that way too."

Chapter Eight

It took time, hours, for Mrs Fairway to confront the real reasons that had driven her to keep her daughter carefully guarded away, the real reasons that she had taken against the possibility of Bridget forming an alliance with the Duke. She had not even been fully aware of it herself, until forced to admit it in that fit of emotion outside the church. Since the death of her husband, Bridget's father, she had done everything in her power to try to preserve life as it had been, as close as she could keep things to the way they had been before the tragic loss of her husband.

Above all things, Mrs Fairway feared change, feared the possibility of the world moving on, and of her being left behind, alone. It was not enough to excuse her for what she had tried to do, but it was enough for the Duke to pity her. As he waited in the front of house with a cup of coffee, he hoped that Bridget and Mrs. Fairway would be able to reconcile their differences, allow their family to move on from Mr Fairway's death, and allow him the chance to be a part of that new family when the time came.

It was late in the afternoon, and the sun was low in the sky when Mrs Fairway emerged with her daughter. The Duke stood, nervously looking between the two women for a sign to indicate what outcome they might have reached. It was Bridget's weak but certain smile that allowed him to feel a measure of relief.

"Thank you for waiting so patiently, Your Grace."

Bridget spoke in a soft voice. As the light from the window lit her face, it was plain to see that she had been crying.

"Is there anything I can do for you... either of you?"

Mrs. Fairway shook her head. She seemed older somehow than she usually did. It was as though, for the first time in years, she had allowed herself to stop and, in doing so, realised just how tired and worn down she had become.

"You have done quite enough, your Grace... and I mean that in the best possible sense. Had you not been so persistent in these last two weeks since meeting my daughter, I doubt I would ever have come to confront the truth of things as I have been made to today."

"The truth of things?" the Duke repeated the phrase with uncertainty.

"That I need to let go of the past and accept that there is a future that awaits us: a future for me and a future for my daughter. Keeping this coffeehouse open the last two years has been taxing for both of us. It has left us without friends and, until you came along, left my daughter without anyone she might have as her own. I thought it was helping me deal with the loss of my dear husband."

She smiled weakly, and continued.

"Yet I know now that all it did was allow me to ignore his absence. I could wake up in the morning and just get on with the day as we always did, pretending that he was just elsewhere, due back at some point in the near future. I sound foolish, I know."

"I know that a death can be hard to deal with, Mrs. Fairway, and I am sorry if I seemed insensitive or accusatory when I confronted you in the churchyard."

"It was necessary, I think." Mrs Fairway sighed and looked at her daughter. "I think that I will leave you to tell His Grace the rest. If it is all the same to you, I would like to be alone for a while."

The Duke watched as Mrs. Fairway walked silently to the door and left the shop. "Will she be alright?"

"Given time, I am sure that she will mend. She has taken an important first step." There was still a note of sadness in Bridget's voice, but her slight smile revealed hope. "I do not know if the offer you made in the churchyard still stands, Your Grace, but, among other issues discussed, my mother did give her consent for me to accept you, if your proposal still stands."

"You know that I will not force you away from your mother, or try to tear you apart from each other. If it would please you and secure your happiness, I would gladly have you both live with me. My house here in London has a spare room she could take up. My estate in the country, meanwhile, has enough rooms that your mother could have an entire wing to herself should she desire it."

Bridget laughed and her body drew closer to the Duke's as their hands entwined.

"That would be wonderful! Just perfect, as I think Mother has agreed that we should sell the coffeehouse and let another take over its running. So, if I did not accept you, we might find ourselves homeless, if in possession of some funds."

The Duke took a deep breath and leaned forward so that his and Bridget's foreheads lightly touched.

"You know that I will look after you. But are you sure about selling this place on?"

Bridget nodded, her fingers tightening their grip on the Duke. "I think it is for the best, and in keeping with the spirit of the season."

"How do you mean?" the Duke asked, curiously.

"I think I have come to realise that Easter isn't about abstaining from bad habits for a finite number of days. It is about releasing oneself from the past and looking forward to the future. After all, at the core of it, we are celebrating the transition from death to new life. Out on the hills, just shy of where my dear father is buried, there will be new lambs taking their first steps. In a sense, my mother and I are just like them, both moving forward into a new world and finding our feet."

The Duke found his lips drawing closer to Bridget's until at last they met. For a long moment, the two held their kiss, savouring the sensation and yet another new beginning for them both.

"I think I like your interpretation of Easter, Miss Fairway," he whispered in her ear, as they held each other.

Epilogue

Eyelids fluttered open and there was a yawn. As tiny eyes adjusted to the light pouring in through the windows, the little baby began to squirm. It did not cry; it rarely cried. Still, its odd sounds and gurgles garnered the attention of those lying in the bed next to its cradle. Bridget left her husband sleeping, and silently lifted her little boy from his cradle, walking him down the corridor as she prepared to give him his morning feed.

Once little Isaac was contented, Bridget bounced him on her arm, eliciting the most curious happy gurgles and squeals of delight as she ventured downstairs towards the dining room. As always, her mother was already up and had taken breakfast well in advance of her daughter and son-in-law.

"You know mother, you are not running a coffeehouse anymore, you do not have to wake at the crack of dawn."

"I know, but I do look forward to seeing my adorable little grandson every morning." As she spoke, Mrs Fairway put out her hands, eager to take the little baby into her arms.

Bridget carefully handed her son over to her mother and smiled as she watched her dote on him. She let out a contented sigh.

"If you don't mind holding him for a while, I shall try to see if I can coax my husband out of bed."

"Good luck with that," Mrs Fairway teased.

As the sound of her daughter's footsteps receded, Mrs Fairway walked over to the window. Outside, on the Duke's lawns, a procession of baby geese were following their mother from the pond onto a stretch of grass.

"Easter will be coming around soon. That's your grandmother's favourite time of year you know... a season for changes. I didn't always approve of change you know. Did I ever tell you the story of the Easter that changed your mama's and my life forever? If it weren't for that Easter, you might never have been born. That's when I first realised how good a change could be."

The End

~~~~~
~~~~~

Thank you for reading! I truly hope you enjoyed
The Duke's Easter Proposal!

If you have any questions or comments I'd be happy
to hear from you.

Feel free to contact me – Katherine Keats at
KatherineKeatsBooks@gmail.com.

You will also receive updates and advance notice of
upcoming releases.

I look forward to hearing from you!

You'll find a special preview of my book, '**Escaping
the Duke**' just after the **About the Author** Section!

About the Author

Katherine Keats writes sweet and clean Regency Romance. She's a hopeless romantic who loves music, dancing, and long walks on the beach. She enjoys writing stories of true love that defy all odds.

You can connect with Katherine on her Facebook page at:

https://www.facebook.com/KatherineKeatsAuthor/

Or follow her on her author page at:

https://www.amazon.com/Katherine-Keats/e/B01N3R8L65/

Get in touch at:

KatherineKeatsBooks@gmail.com

Other Books by Katherine Keats

Clean Regency Romance

The Duke's Unlikely Bride

The Duke's Dangerous Dilemma

Rescuing the Earl

The Duke and the Dressmaker

If you enjoyed reading ***The Duke's Easter Proposal*** then I'm certain you will also enjoy my other recent releases: You can pick them up now for FREE on Kindle Unlimited.

As a special thank you for reading I'm including a preview here for you to enjoy. Turn the page for your preview of 'Escaping the Duke'

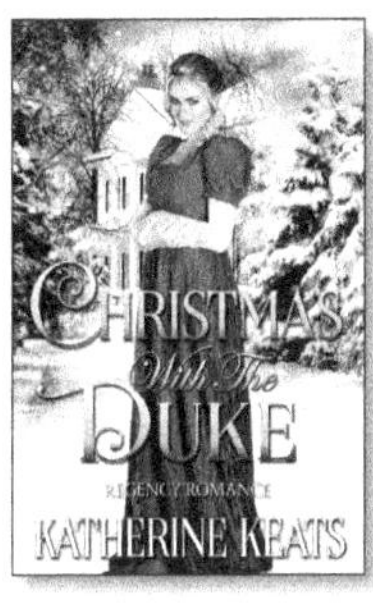

Christmas with the Duke

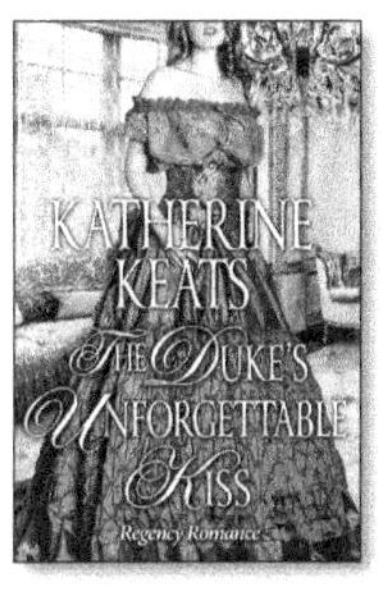

The Duke's Unforgettable Kiss

A Christmas Surprise

A Gentleman's Gamble

ARIETTA RICHMOND, CATHERINE WINDSOR, ISABELLA THORNE, KATHERINE KEATS, KELLY ANNE BRUCE

Here is Your Preview of

Escaping the Duke

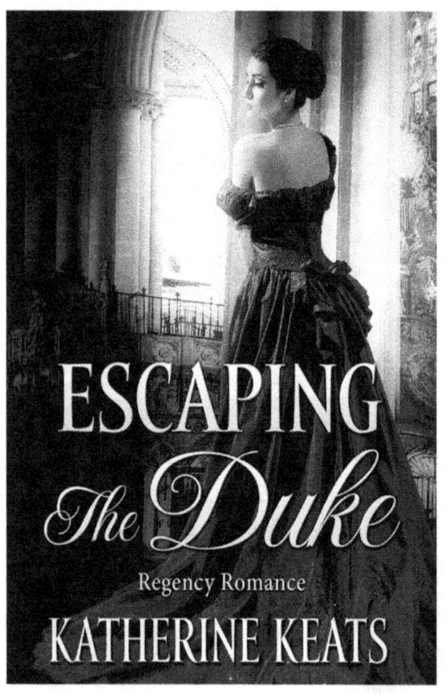

Katherine Keats

Chapter One

Rebecca moved through the bustling crowds with all the skill of a cutpurse. More than a few stopped to stare at her as she fled by in a blur of blonde hair and blue cloth and they clutched their belongings tightly, just to assure themselves that they were still there. Rebecca barely paid heed to the folk; they were only obstacles to be negotiated as she ran home with the biggest smile painted on her face.

Her head was filled with visions of how her mother and father would react. She could imagine squeals of joy and dancing around the table in their small riverside dwelling. Their fortunes were about to change incalculably and she owed it all to the benevolent Mr Clements.

Mr Clements was like a knight from some legend. Goodness seemed to radiate from him and he never let his rank dictate who he could or couldn't talk to. He seemed to take pride in frequenting the lowlier taverns of London and avoiding the grand soirees and parties of the capital's elite.

It made him popular with all within the river-side taverns and many had cause to praise the man for his expansive character and generosity of spirit. However, as Rebecca ran home to meet her parents she could not imagine anyone being more greatly indebted to the man than she was now.

Running up the wooden stairs, which were precariously affixed to the outside wall of her house, she fumbled with the key before bursting into the single floor apartment that she called home.

"Rebecca? I could have sworn someone was trying to drive a herd of cattle up our stairs from all the noise you just made." Mr Johnson looked at his daughter with an air of suspicion. His face grew concerned when he noticed how flushed and out of breath she was. "My goodness girl, what has happened? Did someone try to attack you in the streets?"

Rebecca smiled and shook her head. She enjoyed the way that her father was so protective of her, always assuming that the worst might befall her on any given day, and equally prepared to revenge himself on any who would sully his daughter's honour.

"Please relax Father, it is nothing so bad. I was running because I have good news!"

Mrs Johnson, who had been attending to the gently cooking dinner on the hearth, looked up with fascination.

"I should hope it is good news considering you should be working at the Three Crowns tonight." Both she and Mr Johnson looked at their daughter expectantly, watching her already rosy cheeks glow with pride.

"I have been asked to work at Perryway Hall as a maid to Robert Clements, the Duke of Kent."

Rebecca continued to smile at her parents, her body struggling to remain still and not dance about the room at once. Only her parents' surprised and sceptical faces helped to lessen the excitement that had been whipped up within her.

"A servant to the Duke of Kent?" Mr Johnson exchanged a disbelieving look with his wife. "Who said you were guaranteed such a posting? I very much doubt the Duke himself came to the Three Crowns to offer you such a position."

Rebecca giggled and shook her head. "No. But John Clements, who you might remember I have been talking of for quite a few nights now, informed me of the open position at his brother's estate and assures me that his good word would be enough to convince his brother to take me on."

Mrs Johnson left the food to its own devices, standing up and taking her place by her husband's side. "But the Clements do not live anywhere near London. It is almost a full day's ride to their estate in the country."

"Yes, Mother it is a long way. Still, think of how well paid the position would be. Mr Clements has assured me that I could expect wages of up to twelve pounds a year, plus my room and board included. Imagine what that would do for us were I to save it and send you some back, not to mention the money you would save on keeping me fed and clothed. Don't think I don't know what a burden it is for you, trying to keep the three of us fed each day Father. If I were to take this position it would change all of our fortunes for the better."

Mr Johnson looked up at his wife and his lip curled. "Twelve pounds a year? That is quite a sum for a female servant. Is this Mr Clements absolutely sure his brother will pay?"

"I am quite sure he is capable of paying as much; he is a Duke after all!"

Rebecca continued to fidget, though now her movements were laced with nervousness. Her news had not been met with the enthusiasm she had hoped for, and she began to doubt if her over-protective father would actually allow her take a job so far from his watchful eyes. Mrs Johnson's eyes narrowed as she watched her.

"Has this Mr Clements made any kind of intimation that he is interested in you, Rebecca?"

Rebecca bit her lip and felt her cheeks flush hot. It was something that always made lying an impossibility for her.

"He has not said in words that he is interested in me, no. However, I can't help but think there is something between us. I think that he wants me to accept the post at his brother's estate so that he can continue to know me better. He goes back to the country in the next few days, and we will be unlikely to see each other again if I do not take this job."

Mr Johnson gave a solemn and slow nod, tenting his fingers as he looked up at his daughter from his chair. "I do not mean to sound cruel to you, but what would a man of his standing want in associating with a girl who could never amount to more than a servant among the gentry? Whenever a man of that kind shows interest in a commonplace girl, like yourself, it only ends in illegitimate children and broken promises."

"Father!" Rebecca was shocked by his pessimism and candour. "For one thing, you know me better than that. I would never give myself to anyone but my husband, should I be blessed enough to have one. More importantly, I don't believe Mr Clements is the kind of man to act that way. If he was looking for an easy woman to conquer, there are plenty of other more amenable women at the docksides. Everyone at the Three Crowns and the other taverns has been tremendously impressed by his generosity and virtue. I trust him not to try to injure me in any way. More importantly though, I trust myself not to let a man use me so."

Mrs Johnson took a deep breath, her eyes wavering between her daughter and her husband. She put her hand on his shoulder, massaging it gently as she spoke.

"I do think our daughter is sensible enough not to put herself at risk, and I will admit to having heard nothing but praise for Mr Clements, on my walks through the markets and shops. Were he trying to abuse her in any way, I do not think he would go to such great lengths as to offer her employment in his brother's home. In an estate as grand as Perryway Hall, there will be plenty of other servants about to look after our girl. Plus, if Mr Clements does prove to have honourable intentions towards our Rebecca, it would be a shame to stand in the way of such an alliance. She really could do no better than the younger brother of a Duke."

Mr Johnson's grim expression began to soften. His eyes stopped scrutinizing his daughter and he let out a defeated sigh. "I suppose you are right, about both Mr Clements and the opportunity this presents for us. I would like to meet him for myself though, before I give my final say on the matter."

Rebecca's face lit up and she could not stop herself from running over to embrace her mother and father.

"Thank you! I am sure that Mr Clements will not object to meeting with you to allay any of your fears, and I promise you, you will both find him quite charming and agreeable."

Mr Johnson returned his daughter's embrace with a light pat, hardly enthusiastic.

"Yes, well, we shall see how things go. For now, just be sure to arrange a good time for me to meet with him, to better discuss this opportunity he has given you."

Chapter Two

Exactly as Rebecca had predicted, one meeting with Mr Clements was enough to set her father at ease. He had an uncanny ability to make others happy and to gain their confidence. In the case of Mr Johnson, Clements offered to take the man out for a meal and was willing to devote half the day to allaying the man's fears for his daughter's safety.

"I will admit that Mr Clements is exactly how you painted him - very charming, gregarious and charitable, but not to the extent where you feel that he is rubbing his wealth in your face. Why, by the end of our meeting, I would quite happily have taken a job at his brother's estate myself, if he had offered me one."

Rebecca laughed, reassured to know that her father thought the man as honourable as she did.

"I may go to Perryway Hall then?"

"I do not see how I can stop you. Honestly, if Mr Clements were to ask for your hand this very afternoon I would have a hard time refusing him."

Rebecca kissed her father's cheek.

"I am sure we are some way off such a happy event... but maybe, given enough time, I might be writing to you with happy news."

Mr Johnson smiled and gave his daughter a warm embrace.

"You had best go and pack your things. Mr Clements had aimed to return to Perryway Hall yesterday, and only remained in town so as to see me. I have agreed to have you waiting for him, at the end of the street, tomorrow morning. His carriage will pick you up and take you to your new home."

Though he spoke with pride and happiness, Rebecca could see the tears that her father was struggling to hold back. She did not leave him but for a moment held him in a tight embrace.

The next morning, Rebecca found herself alone on the street corner, waiting for Mr Clements' carriage. She had made her goodbyes in the house and begged her father and mother to wait inside, rather than see her off themselves. The thought of them waving her goodbye,, and slowly disappearing from view, was too much for her to bear, and she did not wish to hold up Mr Clements by forcing him to endure the long tearful farewells which she would likely make, if given the opportunity. So, when the man's black carriage pulled up, Rebecca was able to pass her single trunk of possessions to the driver, and step straight into the carriage, alone with Mr Clements.

Mr Clements was the kind of man who not only embodied the personality of noble knights and princes from fairy tales, but also possessed their good looks too.

Some might have called him a rake, though none who knew his character would dare put such a label upon him. He had a svelte physique, sharp jaw and strong cheek bones framing beautiful hazel eyes that sparkled with the wit and vivacity that his soul possessed. His chestnut brown hair was short and fell in tight ringlet curls like a cherub of Grecian myth.

Combined with his impeccable taste in clothing, tailored perfectly to show off his enviable figure, he was the culmination of every good physical quality a woman should find desirable in a man. When he smiled down at her and extended his hand to help her into the carriage, Rebecca could not deny the butterflies that erupted inside her.

"Miss Johnson, good morning. I cannot tell you how much relieved I feel about returning to my family home, knowing that it will not affect my ability to come to know you better."

Rebecca smiled in return, trying to hold back a tell-tale blush from rising to her cheeks. She strained to remind herself that, most importantly, this was to be a financial, rather than romantic move for her. She should not hold out hope for a man of such wealth and standing as Mr Clements to consider her as a suitable candidate for marriage. He likely only wished for a friend.

Settling onto the opposite seat in the carriage from Mr Clements, Rebecca tried her best to ignore the fact that she was alone with the gentleman. For his part, Mr Clements seemed singularly at ease, lounging on his side of the carriage like he was resting on a couch. His eyes danced over Rebecca from time to time, seeming to have no qualms about being in such close and private proximity with her.

It was a trait that she both admired and feared in him. It was flattering to be the object of his attention, but she felt just a little embarrassed at the same time.

"Is there something on my face I should be aware of?"

Rebecca ran a hand through her hair, brushing a stray auburn curl behind her ear.

"Not at all, your face is perfectly charming. I would not be looking upon it so intently if it were not so."

This time, Rebecca could not hold back the blush that rose to her cheek and she bit her bottom lip in annoyance.

"Tell me Mr Clements, do your compliments stem from a particular desire to ignore the bounds of propriety, laid down for us by society for our own good, or could it be that you simply enjoy trying to embarrass me with such brazen compliments, as a sport?"

Mr Clements grin only grew in size and mischievous intent.

"Why can't it be a little of both?" he asked. "Of course, I do not wish to make the journey to Perryway Hall uncomfortable for you. I shall desist if you find my attentions too much."

Rebecca took a deep breath and looked out of the carriage window. It was easier to calm her heated mind when not looking into the gentleman's playful, hazel eyes.

"Perhaps we can come to a mutually agreeable compromise? I will admit to being particularly flattered by your compliments. In return, you can promise not to try and bait my blushes with such pretty words for the remainder of our travel."

Mr Clements made a show of thinking the matter over, tilting his head up and gazing at the carriage roof. Finally, his eye met Rebecca's again.

"Very well."

He put out a hand to her expectantly.

Smiling, Rebecca put out hers to shake on their playfully made bargain. Once again, she found herself duped by the man as he took her offered hand and planted a kiss upon it. She pulled back at once in shock, but the smile remained on her face.

"A deplorable deception, Sir!"

Despite his playful kiss, Mr Clements was otherwise as good as his word and made no further attempt to embarrass Rebecca during their ride. Even his sly glances at her person were dramatically curtailed, though never wholly ceased. For a few hours, he let himself sleep, stretching his body out on the seat of the carriage and using his hat as a shield with which to protect his eyes from the sunlight that poured into the carriage.

While Mr Clements rested, Rebecca found herself watching him with mounting fascination. Even when he wasn't trying to bait her with honeyed words and irresistible smiles, he still managed to arrest her attention with his curious manner, which was so unlike most of the London elite.

Rebecca reflected; if the man's brother were even half as charming and caring in personality, she would likely find working at Perryway Hall an absolute joy.

It was almost nine in the evening when the carriage finally made its way up the gravel path to Perryway Hall. The grounds of the estate were vast, and the only clue that they were close to their destination was in the way that the trees, hedges and grass took on a sudden uniform and structured quality. Rebecca looked at Mr Clements, who was still sprawled unceremoniously across the seat on his side of the carriage, and shook his arm gently.

"Mr Clements, I think we are almost at your brother's estate."

The man slowly lifted the brim of his hat and struggled upright. His body made audible clicks as he stretched and turned to look out the window.

"Nature forced to obey the dictatorial hand of man and conform to a thoroughly unnatural geometry... Yes, it seems we really have arrived."

Rebecca laughed and crossed her arms.

"You sound awfully put out. Do you always wake in such a foul mood or do you just have a particular dislike for this garden?"

Mr Clements smile returned at Rebecca's jibe, and he shrugged his shoulders in answer.

"Sometime I will show you the landscapes I have locked away in a corner of the house. I much prefer capturing the majesty and beauty of wild places. I think it is presumptuous for man to try to improve upon the beautiful creation the Lord has already laid out for us."

Rebecca grinned, wondering if Mr Clements always had such perfect answers ready for every possible subject he might be called to speak about.

A sharp turn in the path brought the large building of Perryway suddenly into view. Rebecca gasped at its enormity and grandeur. She had not seen a stately home before, but this first viewing did not disappoint her expectations. When the carriage pulled to a halt, however, Rebecca saw one thing that did displease her. It was a man with figure and face roughly approximating that of Mr John Clements. However, his expression was far more stern and cold.

As he looked into the carriage, he raised an eyebrow as his eyes met Rebecca's. Like his brother, the Duke had no qualms about staring at a person. However, Rebecca found little warmth in this man's analysing glare. After a long silence the man began to cough and stepped away. Rebecca studied his retreat, noting the silver flask he brandished in his right hand, and which he at once took a copious pull from. She jumped as the carriage door was opened suddenly by a servant. The Duke gave his brother a single glance before returning his withering gaze to her.

"Miss Johnson, I presume?"

Continue Reading at

https://www.amazon.com/dp/B06X413MKC/

ARIETTA RICHMOND, CATHERINE WINDSOR, ISABELLA THORNE, KATHERINE KEATS, KELLY ANNE BRUCE

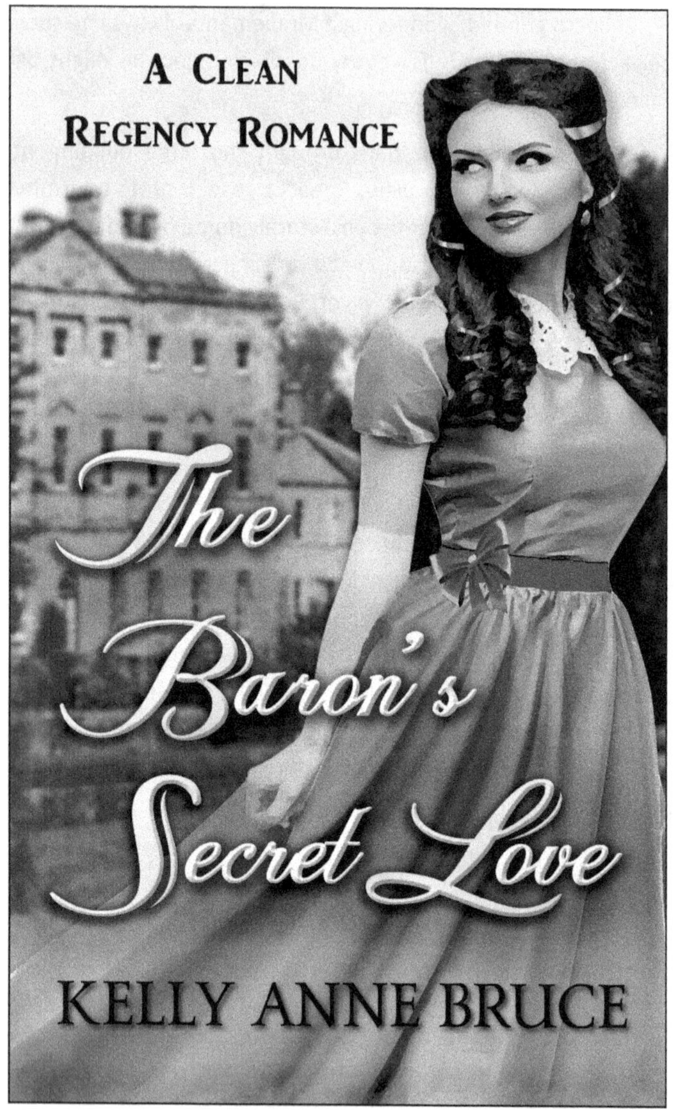

A Clean Regency Romance

The Baron's Secret Love

Kelly Anne Bruce

ARIETTA RICHMOND, CATHERINE WINDSOR, ISABELLA THORNE, KATHERINE KEATS, KELLY ANNE BRUCE

Dedication

This story is dedicated to my grandmother, Jewell. Any holiday was a special time for her. Springtime made her heart sing with joy. She loved all things British and I remember many nights of her reading to me when I was young. She never had the chance to travel to England, but I know she would have loved it!

Her love of reading helped me get to the place I am today. Her example made me want to learn more about a world beyond my boundaries. She's always in my heart.

Chapter One

"...do you think, Grace?"

At the mention of her name, seventeen-year-old Grace Fillmore blinked once. Twice. And then again.

Her closest friend, Leslie Haskett, had asked something and for the life of her, Grace had no idea what it was. She'd been daydreaming again.

Her thoughts had wandered to the upcoming party for the village of Garterrow, in just four short days.

This year, like all the years before, Lord and Lady Forbes would host all of the gentry in the county at their sprawling estate. Grace wondered how exquisite the home was on the inside and if it matched the grandeur of the outside.

"You're not listening to one word I say, are you?"

Leslie's blue eyes were fixed on Grace, who swallowed a tight lump in her throat at being caught and nodded.

"My apologies, Leslie," Grace said, grabbing hold of the other girl's arm as they took another walk around the village pond. "The dance at the Forbes' Manor has my mind going in a thousand different directions. I don't know quite what to expect, but I'm excited about the whole thing."

Leslie smiled and patted Grace's hand.

"I know exactly how you feel," she said with a wink. "Mamma didn't let me attend my first dance until last year and that was only because Elaina had finally landed that proposal from Lord Lampley's son. I was sure that I'd fall flat on my face going down those steps and ruin my prospects forever."

Grace chuckled. It wasn't a large stretch of the imagination to picture Leslie falling down a step or two. Leslie's nose was forever stuck in a book and she rarely came up for air once she began reading.

"Well, did you ruin your chances forever at that first dance?" Grace asked, knowing full well that she hadn't. It had been last year's spring party and Grace had waited up all night, in the girl's dormitory at the Prospect House School for Girls, for Leslie to return.

Prospect House's headmistress, Mrs Margaret Neston, hadn't allowed Grace to attend the party. She hadn't given Grace much reason for her refusal, either — only that her "benefactors had forbidden it."

This year was a different story altogether. Last month, when Grace had casually brought the conversation up at tea, the older woman had agreed that she could attend this year. It was all that Grace could think about since that afternoon.

"Maybe this year I'll dance with someone other than my cousin, Thomas," Leslie sighed wistfully.

"But you enjoyed dancing with Thomas last year!"

It was true. Leslie had returned starry-eyed and breathless over the two dances she'd shared with her older, distant cousin, Thomas Ganfrey.

"Yes, well, that was before his mother made it quite clear that she had her sights set on him marrying that obnoxious Lorna Atkins. Just because Sir Richard is her father, she thinks she's special. Thomas can rot. Lorna, too."

Leslie's shocking declaration was so out of character for the gentle bookworm that Grace couldn't help but chuckle.

"I have no doubt that your dance card will be full within the first hour, Leslie," Grace said. "I just hope you'll be so kind as to toss me a scrap or two and keep me from being a wallflower in some far corner."

It was Leslie's turn to give an unladylike snort.

"You? Relegated to the wallflowers?' she gave Grace a sidelong glance. "There will be a line out of the door for the gentlemen to get a turn about the floor with you and your legendary violet eyes."

Grace dismissed Leslie's compliment. She knew better than to set her hopes too high for the dance. She was a ward with a mystery benefactor, and no known family. The people of Garterrow more or less tolerated her moving about among the peerage, but there would be no long lines of suitors waiting to court a penniless orphan.

Although, it would be a celebration for the arrival of spring and the Easter season, so people would be in a good mood. That might help her chances just a bit.

"You are sad again, Grace Fillmore," Leslie admonished, having notice the change in Grace's mood. "You had better not be mulling over your future again, you stubborn donkey."

Grace gasped at the words.

"Pardon me? I'm not getting melancholy again," she laughed. "Relax."

The girls continued the walk in silence.

Grace loved the village of Garterrow, especially in the spring. The chill in the air had begun to give way to the warming rays of the sun. Most days could be enjoyed without the need of a wool cape. The warmth was bringing about the emergence of blossoms on the trees and early blooms in the garden. The sunny days seemed perfect.

The smell of new flowers blooming nearby danced on the breeze and Grace closed her eyes, letting the indulgent scent of spring and gentle warm air dance along her face. She inhaled deeply and let out a happy breath.

"How do you do it, Grace?"

Leslie's voice cut through her reverie. Again.

"What?"

"That," the older girl made a vague circular motion in front of Grace. "This thing you do when you seem to enjoy every second of life, no matter what's going on around you."

Grace shrugged.

"I have no idea," she answered truthfully. "I just happen to love the smell of flowers and the warmer air makes me happy. The season of rebirth is inspiring for me, I guess."

Leslie closed her eyes and drew in a long breath. A slow smile spread across her pretty face and a wisp of reddish brown hair blew across her forehead on the breeze. She exhaled slowly and opened her eyes, smiling at Grace.

"Extraordinary."

Grace grinned.

"I told you so," she said. "I'm thinking we should go back soon. We'll be late for tea again, and Mrs Neston promised me extra cleaning duties if it happened again this week."

At the prospect of beating wool rugs and scrubbing wood floors, Leslie paled.

"Hurry, Grace," she cried, as she began dragging Grace down the path. "We mustn't be late. Make haste. Make haste!"

ARIETTA RICHMOND, CATHERINE WINDSOR, ISABELLA THORNE, KATHERINE KEATS, KELLY ANNE BRUCE

Chapter Two

Later that evening, after tea and supper had been served, and the dining room had been cleared by the household staff, Grace made her way to the Prospect House library to read.

She found Mrs Neston by the fire. with a cup of tea and a book in her lap. The house cat, Reynaldo, slept near her feet.

"Useless mouser," Mrs Neston sighed when Grace smiled at the fat orange tabby.

Grace knelt down by the creature and scratched him behind his ears as he slept.

"Poor old fellow," she whispered to Reynaldo. "Not allowed a moment's peace on a quiet night like this."

Grace pushed to her feet and wandered toward the back of the room, where the bookshelves lined the walls.

"Anything new, Mrs Neston?"

The older woman chortled.

"Not since the Edgeworth, my dear," she said. "And that was only last week. Takes me longer than that to find new, suitable novels for you to read. What about a nice book of poetry?"

Grace made a face that earned her a stern look.

"Watch yourself, Miss Fillmore," Mrs Neston warned playfully.

"Apologies, ma'am," Grace said with a smile. "Did Bessie return the one about the sisters?"

Mrs Neston scratched her chin a moment while she thought. Finally, she pointed to the desk in the corner.

"'Sense and Sensibility' is the name, dear."

Mrs Neston was forever correcting Grace about remembering details and keeping her mind sharp.

"Oh, of course. 'Sense and Sensibility.' I'll not forget it again."

"And it's on the table near the window. You should know the story by heart now, with as many times as you've read it. Too much prose can't be good for a girl of your age — you're already given to flights of fancy. This can only make it worse."

"We could sit by the fire and talk instead," Grace said, finding a chair near Mrs Neston and sitting. She sensed an opening. "My conversational skills can always use the practice."

The older woman looked up from her book with a raised brow.

"Really, Miss Fillmore?" she asked, setting her book on her lap. "What sort of topics do you have in mind? Shall we talk politics? Humanities? Napoleon?"

Grace gave her headmistress a shy smile.

"I'd like to know more about my benefactor," she ventured, knowing that this topic always led nowhere with Mrs Neston. Grace was determined, however, to learn the truth of her origins and, if it meant asking Mrs Neston about her benefactor every day for the next decade, then she'd settled herself to the task.

"I'm not at liberty to discuss that, Miss Fillmore," Mrs Neston replied with resignation. "You know this already."

"That's fine," Grace ran her finger along the gilded edge of the book she was holding. "What about my parents, then? Do you know anything about them?"

Grace did not miss the sharp intake of breath from her guardian.

"Silent reading is a noble pursuit, Miss Fillmore," the older woman said with determination, opening her book again. "Let us pursue it most determinedly."

With a sigh of defeat, Grace opened her book to the beginning, despite knowing the opening lines by heart.

Chapter Three

Sitting still while Monette worked pins into her hair was pure torture for Grace, but luckily, her hair had enough natural curl to it that she was spared the heating rod some of her companions were currently enduring in their own rooms

"Nearly done, Miss," Monette said, with hair pins between her teeth. "It would be much easier for both of us if you would sit still for just one moment longer.

"I'm a bundle of nerves," Grace said, wringing her hands. "What if I forget every dance step I've learned? What if I don't get asked to dance at all? I'll be mortified and never be able to show myself in public again."

Monette chuckled.

"You're lovely, Miss. No need to fret," she soothed. "And the young gentlemen will swarm to you like bees to honey. It is the spring and everyone will be in a splendid mood."

Grace's cheeks warmed at that.

"Nonsense," she half whispered. "There's far prettier girls than me in this village. I can hardly hold a conversation for longer than a minute or two. And then I start snorting and laughing out loud like the braying donkey Leslie says I am."

At last, Monette set the remaining pins down on Grace's dressing table and clapped her hands.

"You, Miss, are spectacular," she gushed. "The gentlemen of Garterrow are going to be bowled over by one Miss Grace Fillmore."

Despite her excitement at the night ahead of her, a little part of her soured at the thought of being out among the gentry. She was a young woman with no pedigree and a mystery benefactor who paid for her education at a good school. Everyone knew she was a ward.

She was not one of them — she knew this and the gentry knew this. Most were polite, and Grace even had a number of girls here at the school she could count as good friends. But their families kept their distance from Grace Fillmore and she was never invited to dine with anyone the way that Leslie, the daughter of landed gentry, was.

Tonight promised to be magical. She was beside herself with mixed emotions. She had made up her mind to wring every single drop of joy from it that she could, since she had no idea how long it would be before she would attend another party. The evening would also serve up constant reminders that she was different. There was a marked disparity between the children of good families and the child with no family.

"Banish those thoughts, Grace Fillmore," she lectured herself in her best schoolmistress voice.

It was an old habit of hers, which she had never outgrown, and in moments like these the little lectures to herself shored up her courage. Enough, at least, for her to take the few steps from her bedroom door and down the stairs to where Mrs Neston and the other girls would be waiting for her.

In the long upstairs hallway, Grace paused to take in her reflection in the large gilded mirror.

Her eyes widened at the image before her. Gone was the awkward young girl she always saw herself as, and before her stood a lovely young woman. Mrs Neston had helped Grace to choose her gown for the evening and they had done a good job. It was a pale cream coloured muslin with an empire waist that was delicately accented with pale pink ribbons around the cap sleeves and hem.

Long silk gloves that went to her elbows matched the creamy colour of the gown. Her slippers were ecru silk that went perfectly with the dress.

A pale rose-coloured ribbon wound around her bodice and Monette had pinned a silk tea rose into the cascade of dark chestnut coloured curls that tumbled from her crown. Grace's violet eyes sparkled and her lips shone with the light application of Rigge's Liquid Bloom that Monette had applied for a rosy, natural sheen. The maid had even dabbed a little on the apples of Grace's cheeks, after a light pinch to highlight the natural dewiness of Grace's skin.

She gave herself an admiring smile, pleased with how her ensemble had come together.

Downstairs, Mrs Neston clucked her disapproval at being made to wait so long.

She had been rather heavy-handed with the white face powder and Grace fought back the urge to suggest that she soften the harsh, ghost-like effect. Mrs Neston's feelings might be hurt by such a suggestion.

Leslie looked splendid in her white gown with gold ribbon accents. Her strawberry blonde hair had flatly refused to succumb to the heating iron and had denied the curl altogether. It didn't matter, since Leslie was a beautiful young woman, even without the fashionable curls.

Two more girls from the school, Harriette and Annabelle, were part of the Prospect House entourage, and they, too, had been waiting on Grace.

"I'm sorry to have kept you all waiting," Grace said sheepishly, when she noticed the entire party impatiently pacing the foyer.

"Never mind all of that," Mrs Neston clucked. "Off we go. The carriage is waiting out front."

Chapter Four

It turned out that Wentfleet Manor was just as beautiful inside as the manicured lawns and imposing exterior was on the outside. It was just as Grace had hoped.

Twice, she had to be reminded to close her mouth as it hung agape from studying all of the rich furnishings and beautiful décor. She was in awe of everything and nothing was escaping her gaze.

"This is magnificent," she breathed. Beside her, Leslie rolled her eyes.

"Careful, I'm quite certain Miss Forbes doesn't need any reason to inflate her ego any larger," she whispered. "That head of hers will have a hard enough time fitting through the doors into the ballroom as it is."

Eleanor Forbes was the daughter of Lord and Lady Forbes, the owners of Wentfleet Manor. She was near Grace and Leslie's age, but, because her family was one of the richest in the area, Eleanor had been given a private tutor last year and removed from Prospect House.

But all of the young ladies in their small social circle got to hear about every single trip, accomplishment, and possible suitor from Miss Forbes at Sunday service each week.

Dinner for the event included roasted pork and apples in wine and Grace had to remind herself not to groan with pleasure each time she took a scrumptious bite. Twice she congratulated herself on the fact that she was living up to her earlier resolution to extract as much joy as possible from each moment this night. The food was certainly making it easy.

Before Grace knew it, supper was over and it was time for the real fun to begin. She was nervous but excited to see if anyone would ask her to dance.

As the revellers assembled in the great hall and listened to a few obligatory introductory tunes from the gathered musicians, Leslie filled Grace in.

"These opening dances are less and less in vogue lately," she said as the girls watched the young Miss Forbes walk to the centre of the dance floor, escorted by her father. "But the Forbes family cannot miss an opportunity to parade Eleanor around like an overstuffed peacock with all of these suitable bachelors on hand."

"What is the new protocol for dances?" Grace asked quietly.

"More and more in London, the balls are skipping these tiresome minuets completely and beginning straight away with shorter, partnered dances like waltzes or cotillions or quadrilles."

Grace beamed.

"Oh, the quadrille!" She nearly squealed in excitement. "I know that one the best. Do you think they'll have one tonight?"

"I am certain of it," Leslie nodded. "It's quite in fashion and despite this boring performance, the Forbes family loves to flaunt how fashionable and connected to London they are."

Grace smiled, resisting the urge to clap her hands in glee.

"Let them," she whispered. "As long as I get a chance to dance at least once."

Poor Mrs Neston, acting as chaperone to four young ladies, was kept busy for a good part of the evening, fielding introductions from young gentlemen left and right.

Harriette hardly stood still once the introductions began and was claimed for dance after dance by the country gentlemen. Annabelle was caught in a long conversation with a young man recently returned from a stint in the Navy.

Despite the new acquaintances, only Grace had been left without a partner so far. After a particularly vigorous turn around the floor, Leslie returned to Grace and Mrs Nestor with flushed cheeks.

"Oh, dear, Miss Haskett," the woman clucked when she saw the younger woman's appearance. "Pull yourself together. Miss Fillmore, take her to the refreshments room and help her cool off. She's nearly perspiring!"

The girls linked arms and wandered their way around the crowd, taking in the elegant clothes, the dancers, and the throng of guests. Grace was in love with every moment of the experience.

Inside the small room that held tables of small sweet pastries and beverages, Grace held her crystal cup of lemonade and found a far wall to stand against. Leslie had slipped away from her and Grace scanned the crowd in search of her friend. She found her near a table of sweets speaking with a tall gentleman.

The man's back was to Grace, so she couldn't quite make out his features. From the occasional side profile glance, Grace gathered that this young man was very handsome. He had black hair that hung across his forehead and striking dark eyes. His skin was more sun kissed and golden from time in the sun than was fashionable, and, as far as she could tell, he was muscular and athletic.

Grace froze when she watched Leslie point in her direction. When the young man turned to look as indicated, Grace's eyes widened and she swallowed hard.

"Oh no, Leslie," she thought to herself, the panic rising as they both turned in her direction. "Don't do it. Don't you bring that man over here."

But she was doing just that. Terror spiked in Grace's stomach as the two approached.

Fine looking young men like Leslie's friend were perfectly suited for admiring from a distance. That was as far as she was comfortable. Activities that required rational thought, like pleasantries and conversation, were frightening.

"Pull yourself together, Grace Fillmore!" She whispered to herself as she plastered a too-wide smile on her face and clenched her fists behind her back. This was terrible. A failure.

How could Leslie do this to her? She was not properly prepared for an introduction to such a handsome face. She needed time to prepare. Time to practice witty replies and pleasant responses.

Oh, dear. Leslie was speaking. What was she saying?

"...may I please present, Miss Grace Fillmore of Prospect House School for Girls?"

Thankfully, Grace's eyelids fluttered and her head inclined toward the stranger of its own volition. All of Mrs Neston's etiquette training had paid off. At least a little.

"Grace Fillmore," Leslie continued. Her hand swung toward the stranger who was now but a few paces in front of Grace. He was taller than he had appeared from a distance and she had to angle her head up to meet his intense gaze. He was studying her. She swallowed hard.

Leslie continued with the introduction.

"This is Mr William Barnes, son of Sir Edwin Barnes, Baron of Mowbourne."

"I am glad to make your acquaintance, Miss Fillmore," Mr Barnes took her hand in his and placed a soft kiss across her knuckles. Even through the silk of the gloves, she felt the warmth of his lips.

Her traitorous knees threatened to turn to jelly.

"Do you have a partner for the quadrille?" William asked, but Grace didn't miss the conspiratorial glance he gave Leslie.

Grace shook her head.

"No, I do not," she managed.

"Would you do me the honour?"

Grace managed a weak nod and William took his leave, promising to return to find Grace before their promised dance.

Once he was out of earshot, she turned on her friend.

"What have you done?" She hissed to Leslie, the colour finally leaving her cheeks.

"You can thank me later, Grace," Leslie laughed and dragged her friend back to their chaperone.

Chapter Five

No sooner had Mrs Neston and Leslie convinced Grace that there was no reason to be nervous, the next set of dances, which would include a quadrille, was announced and Grace found herself a bundle of nerves once more.

What was this man thinking? He didn't know her from the next girl in the room. She was a nobody, less than that. He was obviously a somebody.

It was obvious by the way he moved through the room that he was confident. She was certain that occasions such as this party were nothing special to him.

Well, they were, in fact, special to girls like Grace Fillmore who never received social invitations. Perhaps this fellow felt some sense of misplaced charity towards her?

Her face grew hot at the thought. He pitied her. How embarrassing. Wouldn't Leslie have let her know if this was the case? Or, more importantly, wouldn't she have thwarted his offer of charity?

Her eyes darted around the room, hoping to find her friend and ask that very question, but Leslie was suddenly impossible to find. Now that she was paying attention, Grace realized, as her eyes darted around the sea of faces, that Mrs Neston suddenly had found a way to make herself scarce.

What was going on here?

Before Grace was able to worry herself into a lather, the quadrille was announced. Feeling the breath in her lungs constrict, Grace found herself in a full-scale state of panic. She couldn't breathe. Her heart raced so fast that she could scarcely hear above the whooshing sound it made in her ears.

Air. She needed air. Now.

And she needed to duck outside before Mr William Barnes came to collect her for the dance she had so foolishly agreed to. She wove in and out of overheated and sweating bodies, carefully stealing glances at her surroundings. The tall, handsome Barnes fellow was nowhere in sight and she was nearly free.

Up ahead, she saw the large glass French doors that led to the gardens beyond. She was nearly there. Just as the cool breeze of the outside whisked along her pink cheeks, a body appeared before her, cutting off her escape.

Slowly looking up, Grace swallowed the lump in her throat and forced an awkward, though pleasant, smile at Mr William Barnes himself. He was even more handsome and arresting than the first time that they had met face-to-face, and Grace did not miss the mischievous smile pulling at the corners of his mouth.

"Are you unwell, Miss Fillmore?" William raised a dark eyebrow at her as he posed the question.

"No, I..." the words were out of her mouth before she could stop them. And just like that, her one chance at escape disappeared like kindling in a flame. Why hadn't she confirmed that she was ill?

"Wonderful," William smiled and easily placed her right hand in the crook of his elbow. "I would hate to miss the quadrille you promised me."

Before Grace could protest, he was guiding her to the dance floor. He found the perfect place for them amongst the assembled dancers.

As much as she wanted to be put out by the dance she had no say in, Grace quickly found herself having a wonderful time. William was a skilled dancer and moved her through the other couples expertly sparing the sore toes that might have been expected.

In no time, Grace was laughing and enjoying the camaraderie that can only be experienced in a group dance like the quadrille. The other couples bounced along merrily and their enthusiasm was infectious. Grace laughed louder and more enthusiastically than Mrs Neston would have approved of, but she reasoned that, if Mrs Neston would like a say in her reactions to people, she ought to avoid disappearing when Grace needed her the most.

Finally, the dance ended and the lines of men and women bowed to each other.

Grace turned to find her party, but felt a warm hand close on her elbow.

"Lemonade, Miss Fillmore?"

Mr Barnes asked the question, but left little room for her to object, as he expertly guided her back to the refreshments table. Walking so close to him through the crowds, Grace couldn't help but notice the way that the other young women of her age stared at him. They must know him. Or perhaps know of him. She caught a couple of unfriendly glances tossed her way as well, but Grace played dumb and simply smiled sweetly in return.

Eleanor Forbes was more overt about her displeasure, however. She managed to block their path as they moved through the room. Standing with one hand placed on her hip and the other offered in William's direction, she smiled triumphantly when he performed the obligatory kiss to her knuckle in greeting.

"Miss Forbes," William said, a little woodenly. "May I present Miss Grace Fillmore?"

Eleanor's eyes slid over Grace for a fraction of a second before darting back to William, effectively dismissing Grace.

"I've left the next dance open, Mr Barnes," Eleanor said matter-of-factly. Grace started with surprise at the other young woman's boldness. Part of her was shocked, but a tiny piece of Grace was in awe that Eleanor could be so bold.

"Ah, yes," William said. Grace noticed he was flustered and nearly sputtering. "Well, wonderful to see you again, Miss Forbes."

He pulled Grace away quickly and they made their way around Eleanor to the drinks table. William seemed relieved when he was out of Eleanor's grasp. He handed her a small cup. Taking the small crystal glass full of the tart, sweet liquid, Grace thanked William and proceeded to look anywhere but at him.

"So you're a school friend of Leslie?" He asked. "Have you known her long?"

Grace nodded.

"Four years," she replied. "And you?"

William narrowed his dark eyes as he thought.

"I first met Leslie Catherine Haskett at her christening," he said finally. "What is that now? Seventeen or eighteen years?"

Grace raised her eyebrows in surprise. "Well, you have me beaten there," she conceded. "I'm sure I can no longer call myself Leslie's oldest friend."

"Our families are neighbours," he said. "I grew up hunting and fishing with her older brother, Charles. Our parents have been friends for years, although I have been out of the country for the past three years. I have hardly seen her since she started attending Prospect House."

Their conversation was light and pleasant and was mostly about current affairs in Europe, from where he'd recently returned, and novels. Much to her delight, Grace found that Mr William Barnes was quite the connoisseur of prose. His chocolate brown eyes danced when he told her stories of the places he'd seen in his travels and of the different types of people around the world that he'd encountered.

She was under his spell in no time.

William reached for Grace's empty cup and handed it to a passing footman.

"And what is your story, Miss Fillmore?"

The question immediately broke the spell and Grace eyed William while clutching her hands tightly together.

Surely, he must be mocking her?

Grace bit her lower lip and willed her mind to stop racing.

She inhaled slowly and blew out a short breath before speaking.

"I have no story, Mr Barnes" she said evenly, choosing to look at a spot on the wall just behind his shoulder, in case she couldn't bear the look on his face.

"Everyone has a story, Miss Fillmore," William replied, that quirk of a smile touching the right side of his mouth. "Yours has to be more interesting than the rest of the girls in this room. Your conversation skills are second to none and you speak about so many topics with ease. Now please, tell me about yourself?"

Grace met his gaze then, trying her best to appear brave and strong, and not absolutely mortified that he had put her on the spot, whilst almost certainly knowing of the rumours and speculation surrounding her.

She drew in another breath before speaking, now more annoyed at this rude bore than ashamed of her own history.

"You insist on a story? Fine, let me tell you one. And once my story is done, I would appreciate you never speaking to me again, Mr Barnes," Grace said through gritted teeth. She didn't take long to savour the look of shock on William's face. "Once upon a time, a baby was born, excuse me if the details are spotty throughout this part, Mr Barnes, as I'm not privy to them. This baby grew into girlhood and beyond, raised by a kind and considerate Mrs Neston, the only guardian she had ever known. Each month, her schooling and expenses are paid for by one mysterious benefactor and no one will speak his name or tell her where he is from. Each month, this young woman asks precisely one million questions in the attempt to discover the truth of who she is and where she comes from. Do you know how many answers she has received so far?"

William's face was ashen. He looked stricken. Good, Grace thought to herself. This is what he wanted, wasn't it? She continued.

"Despite the little whispers and the gossips, who are quite certain that they know the truth, the young woman has received no answers to any of her questions. No answers. No social invitations. No chances to move among the people of society without back-biting comments and being treated as a charity case by misguided young men."

Grace slowed her speech and attempted to slow her racing heart. Chancing one last glance up into Mr William Barne's dark eyes, she smiled sweetly.

"Was that the sort of story you were looking for, Mr Barnes?" she asked, as she drew herself up to leave.

Without casting another glance behind her, Grace bit her lip against the burning tears that threatened to fall and sought out Mrs Neston and the other girls.

She was ready to go home.

Chapter Six

Nearly three days had passed since Grace's painful conversation with Mr William Barnes and, no matter how she tried to close the book on the encounter, she couldn't stop thinking about the way that his dark lashes had lain against his cheek when he had closed his eyes in laughter.

"Traitorous mind," she whispered to herself as the vicar went on with his never-ending Sunday sermon.

Try as she might, she couldn't stop thinking about the man and wondering if her temper had gotten the best of her at the dance. What if he'd truly just wanted to dance with her? What if he'd really just been interested to learn more about her? That thought was utterly foreign to her, but she had to admit that it was a possibility. Grace squeezed her eyes shut and did her best to focus on what was being said.

She failed miserably.

Trying discreetly to look around the chapel and see who was in attendance, Grace's glance through the open doors fell on the beautiful, sunny spring day unfolding outside.

The sky was blue as a peacock feather and the last of the trees had popped out green leaves and blossoms Grace promised herself that, after she changed out of her church clothes, she would take a short walk around the park before tea was called. Mrs Neston usually left the girls with time to themselves after church on Sundays.

A cough from the other side of the chapel brought her back to the present and her eyes searched out the noise offender. She had to bite the inside of her cheek when her eyes rested on none other than Mr William Barnes himself. As if he had heard her thoughts about him, William turned and met her gaze.

Immediately, Grace felt her cheeks grow hot and she quickly looked down at the hymn book in her lap, pretending to be incredibly interested in the psalm that they'd sung nearly ten minutes ago. Her stomach plummeted to her feet and her fingers squeezed the leather book tightly as Grace struggled to regain control.

Sucking in a deep breath and grasping for whatever dignity she might have left, Grace righted herself and looked ahead to the pulpit, forcing herself to pretend to pay attention for what seemed like an eternity. And when she could no longer bear it, she stole a glance out of the corner of her eyes toward William. Not a half-second later, he looked at her again, catching her looking at him.

Grace groaned inwardly. She looked ridiculous now.

Nearly one agonizing hour later, the service was dismissed and Grace filed out behind Leslie and Annabelle as Mrs Neston led the way from the church.

Once outside, the cool air made her feel just a little more human again. The three girls made small talk together while Mrs Neston spoke with two church elders about this year's Easter service.

"Did you see William, Grace?" Leslie struggled to keep a straight face as she posed the question.

"Not funny," Grace bit out. Her afternoon was only made worse when Eleanor Forbes sauntered over, after breaking off from her family's group to the side.

"Hello, Annabelle," Eleanor snaked her arm around Annabelle's waist, causing Annabelle to frown in surprise at the sudden affection from Garterrow's most notorious snob.

"Good afternoon, Eleanor," poor Annabelle stammered, but Eleanor's eyes were on Grace.

"Leslie, it's good to see you. Fillmore." Eleanor's use of Grace's last name as her acknowledgement was a significant and quite rude slight. Leslie's mouth popped open in surprise. When she shot a look to Grace, Grace only shook her head.

Eleanor Forbes was not worth the effort of trying to stand up for herself.

"Good afternoon, ladies."

The unmistakable baritone of William Barnes' voice slid up Grace's spine at alarming speed. She forced herself not to turn at the sound of it and, instead, used Eleanor's face as a sort of mirror to assess William's actions.

"Hello, Mr Barnes. I was disappointed that your family was not able to sit with us today," Eleanor purred at him.

Beside Grace, she felt Leslie stiffen. She apparently did not appreciate Eleanor fawning all over her old friend.

"Yes, well, maybe another time," William said politely, after clearing his throat.

"Miss Fillmore, did you enjoy the rest of the dance? I am quite sorry I did not get the chance to say goodnight."

It was an innocent question, but William's heated gaze made Grace uncomfortable, while the edge in his voice made it apparent that he didn't appreciate the way the evening had ended between them.

"I did, thank you," she said quickly, hoping that his attention would go elsewhere. Lucky for her, Eleanor Forbes was determined to make sure that it did.

"Why would you desire to take the extra effort to say goodnight to Prospect House girls? They would hardly expect the courtesy, seeing as they are only attending these sorts of functions out of the kindness of my mother's heart."

The comment might have included Leslie and Annabelle, too, but Eleanor's beady little blue eyes were locked on Grace.

The barb was meant solely for her, as everyone in the area knew that Annabelle's father was a minor nobleman who travelled often to India. And Leslie came from an old family with plenty of money — her father simply felt that she needed the chance to be more polished, her mother having quite enough to deal with, with her brothers and younger sisters as well.

No, the hint about charity and poverty was meant for Grace alone. All because William kept paying attention to her — attention that Eleanor Forbes was desperate to have.

"Good day, Miss Forbes," Grace bit out and turned back to William. "Mr Barnes."

Spinning on her heels, she walked away from the group with as much dignity as she could muster. She decided that now was the perfect time to take that long, lonely walk around the park's scenic lake.

Tears spilled down her cheeks and she let them fall when she was certain that she was alone.

Grace had never deluded herself about her mysterious upbringing, or her lack of family. But suddenly, the divide between her and the rest of the young people in town seemed like a chasm that was threatening to rip her heart wide open, the more people used her parentage, or lack thereof, to humiliate her.

ARIETTA RICHMOND, CATHERINE WINDSOR, ISABELLA THORNE, KATHERINE KEATS, KELLY ANNE BRUCE

Chapter Seven

"I promise you that William Barnes is not what you think he is."

Leslie was putting a lot of effort into repairing Grace's bad impressions of her childhood friend.

"It really doesn't matter what I think of him, does it?" she pouted.

Nearly a week had passed since that awful encounter outside the church, and Grace had done everything she could to put both Eleanor Forbes and William Barnes out of her mind.

"I think he likes you, Grace," Leslie said and Grace couldn't help but burst out laughing. Leslie frowned. "I am quite serious, you know. Lots of girls have thrown themselves at him over the years and he's always made a game of making them look foolish for chasing his father's money. But you are not chasing him. If I did not know any better, I would swear William was about to chase after you."

The absurdity of it made Grace snort.

The girls were walking to Mrs Hampton's sitting room for tea. She was the vicar's wife and mother of one of their school friends, Mary. She was a year or two younger than Grace and quiet as a mouse. Friendly, though, in a terrified, cornered animal sort of way.

The lane was empty as they walked the modest distance to the vicar's house. The leaves were popping out all around them. Grace knew that they had only a few short days until their world turned green again. She loved this time of year. A time of growth and a new beginning.

"It is a shame Mrs Neston came down with a cough this morning," Leslie said as she fidgeted with her dress. "I am not exactly sure what we are going to talk about with Mrs Hampton. She is a bit aggressive when it comes to conversations."

Grace laughed at Leslie's honesty.

"I am not bamming you, Grace," her friend said as she laughed, too. "I truly am a little terrified of going in there with only you to protect me. I am quite certain that she will ask dozens of questions about my older brothers' marital statuses in an effort to find a husband for Mousy Mary."

Grace swatted her friends arm.

"Stop that," she said, frowning. "Mary is a perfectly fine girl. She'll make someone a lovely wife someday. And she is not even old enough yet."

Leslie glowered at Grace and only shook her head.

"You give her too much credit," she replied. "I am going to fall off my chair in a faint if that girl speaks a complete sentence even once this afternoon. I honestly do not know what her voice sounds like."

When they arrived at the stone gate that marked the beginning of the vicar's property, Grace drew in a steadying breath. Outings lately seemed to be getting more and more difficult for her to handle.

Leslie gave two pulls on the large wooden door's brass knocker and stepped back beside Grace. A maid answered the door and ushered them in.

The Hampton home was nicely decorated and modest — as befitting a country clergyman. Nothing too ostentatious and just enough gilt and gold to make certain that visitors knew that the vicar John Hampton was more than just a parish leader.

Grace and Leslie stood in the hallway, waiting for the maid to return. In her stead, their classmate Mary came to fetch them and led them to her mother's sitting room without so much as a squeak of sound.

As she walked past the girls to show them the way, Leslie raised a single eyebrow at Grace.

"You are being rude," Grace hissed. "She has a voice. I am certain of it."

Leslie's response was a snicker. Mary's head turned back to see what was amusing and she straightened her face immediately.

Inside the comfortable room, the girls found Mrs Hampton holding court like a London duchess. Two older women flanked her on a delicate couch that looked like it was moments away from crumbling into splinters under the women's girth and ornate petticoats. Mousy Mary took a chair in the corner near a window and picked up a book she had presumably been reading.

Another young woman was perched near the fireplace, an embroidery project in her hands, and she gave the girls a narrowed, appraising look that was unmistakably unfriendly, before casting her eyes back down to the linen on her lap.

Grace sighed.

Leslie was right. This was going to be a long, exhausting afternoon without Mrs Neston's verbal sparring abilities.

When the women were all situated around a small table and served cups of tea and delicate cucumber sandwiches, Leslie's predicted onslaught began.

"So, Leslie, dear," Mrs Hampton said a little too brightly. "I hear that you are quite well acquainted with Lord and Lady Mowbourne's eldest son, William. Is that true?"

Leslie took her sweet time responding, inhaling slowly and casting her eyes about the room to drag the silence on even longer. Grace could hardly stifle the smile threatening to spread across her face.

"Moderately," Leslie finally said. "Our families have been friends for many years, but William has been studying abroad for a while now. We fell out of touch when he left England."

"But you must be re-acquainted now, yes?"

The question came from a woman who had been introduced as Mrs Ross. She was a large woman with bright red hair threaded with grey and was the woman responsible for raising the unfriendly girl with the needlework, whose name was Miss Lucy Ross.

The third matronly woman was reed thin and severe, with a sharp nose, a tightly wound chignon at the base of her neck, and severe dark hair that contrasted with her pale skin.

The woman, Miss Bellemare, was the older sister of Mrs Ross. The word spinster had been whispered and bandied about when Miss Bellemare had gone outside for a breath of fresh air.

"Yes, we recently saw each other at the dance at Wentfleet Manor," Leslie replied, her tone making it obvious that she was growing bored.

"And did he speak of any attachments he had formed overseas?" Mrs Ross got straight to the point. The vicar's wife harrumphed in mock dismay, but Grace watched her turn an ear toward the conversation, nonetheless.

"No," Leslie said as she fidgeted in her seat. She gave Grace a conspiratorial glance that Grace ignored. "He did not mention any attachments, but we really did not discuss such subjects."

"You see?" Mrs Hampton nearly squealed. Grace saw Mary roll her eyes. "I told you that he was still very eligible."

Mrs Ross gave a dramatic sigh and fanned herself with a frilly nightmare of a fan, causing her red and grey ringlets to flutter against the lace in her much too daring décolletage.

"I will not lie, I was nervous about this," she said to Mrs Hampton, who nodded in agreement. "I have been afraid that he might have made himself a horrible, match as these boys are wont to do when they go over to the Continent and meet all-sorts of questionable people. My cousin's boy came back married - married to a girl without a family name of any consequence, or a penny in her pocket."

Mrs Hampton and Miss Bellemare gasped in horror.

"What did your cousin do, Gwenneth? How did she handle such a betrayal?"

Mrs Hampton had nearly worked herself into a lather now.

Leslie's eyebrows had lifted towards her hairline as she took in the interaction, and Grace frowned.

"She convinced her husband to cut him from the estate is what she did," Mrs Ross said triumphantly. "What she should have done! The nerve of that boy! To sully their family's name like that for some French trollop. Foolish boy — crying about love and feelings. Let's see how well he feeds himself and his common bride on those emotions now."

Grace blinked a few times, absorbing the malice coming from Mrs Ross and how ardently her daughter Lucy was shaking her head in agreement.

To her, disowning a beloved family member seemed like a horrible thing to do, even if they had married someone deemed unworthy.

"But not Mr Barnes, I'm sure," Mrs Hampton was back at it, looking at them all as if expecting wholehearted agreement, before she continued.

"Despite rumours that he was spending an unfashionable amount of time with people of little consequence, I'm quite certain our handsome Mr Barnes understands how much his family needs him to take over for his elderly father when he dies. Imagine the disrepair and disarray their faithful tenants would fall into if there were no heir to take over the baronetcy?"

Grace did not miss the narrowing of Mrs Hampton's eyes looking at her when she'd spoken of "people of little consequence." She lowered her head to keep from seeing the woman's smug expression.

So the old hen had heard about her dance with Mr Barnes at Wentfleet, had she? No wonder Grace had been invited here today. She was being investigated for crimes against proper young ladies and their marriage chances. She sighed, suddenly tired of it all. It was all a game to these women — the rumour investigating, the gossip-mongering, and the husband hunting for their uninteresting and hostile daughters. Under the table, Leslie's hand squeezed Grace's knee in a show of solidarity. She smiled. Where would she be without Leslie?

"Mr Barnes is a fantastic judge of character, I can assure you," Leslie spoke up. "And he will always make the best possible choice when it comes to something as important as this."

The answer seemed to mollify the ladies and the conversation lulled enough for the tea service to finish. Nearly an hour and a half later, Grace and Leslie were hastily walking the lane back toward Prospect House, trying to beat the sunset and impending darkness.

"Torture," was all Leslie said.

"I should never have doubted you," Grace admitted her defeat graciously.

"I know it has not been easy being raised by Mrs Neston, but every once in a while, I certainly envy the fact that you do not regularly have to put up with social gatherings of that nature," Leslie said. "I hate to admit it, but most of them are like that — or worse. It is just that I am usually ignored altogether. But now my association with William has made me a target nearly as much as it has you."

Grace sighed.

"I am not going to be the topic of conversation much longer, thankfully," she said softly. "You heard them. He is going to have to take a wife soon — a good wife with a good name. Our Mr Barnes is not in a position to choose a wife for something as foolish as love or attraction. It is apparent that many lives hang in the balance, depending on his estate continuing to be run prudently. Him choosing well simply is not a question now, Leslie. So we can lay to rest all of this nonsense about anything you suspect he might feel for me. He does not have that luxury."

Leslie remained quiet as they walked, neither acknowledging nor disputing what Grace said. But she knew her friend, and from the looks of it, Leslie was busy hatching another plot to find Grace a suitable husband in Garterrow.

Grace sighed. She had no idea how she would hold Leslie in check. She was formidable when her mind was set on meeting a goal.

Chapter Eight

By Easter, Garterrow was green again. Leslie was home visiting her family, Harriette had a cold, and Mrs Neston was expecting a visitor. This left Grace as the only person able to collect some items from the village, which Mrs Neston urgently needed.

Her headmistress had offered Grace the use of the school's mare, Tilly, but Grace had refused. She didn't mind the walk. The sun shone down and a good dose of fresh air would do her good.

It was mid-morning and the lane to the village was quiet. A light breeze blew around her and thick puffy white clouds floated high in sky. Glancing up, Grace watched as they covered the sun until the wind blew them away and let the sun shine on her again. She hoped that she'd get back to Prospect House this afternoon in time to enjoy the sun while she snipped flowers in the garden.

Once she rounded the corner of the cobbled street to the village square, Grace went quickly to Mr Potter's store.

On the note that Grace carried, Mrs Neston had written exactly what fabric she needed and how much of it Grace was meant to carry back. Mr Potter greeted her from behind the counter and looked over the slip.

"It will take me a bit to get this cut and packaged, Miss Fillmore," he said, his giant caterpillar eyebrows dancing above his spectacles. "Come back in a half hour or so and it should be ready."

Grace thanked the elderly man and walked back outside, determined to pop into the village bookshop a few doors down.

She had read through the latest arrivals at Prospect House and was eager for something new. Inside the small shop, she moved around the shelves of books, bent low to read the titles on the bottom shelf and ran her finger along their spines. They were costly items, these books, and would eat up the majority of the money she'd saved up since Christmas. Frowning, Grace stood and looked toward the door, the bell on it ringing as someone new came inside — someone tall, dark, and brooding, that is.

Grace's mouth opened and closed wordlessly as Mr William Barnes looked at her. His eyes locked directly on hers, before she could hide or formulate a plan for escape. In the last month, he had invited Grace, Leslie, Henrietta and Mrs Neston to various events and Grace had always managed to find an excuse not to go. She had stood firm on her decisions, no matter how much trouble Leslie had given her.

But now, now she was trapped in a tiny bookshop and William hadn't moved from in front of the only exit.

"Hello, Miss Fillmore," he said, politely inclining his head. "What a pleasure, indeed."

"Good morning, Mr Barnes," she spoke quietly, managing a weak smile.

"I trust you have been well?" He continued quickly, not giving her a chance to answer. "Though I would hardly know, given the way that you have been avoiding any contact with me lately."

William narrowed his inky dark eyes at Grace and from the short distance between them, she could see the emotion roiling behind them. This was more than idle conversation.

"I am sorry," Grace stammered, her mind reeling and searching for a suitable response. "I, well I have been very busy. Have you been well, yourself?"

William gave a curt nod.

"Very well, thank you for asking."

Grace worried her lower lip between her teeth, keeping her eye on the door behind William's back. If he would just go about his way and find his book, she would be able to make her hasty retreat.

"It was good to see you again, Mr Barnes," Grace said, hoping to force the issue by taking a step toward the door. Instead of taking the hint, William held his ground and stood where he was, unmoving.

"Are you here looking for a new book?"

William had ignored her dismissal completely with his arms crossed over his chest. Stubborn man.

Grace shrugged.

"Just looking. And you?"

"Mr Jenkins has a book for my father," he replied. "I thought that the exercise would do me good. Where are Leslie and Mrs Neston?"

As he spoke, William ducked his head and looked outside the window to the village square. Garterrow was essentially deserted which was odd for this time of day.

"Leslie is home visiting her family. Mrs Neston is with Henrietta, who is ill. I am running an errand for the school."

Grace bounced up on the balls of her feet and back down onto her heels. A nervous habit she was hardly aware of, but from William's slight smile and glance at her feet, he had noticed. Promptly, she stopped.

"Are you here for the new Maria Edgeworth novel, then?" William asked. Grace's eyes widened at his unexpected knowledge of contemporary authors. She shook her head.

"Not a fan of hers? My younger sisters gobble up every didactic word that woman pens," William laughed. It made Grace smile. She felt the popular author's works incredibly heavy handed and preachy as well.

The conversation evolved on its own from that point and Grace was powerless to stop it once the subject of literature was brought up. She consumed the written word as quickly as she could manage it, and it seemed that William had used books as a lifeline through the darker periods of his travels abroad.

Once he'd picked up his father's book, he escorted Grace outside. It was still a little early for her to get Mrs Neston's fabric, so William offered to keep her company at the tea shop across the street.

"…and that's why we're forbidden from visiting the Abway farm ever again," Grace said, tears from laughter nearly streaming down her face.

"You wrestled a goat to retrieve Leslie's parasol?" William was shaking with laughter.

"I won fair and square," Grace replied with a grin.

William scrubbed his hand over his face.

"You are too much, Miss Fillmore," he said with a sigh.

Grace glanced out the window toward Mr Potter's store.

"I suppose I should go and collect Mrs Neston's parcel now," she said, standing up. "Thank you for the company. I appreciate it."

William stood as well, but followed her to the door.

"I will see you home, Miss Fillmore."

"Really, I'm quite capable of walking a quarter mile back to the school. I did get here alone, after all."

William followed her outside and across the street anyway.

Mr Potter handed Grace the bundle but William swooped in before she could get her hands on it.

"Thank you, sir!" William smiled at Mr Potter and then looked over at Grace. "I'll carry these back to Mrs Neston for you."

His quick response gave Grace no chance to protest.

Mr Potter grinned as he looked from Grace to William. The sly old man even tossed William a wink when he thought Grace wasn't looking. She felt warmth creeping up her neck at what the shopkeeper must be thinking about the two of them.

With a hasty departure, Grace was outside and on the path back toward Prospect House, William in step beside her.

After a long silence, William spoke.

"You haven't been busy, have you?"

It was more than a simple question about her social calendar, that much she knew from the emotion she could hear in his deep voice. She drew in a shaky breath.

Be completely honest with him, Grace Fillmore, she mentally lectured herself. The advice was sound, though. Grace knew that she would have to wake William up if he was too blind or too stubborn to see that there was no chance for happiness between them.

"No, I have not."

"Did I offend you in some way? Have you found fault in me that you cannot look past? For the life of me, I cannot come up with any sound reason for you to avoid me. Even if you felt only a fraction of the esteem I have for you, you would not be able to stay away completely. I am at a loss, Miss Fillmore."

Grace's heart constricted at his words.

"The truth is, I think you are quite wonderful, Mr Barnes."

She blurted the words out before she could find a more eloquent way to put it. Then her cheeks coloured in embarrassment.

He raised an eyebrow at her.

"Then why have you shut me out?"

She took a steadying breath and stopped in the middle of the lane, turning to face him.

"I am not your equal and you are well aware of that. And it might be the dream of most girls in my unfortunate position to steal a rich, gentry husband, but I know better, Mr Barnes," as she spoke, her voice started to shake. "I know the position you and your family are in. I've been told to my face what a bad match will do to your family and I don't want to be the reason you or your family face disgrace of any sort."

William closed his eyes for the space of a second and Grace held her breath.

"Leslie told me what the vicar's wife and her friends said, Miss Fillmore, and I'm sorry," he said. "You don't deserve to be treated like that."

Trembling, Grace exhaled to steady herself.

"As vicious as the words are, they are true. If you were to associate with me, would your father disinherit you? Would the people who depend on your family suffer? Would you suffer?"

William didn't answer. He didn't have to. He simply turned his face and looked up the lane, his hands shaking.

Unable to continue talking, Grace began walking toward Prospect House once more.

"It is fine," she said quietly, her voice shaky and unsteady. "You will find someone wonderful who your parents approve of. You'll keep the people who depend on you safe and healthy. That is how it is supposed to be."

William had caught up to her and gently grasped her elbow, pulling her to a stop. Grace could not stop the single tear that rolled down her cheek.

"And you, Grace?" Her heart leapt at the sound of her given name on his lips. "What will become of you?"

She met his gaze full on, tears and all, and lied the bravest lie that she could muster.

"Oh, I will be fine as well. I will find some merchant's son, let him court me, and have a simple country life with a simple country man."

The package William was holding dropped the ground and his other hand gently grasped the back of Grace's arm, pulling her closer. When he was half a breath away, he leaned down and stopped just before their noses touched.

"That will never happen, Grace," he said and before she could stop him, he gently pressed his lips to hers and set her world on fire. "I will not allow it."

Chapter Nine

A week after William Barnes gave Grace her first grown up kiss, her life spun out of control.

Prospect House was a flurry of activity and Grace was in the middle of it all, helping the girls decorate the house in greenery and gold ribbons. Leslie and a group of girls were headed to Mr Potter's store for another load of decorating materials. Grace was going to accompany them, but decided at the last moment that her efforts might best be served cleaning the downstairs sitting room.

The school's Welcome Spring Party was less than four days away and there was still so much to do.

"Are you sure? There is a chance that a certain tall, dark and handsome man might be in town," Leslie was half teasing. Grace shook her head.

"No," she said with a laugh. "Our day will go much faster tomorrow if we have everything cleaned and ready for those last decorations. I will be fine here alone, I promise."

"Fine, but if I see him, I am not offering another one of your lame excuses. I will tell William, truthfully, that you chose to clean wood floors over the opportunity to bump into him by chance on an official Prospect House errand. Imagine his heartbreak, Grace!"

Grace shook her head with a smile and would not be swayed.

Reluctantly, Leslie and the other girls left her to her scrubbing rags and cleaning agents. She attacked the sitting room with un-paralleled fervour, thinking about the impression that their guests would have of Prospect House and its students if the room had a single speck of dust.

The chance to clean alone also gave her time to think and sure enough, her thoughts drifted to Mr Tall, Dark, and Handsome himself. If she thought of that stolen kiss too long, a tell-tale blush crept onto her cheeks. It had taken her by surprise, had shocked her, but had utterly thrilled her and set into place any feelings about William that might still have been uncertain.

It was official now. She was completely and hopelessly in love with a man she could never marry, no matter how William tried to convince her otherwise.

She had seen him at Sunday service once, since the kiss on that fateful day.

When they had locked eyes outside afterwards, her face had flamed, giving him cause to laugh a little. He obviously knew what she was thinking about and was amused by it.

How could he function like a normal human being around her? She was utterly tongue-tied whenever she saw him. Lucky for her and her wits, the Barnes family had gone to London for a few weeks, to visit the family of William's mother. She missed seeing him, but at least it gave her heart a little break from the constant flutters the sight of William gave her.

She knew that she would eventually have to make a more concerted effort to discourage his attentions, to be fair to both him and her. She just was not ready for him to be out of her life yet. Grace was being very selfish about savouring as much time with William as she could. She promised herself that, sometime this summer, she would let him know, in earnest, that they should stop whatever it was they were doing.

She would tell him for certain that their attention toward each other would only result in heartbreak, at the very least. At worst, it would result in ruin for her. She did need to take care of her own heart. She was the one responsible for it, after all.

Sighing, Grace scrubbed until her hands were raw. She decided that she would enjoy the spring as she always did. But once it was summer, she would do the right thing. For both of them.

The sound of voices behind her in the hallway caught her attention. She recognized Mrs Neston, but the man speaking with her was unfamiliar. His voice was not recognizable at all.

"All of the girls have gone to the village. We will not be disturbed," her headmistress said.

Their voices were getting closer and Grace shrunk further. She did not want to be discovered eavesdropping when Mrs Neston had expected her to be with the rest of the girls.

"… she is doing remarkably well and is a favourite amongst the other girls. A good girl on every level," Mrs Neston was saying as the two passed by the doorway into the sitting room.

Grace caught the briefest of profile glimpses of the man with her. He looked to be near the same age as Mrs Neston, somewhere in his forties, with sandy blonde hair and laugh lines around his bright blue eyes.

The look was fleeting but something struck Grace about this stranger. He seemed so familiar to her, but she was quite certain she had never seen him before in her life.

The door to Mrs Neston's office closed with a soft snick, cutting Grace off from the rest of the conversation, but a fire had been lit deep within her. There was something about the man that resonated with her. Was this her guardian? Had she met him before? Is that why he seemed so familiar?

The two adults stayed in the office for a long time and Grace began to retrace her cleaning steps, scrubbing parts of the room that were already immaculately clean. Anything to stay hidden in the rarely-used sitting room and to avoid discovery when all that Grace wanted was another look at the stranger.

Finally, after what seemed like ages, the door opened and their voices returned.

"I am quite pleased with everything here today," the man's voice was smooth and clear. He sounded friendly and jovial.

"Please, let me know if she needs anything else in preparation. It is all going to be quite a shock, but I would like to make it as easy as possible for her."

Crouching behind a potted plant, Grace watched Mrs Neston and the man walk toward the front door. Again, her eyes raced over his features, trying to burn them into her memory in case she recalled where she might have seen him before.

Mrs Neston showed the man out and walked back to her office and sat at her desk. Moments later, Grace went in and stood quietly in front of her. She was wringing her hands, unsure where to begin. She wanted to know so badly, but knew that if the man had anything to do with Grace or her past, Mrs Neston was sure to become a giant stone wall with no information to share.

Still, she had to at least try. There would be no sleep for her until she tested her theory.

Mrs Neston looked up at Grace in surprise when she realized that the younger woman was standing there.

"Oh, Miss Fillmore," she said, dropping the paper in front of her and then quickly shuffling it away into a large green envelope that was promptly stuffed into a desk drawer. Grace did not miss a single pertinent detail of what had just happened and filed it away for later use. "I did not realize that you girls had returned from the village. Did you get all you need?"

Grace inhaled slowly, mentally preparing herself for the delicate approach to his conversation.

"I did not go to the village, Mrs Neston," she said, slowly. "I have actually been cleaning the sitting room to get it ready for tomorrow's decorations."

She did not miss the way Mrs Neston's eyebrows raised toward her hairline slightly.

"Oh, you have, have you?" The older woman spoke slowly and deliberately. Her eyes narrowed as she looked at Grace.

"Yes, ma'am," Grace said. "And I could not help but notice the gentleman you had a meeting with. He seemed very familiar for some odd reason."

Grace let the sentence hang in the air between them for a moment while she gathered her racing thoughts.

Mrs Neston did not respond. She sat quietly, saying nothing.

"Is he, by chance," Grace blurted out suddenly, "my benefactor? Or perhaps a distant relation?"

Just as she had expected, Mrs Neston's carefully crafted wall crossed her features and Grace knew that she'd already lost the battle before it had begun.

"You know better than to pry into other people's business, Miss Fillmore," the older woman said curtly. "Sticking your nose where it does not belong will bring you nothing but trouble."

Normally, Mrs Neston's tone would have ended Grace's effort. But something about the stranger would not leave her mind and Grace pushed further.

"You have not denied what I asked, though," she said, quiet but resolute. "Is he someone related to me?"

Mrs Neston heaved herself to her feet in a rush, slamming her hands down on the wooden desk. Grace jumped at the noise, despite her attempts to be brave.

"You have gone too far, Miss Fillmore, and this insolence will not be tolerated!" Mrs Neston's face was flushed pink with anger. "Leave now or lose all of your privileges for the entire holiday. Easter and spring will be lonely and dull for you. And do not ask me again about my own personal business or you will be sorry for it!"

Grace knew that there would be nothing else to be gained from her headmistress, and the tears from the outburst were already stinging her eyes. She turned on her heel and ran to her room, slamming the door behind her.

Mrs Neston had stopped her for now, but Grace knew it was not the end of the search. For her, it had only just begun. She had to know who she really was.

Easter and spring this year would be her time of new beginning. She would see to that.

ARIETTA RICHMOND, CATHERINE WINDSOR, ISABELLA THORNE, KATHERINE KEATS, KELLY ANNE BRUCE

Chapter Ten

"You cannot back out now," Leslie said as she shoved Grace out the front door. "Everyone is waiting!"

Everyone was most of the girls at Prospect House, and some of the villagers of their own age. And William would also be there. Her heart fluttered.

The church was having a special Palm Sunday service. The choir was presenting a song which they had practiced for weeks. Grace knew the words and harmonies by heart. Not many would miss this special service, even though it would be done in the village square instead of in the church.

"You have the voice of an angel! You cannot let the others down," Leslie said, as Grace complained one more time about having to sing in the village square.

A large wagon was waiting for them. The girls and Mrs Neston climbed into the back and covered themselves with blankets for the short trip to town.

Leslie sat down on one side of Grace and Mrs Neston on the other, both providing ample body heat against the frigid evening air.

"Will you be going home for Easter?" Grace asked Leslie. She shook her head.

"Papa said it would be too much of a headache for me to travel for just two days. I am staying here."

Grace could tell that her friend was disappointed.

"Cheer up, dear girl," Grace said with a smile. "You know I will be around to amuse you."

It was a bit of a joke between the two, but true at the same time. Because she had no family to speak of, Grace never left Prospect House and was under the guardianship of Mrs Neston. There was nowhere for her to go.

The bells on the horses' harness jangled a cheery tune as the wagon bumped along the narrow lane toward the village. Grace loved Easter and spring time in Garterrow. The villagers were so happy welcoming each year, that the entire town seemed to come alive with the changing season.

Soon, they'd come to a halt in the village square and Grace and her party joined the other choir members who had already assembled. Without meaning to, her eyes danced from face to face in search of one set of dark eyes in particular. But William was nowhere to be seen.

Instead, Eleanor Forbes pushed her way over to Grace and Leslie's group with Annabelle in tow. Leslie didn't bother to hide her groan. Grace bit the inside of her cheek to keep from letting her displeasure be as obvious.

Word had travelled among the gossips that Eleanor and her mother had their sights set squarely on William as a match for Eleanor. Apparently they were not happy about the amount of time he spent with the girls from Prospect House.

Grace should have known that this would happen. She should have cut this off much sooner.

"Ladies," Eleanor said as she came to a stop in front of them.

"How is the husband hunting going?" Leslie asked, managing to keep her face straight. Henrietta snorted laughter and turned it into a cough in a poor effort to hide it. Eleanor's eyebrow raised and her lip curled.

"It is a pity, really," the girl said, plastering a neutral look back onto her face. "None of you will ever know what it is like to think about a happy future with a prosperous husband," she smiled sweetly and, before anyone could react, she continued, "You are too fat," she jabbed Henrietta in the sternum, "You are too plain," she pointed at Leslie, careful not to touch her since Leslie had a village-renowned temper, "And you," she levelled her gaze on Grace and pointed at her, "Are simply a nobody."

The air grew heavy around Grace and she saw the red flush heating Leslie's cheeks. Before either of them could react, however, the rich baritone voice that set Grace's heart aflutter broke in.

"I don't think you could be more mistaken, Miss Forbes," William said as he came to stand directly behind Grace, keeping a proper distance to avoid wagging tongues, but sending a chill down her spine nonetheless.

"Miss Mansfield is quite pretty and has triple the inheritance that you have. Miss Haskett has both looks and an impeccable pedigree. And Miss Fillmore is most definitely a somebody worth knowing. So much so that there are rumours that men of fortune throughout the county would count themselves lucky just to be able to have a conversation with her."

Leslie's scowl was now a beaming, victorious smile, and Henrietta looked like she was about to burst with happiness from William's compliment.

Eleanor's face went ruddy as she tried to salvage the conversation that had so quickly turned against her.

"Mr Barnes, you have me all wrong," she shrilled a little too loudly and vehemently. "These three are dear, dear friends of mine that I was lucky enough to call classmates until this past year."

William merely nodded, but his knowing smile remained.

"Have a wonderful night, Miss Forbes," he said, effectively dismissing Eleanor, whose mouth dropped open in disbelief. He looked to Grace and her friends. "Ladies, shall we?"

Chapter Eleven

"I think you owe it to yourself to find the answers you need."

William's words as they walked through the town of Garterrow hit Grace like an arrow in the chest. She had decided to confide in both him and Leslie about what had happened two nights prior. And how quickly Mrs Neston had shut her out.

"I am not sure how I am going to find the answers if Mrs Neston seems so determined to keep them to herself," she said quietly as they approached the next home. "I am at a loss as to what to do now. I just know I cannot give up."

Leslie had listened intently and not said much. But when she finally spoke, she had both Grace and William shocked.

"Here is what we are going to do, Grace Fillmore," Leslie said. "We are going hurry home from church on Sunday when Mrs Neston is in her meeting and we are going to look through that desk of hers for ourselves."

Grace laughed at the idea at first. It had been bad enough that she had eavesdropped the first time, but breaking Mrs Neston's trust and going into her personal belongings? Grace was sure she could not do that and said so.

William shrugged his shoulders.

"I think that you have been more than patient," he said quietly and Leslie nodded. "If it really is nothing, then you can go back to the way things were before. But if there is something to your suspicions, maybe you will be one step closer to finding the answers you desperately need."

Leslie nodded once more.

"You are such a wise young man, William Barnes," she teased. William brushed aside her backhanded compliment.

"You know that I will help you however I can," he said earnestly. "I know I will not be able to do much, but even if you can find me a name, I can find out more information for you. My father's family has been in the county for generations and my mother is well-connected in the London circles. If there is a mystery to be had, we can definitely get you pointed in the right direction to the solution."

Grace's heart swelled a little with emotion.

"I do not deserve such good friends," she said quietly, trying to tamp down the emotions welling up.

Leslie burst out laughing.

"Good friends? Grace, we are encouraging you to break into a locked office and look through very personal, very protected files. I would hardly call that good friends!"

Chapter Twelve

"Keep your voice down, Leslie!"

Grace's hands were shaking as she wedged the butter knife into the lock and pushed. The heavy wooden door groaned a bit but didn't budge enough for Grace to think it was working.

"This is pointless," Grace sighed, leaning her head against the door. She had already tried to quit twice and they'd only been at it for ten minutes. "She is going to return soon and then our gooses will be cooked!"

Grace hovered between understanding the importance of finding answers and the absolute terror of being caught by Mrs Neston. The woman would certainly not appreciate this obvious breach of privacy. Would she turn Grace out? If so, where in the world would she go?

"You had better be prepared to hire me as a governess for your future children when Mrs Neston kicks me out of here," she groaned as she leaned on the knife one more time. It did the trick and moments later, the door to Mrs Neston's office popped open.

"Victory!" Leslie hissed excitedly. "You go in and I'll keep watch. If we have to, we can sneak out the window into the garden."

It was a solid plan – or at least as solid as they were going to be able to come up with – and Grace walked quickly toward the desk. She knew what she was after and, if providence was on her side, she would not have to look too hard to find it.

Mrs Neston's large oak desk was the picture of organization and efficiency. The top of it was polished smooth and bare, save for two pencils neatly lined up in the centre. Grace plopped herself down in the chair and retraced the confrontation she had with Mrs Neston days earlier. There had been paperwork and a large green envelope.

She pulled open the top drawer and found little else but a few writing supplies.

The second drawer was nothing but blank order slips from the various shops around Garterrow.

But the third drawer held all of the paperwork and files.

Grace hummed a nervous tune as she thumbed through each individual paper. Outside the door, Leslie whispered in to her.

"I think you should hurry. I think I hear something."

Grace panicked and moved her hands quicker, picking through each file. At last, she came across the familiar green folder and pulled it free from the drawer.

Setting the desk back to rights, Grace flew across the carpeted floor to where Leslie was waiting.

The girls locked the door to the office and pulled the door shut before turning to dash off toward the staircase that would lead up to their rooms.

Just as they reached the landing to the second story, the front door opened and Mrs Neston and their classmates filed in. Leslie shot Grace a look of relief and added a wink to it for good measure.

"I will go downstairs and keep everyone distracted while you read through everything."

Grace nodded.

"Have you considered how we are going to get the paperwork back into its proper place?" Grace said, the reality setting in. She might have been successful in the taking of the papers, but she was going to have to return them without being caught.

Leslie shrugged.

"Maybe there will be something so good in there that you will not care about returning them unnoticed," she said as she made her way back to the staircase.

ARIETTA RICHMOND, CATHERINE WINDSOR, ISABELLA THORNE, KATHERINE KEATS, KELLY ANNE BRUCE

Chapter Thirteen

Oh, how right Leslie had been.

Mrs Neston was on her feet, pacing in front of the fire. Grace couldn't help but appreciatively take in the pots of flowers and the golden ribbons everywhere, despite the unpleasant conversation happening in the sitting room.

"I cannot believe that you would go so low as to snoop through my personal belongings." Mrs Neston was pacing the room. She had been more than just angry that Grace had approached her in the sitting room that evening with the green folder in hand. Grace had not even needed to explain anything. Mrs Neston knew immediately what it was all about.

"I apologize, ma'am," Grace said, not really meaning it. She was shaking and found it hard to keep herself upright. The papers had contained so much. So many answers all at once that Grace thought she might fall over where she stood. "But that does not give you the right to keep all of this from me for so long. Please. Tell me the details that these papers leave out."

The tears welled up behind Grace's eyes again and this time she didn't bother trying to wipe them away before they fell slowly down her cheeks.

Mrs Neston immediately softened.

"Grace, there is so much to your story that is not mine to tell you," she said, her harsh tone gone in an instant. "All of these years I have cared for you like you were my very own and it has been my pleasure to do so. And every single time you asked me about your past, I wanted to tell you everything — please believe me. But everything that centred on your wellbeing I was sworn to keep secret. Had I told you too soon and if word had gotten out, so many lives, including your own, would have been ruined forever."

Grace drew in a shaky breath.

"Who is Frederick Sargeant?"

Within the papers, a history of her education, expenses, and legal decisions had been dictated and managed by one Frederick Sargeant and overseen by Mrs Margaret Neston.

This mysterious Mr Sargeant had receipts and missives that dated back to Grace's days in foster care. He had been her benefactor from the day she was born, but who was he?

The question hung between the women for the space of a breath. Mrs Neston closed her eyes.

"He is my older brother, the son of the late Sir Bonner Sargeant, Baron of Guilford, widower of Rebecca Sargeant," Mrs Neston said with a sigh, "and he is also your father."

The answer hit Grace square in the chest and she had no choice but to sit down on one of the overstuffed chairs.

Her face flushed with emotion and before she knew it, she was crying again. She was certain, by the way that Mrs Neston was answering the question, that the news was about to take a turn for the worse.

"What are you not telling me, Mrs Neston?" Grace croaked. "Is it bad?"

She almost regretted her incessant push for answers now. What if it was too painful for her to bear? What if there was a secret shame that now she had to carry with her, just because she had been determined not to be shut out from the truth.

"It is not good, especially the past," the older woman replied honestly. "But it is about to get much, much better. Listen to the story and decide for yourself."

Grace nodded and sat still, waiting to hear the story. She opened her heart and her mind in the hope that her life was going to change for the better.

"Frederick Sargeant was the eldest son of Lord Guilford, a wealthy Baron from the south. He had been a dutiful son and learned the workings of the family estates, just as his father had wanted. He would be an heir who would take the Sargeant name and bring honour and prestige to it, just as his ancestors, dating back to Charlemagne's time, had done.

"But Frederick met and fell in love with a young woman named Rebecca Hamilton, the daughter of a local merchant. The merchant was wealthy and his daughter was well-provided for, but what she had in dowry and wealth, she lacked in pedigree and prestige. Lord Guilford would not hear of a match between his heir and a commoner and strictly forbade Frederick and Rebecca from seeing each other again.

"Before anyone could stop them, they travelled to Scotland and eloped. Lord Guilford was beside himself with anger and had all but cut Frederick off. It was only Lady Guilford's love for her son that kept cooler heads prevailing. She set the newly married couple up in a small home, two counties over, and told nobody of the marriage.

"When Rebecca became pregnant, Frederick was overjoyed. But the joy was short-lived, as he lost his love just as she gave birth to Grace Rebecca Sargeant."

According to Mrs Neston, Frederick had nearly lost his mind to his grief and it was the future of his daughter that mattered most to him now. To keep his father from punishing them further, he sent his newborn daughter to his younger sister and her husband in Garterrow. They found her a loving foster family who would raise her until she was old enough to attend school.

Frederick returned home and worked his way back into his father's good graces. Attending the functions that he was required to attend and learning what it took to be a decent peer. His plan was to keep his daughter hidden until he was in a place to rightfully claim her and ensure that she would not suffer because of his love for her mother.

"And so, he watched you grow from afar, while our father aged and nearly forgot about dear Rebecca and that short marriage," Mrs Neston said, wiping a tear from her eye. "Lord Guilford died in late summer this last year and Frederick has been working furiously to get the estate set to rights before coming for you. You just managed to snoop your way into spoiling the surprise early."

She said the last part with a short laugh.

"Was he the man who came to visit you last week?"

Mrs Neston nodded.

"I told him he was being careless, but he reminded me that the danger had passed away with our father," she explained. "The marriage to Rebecca was valid and, thanks to my mother, our father never took the legal steps to disinherit Frederick or his heirs. And now that Frederick is the new Baron Guilford, it is time for you to be with him."

It was all wonderful news and Grace was going to need at least a lifetime to process it all, but the part about leaving with him unsettled her. Her friends and everything she had known was here in Garterrow.

"Do I have to leave?"

Mrs Neston looked up in surprise.

"Why would you not want to?"

Grace took a deep breath.

"You. My friends. My school," she said, looking out the window.

"Dear girl," Mrs Neston breathed. "You have so much changing in your life right now. You should just take it all one day at a time, yes?"

So Grace decided to do just that.

ARIETTA RICHMOND, CATHERINE WINDSOR, ISABELLA THORNE, KATHERINE KEATS, KELLY ANNE BRUCE

Chapter Fourteen

A party gathered at Prospect House and the revellers had many things to celebrate. First and foremost, was the Easter season. Springtime had come at last to the tiny village of Garterrow and the citizens were hailing the new beginning.

A gathering of friends and family for any reason was a wonderful thing.

True to her word, Leslie had stayed at Prospect House. What was even better, was that one of her older brothers, Marcus, joined them as well. They laughed and teased each other for most of the night. Henrietta and her mother were there, as well as a few other girls who were not able to travel.

Grace's aunt, Mrs Neston, made a fantastic hostess. Along with a few of her matronly church friends, she made sure that no plate was less than filled to capacity with sweets and treats, and that no cup was empty.

And Frederick Sargeant, who came the very next day after the truth came to light, was celebrating with them.

Grace had expected some awkwardness between them. Possibly there would be the stiff formality she had often observed between family members in noble families. That had not been the case.

The moment he walked through the front doors at Prospect House, he had gathered Grace up in a fierce hug, which had left both Grace and Mrs Neston in tears. He apologized over and over for having to leave her.

"I could not let you grow up with nothing," he had told her later. "I knew that, if we could weather the time apart until I was confirmed in my inheritance, then it could all be worth it. It was the hardest, most heart-breaking seventeen years of my life, Grace."

And she believed him. Together they mourned her mother. According to her father, her mother had displayed a sharp mind and a tender heart.

"Much like I have known you to be, through Margaret's correspondence. The few times that I have chanced a visit to observe you from afar, I see so much of your mother in you."

Grace had expected him to push her on the issue of leaving Garterrow for Guilford, but so far, in the four days he had been there, he had not mentioned it. She knew that she would have to make a decision soon, but she was determined to soak in the love and atmosphere of such a perfect night.

To Grace, there was only one thing missing in a most perfect celebration time. When everyone had settled around in chairs and in comfortable conversation, the one missing element from Grace's perfect life arrived, as if on cue.

William's tall frame blocked the door and her heart raced at the sight of him, no matter how hard she tried to tamp down her excessive reaction to the man. No matter when, no matter what, William Barnes set her heart aflutter simply by being near her.

After the obligatory round of greetings and introductions, Mrs Neston bade Grace to be a good hostess and show William to the dining room where the food was. Shocked at the informality of the introductions between William and her father, Grace decided to let the matter drop. The mood was light, with spring time here and their newfound relationship, so possibly her father's jovial mood was to blame.

William was less relaxed than he normally was, as they made polite small talk in the short walk through the hallway.

"Have you been well?" His voice lilted a little too high, giving his nervousness away.

"Yes, thank you," she said slowly, studying him as they turned into the dining room. She walked William through all of the dishes, but he selected none of them.

"I hope that you do not mind that Leslie informed me of your exciting news," he said, after he cleared his throat. They stood by the stack of porcelain dishes and Grace waited for William to begin serving himself.

"Not at all," Grace replied. "I would have loved to tell you myself, to thank you for your encouraging me to be brave enough to search for answers, but I have not seen much of you these past days. Is your family well? I imagine that you are all busy with the holidays."

William nodded, seeming somewhat absent minded.

"Has the shock been hard for you?" he asked, bringing his attention back to Grace.

She frowned, considering the question.

"No. It has been wonderful getting to know my father," she said. "Going from nobody of consequence to a Baron's daughter has been easier than I expected it to be — mostly because I have not really left Prospect House much."

Grace laughed at her own joke and William smiled.

"The part that I am struggling with now, if I am to be totally honest with you, is that I am not sure I want to leave Garterrow and go with him to Guilford. I know it is my place to go with him and that I probably belong with him. I want to get to know him. But everything and everyone I love is here," Grace sighed and looked at her hands.

"Do you have a reason to stay?" William's voice was quiet, barely above a whisper.

"I suppose if I wanted to, I could stay on here at Prospect House and teach with my aunt," Grace began, but stopped when William stepped forward and grasped her hands in his. Stunned, she looked up and met his intense gaze.

"Would you like a more compelling reason to stay?"

Grace could hear her pulse racing in her ears and could hardly form a thought.

"Do you have a more compelling reason for me to stay?" she managed to squeak out.

Her heart knew where this was leading and could hardly believe it. Her head refused to believe it was possible.

"I believe I might have," William said, his normal grin easing back onto his face. "Three days ago, I had a mutual friend make the introductions for me to your father. I laid out my plan to make me the happiest man in the world. While he was not exactly keen on the idea of giving you away before he had really had a chance to get to know you, I assured him that we would spend plenty of time visiting him in Guilford should he agree."

No wonder her father and William hadn't required any introductions — they had already met!

"So, do you agree?"

He was grinning from ear to ear now, but Grace was not going to allow him to get away with it quite so easily.

"Agree to what, Mr Barnes?"

She batted her eyes at him coyly.

A smile quirked the corners of William's lips as he bent his tall frame down to one knee and wrapped both of his warm hands around Grace's.

"Will you agree to be my wife, Grace Sargeant? To bind yourself to me for the rest of your life? Will you make me the happiest man in the world, as spring abounds all around us? Will you honour me with a late spring wedding? I must be your husband as soon as possible!"

The tears were out before Grace could get the words onto her lips, so she only nodded and then immediately wrapped her arms around William's neck. He stood and locked her into a tight embrace, whispering into her hair.

"I would have married you no matter what," he said softly. "I want you to know that. Leslie and I were hatching our own plot to convince you, too. The fact that you are a wealthy heiress from one of the oldest names in the country has certainly made things easier, though."

Through her tears of joy, Grace laughed as William set her on her feet and smoothed down the sleeves of her gown.

"They are all waiting in there, you know," he said, motioning back toward the sitting room.

"Waiting for what?"

William smiled and stole a warm, chaste kiss from Grace's lips.

"Waiting to hear that you have agreed to be the next Lady Mowbourne."

"Yes! I will! I cannot believe this new beginning is mine. I will be so happy to be your wife, William."

"I love you Grace, but I loved you long before I knew you had a title. You are my new beginning. Now, let us go and celebrate!"

The End

Thank you for reading!

I truly hope you enjoyed

The Baron's Secret Love

You'll find a special preview of my book, '**Arabella**' just after the **About the Author** Section

Kelly Anne Bruce has enjoyed reading about the Regency period since her teen years. Intrigued by the society mindset, the elaborate dress, and the lovely parties, she starting doing research. The people of the era are fascinating! That's what drew her to write about this time in English history.

Kelly Anne is an American, married to an Englishman. They live in Cambridge, which happens to be her favourite city in England. Their two cats and a dog run the household remarkably well!

If you're interested keeping up with Kelly Anne and new releases, you can sign up to receive notices.

Join the Readers Group! at

Connect with Kelly Anne on Facebook at

https://www.facebook.com/Kelly-Anne-Bruce-703936873079553/

or visit her website at www.kellyannebruce.com.

Want to find more sweet and clean Regency romance stories from Kelly Anne? Check out the listing on her website.

If you prefer, you can visit her Amazon Author Page at

https://www.amazon.com/Kelly-Anne-Bruce/e/B01EG7RSD4/

Other Books by Kelly Anne Bruce

The Jilted Earl

The Duke's Heart

Arabella

The Corbyn Sisters Book 1

Helena

The Corbyn Sisters Book 2

Charlotte

The Corbyn Sisters Book 3

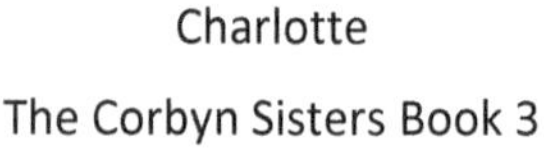

Also available :

All She Wanted

The Earl's Unconventional Bride

The Marriage Arrangement

The Baronet's Daughters

The Captain's Lost Love

To Marry for Love

Rival Cousins

Second Son

The Earl's Choice

Their Second Chance

Regency Romance Adventures - Eight Book Boxed Set

Changing the Earl's Plan

A Rogue's Transformation

The Duke's Big Surprise

The Duke's Happy Holiday

The Earl's Christmas Spirit

The Earl's Yuletide Surprise

A Lady's True Fortune

Here is Your Preview of

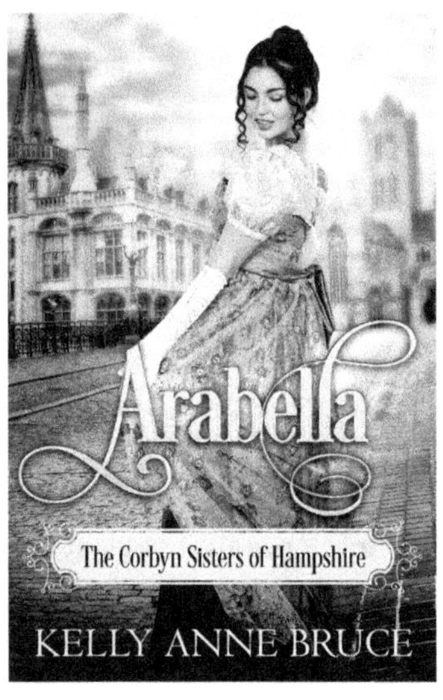

Arabella, Helena, and Charlotte are the Corbyn sisters. The sisters are quite different and their lives are heading in different directions, much to the dismay of their social-status-conscious mother.

Arabella is the oldest and this is a preview of her story and a chance for you to meet her and her sisters.

Chapter 1

"What are you doing in here?"

Arabella looked up to see her sister standing in the doorway of the library.

"Shhh," she said and motioned her into the room.

Helena carefully looked down the hall before stepping into the room and closing the door behind her.

"Whatever is going on?"

"I came in here hoping to avoid Mother." Arabella sank into one of the upholstered chairs near the window. "She is in quite a frenzy today."

"Yes, well, that is not much of a surprise, now is it?" Helena asked. "You know how much she loves going to London for the Season."

It was common knowledge in their household that their mother and father expected their daughters to marry well, especially Arabella.

She grimaced before saying primly, "Yes, of course, and that is why I am in the library."

"Smart thinking," Helena said with a raised eyebrow. "She will never look for you here."

Arabella looked around as though she had never been in the library before. "It is quite nice. It is no wonder you spend so much time in here."

"I spend time in here because of my books and research. Not because of the decoration of the room." Helena tilted her head. "Although the light in the afternoon is quite delightful, if not helpful when I am reading."

Arabella nodded.

"Perhaps I shall bring my embroidery in here rather than sit in the drawing room."

Helena frowned at her. Arabella smiled, sure that her sister was not excited about the idea of having company in what was normally her domain. Their father hardly used the library, as he had a study across the hall that he used for his business work.

"Helena!"

Arabella stood up as the library door opened and Mother looked in. Both girls drew in a deep breath.

"Oh, Arabella, there you are. I was just going to ask your sister if she knew where you were."

"I came in to remind Helena to gather her books for London," Arabella said quickly.

Mother frowned. "Oh, Arabella, she can leave her books here. Once we are in London, Helena will not need anything such as a book to keep her busy."

Helena narrowed her eyes at Arabella behind their mother's back.

"Mother, you said you were looking for me?" Arabella asked, taking pity on her sister. She led her mother to the door and made a waving motion behind her back. Hopefully, Helena would have a few moments to pack up what she needed.

"Mother!" Arabella heard her youngest sister call from the top of the stairs.

Mother walked out into the hall. "Yes, Charlotte?"

Charlotte stood at the banister. "Bridget wants to know which dresses you want her to pack."

"Definitely the emerald, and the sky blue," Mother paused and scowled.

Charlotte came down the stairs, a distressed look upon her face.

"Mother, what is wrong?"

"Oh, I only wish that we had planned on leaving a few days earlier," Mother lamented. "We should have gone to the modiste first. I am not certain that any of you have dresses that are fashionable enough for London society."

"Charlotte, I am sure that your dresses are perfectly acceptable." Arabella patted her sister's arm, trying to calm her. It was to be Charlotte's coming out and Arabella did not want her to fuss over things.

Clearly, their mother did not share Arabella's concern.

"What if the patronesses of Almack's look at the dresses and decide that you are not worthy of vouchers?" she replied, wringing her hands.

"No need to worry, dear Sophia. Once we get to London you can visit Bond Street and get whatever you need."

Their father had come out of his study at the end of the hall. He had been standing quietly, taking in the conversation.

"We don't have much time. Perhaps we should try to leave a day earlier." Her mother sighed. "No, I suppose Tuesday is fine. It will not be easy, but I suppose it will be enough time for the modiste to see Arabella."

Arabella tipped her head. "I am sure that there will be enough time for all of us to visit Bond Street."

"Arabella, you have no idea how important your wardrobe can be. It would be disastrous if you were to show up looking as though your father's pockets were bare."

"Mother," Arabella started as Charlotte's smile had faltered again. "Surely, you mean to have Charlotte see the modiste first."

"We are expecting that great things are ahead for you, Arabella. You are the beauty of the family after all."

Her mother started up the stairs and then seemed to finally understand Arabella's meaning. She paused and smiled down at them. "Oh, and of course, Charlotte, too. Your coming out Ball will be quite the event. I promise you that, indeed."

Chapter 2

Arabella watched her mother go up the stairs and stifled a sigh. She truly wished that her mother was not so enamoured of the fashionable elite of London. It was embarrassing how intent her mother was about having her garner such a good social match.

She smiled at her sisters. "Who fancies a ride?"

Helena came out of the library with a stack of books in her arms. "I would think Mother will want us to help her get ready to go to London."

"In the last three Seasons, have we really done anything useful before leaving for the city?"

After a moment, Helena shook her head. "No, I cannot remember anything but Mother running around calling instructions out to Bridget."

"I think Arabella's idea is splendid. There is little chance we will be able to take a ride before we leave for London if we don't do it now." Charlotte started up the stairs. "I want one last afternoon with Betsey."

Arabella turned to her other sister. "Helena, what would you like to do?"

"Help me carry my books upstairs. I will need to pack them before I change into my riding habit."

Arabella laughed and took several books off the top of the stack and handed them to Charlotte. "You two get changed. Meet me by the door to the garden."

Charlotte frowned.

"But where are you going?"

"To talk to Gregory. Wait for me at the garden gate. That way Mother will not happen upon you."

Arabella turned back down the hall. Gregory was probably in the kitchen chatting with Maggie. He was most likely avoiding Arabella's mother, too — not that she could, or would, blame him for that. After all, she and her sisters endeavoured to do the same thing at times like this.

She got to the far end of the hall before calling his name.

"Gregory!"

Arabella waited. Perhaps she had been too quiet.

It was not long though, before the door closest to the dining room opened and Gregory appeared.

"Yes, Miss Arabella?" He looked cautiously down the hall. "Is there something I can assist you with?"

"Yes, thank you, Gregory. My sisters and I will be going for a ride. Could you let Burke know that we will be down to the stables shortly?"

"Of course, Miss Arabella. I believe that one of the boys is refilling the wood bins. I will send him at once."

"Thank you." Arabella began to step away but paused. "Mother is quite busy upstairs. There is no need for her to worry over our ride."

"Certainly," Gregory nodded, his face serious, although Arabella detected the faintest smile as he said, "I have more than a few tasks I need to tend to down here."

His reaction proved Arabella's earlier assumption that Gregory was staying far away from her mother, too. It was easier for all of them if they gave her a wide berth. Arabella smiled at Gregory.

"I hope it goes well for you."

She hurried back down the hall, relieved to hear her mother talking to her Father in his study. Arabella continued up the stairs and to her room and changed into her riding habit as quickly as she could. She nearly left the room in her slippers instead of her riding boots in her haste.

She opened her bedroom door quietly.

"Bridget, I want you to take all of the dresses, except the dark blue and the white with the ribbons." Her mother's voice came from the direction of Helena's room. Arabella hoped that Helena had her books tucked into a good hiding place.

Arabella took the opportunity to dart to the stairs and down to the drawing room. She slipped out the door into the garden and was quite relieved to see both of her sisters at the garden gate.

"There she is," Helena told Charlotte. "I told you that you were worrying for no reason."

Arabella glanced back toward the house. "Let's get to the stable before Mother finds something for us to do."

The stable was a quick walk from the garden gate and Burke had already brought out Betsey, and Primrose, Helena's horse.

Burke looked up and smiled. "Give me just a moment and I'll have Morgan out for you, too."

"Thank you, Burke," Arabella said as he turned away.

Using the mounting block, Charlotte adjusted herself into the side saddle and then rode a short distance away. Helena and Primrose followed behind.

"Where shall we ride?"

"To the creek and back," Charlotte said and took off before Arabella or Helena could reply.

"She seems a little excited," Helena said dryly.

"Quite." Arabella watched Charlotte and her horse gallop out ahead of them.

"Arabella, I must confess, I am not looking forward to London or the Season."

She sighed and looked over at Helena.

"I would rather we stayed here in Hampshire, too."

Arabella did not really mind going to the Balls and other parties.

She would enjoy seeing some of the friends she had made the previous season. It was her mother's role in the endeavour that she dreaded.

Arabella had hoped to find love, but with her mother's affinity for London's social elite, she feared that her wishes would fall by the wayside. Love was the last thing on her mother's mind.

~~~~~

If you're interested in reading the rest of Arabella's story, you can find it here on Amazon:

https://www.amazon.com/dp/B01N0VBZMV/
~~~~~

Other Books from Dreamstone Publishing

Dreamstone publishes books in a wide variety of categories – here are some of our other bestselling books:-

We have books in many categories, ranging from Erotica and Romance to Kids Books, Books on Writing, Business Books, Photography, Cook Books, Diaries, Coloring books and much more. New books are released each month.

Be the first to know when our next books are coming out

Be first to get all the news – sign up for our newsletter at

http://www.dreamstonepublishing.com